Lizardskin

Also by Carsten Stroud

Sniper's Moon
Close Pursuit

Lizardskin

CARSTEN STROUD

BANTAM BOOKS

NEW YORK • TORONTO • LONDON • SYDNEY • AUCKLAND

LIZARDSKIN

A Bantam Book / September 1992

Book design by Richard Oriolo

Library of Congress Cataloging-in-Publication Data
Stroud, Carsten, 1946–
  Lizardskin / Carsten Stroud.
    p.   cm.
  ISBN 0-553-08935-8
  I. Title.
PR9199.3.S838L59   1992
813'.54—dc20   92-833
                                                        CIP

Published simultaneously in the United States and Canada

PRINTED IN THE UNITED STATES OF AMERICA

BVG   0   9   8   7   6   5   4   3   2   1

A Note on the Details...

I've walked a narrow track through this book, trying to balance the requirements of fiction with my affection for hard facts. Those Montana residents lucky enough to live around Billings and Hardin and the Crow lands will know that Pompeys Pillar is rather less than I've described, Hardin rather more, and the valley of Arrow Creek considerably changed. I hope they'll understand I made these changes with care and out of a writer's necessity. To my cousin Michael Spence, whose love for the West sparked this story two years ago, I offer my affectionate gratitude.

And for those Lakota, Crow, and Cheyenne people who may read this book, and see the names of great men and women from their histories, and see those names carried into this age by some of my fictional characters, I want them to know it was done as a kind of remembrance, with the hope that their names might be spoken again by those who loved them, among their own peoples, and, with respect, among those people who are not of the First Nations but who, when the day is slipping away and a soft amber light is on the land, sometimes go to their windows and look out across the hills and the coulees and think about how much that was fine and true has passed away under the sweetgrass.

Beyond these caveats, and always remembering how much I owe to my editor, Beverly Lewis, the book is mine and I stand or fall on what I have written.

For Linda Mair,
who crossed the Missouri with me,
and brought me to the bluffs above Chamberlain,
and showed me how to see.

CARSTEN STROUD,
Thunder Beach, 1991.

God made the universe
out of nothing . . .

and if you look real close,
you can tell.

—11 Bravo Helmet, I Corps, RVN

From the high hill of my old age,
I look back on the ways I have taken,
and the rivers I have crossed,
and the broad valleys under the mountains,
and the people who once walked there,
the voices and names of my youth,
all gone now, and the hoop broken,
and I say that it was enough
that I lived to walk in these places,
and come to the high hill at last,
and see cloud-shadows on the peaks
and the light that is in the world.

—Blue Coat's song

Prologue

Sunrise – June 7 – Hardin, Montana

When the light outside her window turned the color of milk and blood, Mary Littlebasket closed her eyes and pulled at the intravenous line. It came away from her vein like a snake letting go, a skin-pop sound, and then a small blossom of her blood rose out of the brown skin on the back of her hand. From the glittering tip of the needle, drops of clear liquid swelled and fell onto the wrinkled pink hospital linen. She closed her eyes again and for a long moment thought about putting her head back on the hard pillow and trying once again to drive her soul from her body by singing the leaving song. But there was no belief inside her to give the song power. She let out a long trembling breath through her taut lips, paused at the edge of this moment to summon her intentions, then rolled to her left, feeling the stitches in her belly as they tugged at her like hooks.

Now she was on her feet. The room reeled, and a soft white cloud seemed to fill her head, dimming the pooled yellow light from the lamp over her bed. She steadied herself on the bedside table, seeing her hand and her bruised arm as if from a distance, oddly distorted and elongated.

She found her clothes in a brown paper bag; her flower-print dress and the sandals and the blue ribbon that Charlie Tallbull had tied in her hair when the ambulance came to take her to town.

Mary Littlebasket dressed herself, trying not to be frightened at the incision that violated her belly and the bandages that girdled her body.

She stepped into the bathroom and turned on the shower. Pausing at the mirror, she stared at her reflection, at the ochre tint in her cheeks and the coal-fire light in her brown eyes, at the wild aurora of blue-black hair and her blunt strong face. Taking a tube of lipstick—Tahiti Dawn—she inscribed a sign on the chilly glass, doing it slowly and carefully, out of respect for the gesture, perhaps for her parents and her relatives if they should ever hear of it, but it still seemed a slight thing, as futile as a rabbit's shriek.

Finishing, she came out again and closed the bathroom door. Perhaps they would be pleased that the stupid Crow girl had finally decided to take a shower.

Out in the hall she heard the nurses talking at their station, bright brittle chatter and one voice carrying above it. They were changing the shift, each one describing her patient load and how they had passed the night. It would take them a half-hour, and then they'd spread out through the ward, full of cold comfort and metallic efficiency, like the sisters at the Mission St. Labre. Mary shook the memory out and stood awhile at the door, trying to transcend the white fog and the pain in her belly. She stepped out into the hall, turned to the right, and pushed her way through the doorway into the nursery, the heavy door closing behind her with a hissing reptilian slither.

The hallway was empty. Through the plate-glass window she could see the plastic shells where they kept the babies. There was no one in the room. The attendant must be at the shift meeting. She came into the room and went over to the one where her baby slept. She stood over the alien machine, watching him draw in his breath and let it out, a small brown monkey-creature bound up in a web of tubes and needles and monitors.

The monitors.

If she pulled at the wires, surely a bell—an alarm—would ring at the nurses' station. She studied the machine for a while, then she reached out and flipped a red switch on the panel. The tiny green screen went dark, but there was no change in the baby's breathing. With her breath held and her heart pounding in her ribcage, she forced herself to look at the baby's face, at the—wrongness—of the features, the flat misshapen skull and the eyes that seemed to be sewn shut. Yet there was breath and a heartbeat. He was alive. Surely this was a kind of life.

She took the covering off him and carefully disconnected the monitors. She lifted him—so light! so delicate—yet warm, and breathing; he radiated a perfect sweet stillness, calm as a pool under a gliding moon. His body was hot and dry, and she covered him with a blue blanket, wrapping it around him, pulling him to her aching breasts; turning now, leaving, she glided, wraithlike, a sweep of cotton flowers and the whisper of sandaled feet on the polished floors. She passed away down the long hall, her blue-black hair shining with yellow lights as she moved into and out of the glow of the overhead lamps toward the glowing green sign that said EXIT.

Holding the child in her right arm, she leaned into the door and popped it open. A warm wind coiled inside around the door, smelling of dry stone and dust and baking asphalt.

In the security office on the second floor, a red light began to blink on a control panel showing a floor plan of the clinic. The guard put down his copy of USA Today and leaned forward in his chair, his leather creaking, the Ruger digging into his waist, hesitating, his right hand poised over a phone set.

Mary Littlebasket went through the door and closed it with her back, feeling the lock set again. She was in a parking lot, newly painted white lines intense against the sticky surface. The air was warm and harsh against her cheek as she ran across it toward the street. Past the tiny brick homes and the stunted cottonwoods at the edge of the schoolyard, she could see the low weathered hills of the Arapooish, the grasses still soft and blue-green in the dying June days.

The Changing Grass Moon, she thought, going out across the school-yard, looking for the pickup truck, listening for a motor.

The guard stared at the blinking red light for another thirty seconds. Sighing, he tapped the panel twice, hard. When the light did not go off, he picked up the telephone, spoke into it for a few seconds, then he pushed himself up out of his oak swivel chair and adjusted his belt. He sighed again, theatrically, for his own pleasure, put on his cap, setting it just right in the reflection of the office window, and stepped out into the stairway. He was halfway down the stairs when he met a nurse coming up around the flight, her face hard and white.

Charlie Tallbull was slouching low in the driver's seat of his Ford pickup, a straw cowboy hat pushed back away from his seamed and craggy face, his big scarred hands crossed on his wide belly. He saw Mary Littlebasket crossing the dried grass of the schoolyard, a flutter of flowered cotton and black hair and a small blue burden in her arms. He started the engine of the pickup and eased it out into the side street.

Dell Greer and Moses Harper were sitting in their Big Horn County cruisers a couple of miles away up the Whitman Coulee toward Lizardskin, parked driver-to-driver, drinking coffee laced with Bailey's Irish Cream out of Styrofoam cups.

Greer had a part-time cattle operation that he and his wife were trying to run up in the Bulls. He and Harper looked a lot alike, thick-bodied, late twenties, both blond and crew cut, as nicely matched as artillery shells. Harper was a little older than Greer, and maybe a little slower to get angry. They were arguing the relative merits of Black Angus and Aberdeen when the dispatcher came on the radio and told them there was a break-in alarm at the Julia Dwight Clinic.

Moses Harper took the call, and the morning being slow and the hours heavy, Dell Greer decided to follow along. They turned south onto the Lizardskin road, a couple of brown and tan cruisers with the gold crest of Big Horn County on their doors. Accelerating, they cleared the rise and saw Hardin in the flats, a collection of red-brick and wood-frame houses under twisted cottonwoods, hazy in the growing heat. Behind them a tail of yellow dust rose into the changing sky, burning amber in the hard light of the rising sun.

It was thirteen minutes after five, on a warming June day. A high-pressure area centered in Coeur d'Alene had spread itself out over central Montana, driving the thunderheads north into Alberta and Saskatchewan and east into the flatlands of the Dakotas. The air was muted and gauzy, softening the edges of the rolling green hills and the spires and peaks of the Bighorn range into a wash of glowing blues, rich deep browns, wide bands of ochre, russet, and sage, the dusty blue of high pines, and the sudden bright arc of copper and black granite. A few miles north and west, the smoke and fumes from the Cenex refinery were drifting westward down the Yellowstone Valley between the Rimrock and the southern bluffs, settling down over the skyline and the railheads and the shipping yards of Billings like a dirty brown blanket. But here along the Bighorn the air was as bright and clear as the edge of a straight razor.

Except for the small shape of Mary Littlebasket running across the drying grasses of the empty schoolyard, and the rust-red pickup moving toward her along a side street, and a few blocks to the north near the I-90, the two Big Horn cruisers rolling into the little town, Hardin was soundless in sleep and dreams.

The security guard was a forty-nine-year-old man named Bill Haugge, three years divorced from a check-out clerk named Violet who had stapled weekly summaries of his serial shortcomings to his forehead for eleven years before he finally left their house in Billings and took this job at the Julia Dwight Clinic. Haugge was emphysemic and overweight and he drank too much, but he had good eyes and he saw Mary Littlebasket right away, running through the cottonwoods. At the same time he saw Charlie Tallbull's old pickup come around the corner, and he remembered the nurse saying that a baby had been taken, and he knew right away that there was no way that Fat Bill Haugge was going to catch her in a footrace. So he tugged out his Ruger—first time he'd had it out of the holster since he'd passed the Highway Patrol Firearms Certification Test in Laurel two years ago—and he raised it above his right shoulder, muzzle skyward, and squeezed one off.

The muzzle blast blew his right eardrum in and knocked him sideways into the iron handrail to the left of the stairs, where he hit his head—hard—on the spur of it, and his Ruger fell out of his hands and clattered down the concrete stairs to the pavement. The deep booming sound of the blast carried over the rooftops of Hardin in the dense warm air, and Dell Greer got on the horn with a shots-fired signal as they both accelerated.

The muzzle blast woke up every crow on the roof of the clinic. They exploded into the air, a black shout of crows shooting skyward. The concussive wave that traveled out across the schoolyard shook several hundred bats out of the cottonwood branches—they flew upward in a fluttering mass of leathery brown wings. Mary Littlebasket felt it as a puff of breath on the small of her back, and her heart flew upward in her chest until it slammed into the back of her throat and she was flying, flying, across the dry grass toward Charlie Tallbull, where he was pulling the pickup to a stop. The passenger door was now wide open—she could see him leaning forward at the wheel, a big old mahogany bull of a man in faded jeans and a straw hat, waving her on, and she was just slipping into the cab of the truck, her baby tight to her chest, when the two Big Horn cruisers came around the corner, flat-out and sliding a bit in the gritty ochre dust that covered Hardin in the summer. Moses Harper went for the pickup, and Dell Greer peeled off to check out the alarm call at the Dwight Clinic.

Charlie Tallbull slammed his accelerator down and cut the truck hard right onto the access road for I-90 and then hard right again, seeing the eerie geometry of the interstate and the infinity of the hills all around him and the smoky blue peaks of the Bull range far away at the vanishing point of the endless curving road. He powered up the ramp, and then he was running the YIELD sign and blue smoke was pouring out of the pickup's tailpipe, and

Moses Harper was getting blue smoke and raw carbon monoxide in his face as he pushed the cruiser right up the man's tailgate.

Dell Greer slid his cruiser to a stop and ran across the parking lot to the clinic stairs, where Bill Haugge was just now sitting up with blood running from his right ear and his left temple. A small nosebleed stained his uniform shirt.

Moses Harper heard Dell's voice on the radio saying that a man had been shot at the Dwight Clinic and that 229 was in pursuit of a brown— Moses was thinking it wasn't really brown, it was more of a red-rust color— 1974 Ford pickup—Dell was really pretty good at identifying running vehicles. He was about to cut in with the license number—it was red and white, a South Dakota plate—victor alpha niner seven four—in fact, he was reaching down—now isn't that—hell, that's Charlie Tallbull's truck—why the hell is—looking down for the handset—shouldn't have done that—so when he looked up again, all he really saw was a massive blur of chrome and blue paint as a Kenworth eighteen-wheeler came over the hilltop, and then Moses saw Charlie Tallbull's pickup dive—the taillights suddenly bright red—and then the blue Kenworth sounded its horn and that was all Moses could hear—that tremendous buffeting blast—he hit his own brakes and pulled hard to the right as the Kenworth skimmed his door, huge wheels spinning at his shoulder, a wall of sound and iron and smoke and it caught— met—*butted* the rusted pickup.

Broken glass flared in the sunlight like a spray of water.

Folding, the pickup bounced away, the Kenworth climbing up and over it. The pickup rolled over, a shimmer of sun on the black greasy underbelly as it rolled, and the Kenworth kept riding up on top of it. There were sparks now, as the cab of the pickup was driven into the road, the metal grinding away on the stones and gravel at the side of the highway. Moses got his cruiser stopped and sat there, maybe fifty yards back now—a ringside seat— as the Kenworth rode the pickup down the side slope and settled onto it like a cast-iron avalanche, and then the dust cloud rose up, billowed, spread, settled back down over the scene, shading it and softening it, tinting it amber and sepia so that it seemed to Moses that he was watching something through stained glass, something that took place a long time ago.

At the Julia Dwight Clinic, Dell Greer got Bill Haugge some help, and after a while he got enough out of the distraught nurses to figure out that Mary Littlebasket had simply taken her own child out of the hospital and that what had happened here this morning could very well turn out to be the kind of career-blasting, sixteen-ton, great-bellowing-balls-to-the-wall fuckup that would pass into Big Horn County legend and make for interesting sunsets in eastern Montana for years to come. Dell Greer went up the back stairs to Mary Littlebasket's room and stood in the doorway, thinking about it all, listening to Moses Harper's voice on his portable radio trying to sound in control, Harper calling in Fire and Rain and the ambulances. The bed still showed the impress of her body. A pair of paper slippers sat neatly in the near corner. A damp handkerchief lay twisted beside a Bible on the bedside table. Greer went into the bathroom and saw Mary Littlebasket's sign in lipstick on the dripping mirror.

> > > = = = = = = = = = = = >   < + >   < = = = = = = = = = = = < < <

It meant nothing to him.

Well, whatever had happened here, it looked like it was still happening. As he turned to leave, he looked down and saw a ribbon on the floor. Cornflower blue, grosgrain, it must have fallen from her hair. He left it there. It all belonged to the detectives now. He was just Patrol. The state boys would have to unravel all this. When it was over, maybe someone would tell him what it all meant.

1

1600 Hours – June 14 – Pompeys Pillar, Montana

Engine racing, rear wheels spinning in the dry wash, McAllister's patrol car butted through a windbreak of gorse and dry sage. He hit the brakes. He was right at the crest of Bull Peak, and fifty square miles of Yellowstone County stretched away south and west, a watercolor wash of greens and blue-gray, ochre and amber and copper fading out along the distant horizon where the last of the spring snow on the roof of the Beartooth range glimmered pink and silver in the waning sunlight. It would have been a sight to raise a man's heart if it weren't for the little corpses scattered all around.

To the right of the cruiser, like a deep cut in old green hide, a massive crater scarred the slope. New earth and cracked rock covered the prairie grass. Prairie dog corpses were scattered around like pillows in a cathouse.

Some of the bodies were about to pop. It looked like a tailgate party for crows and coyotes.

He powered down the window. The midafternoon heat moved across his face and down into the cool of the car.

Even McAllister could read this kind of trail sign in the roadway. The little tiptoed skitter of the coyotes. Those crisscrossing hatchwork trails under the coyote sign would be the crows. Shiny blue-black, as big as dogs. Waddling back and forth between the bodies like lawyers at a nine-car pileup.

And this track here . . . he leaned out the window to follow it. A kind of shallow trench with hills of yellow dust looking a little like waves. Fresh, since the wind up here in the hills was always pretty good. And big . . . a full-bore male.

So he'd be . . . close. Good to know how close. Not that McAllister was getting out of the patrol car. But it was an interesting problem. It was always good to know who was where. He shut down the engine and opened all the windows. The car needed an airing anyway. He tugged his garrison belt off and dumped it in a pile on the passenger seat, the Browning on top.

It would have been Walker's crew. They were working up this slope, trying to cut a roadway through the crest over to Musselshell. God knew what for. The best thing about Musselshell was there were two ways to get out of it.

Walker must have hit bedrock here. No county bulldozer could have done this. McAllister had never been on a battlefield, not a fresh one anyway, but this was what he thought it would look like. Bodies all over the place. New earth ripped up in heaps and piles. New white stones that hadn't seen the sun for a half a million years. Wind in the grasses—he looked up at the skyline, and as usual it hit him that this was possibly the finest work God had ever done, this fifty square miles of Yellowstone County, sea green and rolling from the massed blue line of the Big Horn Mountains in the south all the way west to the Beartooth range. Most of it as full of little murders as this ridge.

When Walker's charge went off, it had blown away a section of this hillside up here to his right. It had opened up a prairie dog town and spread it down the grassy slope. Most of them had died right then. The rest, those who could, had split for a better neighborhood. But since it was June in Montana, everything that had lived through the winter was breeding furiously. There were some mothers with litters around, trying to get whatever was left of their broods into a safe place.

What had looked to McAllister like a pile of pebbles in the roadway was now sitting up and looking around. One large gray-brown prairie dog. The mama. And one—kit? pup?—at her forelegs.

And another about a yard away.

So where was the rattlesnake?

There he was—where the waving track went into a low screen of sagebrush. He must have been making his run when McAllister came up the hill and scared everybody. A *big* old son of a bitch from the look of him, a dirty-brown loop of thick rope with a pattern along his spine. A diamondback maybe, although the purple shadow made it hard to tell. He might go six feet, judging by how thick he was, coiled up there. Under the sage, Scratch was perfectly still, except for his tongue. Now and then, McAllister could see it flutter out and back. Scratch was tasting the air, tasting the oil and gas smell of McAllister's cruiser. Calculating the odds and the distances.

McAllister glanced down at his Browning, trying to work out his position in this thing. Knowing he didn't really *have* a position in whatever happened next.

The mama-dog was up now on her back legs, looking sideways at McAllister. She couldn't smell him in the car. Her tail flicked and trembled, and the pup at her feet started to move. McAllister could hear it making a little beeping sound.

That was enough for Scratch. He started to slide out of the shadow, like a wave curling across a pond.

McAllister picked up the Browning and thumbed back the hammer.

This was silly—he'd shot more prairie dogs than this snake could eat in three lifetimes. Why was he getting involved now?

Was it because of the two babies? He had babies. Well, not babies. Girls. One grown now, twenty-two and somewhere down in Wyoming at an archaeological dig. And Bobby Lee, six this very day, waiting for him at what used to be his house and was now generally known as the Bitch's Bungalow.

No turning back now. Scratch was committed. He'd get to within a lunge of the prairie dog, and suddenly he'd be *on* them. You'd never see the move. There'd just be a snake with a dead prairie dog in his jaws. Mama was still thinking about McAllister's cruiser. She was not paying enough attention to what was going on around her.

Cold little brown eyes on her. She reminded him of Maureen, which reminded him about his date—no, *appointment* was more like it. His appointment with Maureen to pick up Bobby Lee at six tonight. It was four now, and he still had to get the car into the station house, shower and change, wrap the present.

Maureen did not *like* it when you were *late*. That was *your problem,* Beau. You were always *late*. That isn't *nice,* Beau. So don't be *late,* Beau. Thinking on that, he reached down and turned off his radio. What could happen this late on a slow Friday?

Well . . . just about anything, but they could get into it without any more help from Beau McAllister. He'd pulled his weight long enough to get some slack.

He watched the snake sliding through the grasses, in and out of the sunlight. It was interesting to watch. You could pick a portion of that body and focus on it, and it would be as if that part didn't move. The pattern there would compress, and the rest of the snake would just flow through that section. It was like watching the light bulbs on the roof of the Cineplex in Billings. You watched the bulbs and you missed the pattern, or you watched the pattern and the bulbs seemed to move.

Scratch was picking up a little speed here. Jesus, these things could really cover the ground. McAllister moved the Browning across his chest and lined the sights up on Scratch's head, tracking it as it made that little sideways move, back and forth, the tongue out and flickering. A few yards away, a soon-to-be-*ex*-prairie-dog mama continued profoundly misunderstanding her situation. Come *on,* Mom!

Then she seemed to vibrate for a half-second—a flicker and a spurt of dust and she was—*gone*. A rustle in the grass at the far side of the road. A flash of gray tail. Leaving the kids in the roadway.

Christ, what a cold-assed *bitch*!

So much for motherhood.

And here comes Scratch, making his run at the half-blind pups in his path. McAllister tightened his grip and began to pull. He had maybe a couple of seconds.

beep beep beep

Christ! He'd forgotten to shut off his beeper. God-*damn* all beepers! Somebody was trying to get him and knew his radio was off. He flicked the switch to his radio and picked up the handset just as Scratch got to the first pup.

"Five eleven."

Man. Just like that. A cocktail sausage.

"Beau! Where the hell are you?"

In the background of the transmission, McAllister could hear the tone-beep of the emergency system. Armed robbery, or a gun run. Nice timing, Beau.

"Up on Elbow Hill, a coupla miles, Eustace. What's up?"

"Well, if it's not an imposition, maybe you might get yourself down to Joe Bell's place. He's got a robbery in progress, wants to know if we feel like helping out."

McAllister started up the cruiser, not soon enough to distract Scratch from the next pup down the road.

"Why me? That's a County call. Get the Yellowstone guys onto it. Get the Big Horn guys. Get anybody but me."

"Bell's place is on the interstate, last time I looked. That's us. Quit jerking me around, Beau."

"Any guns?"

"One thing for sure—Bell's got one."

By now, McAllister had the white Ford LTD rocking down the dirt road toward Pompeys Pillar.

"He tell you that?"

"He didn't have to—I heard him doing it. Ronny's on the way. And Rita. The rest of the guys are all over the County."

Shit, thought McAllister. Never answer the phone on a Friday afternoon.

Joe Bell was a retired railroad man who ran Bell's Oasis, a huge truck stop and Shell gas station on I-94, at the east end of Pompeys Pillar. Bell's Oasis was *the* major business of Pompeys Pillar. Joe Bell was a big bald cracker with his hand in all sorts of pockets around Yellowstone County. Like everybody in Montana, Bell had a do-it-yourself attitude about law enforcement, and he seemed to be doing it himself right now. McAllister had the Ford shuddering over a washboard track as the radio popped and snarled with chatter.

"Four nine nine, come on?"

"Yes, Sergeant?"

"Where're you, Rita?"

"I'm behind an RV, 'bout a mile out. No—wait—*shit*!"

"Rita? Rita?"

"I'm fine—I just took him on the shoulder there."

McAllister could hear the siren in the background as she talked. Rita was new and very intense.

Eustace Meagher was back on the air. "Rita, cut the chatter. Beau, you there?"

"I'm here, Eustace."

"It looks like Joe's out there by the pumps, shooting the buttons off everything."

Christ.

"By the pumps?"

"Yeah—I called Fire and Rain. ETA is ten minutes."

"I'm just about there."

"Sergeant?"

"Rita?"

"Yeah—I can see it now. You want me to wait for you?"

"You block the east end. Where the hell is Thornton?"

There was an explosion of static and then Ronny's voice, breathless and wired up.

"This is 495. You're gonna blow right by me."

McAllister could see the town now, a ragged line of low buildings set in the lee of a dry wash. The Shell sign was the tallest thing in town. At the point where the gravel road hit the pavement, McAllister could see Ron Thornton's cruiser.

"Sarge, I can see you!"

"Yeah. Rita, stay put! We'll come east on the service road. You block the far end. Ronny, when we get there, keep that goddamned werewolf in the car. We don't need him ripping up the citizens. Rita, you read me five by five?"

"Ten-four, sir. I'll hold."

McAllister was doing a flat eighty as he flew by Ronny's cruiser. Ron Thornton was a heavy-set, barrel-bodied youngster with a pencil-thin moustache that made him look like a Mexican pimp. His dark face was hot and bright. Through the slots in an aluminum barrier, McAllister could hear Ronny's police dog howling and snarling.

Ronny stayed right on McAllister's bumper all the way up the main street of Pompeys Pillar, sirens yipping and the people all lined up on the walkways. Bell's Oasis was at the far end of town. At a hundred yards out they heard the solid percussive boom of a shotgun.

Ronny and McAllister slid to a stop in the lee of a J. B. Hunt tractor-trailer. The driver was already flattened up against the wheels. He grinned weakly as they ran over and got their backs up against the trailer.

"What the *hell's* goin' on here?" McAllister asked the driver.

"Beats me, Sergeant," said the driver. "All's I know is, one minute I'm sitting in my cab, and the next Joe's shooting the shit outta a bunch of Indians at the pumps."

"Indians? What kind?"

The trucker's lean face split along his worry lines. "Jeez, man! Indians! Crows, likely, or Cheyenne from Busby. Bell give one of 'em a bellyfull of shot, I know *that*!"

McAllister ducked down to take a look under the trailer bed.

Across the tarmac, Joe Bell was crouched down beside a line of gas
pumps, head down, feeding shells into a semiauto twelve-gauge Winchester
shotgun.

Twenty feet away, a dark-skinned boy in faded jeans and a blue plaid
shirt lay on his back in a widening lake of thickening blood. One of his boots
was off. It was standing, oddly, upright. A black Stetson with one eagle
feather lay on its peak a foot away. Most of the boy's side was scattered in
a pulpy red fan over the pavement. McAllister could see his chest rising and
falling. Still alive.

"Ronny, you get back to the car, you tell Fire to bring the paramedic
van and not to screw around doing it!" Fire and Rain was what they called
the Emergency Service Unit.

Ronny jumped and ran. McAllister peeked back around the end of the
van. A dusty blue Chevy pickup was parked at the pumps. Its hood was up,
and the oil dipstick was on the ground in front of the truck. Jubal's pickup.

"Hey, Bell!"

Bell pivoted with the shotgun, shouldered it, and fired in the direction
of Beau's voice. The back of the trailer rocked, and a license plate flew fifty
feet into the ditch.

"Christ, Bell! It's Beau McAllister!"

Joe Bell's bald head and heavy red beard rose up above the top of a
gas pump.

"Beau?"

"Yes! For chrissake, Bell!"

"You see 'em, Beau? Over by the propane tank?"

Oh, great, thought McAllister. About fifty yards away, there was a big
enclosure marked off by a Lundy fence. Inside, a huge white torpedo tank
sat atop a series of concrete supports. He could just see some huddled shapes
through the support pillars.

"First thing, Bell, you stop firing at that thing. You hit that tank right,
we're all gonna go way up high and come back down as pink rain."

"It was just grazing fire, Beau. I know what I'm doing!"

Sure, thought McAllister. You sure grazed that boy pretty good, didn't
you? "What the hell's goin on, Bell?"

"There's five of them. Look like reservation Indians. I got this one.
There's three men and a girl. They come in with that old blue pickup there,
and I braced 'em. Then they go for the weapons."

"What kind?"

"A knife. A *big* one. Other weird shit. I didn't stop to make a fuckin'
list!"

"What'd they do?"

"*Do?* They go for weapons, I figure it's a fight!"

McAllister turned to Ronny, who was once more pressed close to the truck. "Go get me the hailer, Ronny. I'm gonna see if we can talk our way outta something here. I don't have time for this shit."

Ronny came back with the Motorola hailer. McAllister crawled back to the end of the tractor-trailer. "You there, by the tank!"

Nothing. Maybe some movement.

"This is the po—"

Something went *thoong* and then—unbelievably—there was the whirring sound of—a kind of whistle—what the?—then a huge metallic clang hit the tractor-trailer near Beau.

There was—there was a god-*dammed arrow* stuck ten inches into the back of the tractor-trailer. It had pretty blue feathers and a dark metal shaft, stuck in there good and solid. McAllister stared at it for maybe five seconds, not ready to believe what he was seeing.

"Ronny, are you seeing what I'm—"

Another basso *thoong* sound. McAllister scrambled back into the cover beside the driver and Ronny. The trailer caught another shaft. It hit the outside wall like a hammer blow.

Arrows, McAllister was thinking. He couldn't get his mind around it. Somebody was shooting *arrows* at him.

Two more *thoong* sounds, and two more shrill whirrings.

Chunk!

Chunk!

Joe Bell felt the need to respond. The three of them heard Bell pull his slide back.

"No!" McAllister shouted. Ron and the J. B. Hunt driver were already running for the ditch at the side of the road.

"I'm just gonna—" That sound again, and the whistling whirring. Joe Bell was up and leaning across the pump. The shaft came in like judgment, sliced into his left shoulder. Beau could see the plaid shirt open up and the vivid red flesh underneath.

Bell stood up and bellowed once. He still had the shotgun in his right fist. That gun had everybody's full attention now, the arrow stuck in his shoulder. Round and round she goes, thought McAllister, not able to drop, just watching the barrel and watching Joe Bell stagger around the end of the pump island, watching him come forward now, blood running from the slice in his upper arm—Christ, that would hurt. Everybody in the area who could see what was going on tried to dig a little farther into the dirt or tiles on the snack-bar floor or the bottom of the truck cab—but Bell wasn't dropping that goddamned Winchester.

Bell squeezed one off. The big gun kicked back in his hand.

A swarm of fat black bees hurtled off into the blue.

Jesus, thought Beau. He's got double-ought in there. Twelve steel balls as big as marbles.

So it came to McAllister that maybe he should just plain shoot Joe Bell. Otherwise they were all going to die.

"Bell! Put the gun down!"

Bell was out there, beyond control. His face was sweaty and bright as a road flare as he came out in the open now, bringing that big barrel around one more time, leaning back in his Tony Lamas, his big white belly out over the top of his jeans, his shirt ripped and flapping in the wind, his mouth wide open in the middle of that huge red beard.

Beau pulled the Browning out and lined the red foresight up over Joe Bell's right foot.

"Bell! You gotta stop firing!"

Boom! Bell got off another shell. Maybe he had visions of Wyatt Earp in his head. Maybe he was seeing it all on *Eyewitness News*. This one zipped and zanged into the gravel about ten feet to one side of the propane tank. Steel shot skittered crazily off across the highway.

Beau saw a couple of things in a crystalline bubble of hallucinatory intensity.

He saw the way Bell's blue jeans had faded to white along the top of his right leg and the darker indigo color along the rumpled sideseam.

He saw the frayed threads on the cuff of his own right sleeve and the sheen of silicon grease on the dull black slide of his Browning.

And in his mind, he saw Lieutenant Eustace Meagher in front of a line of his fellow cops, McAllister standing there while Eustace pulled off McAllister's stripes and somebody off to the left beat an accusatory rattle on a little muffled drum.

McAllister breathed out slowly and squeezed off one round, aiming for Bell's right foot. The Browning bucked in his hand, and his ears rang from the blast.

Damn, thought Beau, watching in a cold detached way as the round hit Bell in the muscle of his ass, square in the middle of his wallet. Why do they make these things so goddamned *loud*?

Bell jerked, reeled, and staggered left. He looked across at McAllister, his face the very picture of outrage and injured dignity. He twisted to regard the damage in his back pocket, then looked up at McAllister again.

"You god-*damned* asshole! You *shot* me!"

"*Somebody* had to, Bell! You were gonna—"

And now Bell felt the muscle give, and he started to go down to his right. As he came down he brought the shotgun around and he was trying to . . .

. . . get that barrel lined up . . .

. . . on what?

. . . on me, thought McAllister.

Now what? Do I kill Joe Bell?

When Bell hit the ground, the shotgun bounced out of his hand and clattered across the pavement. McAllister was out around the J. B. Hunt trailer and halfway to Bell when he remembered that somebody had been shooting arrows at him only a minute ago.

"Hey, over there! No shooting, eh?"

Jesus. Listen to yourself, McAllister. Like it was half-time or something.

The way the sun was lying, it was hard to see into the enclosure. He stood there in the open for a second, waiting for another one of those lunatic arrows to come flying across the parking lot. Bell was trying to crawl toward the shotgun. McAllister could hear him swearing to himself.

Ronny Thornton came out from the front of the tractor cab and put his Smith over the propane area.

"Ronny, don't shoot into that tank."

Ronny's hair was in a tangle, and a clump of grass was stuck to his shoulder. "I'm not gonna shoot, Sarge. Anyway, I think they're gone."

"Then why the hell're you pointing your piece over there? Get back on the air, tell everybody in Charlie Sector—tell everybody in District Four, get Radio to notify the Counties and get a BOLO out for three male Indians and a juvenile female. They're armed and dangerous. Last seen this ten-twenty. Tell 'em what's happened here. Now. Go do it!"

Thornton nodded once and went back to the cruiser at a jog.

McAllister walked over to the shotgun, picked it up, and jacked it empty. Joe Bell rolled over onto his side and said something. Beau couldn't make out anything but "McAllister." He figured it had something to do with lawyers.

"Ronny, get on the radio and find out where the hell Fire and Rain is. We're gonna need them."

He walked over to the Indian boy on the ground, got down on one knee, and put two fingers of his right hand under the boy's shirt, just where the ribs met the breastbone.

Not a sound. And nothing at the neck. The kid had a look on his lean

unmarked face that McAllister had seen before. Although we all live surrounded by death and dying, every one of us believes he will live forever.
The truth is always a surprise. The boy had long blue-black hair; it would
have run down past his shoulders if it hadn't been matted with drying blood.
He had a Plains Indian look about him. Clean lines and that heavy-bodied,
skinny-legged shape.

McAllister touched one of the boy's eyes. No reflex. No pupil change.
Down at his left side, a loop of intestine and a pink bulb of kidney projected
through the bloody ruin of his shirt.

Bled to death while I was jerking around with Bell. Poor little bastard.
One more sorry-ass useless killing. Kid had good taste in boots, too.

McAllister patted the boy down. He found an eelskin wallet in his back
pocket and a large bowie knife in a beaded doeskin scabbard at his right
side.

He tugged the knife out. A buck knife with a solid bone handle. A foot
long, and sharp as an ex-wife.

So what? He could pat down half the citizens of Montana and find some
kind of knife.

He headed across the lot toward the propane tank, holding the Browning
out to one side, trying to look like a reasonable guy, the kind of guy you
wouldn't want to shoot an arrow into.

Still, it was a long walk in the afternoon sunlight.

The little fenced-off yard was empty. Behind the tank he found a sliver
of blue feather lying in the dirt.

Now that would be your basic clue, right?

Or was it a sign?

A sign of *what*? Times like these, Beau was glad he was just a patrol
sergeant. Let the boys from the Criminal Investigation Bureau figure out this
Indian voodoo.

The dirt was scuffed up. Bootprints and some kind of patterned grid,
maybe a running shoe. The sign ran to the back of the fence and continued
on the far side. Wherever they had got to, they had done it on foot. Behind
Bell's Oasis there was a low coulee that ran a couple of hundred yards up
into the hills. And beyond the hills, half of Montana, the Bull Mountains,
Canada. He could see a faint trail running up into the brown prairie grass.

McAllister had no inclination to go tear-assing up the slope and into
the hills after anybody with arrows as mean-looking as the ones stuck into
the rear of that van. He was too old and too smart. Maybe the National
Guard would let them borrow one of their Hueys and a pilot.

Rita Sonnette pulled up into the yard as McAllister got back to where Ron was using a field dressing on Bell's wound. She got out of her cruiser and started pushing tourists and truckers away from the dead boy by the gas pumps. Rita was a short, well-constructed lady with green eyes and deep copper-colored hair.

Joe Bell was putting out a fair amount of unfriendly vibrations in spite of the hole in his butt. They could hear a siren in the distance.

"Bell—I *tried* to—"

"I got nothing to say to you, McAllister."

"I told you to stop shooting that artillery piece all over the place. You know the blast radius of that tank better than I do."

"You ever hear of fire control? I was in the war!"

"Yeah? You weren't controlling a damned thing."

"I was protecting my property and my place of business. And the citizens. I got a constitutional right. You had no call to shoot me. Why didn't you shoot one of those Indians?"

"You shoot that boy over there?"

"You're damned right I did! It was him or me."

"He drew on you? He showed a weapon?"

"Of *course* he did! Otherwise I wouldna hadda shoot him. I don't usually shoot my customers. Word gets around."

"What exactly did he do?"

"They all come in in that blue Chevy pickup over there. Soon as I see the weapons out, I know what's happening. The one I shot, he comes right into my office with a knife out, so I braced him and backed him down."

"What time was this?"

"Now! It just happened. Christ, Beau! Ain't you got a watch?" Bell jerked as Ron taped the pad down. "Jeez, Thornton, where'd you get your training?"

The Fire and Rain wagon rolled up in a cloud of dust and a hearty hi-ho-plasma, the way those guys like to do. They came running across the lot, and McAllister could almost hear them going *hut-hut-hut* to themselves, the way they saw it done on *Rescue 911*. Same as the young cops nowadays—Ray-Bans and black leather gloves and zombie cool. Television was taking all the fun out of being a cop.

McAllister patted Bell on his good shoulder. "I'm sorry about shooting you. We'll haveta talk later. You hang in there, Joe."

"I got a hole in my wallet you could stick your dick through, McAllister. Fucked up all my cards, my ID, everything!"

"I'll buy you a new wallet."

"Hey, this ain't no joke! I can't walk, I can't work. Somebody's gonna have to make good on this."

"Man, don't tell me you're gonna *sue*? What the hell's Montana coming to, a hard case like you goes squealing to a lawyer?"

"Jesus, McAllister. We'll see if you can still laugh with a lawsuit stuffed up *your* ass."

"Long as you're somewhere in Montana, Bell, I can always find something to laugh at."

"We'll see, McAllister. We'll see."

"No doubt, Joe. No doubt. You go with him, Ronny. Get a complete statement, and get a Polaroid of that wound there. And go around, take some shots of those arrows right where they are. The CIB guys'll want that."

He stepped back as they hoisted Bell onto a gurney and *hut-hut-hutted* him away to the van.

They'll hit the siren as soon as they get the back doors slammed, thought McAllister. He sighed. Another lawsuit in the works there.

He walked across to where Rita Sonnette was standing next to the dead boy. A circle of the curious and the bored stood a few yards away, staring at the body with that kind of face people get in the presence of violent death. Sick, avid, hungry. McAllister thought they looked like those walking corpses in *Night of the Living Dead*. They all had that blankness.

"You're standing in the blood there, Rita."

She jumped and stepped back.

"God. I'm sorry, Sergeant."

"No problem. Go get some of that crime scene tape. We might as well get this place organized for the CIB guys. Seal off that blue pickup, but don't touch it and don't go inside it. I wanna be able to tell the dicks that no patrolman of mine screwed up their crime scene. I'll get these people on the move here. And get those arrows outta that J. B. Hunt trailer. Do it without screwing up the shafts, okay? We might get prints off them."

It took Rita and McAllister awhile to close down Bell's Oasis and empty out the snack bar. They put a tarpaulin over the dead boy and wrote down the names and numbers of anybody who would admit to seeing anything.

Most of the witnesses agreed that the first thing they noticed was Joe Bell coming out of the station with the barrel of his shotgun stuck into the belly of that dead boy over there.

He got the same story from the waitress on duty. She was a weathered-looking number with pale yellow hair that floated around her head like cotton candy. She said her name was Marla LeMay and had ID to prove it, which was good enough for McAllister. She had that seen-it-all-and-seen-it-first look that made McAllister think of cops, hookers, and old nuns.

"How long you been working for Bell, Marla?"

"Six weeks. Maybe seven. I got a place over in Hardin, near the post office? I work double shifts here 'cause Joe can't seem to keep his help."

"Yeah? Why's that?"

"He lets his little head think for his big head."

"Oh—that doesn't bother you?"

"No. First time he tried anything, I put my hand down the front of his jeans and give his tail a twist. Then I told him if I leave I'm goin' straight to Montana Labor and sue his ass off. Plus I'd come back and kill his dog."

"You sure Bell has a dog?"

"If he doesn't I'll buy him one and *then* kill it."

They both laughed.

"Okay, Marla. What'd you see today?"

"Can I just not say anything?"

"Why?"

"I need this job. I just don't like lying to cops, either."

"Why would you have to lie to me?"

"Because I ain't at all sure anybody had to get shot today."

"Why don't you just tell me what you saw, and I'll work out where I mighta heard it?"

"Bullshit, Sergeant."

"Call me Beau."

"Bullshit, Beau. Call me Marla."

"I've been calling you Marla."

"Yeah. But now you got my permission."

"Why's it bullshit?"

"I been to court a coupla times. You guys are always saying hey, well now, *you'll* never have to testify. Then you go back to the office, and some college-kid DA says fuck that. Subpoena the bitch."

He smiled down at her again.

"You're a smart woman. You can see how sometimes shit happens and all you can do is try to scrape it up. I got a poor dead boy over there, died while Joe Bell was playing at Wyatt Earp. Bell says it was self-defense, but all I can see is a dead kid. I don't see a cash bag. I see arrows—an odd choice for armed robbery, but that's okay. Everybody says the first they saw was Bell backin' the dead guy out of his office with his Winchester. Is that what you saw?"

"I saw the boy go into Joe's office. I heard them talking. Then I seen the boy backing out, and Joe's got that shotgun shoved right into the kid's belly."

"Were they fighting?"

"It *looked* like a fight from where I was at."

"Yeah, but what was being said?"

"I really couldn't hear. By that time, some of the customers were screaming and a lot of people were trying to get out of the way."

"And the kid?"

"He wasn't saying anything. He was just trying to back up without falling."

"You see a weapon?"

"Yeah. I saw a knife. The kid had it in his hand when he came backing out."

"Was it in his hand when he went in?"

"I didn't see it. Knife like that, you notice it."

"Was Bell in his office when the kid went in?"

"Yeah. He's always in there. Has a bunch of skin magazines under the desk. We call him Zamfir."

"Why Zamfir?"

"Bell's a master of the skin flute."

McAllister thought it over. Bell said he saw weapons. When? Not from his office. His office had a window that opened onto the snack bar and cash area, which led out to the pumps. There was a large plate-glass window cluttered with oil cans and antifreeze bottles. There was too much inventory stuck in the window for Bell to see out into the pump area. So you couldn't see the pumps from Bell's office, just out into the snack bar and the store. So when did Bell see the weapons?

"What happened then?"

"Bell backed the kid outside. Then he . . . "

McAllister waited. She'd either say it or not say it.

"Kid *did* have a knife, Beau."

"True."

"So that makes it self-defense, right?"

Not exactly, thought McAllister. Something about this thing just hit him as strange. Bell had a shotgun over the kid. The kid was backing away. Any cop who used deadly force in that situation would be looking at permanent administrative leave and maybe even criminal charges.

"Where were you standing then?"

"Over there. By the door. I could see pretty good."

"Could you see both of them?"

"Yeah . . . well, not really. I could see Joe's back and see some of the kid. Joe's a big guy, and the kid isn't very big."

"Could you hear what was being said?"

"Just Joe. Joe was being pretty loud. The kid was talking fast, but I couldn't hear him over Joe's voice."

"What was Joe saying?"

"Threats, mostly."

"Where were the rest of them?"

"The other ones? There was four of them, three big guys and a girl. The girl was in the cab. One of the guys was standing at the front of the truck there, checking his oil or his coolant or something."

"Odd thing to do during an armed robbery. What did they do when they saw Bell coming out?"

"They kind of froze solid. The girl tries to get out of the truck, and the biggest Indian, he goes for the back but keeps the truck between him and Joe, and then Joe starts firing."

McAllister thought it over for a bit.

"Okay, Marla. You tell it like you saw it, I don't think Joe Bell will hold it against you." McAllister thought she was the least of Bell's troubles.

"We'll haveta see, won't we?"

"Yeah. You have a ride back to Hardin?"

"Yeah. I got an old Riviera out back."

"Okay, Marla. We'll have to talk again. You don't worry about it, right? There'll be a shooting board sometime in the next couple of days. We'll need you to appear, tell the board what you saw."

"What's a shooting board?"

"Every time an officer in Montana fires his weapon, there has to be a formal inquiry. The DA and a couple of experienced detectives talk to everyone who witnessed the event, and then they decide whether or not the officer was justified in using his weapon."

"So it's about you, and shooting Joe Bell?"

"That's right."

"Why did you shoot Joe, anyway?"

Beau inclined his head toward the propane tank.

"That tank. Bell was shooting right at it. If he'd punctured it, we'd all be dead."

Her eyes widened, and she sighed.

"Hell of a day. Burned my dress, broke three nails, then we get robbed. You ever have a day like that, Sergeant?"

"You're looking at one right now, Marla. You take care of yourself."

Marla shrugged and walked back toward the kitchen. McAllister went into Joe Bell's office. The first thing he saw was the phone on Bell's desk. Bell had a business phone, a multiline with a board full of push-buttons and lights. The machine was howling. Beau recognized the electronic warning for a phone off the hook. He searched around the thing for a bit until he found a button that said SPK. It was lit up red. He punched it, and the light went out, and the noise stopped. He picked up the receiver and got a normal dial tone.

McAllister sat down at Bell's desk and flipped the dead man's wallet out onto the top. The kid had died with . . . close to seven hundred dollars! And what was this? Gold American Express card in the name of Edward Gall. A whole packet of gas receipts. A cash card for one of those electronic machines. BankAmericard. A California driver's license, picture ID of a young man who looked like the boy out in the yard. Showing an address of 1623 Vallejo Canyon Drive, Los Angeles. Also a plastic hospital card showing that an Edward Gall had been admitted to something called the Sonesta Clinic in March of this year.

And a couple of photographs of a strong-featured young Indian woman in what looked like a school uniform, a pink tunic and a white blouse. It made McAllister think of reservation schools like the one his first wife had attended, a long time ago.

Interesting . . . looked like young Mr. Gall here wasn't exactly hard up for cash when he apparently set himself to rob Joe Bell at knifepoint in the middle of the day in the middle of a crowd of people. *And* they brought along a young girl to watch them do it.

There was an old joke about only an Indian being dumb enough to bring a knife to a gunfight, but this was pushing it. It ran contrary to everything in Beau's experience of armed robbers, which was considerable. He moved his leg and felt something along the side of the desk.

Bell had a rifle sling bolted to the inside well of his desk. Big enough for the Winchester. The top was a litter of bills, receipts, yellow pads, assorted junk. McAllister pulled open some drawers. The first one had checks and some loose cash. The second drawer was locked. The third one was full of magazines and videos.

Swedish Nights. Ballbusters. Seka's Greatest Hits. The usual full-color hardcore entertainments, based largely on having low gag-reflexes and being double-jointed. This stuff always reminded Beau of autopsies, all that red flesh and slippery skin. Sexy as a federal audit. There was a television set on top of a filing cabinet, and a VCR beneath the TV. Bell's wastepaper basket was stuffed full of old wadded-up tissues. Best thing to do with that was to take it out back and set it on fire.

Porn videos and skin mags.

This garbage was illegal in Montana, but McAllister had better things to do than police other people's entertainments. A lot of unmarried men had worse than this under their bunks. At least it kept them away from the schoolyards—

Oh, Christ!

He grabbed up the handset and punched in seven numbers, looking at his wristwatch as the line started to ring.

"Hello."

"Maureen, it's Beau!"

"You've done it again, haven't you, Beau."

There was that tone—all sweet reason and razor blades.

"Maureen, we've got a real thing going on down here at Joe Bell's."

"Don't you always? How do you think Roberta Lee's feeling right now? Or do you care?"

"Of course I care, Maureen. You know that."

"I do? She's six years old today, Beau. In case you forgot that, too. She's been out on the front step for an hour. She won't come in because she knows you're coming soon. She's got her blue dress on, and she won't come in. Do you *care* about that?"

"I know, Maureen, I do care. I've got a whole party set up. Everybody's gonna be there, and we have it all—"

"You know the rules, Beau."

McAllister tried very hard not to pull out his Browning and send a round down the phone line. He imagined it hitting Maureen in the ear and going right through her head and out the other ear.

"Maureen—"

"You signed the agreement. Dwight says I've been more than fair about access."

"Let's leave Dwight out of this, can we? Just for now? I can be there in half an hour!"

Less, if I take the cruiser and don't change. Use the siren. He sniffed at his shirt. God, he smelled like a dead bat dipped in gasoline.

"The agreement says if you're late one more time—"

"Maureen, it's her birthday. She's just six. Don't make her part of this. She's too young to understand. All she'll think is I don't—"

"She'd be right."

"You *know* that's not true, Maureen. I've had to fight you and that son of a bitch Hogeland for every minute with her. Would I do that if I didn't care about her?"

"Dwight's twice the father you are to her. She—"

"Dwight's your goddamned *lawyer,* Maureen! He's not her father. I'm her father, and I have a right to—"

"Take her to Fogarty's so she can hang out with a bunch of lesbians and bums and cops? Dwight's been telling me about that crowd. No, Beau—"

"Maureen, don't do this again!"

"You've got to learn a lesson. You have to take your responsibilities *seriously,* Beau."

Jesus, that voice. It was in his ear like a wasp. He fought to keep the tremor out of his voice.

"I have the right, Beau. The agreement says—"

"Hey, Maureen. *Fuck* the agreement! And fuck Dwight!"

"Thanks, Beau. Maybe I will."

And she was gone.

McAllister stood there for a long time, breathing in and out rapidly and looking at his reflection in the black screen of the television on top of the filing cabinet.

He saw a forty-five-year-old cop in a rumpled tan uniform with two days of beard on a face like old leather and more gray than black in his hair. He saw a man with a large ragged salt-and-pepper moustache and tired blue eyes who had done a lot of damage for one Friday shift; he'd shot a man in the ass when he was aiming for his foot, he'd let a bunch of Indians shoot *arrows* at him and then walk away smiling, and he had just now totally torched his chances of getting to see his daughter on her sixth birthday.

What he saw did not impress him.

He put both his hands on the inside lip of Joe Bell's desk and heaved it hard upward. It flipped over away from him, papers and drawers flying, pens and pencils clattering and spinning, a tremendous crash and clang as the gray metal desk hit the floor ten feet away. The drawers spilled out all over the greasy tiles, a ragged fan of porn magazines, slips of paper, loose bills.

There was a large mass of duct tape attached to the underside of the bottom drawer. If Bell had put that packet there, whatever was inside it was kind of important to him.

But Joe Bell wasn't the target of an investigation right now. McAllister had no legal right even to be *inside* Bell's office, let alone throwing his furniture around like a drunken cowhand in a bar fight.

And *if* Joe Bell did become the target of an investigation, then anything McAllister found inside Bell's office *before* getting a legal search warrant would be inadmissible in a court of law. Fruit of a Poisoned Tree. Fourth Amendment. Weeks. Mallory. All that voodoo.

Beau knew damned well what a good cop would do now. He'd leave it alone. Yes sir—that was what a good cop would do.

McAllister got down on his knees and used a corner of a stapler to pry up a section of the silver mound of duct tape. It came away from the gray metal easily. There was a flat plastic box in the center of the mound. And inside the plastic box, something flat and rainbow colored glimmered like a jewel.

Hell, it was a computer disk!

Why the hell would Joe Bell be hiding a computer disk under his desk? He started to rip the tape away when he heard somebody clearing his throat in a theatrical way.

A short black man in a starched and razor-pressed Montana Highway Patrol uniform was leaning on the doorjamb. He had his hat pushed back away from his shiny bald blue-black head, and his exceedingly muscular arms were crossed over his weightlifter's chest. His badge glittered in the downlight. His shoulder bars gleamed. His clean-shaven face was fine-boned and hard-looking. He was grinning the kind of grin you give your kid when you catch him with his head stuffed inside a bottle of your favorite bourbon.

Beau McAllister got slowly to his feet. They both looked around the room awhile. McAllister tried a smile.

"Afternoon, Eustace," he said, shuffling a boot through a pile of papers. "I suppose you're wondering what the hell's going on in here."

"No," said Eustace, "I wasn't. I can *see* what's going on in here. What's going on in here is either a class C felony or a violation of several elements of the Fourth Amendment."

"Look . . . aah . . . "

Meagher held up one elegant pink-palmed hand. More gold glittered from his FBI Academy ring.

"Beau, you only call me lieutenant when you're gonna tell me something I don't wanna hear. Like when you've shot the wrong guy or something. Is this gonna be one of those times?"

"Well . . . Lieutenant . . . "

1500 Hours – June 14 – Los Angeles, California

Braced against the wind, Gabriel Picketwire walked back to the edge of the roof and looked out at the Pacific. One hundred feet gave you a lot to look at. The sun was still high in a sky the color of sulphur. On the windward shore of Catalina Island a heavy sea boiled along the rocky shores. Gulls screamed and dipped at the rockline, snatching at crabs and dead fish. The sun broke up on the whitecaps like yellow glass. In the San Pedro channel, butting like rams through the surge, bluewater trawlers heading in to Long Beach harbor dumped their old bait into the churning current. Yellow lances of sunlight shimmered in the hazy water.

Gabriel knew that twenty feet down, drawn by the chum and the smell of blood washing off the trawler decks, bulls and makos and whitetips circled and darted, jaws working, gills extended, dead eyes swiveling in powder-blue flesh. He had seen them. Once, on a shoot at Catalina, he had killed a bull shark with a compressor-gun. Broken at the spine, it had slashed and twisted at the wound. It had been eaten by the others before it could die. He remembered its one black eye and his image in it as a whitetip struck from beneath and tore out its stomach.

A hot wind thick with dust and the iron smell of the open sea drove a flutter of white sails over the hammered bronze surface of the water. Close to the shoreline at Sunset Beach, a few surfers in acid greens and hot pink rubber cut lacy arcs into the green shoulders of ocean rollers, and the hot wind drove the salt spray back north along the edge of the waves. Along the beaches a few sunbathers dug in behind dunes and jerry-built windbreaks, working through Styrofoam boxes of warm beer, chasing the old dream of sunset days and California nights. Across the coast, highway oil derricks rusted into ruin in a clutter of warehouses, dead cars, and empty lots.

Gabriel looked down at the second-unit film crew working at the dumpster a hundred feet below him. They were trying to get the air bag pumped up, and it looked as if they were having trouble with the compressor again. He could hear them yelling at each other, a strange high sound like the cry of the gulls out there on the ocean.

The lot below was a crowded litter of trailers and cars and catering trucks and lighting rigs. Black cables snaked everywhere from a big transformer truck near the chain link fence. As usual, the talent was hiding out in their Winnebagos, four in a row, one for each of them, the size and placement of each Winnebago the consequence of weeks of talk and six full pages of legal terminology.

Around the set, hundreds of people were in constant motion with clipboards and radios. From a hundred feet up they all looked like brightly feathered birds in a box. They were like that when you were down there with them, too—all herky-jerky motions and chatter and that same kind of birdbrain self-satisfaction you could see in a budgy or a parrot.

Well, if you don't like the company, find another line of work. Stop whining to yourself. What was bothering him wasn't putting up with the people or even an asshole director like Nigel Hampton. It was that hot wind from the south that was whipping up the ocean out there and tugging at his flak jacket and flaring his thick black hair. He had a hundred feet to cover, at thirty-two feet per second squared every thirty-two feet. He was carrying an M-16 that weighed ten pounds, and he had six pounds of calf liver taped to his chest, over three explosive squibs and the radio detonator. Under the liver and the black-powder squibs he had a Kevlar and asbestos vest. Under that there was only him. He drew a long breath and felt the wind at his cheek. Holding a palm up into it, he stood awhile, lost in that sensation. Then he pushed the jump-marker a few inches to the left. It would be like throwing a Hail Mary pass the length of the field, with a bad side wind. He would have to allow for that.

Gabriel was six feet even, and the last time he'd weighed himself, he had been a reasonable one sixty-five. He was good at his work. There wasn't much that worried him. Dying like a putz in a fucked-up gag was one thing that did.

They had rigged a transmitter under his flak vest. He keyed it on again. Mike's voice buzzed in his left ear.

"Mr. Picketwire—you reading?"

"I'm reading you, Mike. What's the story down there? This wind isn't getting any better up here."

He saw one of the crewmen around the dumpster step back and look up at him.

"We're okay now. The compressor was fucked. Jody hadn't changed the filter, so we were pushing crap into the nozzle. This bag'll be up in about a minute. You still gonna do this thing?"

"Is Nigel ready?"

"Yeah. . . . He's got Silverman here with him, so he's gotta show her pages, and we been stuck on this gag for two days."

"I told him to second-unit the gags. The rest of these people could be doing interiors in Vancouver. He could shoot around this scene."

"Yeah. Well, you know Hampton. He's an *auteur,* right?"

"Yeah. Well, buzz me when it's up. I stand around here any longer, I'm gonna talk myself out of it."

"Mr. Picketwire—Gabriel—why don't we rig the harness instead? Drop on a line. Use the drum."

"Don't trust the line. Someday somebody'll die on one."

"Okay. One minute, then I'll cue you."

Gabriel stepped back away from the edge. The tiles grated under his combat boots. The wind was a steady force up here, dry and dirty as truck exhaust. Under the soldier's gear—so familiar and so strange—he could feel sweat running into the small of his back. Far into the east he could see the low black line of the San Bernardino Mountains. Beyond that there was desert, and then the big range. Home was back beyond that, as much as any of his people had homes anywhere now.

He let his mind go that way for a while, wondering about Eddie and Earl Black Elk and old Jubal and his emphysema and whether that blue truck had made the climb through the passes. Well, if they had trouble, they'd call him. They'd promised him that.

Something was moving against the smog and the haze. He strained to focus on it. Something flying out there. A small plane, maybe. Or a large bird. It rose up on a thermal and banked in a huge arc and dipped down again. Then it disappeared.

Be good if that were an eagle or a hawk, thought Gabriel. How good it would be to believe in that kind of sign now. If that were really a hawk, it would mean something. It would be good to be able to believe in any kind of sign.

That was the thing about working with these people out here. They knew about everything and believed in nothing. It was contagious. Now he had to turn around and walk over to the edge of the roof and step off without believing in anything but physics and gravity.

He felt the need to urinate. He ignored the radio and walked over to an elevator cage. Better to leave this here, he thought. He'd seen men with belly wounds, seen how a full bladder of urine could kill you with a wound like that. If he drifted on the way down, he'd miss that bag. Maybe miss the whole dumpster. Maybe not. That would be worse. He might live.

"Gabriel. Hey, you there?"

He finished and walked back to the jump-marker, waved down at the crew. A hundred white faces looked up at him. Birds in a box.

"You ready?"

"I'm ready."

"Just a minute—Gabriel, Nigel wants me to say how much he appreciates this take. He knows you'll give it all you've got."

"Tell Nigel he's gonna see everything I've got if I miss that bag."

"Squibs armed. Okay . . . they're rolling . . . when you're ready, Mr. Picketwire. When you're ready."

He was at the edge of the roof now. He looked out to sea again, saw the curve of the world and the tiny white sails in the bronze light and the color of everything. He smelled salt and blood and sensed the things moving under the surface out there. Life was everywhere around him, and the wind was sliding over his left cheek. A hundred feet below him the black rectangle of the dumpster looked like a small door to somewhere far away.

He raised the rifle and drew back the bolt and let it snap home, feeling the first round grate up out of the magazine and slide into the chamber. It all felt very familiar, and he remembered a time when believing in nothing at all was the only way to come out alive.

"It is a good day to die," he said, not believing in the words. He moved forward.

Bullshit—it's never a good day to die.

He felt the explosions tearing at his chest. The wind was all around him. The flak jacket spread open, and he dropped through the light. The M-16 was working against his ribs. He held it in close. White flame seared his cheek. The black door rose up at him, a flat denial of metaphysics. Maybe he had seen a hawk.

Maybe it was a hawk.

Maybe it was a

1900 Hours – June 14 – Billings, Montana

McAllister followed Lieutenant Meagher's navy-blue Town Car all the way back to the station house in Billings, trying to enjoy the sundown on the ancient slopes and the way the light was always changing along the valleys, trying not to think about how it would go once they got there.

He hadn't exactly covered himself in glory back there at Pompeys Pillar, although he was damned if he could think of any other way he could have handled the situation.

One thing for sure, Eustace had no intention of letting McAllister root through Bell's office with no particular idea of what he was rooting for. Meagher had made sure that Beau put the office back together—the compact disk still in the case, the tape mound intact—and then he walked him out of the office and back to the crime scene.

By then, the Criminal Investigation Bureau guys from the state were there, a couple of plainclothes guys named Finch Hyam and Rowdy Klein. Klein was a long bony bundle with large pale hands and floppy feet whose real name was Rudy but who refused to answer to anything but Rowdy after seeing a bunch of *Rawhide* reruns on cable TV. He kept it up so long that the rest of the men and women on the force had been plain worn down. Even Eustace called him Rowdy now.

Beau always made it a point to call him Howdy every chance he got. By way of getting even, Rowdy always called Beau by his full name, pronouncing it *Bo-ree-gard*.

Finch was just Finch, a silly bird-name on a man his size, but Finch was a solid investigator and a reasonable man with a very sweet wife who made it a point to try to match up Beau with any spare woman she could find. Like all good wives, she hated to see a man running loose. It offended her sense of order.

Rowdy and Finch looked up as they walked over. Rowdy had the kid's shirt pulled up, and they were looking hard at something on his chest.

"Hey, LT," said Finch, smiling at Beau but talking to Lieutenant Meagher. "Whaddya make of that?"

They had the boy's bloody plaid shirt pulled up to his neck. There were four ugly scars on his chest, just above the nipples. Fresh. One of them was still weeping. They were odd, paired scars, each cut about four inches long, running parallel, one set about three inches above his right nipple, the other set over his left.

"Jesus!" said Eustace, who always got a little sick around blood and wounds. "What the hell did that?"

"Beats me," said Rowdy, shaking his head. "Got into a fight, maybe? Somebody with a knife?"

"Real regular, aren't they?" said Finch. "He'd haveta stay pretty still to get himself cut up like that. You figure he'd be jumping around a bit, somebody cutting him like that."

"What's Bo-ree-gard got to say?" asked Rowdy, looking at Beau like a mortician sizing up a client.

"Beats me, Howdy. Maybe an animal did this. Some kinda cat or something?"

"Nice deduction, Beau," said Finch. "Don't quit yer day job. Sure as hell isn't any cat I ever saw."

Eustace had his control back now. He dusted his palms together, although he had never touched the body. "The doc been here?"

"Yeah." Finch inclined his head toward a Jeep Cherokee parked a few yards away. Inside a young man in a gray suit was talking into a cellular phone. "Vlasic's calling Bob Gentile's people now. They'll get a wagon out here and take him in to the hospital. You want an autopsy, LT?"

"It's a homicide, isn't it?"

"Looks like self-defense to us, LT."

"Yeah . . . but we do the thing right."

Beau felt a kind of sadness for the boy.

"What're we gonna do about Bell?"

"*You're* not gonna do anything about Bell, McAllister!" said Eustace. "You and me, we're gonna go back to the station and sort out some divergent views on operational procedure."

"Hey, LT," said Rowdy. "You shouldn't talk about Bo-ree-gard that way. He's doing the best he can with what he got."

"Thanks, Howdy. And here I was just thinking that you probably couldn't talk at all unless somebody had his arm shoved up your ass. Say hi to Clarabelle for me, willya?"

"Fuck yourself, McAllister."

Beau was going to say something else, but he caught the look Eustace was giving him and he shut up.

He had rolled these thoughts around in his mind all the way back to Billings. They parked side by side in front of the low yellow breeze-block building next to the Highway Department's truckyard on Foote Street, in the middle of a sprawl of warehouses, truck depots, gas stations, and roadhouses.

PUBLIC SAFETY BUILDING
MONTANA HIGHWAY PATROL

Behind the new bulletproof glass wall, Sergeant Myron Sugar was typing away at an old Remington machine, his fine Mediterranean features taut with concentration. He raised a languid hand without looking up.

The rest of the desks were empty at this time on a Friday. Most of the patrol guys were out on the six-six night shift. And it was still too early on a Friday night for the usual crowd of drunken ranchers and maudlin cowhands and grifters off the interstate to build up in the waiting rooms and the cells downstairs. Finch Hyam and Rowdy Klein were the only Criminal Investigation Bureau men stationed at this branch, and they were still back at Bell's Oasis, tagging arrows and telling each other war stories.

"Hey, LT—Beau—I hear you shot Joe Bell. Good for you. He gonna live?"

"He'll live," said Eustace.

"Too bad," said Myron, who had once locked horns with Bell during a pool game over at Fogarty's New York Bar in Pompey. Bell had called him a kike. Myron had expressed his dislike of that term with a cue ball.

In Meagher's office, a large room with a massive metal desk and a long row of filing cabinets with a coffee machine on top, Eustace poured them coffee. Eustace got his favorite, a big china mug with the FBI seal on it. Beau got one shaped like a pig in a blue uniform. Beau hated it because to get any coffee out of it you had to look like you were kissing the pig on the snout. It was one of Meagher's little jokes.

Beau looked around at the pictures and certificates on the wall while Meagher riffled through his While You Were Out slips and made a few apparently urgent calls. Letting McAllister sweat a bit. Beau went back to looking at the pictures all over the office walls.

Meagher had a poster on the wall behind his desk. It read:

WHAT PART OF "NO!" DON'T YOU UNDERSTAND?

And the pictures—there was Eustace in his graduation class at Quantico, in a lineup of sixty guys as tightly wrapped as he was, everybody grinning like they had a secret you'd *never* guess. And Eustace with Robert Ressler, head of the FBI's Behavioral Sciences lab, and Eustace with Dan Quayle and the governor. Eustace with Doc Darryl Hogeland—Dwight Hogeland's famous father and a great argument against evolution, since the father was a fine man and the son was a legalistic weasel: Eustace was standing beside the doctor's navy-blue Learjet. Eustace with Doc Hogeland again, at the opening of the Hogeland Oncology Wing at Sweetwater General here in Billings; Eustace holding one end of a blown-up check, money raised from District Four of the Montana Highway Patrol last year.

Beau had to smile at that one. The lieutenant's fund-raising method was sort of like the IRS—he had it taken off their paychecks. When he looked back at Eustace, the lieutenant was looking at him and tugging on his lip. Beau tried a big disarming smile.

He got a thin grin back.

"This part of a campaign you're on, Beau? Discourage the citizens from cluttering up the 911 line? Every time one of 'em calls in, we send you out there and you shoot 'em?"

"Not a bad idea, LT. I say, why wait till they call? I'm out there, I could just pick one at random, smoke him. Be like the lottery, only instead of going to Hawaii, you die."

"You give them a running start?"

"Nah—just blast away at 'em. They'll figure it out."

"That's true. Way you shoot, never know, they might just die of old age waiting for you to get the windage. Thornton tells me you were aiming at Bell's foot."

"Yeah. You can always tell what I was aiming at by what I hit. Take fifty feet of string and a piece of chalk, draw a big circle around the bullet hole. It's probably in there somewhere."

"Yeah. Shoot at his foot, hit him in the ass."

"It was a larger target. Bell's got an ass like a harvest moon. Bell gets any fatter, they'll give him his own area code."

"And while you're popping away trying to hit Bell's ass, three, maybe four armed robbers are zipping off into the hills. I'm gonna *love* writing this one up for the brass in Helena. So just for the record, why'nt you tell me—in your own words—just how this all happened?"

"This a Q and A?"

"You see a tape recorder? You see Vanessa down here?"

"Oh, Christ—Ballard catching today?"

"None other. She's the duty DA all weekend. Your luck."

"Jeez, I thought she was down at her place in Red Lodge."

"Nope. So we better get this right."

"Hell. Why can't women just do what God made them for?"

"Beau, I tell you, that's what God made her to do. She's the best DA in eastern Montana."

"I know that. She still makes me jumpy."

"When they told you these were the nineties, Beau, they didn't mean the *eighteen* nineties."

"Damned affirmative action."

"That's not how Ballard got here. You saying that's how I got here?"

"You know what I'm saying, Eustace. You didn't get here because you're black. You got here because you were a hotshot fed and a good cop. Nowadays, the only way to get into the force is to be a Native American lesbian dwarf with a wooden leg and an ACLU card. Cover a shitload of federal quotas there. Just don't be tall enough to reach the pedals on the cruisers or help out in a bar fight. Last week, remember that go-round at Twilly's?"

"I remember."

"So do I—I'm getting the shit kicked outta me by Johnny Karpo and that huge Crow girlfriend of his, Brenda Roan Horse? Who shows up but the Munchkin."

"He did okay, I hear."

"Oh, yeah—pulled some of that oriental martial arts stuff, and Brenda comes up behind him and throws him over the bar. That was fun to watch. Only reason I lived, Karpo turns to watch and I maced him."

"*Maced* him? Why the hell? Mace is for wimps."

"Left my gun in the car, Eustace. Somebody's always pulling it outta my holster in Twilly's, and then I gotta kick ass to get it back. Lately I just leave it in the cruiser—all they ever wanna do is brawl. No harm in them."

"How'd Karpo take to the mace?"

"He didn't like it."

"What'd you do then—hit him with a chair?"

"Nah, a bottle. Word of advice there, LT. Never hit a man with one of them foreign Scotch bottles. The ones with the dented sides? They don't break."

"What happened to the Munch—to Patrolman Benitez?"

"He got the cuffs on Brenda. Finally. Guy's so dumb, he couldn't pour piss out of a boot if the instructions were written on the heel. That's not the point. We got a lot of stupid troopers. That's what traffic duty is for. Point is, he's too short. He's only on the job because he's Hispanic."

"Well, at least you didn't say spic."

"Don't get on me about that shit, Eustace. You brought this up. I'm no racist. No sexist either. I think that Sonnette broad has the makings in her. And Myron out there, he's one of the best we got. Today's Friday, right? After six? That's sabbath for Myron. You ever think of *that* when you're setting up the duty rosters around here? You notice, he's using the only manual typewriter we have so he can stay in line with the sabbath restrictions. He ever bitch to you about it?"

"Can't say he does."

"Can't say? I know you can't. Now Myron could pull some of that racial religious equal opportunity shit on you, say he'll go to the union or the civil liberties people. But he doesn't, because he's a cop first and something else afterward. That's all I'm saying."

"Christ, Beau. You get up on the wrong side of your cage?"

Beau leaned back in the chair and let out a long slow sigh. "Not my best day, Eustace."

The lieutenant thought it over for a second.

"Oh, hell. You're not even supposed to *be* here, are you? You're supposed to be taking Bobby Lee over to Lizardskin for a party! Why'nt you *say* something?"

"Oh yeah—excuse me from the firefight, LT, I gotta take my kid to a party. That'd get me a citation for sure!"

"That why you were hiding out up at the Elbow?"

"Two hours left in the shift—well, there y'go."

"You wanna go now? We can do this tomorrow when things are slower. I'll call Vanessa, tell her some story."

Beau tried to keep his smile in place, but inside he could feel that old blackness rising up. "No point now. Maureen pulled the plug."

"She did? How'd Bobby Lee take it?"

"I don't know. I never got the chance to ask her. I ended up saying something stupid, and Maureen hung up on me."

"What'd you say?"

"She was quoting Hogeland at me. Guy's all over me like a bad suit. I said *fuck* Dwight Hogeland—and she said thanks, Beau, maybe I will."

"Dwight's getting real tangled up in this, isn't he?"

"I think so. I think he and Maureen—hell . . . it couldn't be worse, Eustace."

"Ethically, if he's involved with her—you know—then he oughta get someone else in the firm to handle her file."

"Ethics are something Dwight doesn't seem to have inherited from his father. Doc Hogeland—man, I can't see how Doc can stand his own kid. Anyway, I screwed it up good with her."

"This before or after you whacked Joe Bell?"

"After. That was when you came in on me, in Bell's office. I sorta lost it and flipped his desk."

"That I had noticed."

"I *still* say there's something rocky in his bedroll, LT."

"That more of your cowboy shit? Don't tell me. What'd you get from the witnesses?"

Beau ran it down for the lieutenant: the time of the call, their attendance at the scene, being fired upon by Bell, receiving hostile fire from the area by the propane tank.

Meagher nodded through it all, considering how it would look to the district attorney.

When Beau reached the point where he had fired to wound Joe Bell, Eustace shook his head slowly and made a couple of notes on his desk calendar.

Beau was wrapping up his story when the intercom on the lieutenant's desk buzzed.

"Meagher here. What is it, Myron?"

"Ballard's here. You want her to wait?"

"Tell her just a minute, Myron. . . . Well, Beau. This is it now. She's gonna want to tape the whole thing. Not a formal Q and A, but it'll be part of the official record. Also, she's gonna be a tad pissed as well. I hear we're getting sued. You want to go ahead now, or I can say you're still in a reaction from the stress of the encounter, tell her to do this later tonight?''

"Oh yeah—tell the Dragon Lady I'm stressed out? No way, Eustace. Bring her on, and damn the torpedoes.''

"Well, I think we're in good shape here. There's a precedent for wounding fire if an officer perceives a danger to citizens. Just stick to your notes, and don't let her get you rattled, okay?''

Meagher leaned over and hit the intercom button. "Please ask Ms. Ballard to come in.''

Beau and the lieutenant waited in taut silence for a minute. Beau tried to keep his heart from speeding up, tried to breathe slowly and steadily through his nose.

"Cut that out, Beau. You sound like a church organ—*Hello* there, Vanessa!''

Eustace and Beau got to their feet as the assistant district attorney for Yellowstone County came gliding into the room on a wave of poison and the squeak of rubber on hardwood.

Vanessa Ballard was a problem for Beau. He was always a little off balance when he was in the same room with this tall, slender horsewhip of a woman with a golden bell of blond hair and creamy white skin, eyes a little too far apart and as blue as glacier ice, a rich red dahlia of a mouth, always a little breathless, long-fingered surgical hands ending in blood-tipped nails as red as taillight glass, and legs that went, Beau assumed, all the way to heaven in a flawless sweep of jazzercise and good genetics.

Today The Ballard was exquisitely fine-tuned in an imperial purple suede suit with a radically abbreviated skirt and little touches of solid gold at the silky hollow of her throat and the supple turning of her wrists. She wore, as usual, one of what seemed to be hundreds of different pairs of expensive jogging shoes in a spectrum of shades. Today's shade was pale lavender.

"Hello, Lieutenant Meagher.'' She shook his hand twice, hard, making excellent eye contact. Ballard was radiating testosterone today, as she always did when she had to go out and tolerate policemen, a breed she seemed to consider an evil necessity, like tick birds on a rhino.

"I'll need the desk,'' she said, and seated herself behind it. She began to riffle through her black snakeskin attaché case, head down, a glittering sweep of heavy golden hair hiding her face. Her voice was a velvet growl, her enunciation as honed as a glass blade.

"This situation, gentlemen—I'd say the word *sucks* catches the essence of it. Joe Bell is sitting on his ass in Sweetwater''—at this point she looked up through her waterfall of cornsilk hair and fixed Beau with one steel-blue eye—''perhaps I should say lying on his belly over in Sweetwater General, having a seance with Dwight Hogeland even as we speak. And if I know Hogeland, that man will do his level best to sue us all into Go-Home Bay for his two-thirds contingency fee and all the troopers he can butt-fuck. This means *you*, McAllister!''

''Hey, Vanessa!''

She slammed a tape recorder down on Meagher's desk and threw her hair back in a kind of wild-horse twist Beau could feel in his belly.

''How many times are we going to have to explain this stuff to you, McAllister? If you *must* shoot the citizenry, *shoot to kill!* It's a hell of lot cheaper to kill one—only eighty cents a round for your revolver, use as many as you want—plead *you* criminally stupid, for which we'd get the thanks of the regiment *and* the Nobel Peace Prize, *plus,* all we pay for then is some bereavement settlement, and we're all off to the Ramada for blab-bermouth soup. But *noooh!* Our Beau must have his jest! And *another* opportunistic scumsack limps straight to a lawyer, and *bingo*—we find our-selves up to our earrings in alligators!''

Beau sat up and raised a hand.

''Now, Vanessa, if you're gonna get into that thing, the guy from Deer Lodge last year? I did shoot to kill on that one. It's just that when you're being shot at, it affects your concentration. And everybody was screaming and running around.''

''It was the Hilltop Mall, Beau! Of *course* people were running around. *And* screaming. Not to mention, it was a *County* call you should have left to the Yellowstone guys.''

''I was *shopping,* for God's sake. I was off duty.''

''And you got involved anyway. You could have ducked it.''

''He was endangering the citizens, Vanessa. I'm supposed to stop that kind of thing. Anyway, I'm just making a point.''

''I agree. And *my* point is, if you'd just plain *killed* him, then there'd have been nobody around to sue us for excessive force. He didn't have any relatives.''

''So why'd you let 'em settle?''

''Beau, nine times out of ten, the County settles out of court, and the County settles because it's just plain *cheaper!*''

''Even when the plaintiff is a paroled con committing an armed robbery? Even when he's firing on a law enforcement officer?''

''I've seen worse. And you fired first.''

"Jeez, Vanessa! What do I do—give him a free one? I'm *supposed* to fire first! That's how it works!"

"Beau, read the papers. Everybody has rights except those who really need them. It's the American way. You used your firearm in a crowded mall. The guy said he was just trying to get away, that you provoked the exchange."

"You actually *believe* that?"

"What I believe and what I can prove in an action are different things. The law isn't about belief. It's about advantage and disadvantage, about technical distinctions between separate realities."

"Well, that asshole was sure as hell trying to separate me from *my* reality. With a Delta ten-mill, too."

"That was real for then. It wasn't real for later."

"So what was I supposed to do?"

"Learn to shoot straighter."

"So I should have killed Joe Bell?"

She sat back in Meagher's leather wing chair and swiveled back and forth in silence, looking across at Beau. The lieutenant leaned against the wall and tapped a finger on his brass buckle.

"No . . . look, Beau, I'm sorry to come on so hard here. The County barely has enough money to run a decent court system as it is. You guys are still hung up in Helena trying to get two officers in a car for night patrol. And you need three more troopers we can't give you. Over in Big Horn County, we have two troopers on administrative leave while we sort out what looks like a police chase that didn't have to happen and got a young Crow girl and her baby killed. Indian Affairs is onto us for *that* one. Now Joe Bell's talking to Dwight Hogeland about another lawsuit. *This* we don't need."

"You mean Harper and Greer?"

"I do."

"What happened there, anyway?"

"A woman named Mary Littlebasket was killed, along with her newborn baby. Her uncle—Charlie Tallbull, Eustace, you know him, don't you?— he's in Sweetwater General with internal injuries. The whole thing was just one overreaction after another. We're going to—hey! Don't try to change the subject, Beau. I'm saying we didn't need another law enforcement sideshow right now."

"We didn't need Pompeys Pillar blown all the way to Bozeman, either. I did what I had to do to stop him."

"What happened to the robbery guys, Beau?"

"They, ah, sorta slipped away."

"Sorta slipped away? You mean, while you were drilling Joe Bell a new asshole?"

"That's not how it went, Vanessa."

"Okay." She set her Pearlcorder up on the desk and punched the button. "Let's see how it did go. My name is Vanessa Ballard, assistant district attorney for the counties of Yellowstone, Big Horn, Powder River, Treasure, Custer, and Rosebud. In connection with the wounding by gunfire of one Joseph Bell, a citizen of Yellowstone County, this day and date, in Yellowstone County, we are questioning the officer of the Montana Highway Patrol who answered the emergency call. Please identify yourself."

"Staff Sergeant Beauregard McAllister, shield number 2211, District Four of the Montana Highway Patrol."

"Staff Sergeant McAllister, did you have occasion to make entries in your notes concerning the events of this date as they affect the matter in question?"

"I did."

"Would you feel it necessary to refer directly to your notes as they concern this matter, should you be required to testify in court or in a pretrial hearing or in an examination for discovery, Sergeant McAllister?"

"I would."

"Duly noted. Now . . . are you prepared to answer direct questions in this matter at this time, if such questions fall within your area of knowledge as they affect the discharge of your firearm while responding to this ten-seventy call?"

"I am."

"And do you wish to have legal representation as is your right under the terms of the police act and the Escobedo decision?"

"Are formal charges being considered against me?"

"Not at this time, Sergeant McAllister."

"Then I do not wish to have legal representation."

"You agree to make this statement of your own free will. No one has made threats or offered you inducements or guarantees?"

"No, ma'am."

"Very well. Can you tell us in your own words what you know of the events under investigation?"

Beau flipped out his notebook, ran a thick forefinger down the pages. "Okay. Got the radio call at sixteen-thirteen hours this date, a ten-seventy, an armed robbery in progress, at Bell's Oasis. I attend scene accompanied by a Four car, the dog car, Trooper Thornton, and that wild-assed mutt he lives with—"

"You have that phrase in your notes, Sergeant?"

Beau grinned and kept reading in an official monotone.

"—and as we arrive at the scene we become aware of gunfire coming from the direction of the pump island. Trooper Thornton and I acquire tactical defense positions—"

"I beg your pardon, Sergeant?"

"Positions out of the line of fire, possessing sufficient material obstruction as to deflect or absorb such lethal ballistic energy as may be directed at the officers, Ms. Ballard. Tactical defense positions. We reconnoiter the scene. We observe citizens in various positions of hiding, having taken cover from the line of fire. We also observe one white male in possession of Winchester semiautomatic twelve-gauge shotgun. White male known to this officer as Joseph Arnold Bell, D.O.B. the eleventh of the seventh 1939. Mr. Bell is the owner of Bell's Oasis, at Pompeys Pillar in Yellowstone County in the sovereign State of Montana. Upon attempting to identify ourselves to Mr. Bell, these officers received immediate return fire from Mr. Bell."

"Let me understand you there. Mr. Bell *shot* at you?"

"Yeah. Didn't I mention that?" Beau's smile was guileless and sweet. "Anyway, the officers received immediate return *shotgun* fire from Mr. Bell, whereupon the responding officers returned to their defensive positions and another attempt was made to identify ourselves to Mr. Bell. This attempt was successful, and Mr. Bell informed us that there was an attempted robbery in progress at his place of business."

"That would be the Shell gas station known as Bell's Oasis?"

"Yes, ma'am."

"Please continue."

"Yes, ma'am. An attempted robbery in progress. At that time I observed a young Native American male lying approximately twenty feet from Mr. Bell's position by the pumps. This young male appeared to have sustained a wound in his side and was in a prone position on his back."

"Did you attempt to provide emergency aid at this time?"

"No, ma'am. At that time, we were advised by Mr. Bell that he was receiving hostile fire from a location in the vicinity of the propane tank on his property. I studied that area and did observe figures in that vicinity."

"And you made no attempt to reach the wounded male?"

"I identified myself as a law officer to the people by the propane tank. I was then fired upon by one of those individuals."

"What kind of fire did you receive?"

"It was arrows, ma'am."

Ballard picked up the Pearlcorder and shut it off.

"Arrows! Some Indians shot at you with *arrows, Beau?"*

"Yes, ma'am."

"Well—how dangerous could that have been? Toys."

"Vanessa, Finch Hyam's got them in his evidence kit. You go look at 'em."

She shook her head and turned the machine back on.

"You confirm that the fire you received was—were arrows?"

"Yes, ma'am, arrows. So we again secured a tactical defensive position"—Eustace was trying to restrain a smile—"and we commenced to deploy for a flanking maneuver."

"Did you execute this flanking maneuver, Sergeant?"

"No, ma'am. At that time, Mr. Bell was attempting to return fire from his position, and I felt it was necessary to attempt to stop him from returning fire."

"Why was that, Sergeant?"

"Because Mr. Bell was discharging a twelve-gauge shotgun in the direction of a fifteen-thousand-pound tank of liquid propane gas, and I considered this course of action to be unwise."

"Why did you consider it unwise?"

"Why did I—jeez, Vanessa!"

"Please answer the question."

"I considered it unwise because this tank has a dual-steel wall that can be punctured by a double-ought ball fired at a short range. Each twelve-gauge shell of double-ought contains twelve steel balls, each ball being of approximately .38 caliber and leaving the muzzle at approximately eleven hundred feet per second with a normal choke. I considered it to be highly likely that one of the double-ought balls being fired by Mr. Bell in the direction of that tank would penetrate the skin of that tank, thereby causing a violent rupture of said tank, resulting in the rapid dispersion of highly volatile gaseous material with a high explosive value, and that a blast of that magnitude would be likely to kill and injure anyone within the blast radius."

"Are you in a position to *know* the blast radius of a fifteen-thousand-pound propane tank, Sergeant McAllister?"

"I am, ma'am. I witnessed such a blast while working as a truck driver for Steiger Freightways in 1971. I witnessed a head-on collision between a propane tank truck and a touring bus on Interstate 94 outside Miles City, Montana, on the second day of July of that year. At the time of the blast I was approximately one half-mile away, and the blast wave blew in the front windshield of my truck and caused severe injury to myself and my co-driver, who subsequently died of her wounds."

There was a long silence in the room.

"So yes, I would say I know something about the kill zone of a propane tank. Ma'am."

Ballard shut off the recorder again.

"Eustace, did you know about this?"

"Yeah. Sorry, Vanessa. I didn't think it would come up."

Ballard looked at Beau for a long time.

"You never told me about this, Beau."

"It's not the kind of thing you bring up over lunch."

"Is this the . . . Doc Hogeland worked on her, didn't he? I remember the . . . she was in the Sweetwater burn unit for a while, wasn't she? Her name was—"

"Alice Manyberries. She was a Crow Indian."

"I—didn't Custer County prosecute on that? Contributory negligence? Wasn't there also a suit?"

"Manyberries *versus* Provo Gas Transfer, Felcher, et al. We lost the criminal on a faulty pathology report, but Provo Gas Transfer agreed to an out-of-court. Five years after." It had paid for his daughter Laurel's college tuition.

"Yes. And didn't Doc Hogeland—"

"It took Alice three months to die. Doc Hogeland paid for all of her medical expenses himself, as well as mine. He said the State owed it to the Crow Nation."

Ballard was quiet for a while. Beau tried to see something other than blue fire and flying glass and red blood.

"I'm sorry, Beau. That was a big case. Spellman Sterling wrote a paper on it for the law review. I remember reading it in school. I didn't get the connection. I never knew she was your wife."

"She had to keep the Manyberries name, or Indian Affairs would have taken away her status. We married under Crow ritual. Never mind, Vanessa. It's a long time back."

There was another long silence.

Finally, Ballard reached forward and turned the recorder back on.

"Ah . . . yes, Sergeant. That would seem to be persuasive. So the—the—kill zone would have been somewhere in the area of one half-mile, in your informed opinion?"

"Yes, ma'am."

"And can you tell us what buildings and people might lie within a half-mile of Bell's Oasis?"

"Yes, ma'am. About half of the town of Pompeys Pillar, including most of the main shopping area and two other gas stations that might have become involved in the subsequent fire.''

"We have noted that these events took place around four-thirty on the afternoon of Friday this date. Can you estimate for us how many citizens might have been within the blast radius of this tank at that time?''

"I can try—say, fifteen hundred people.''

"I see. Fifteen hundred men, women, and children. Can you tell us what steps you considered taking to prevent this explosion?''

"Yes, ma'am. I made several verbal attempts to dissuade Mr. Bell from discharging his weapon in that direction.''

"With what words, Sergeant?''

"What words?''

"Yes. What words did you use to dissuade Mr. Bell from shooting at the tank?''

"I said . . . I said if that tank went up, we'd all come down as pink rain. I may have called him an asshole, too.''

"I see. And what was Mr. Bell's response?''

"He stood up and prepared to fire again.''

"And at this point, what did you do?''

"At that point, nothing. At that point, one of the Indians—Mr. Bell was struck in the left shoulder by an arrow that seemed to have been fired from behind the propane tank.''

"And what effect did this missile have upon Mr. Bell?''

"Jeez—what effect!? He didn't like it. It made him angry. He came out from behind the gas pump and fired another shell at the tank.''

"And what were your actions then?''

"Then I yelled at him to stop, and he said he was going to get some payback—''

"Pay back? Were those his words? Pay back?''

"One word. Payback. It's an army term, ma'am. Bell was in the army for years. It means to get even. To get some.''

"I see. And did Mr. Bell continue firing after you had given him this verbal warning?''

"He fired that once, ma'am.''

"And what did you do?''

"I had the Browning on him at that point—''

"The Browning being your service revolver?''

"It's not a revolver, ma'am. It's a semiauto pistol.''

"Was it loaded at that time?''

"If it ain't loaded, it's a paperweight. Ma'am.''

"And you pointed this device at Mr. Bell?"

"Yes, ma'am."

"And you issued a verbal warning?"

"Yes, ma'am. A loud one."

"What was the distance between you and Mr. Bell?"

"About seventy feet."

"What happened then?"

"Mr. Bell was moving around some and screaming. He was trying to raise the weapon and get off another shell."

"At this time, he had an arrow in his body?"

"In his shoulder, ma'am."

"And yet you still considered him capable of formulating the intent to discharge his weapon in a careless or unlawful manner?"

"He had already fired it once with an arrow in him."

"And he showed indications of intending to do so again?"

"Yes, ma'am."

"And at that time, at that juncture, when you observed that Mr. Bell was not appearing to heed your verbal warning and seemed to be preparing to discharge his weapon again, what did you do?"

"I took aim and shot him."

"At what point did you aim?"

"Ma'am?"

"At what part of Mr. Bell's body did you take aim?"

"At his . . . lower body."

"You aimed at his lower body. Can you be more specific?"

"Yes, ma'am. I aimed—I aimed at his foot."

"At his foot?"

"Yes, ma'am."

"So your intention was to disable Mr. Bell?"

"Yes, it was."

"It was not your intention to kill Mr. Bell?"

"No, ma'am. It was my intention to use sufficient force so as to prevent the individual from continuing with his careless discharging of that shotgun."

"And where did the bullet strike Mr. Bell?"

"He was moving around a bit."

"Yes, duly noted. Please answer the question."

"Ah—the bullet impacted him on his lower anterior quadrant of the gluteal muscle. At that point—"

"The lower anterior quadrant of his gluteal muscle? That would be in Mr. Bell's buttock, then?"

"Yes, ma'am. In his right buttock."

"Am I to understand that you took aim at Mr. Bell's right foot, then contrived to shoot him in the *ass,* Sergeant?"

"Not actually in his ass, ma'am. More like in his wallet."

"Do you receive firearms training in your capacity as a Highway Patrol officer, Sergeant?"

"Yes, ma'am. Twice a month. And you have to qualify once a year."

"Are you considered a marksman by your department, Sergeant?"

"I am qualified to carry a weapon."

"Did you consider the—I believe the phrase is backstop? Did you consider what material or structures might receive the round in the apparently highly likely event that you should *miss* Mr. Bell's prodigious ass, Sergeant?"

"Yes, I did."

"And what manner of devices did you observe to be *generally* within the region—I think we may use the term *region* to encompass the statistical probabilities suggested by your talents as a marksman—in this region, what devices were likely to receive an errant round from your less-than-surgical service Browning?"

"Ah . . . there was a big empty oil drum and also some tires."

"Were there no gasoline pumps, Sergeant? Since Bell's Oasis is referred to as a Shell gas station and since many citizens attend this location regularly to acquire gasoline, it seems reasonable to infer that one might expect to find gas pumps in the region. So were there?"

"Yes, ma'am."

"And yet you saw fit to discharge your weapon nevertheless?"

"I did."

"And you admit that you missed your target?"

"No, ma'am. I intended to hit Mr. Bell, and I did."

"I see. I suggest to you that Yellowstone County owes its narrow escape from a large gasoline-fueled explosion at this location at least as much to the height and breadth of Mr. Bell's butt as it does to your skill as a marksman, Sergeant."

"Well, ma'am."

"Would that be a fair inference from the facts as you have reported them here, Sergeant?"

"Well . . ."

"Please answer the question!"

The intercom on Meagher's desk buzzed. They all jumped. Ballard reached for the Pearlcorder and shut it off. Meagher leaned across her to answer the call.

"What is it, Myron?"

"Well . . . seems we got a problem with the County morgue guys."

"What about 'em?"

"Vlasic called 'em out to get that kid, the one Bell popped?"

"Yeah. They not there yet?"

"No, they showed up okay."

"So?"

"So they left with the stiff an hour ago."

"So yeah?"

"So nobody's seen 'em since."

"So they stopped for coffee. Kid'll still be dead in the morning. Vlasic got a heavy date or something?"

"No, they didn't. And they're off the CB. Rowdy and Finch been all up and down the road between there and here."

"Oh, shit."

"That's right, LT. That wagon's gone."

4

2100 Hours – June 14 – Billings, Montana

A t the start it was no big deal. They figured one of the guys had remembered
some business somewhere, or maybe they had detoured south to Hardin
for a drink at Twilly's, or they could have gone cross-county to Roundup
for some God-cursed reason. They could have gone west to Laurel on another
call, because Ron Thornton suddenly remembered that Danny Burt, Gentile's
senior driver on duty, had mentioned a pickup at Zweibeck's Nursing Home
in Laurel—that turned out to be wrong. Or maybe they'd gone up to Musselshell because Burt had a girlfriend in Musselshell, and Sugar remembered
that once before Danny had taken a load of stiffs up to Musselshell and left
them cooking in the wagon while he did the horizontal bop with this girl—
what was her name, Lorraine? Something like that.

When Sugar started talking about horizontal bopping, Ballard snapped the gold locks on her snakeskin briefcase and started to weave her way through the growing crowd in the squad room. She stopped at the glass doors and looked back at McAllister through the sweep of golden hair. McAllister thought she was going to ask him if he knew how to whistle.

"You keep your notes, McAllister. I'm going to want a copy of your pages, too. When can I have that?"

"I don't like copying pages out of my notebook."

"I don't like stories that go all pale and shaky in cross. When will I see them?"

"Notebooks belong to the man, not the department."

"Your notes constitute a substantial evidentiary component of a pending civil action affecting the State. As such, they are subject to subpoena and may be seized by bailiffs."

"Hey, Vanessa—how about the bailiffs seize this?"

She smiled at that. "God, McAllister. Mutate soon, will you? The suspense is killing us. Just get your story straight. Eustace will set up the shooting board, right? Internal guys are all your buddies anyway."

Eustace grinned. "I'll put Finch Hyam on the board."

"Yeah. I'll be in touch."

And she was out the door, a curved space in the air, and gone.

Meagher set his phone down and looked across his desk at Beau.

"You really have a way with women, Beau. You want to heat her up some more, we could use her to take paint off a wall."

"She gets to me. They all do."

"Who all?"

"Women. I don't seem to have a handle on them."

"Yeah? Well, *you're* the one with the handle. You keep wanting them to grab that—you don't think about Tuesday morning."

"What's Tuesday morning?"

Meagher sighed, reached for his phone. "*Any* Tuesday. I mean the domestic stuff. You never think how it is for women, what *they* need."

"If you mean shifts, that's why I married Maureen when she got pregnant. She was working shifts down at the clinic in Hardin. She was used to the life."

Meagher was listening to his phone ringing down the line. He put a hand over the receiver. "Look, Beau, we have to find this wagon. It's probably nothing. Danny's done this before. You had a party to go to— what's left of it?"

"I *had* a party. Now I don't. I'm here. Let's do it."

"Good. All your watch got their beepers now? Go beep 'em, the off-duty guys, see if they'll ride around some, get a BOLO out on that wagon. Finch ran the plates on that blue pickup and got a registered owner named Jubal Two Moon, sixty-six, listed address on the Rosebud Reserve. Bought it in Pierre."

"Any priors on him?"

"Dinged once, in Rapid City. Drunk and disorderly. June 25, 1976. Guy's a carpenter. Might be something military on him, but we can't get that after business hours without help from the feds. Rosebud Reserve makes him a Sioux."

"You mean Dakota. Sioux is a white name.

"Okay. Anyway, the CIB guys'll take care of that. You think about getting some men out there and find that morgue wagon."

"We don't have enough cars."

"So tell 'em to use their own. We'll spring for the gas. Hello, Barney? It's Eustace, over here in Billings—yeah! You got the printout on these Indians? Well, we're all over the county looking for them. Now Barney, I got something else. Can you get your guys to keep an eye out for one of Gentile's wagons? . . . yeah . . . Danny Burt . . . and some kid—'' Meagher looked at McAllister, raised his eyebrow.

"Peter Hinsdale. He's nineteen."

"Hinsdale . . . yeah . . . no . . . we last saw them out at that ten-seventy in Pompeys Pillar, maybe ninety minutes ago . . . Yeah, he's right here— Barney says hi . . . says your shot should have killed Bell . . . you hit him in the brains . . . Anyway, the plate is echo delta five niner tango four, a gray Ford wagon. Hell, Barney, even your guys can't miss that . . . sure . . . same to you, only sideways. Have a good one. . . . ''

McAllister stood and gathered up his gear. "Okay, Eustace. I'm gonna go beep the watch. I'll take a run out to Pompeys Pillar and do the back roads, see what I can see. You see to it your people in Commo get the best descriptions of Jubal Two Moon and the rest of them. I'll ask the Big Horn County guys in Hardin to do a pass over in the Crow Reserve. They might make it that far. Can't see a Dakota going to a Crow for help, but you never know these days. Somebody'll know something . . . just do one thing for me?"

"Sure, Beau."

"Rowdy and Finch'll see this Bell thing as self-defense."

"Looks like that from here."

"Yeah, but I got—"

"One of your feelings?"

"Yeah."

Meagher looked at him as the squad room started to fill up with troopers and the first of the Friday-night prisoners. The tempo was rising as the citizens swallowed up a Friday-night skinful and started to take exception to each other in more direct ways.

"You think it was . . . what? A setup?"

"I think Bell had more on his mind than he was saying. The whole thing seems wrong. Has the wrong rhythm. I don't know. And what's with the hideaway disk? There's something—"

Meagher looked at him, his eyebrows raised.

"Now *that's* what I call a real professional assessment. And there's nothing in the statutes that says a guy can't hide something in his office. You know Bell. He's got his finger in a lot of pies. He's trying to get into that Rancho Vista development out near Musselshell. He's moving money around on the market. There's any number of reasons for the guy hiding something in his office, and not one of them is any of our business."

"Well, this Gall kid. No record. Now the RO on Jubal Two Moon, turns out he's clean too, and—"

"He's not clean. He's got a sheet."

Beau rolled his head and gave Meagher a pitying look. "He's got a drunk and disorderly. Look at the date."

"Nineteen seventy-six. June 25."

"Ring a bell?"

"No."

"Christ, LT. I talk about it all the time!"

Meagher looked blank, then his face changed. "Oh, hell. The Little Bighorn?"

"June 25, 1976, would be the centennial. Exactly one hundred years after. Jubal Two Moon's a Dakota. Hell, I think there was a Two Moon *at* the battle. Probably an ancestor. I'd say, the guy who doesn't get pissed on that day has no soul."

"Any other witnesses?"

"Not really. The gas station was pretty empty. The truckers get their diesel over by the repair yard. No other citizens on that pump island. One other thing—"

"Yeah?"

"How'd you know Bell shot somebody? When you called me, you said you could hear Bell shooting."

"Yeah. I heard it on the phone."

"So he was on the phone when the thing started?"

"Yeah—oh, I see."

"Yeah. Why'd he make the call in the first place?"

"Actually, he didn't. It was somebody else called."

"Who was it?"

"A woman. Marla, the waitress. Didn't she tell you?"

"Must have slipped her mind," said Beau.

"Right. A little odd, huh?"

"Yeah. They call in direct, or 911?"

"911. Then Beth calls me in on it."

"So there'd be a tape?" Beau asked.

"Should be. You want me to get it?"

"Well, is it evidence now?"

"Not till I say so. What're we looking for?"

McAllister took a long breath and set his Stetson back on his head. He hooked his hands in his garrison belt.

"This is all CIB territory now," said Eustace. "You're just patrol. And when Bell's lawyer gets to the courthouse on Monday, you'll be warned off anything to do with this investigation until it's settled."

"Both ways? Civil *and* criminal?"

"Depends. Don't get into any more trouble in the meantime."

"You'll think about what we been talking about?"

"I'd rather not."

"But you will?"

"Yeah, Beau. I will."

McAllister spent a few minutes rousing the off-duty troopers and talking them into doing some cruising around the county. He told them to watch out for any Indians on foot or hitchhiking, and if they did spot any, to use the CB to call it in. There was to be no attempt at a singlehanded arrest. Not even a check-out. Just mark the location, get to a phone, or get on channel nine of their own CB and call in some backup.

Out in the waiting room, the citizens were belly-up to the duty desk, all bitching and whining at once about illegally parked cars or missing dogs or noisy parties or kids drag-racing on the back roads. The radio in the squad room was crackling with more of the same. Cowtown Friday nights. McAllister pushed through them and walked out into the evening.

The air was clear and soft, with that first faint scent of spring grass and bitterroot flower. The sky was a mist of red fire and deep green night, showing a few stars. There was a little evening dew on the window of his cruiser. He leaned against the door for a minute, filling his Petersen pipe with some

Virginia tobacco. He fired it up with a kitchen match, the flare lighting him up under the brim of his patrol Stetson, deepening his lines and creases. His hands looked blunt and rough. A glint of old gold on his left hand. He looked at the wedding ring for a long moment.

A way with women . . . no, that he did not have. Either loving them or keeping them safe. The match flared, and pain lanced along his finger. He shook it out and dropped it on the ground.

It had been like a bright white flower suddenly blossoming in that late afternoon two decades ago. Way off down the lizardskin ribbon of blacktop, one truck had swerved, a big silver tube. There had been one short, shouted curse on channel nineteen of the CB. The silver tube met a square blue bus. They locked. That flower grew in a massive silence. He remembered feeling the wheel under his hand, and Alice saying his name, and then the Kenworth rocked and the windshield blew apart in a scintillation of tiny prisms, and in each one there was a bright flower growing, like a bitterroot flower, yellow as sulphur in the center, then white and purple at the petals.

He had instinctively reached for her, leaning across the cab as the windshield came in and that huge silence followed, and then a massive wall of packed air as tight as hardwood had hit them both. Turning that way, turning to his right, to Alice, and trying to cover her, that had saved his eyes. But the seat belt had stopped him and he had never reached her, just got one hand on her arm and then he was close enough to see the glass hit her full on, like a shotgun loaded with broken glass. She rocked back and her face disappeared . . . another-color flower.

Laurel had been two then. He remembered the long hospital time in Sweetwater, and then the night there had been an empty bed in her room and a nurse saying, why, Mr. McAllister, I was sure someone would have called you. . . .

Alice Manyberries had been a full-blood Crow from the Whistling Wind clan, who held the Little Bighorn River country as much as any Crow holds his own land. She was working in the bookshop of the Custer memorial near Crow Agency when Beau first saw her.

He had been with Steiger Freightways for a couple of months then, back in 1968. He was still angry about the army turning him down for bad knees. Football knees, they said, as if it were a lucky break for him. You'd never clear boot, son. Thank your stars. McAllister hadn't seen it that way at the time, although later on he'd learned to live with it. Not every young man finds his war.

So it had been high summer, on a long haul from Gary to Coeur d'Alene with a flatbed of steel rods. The load had been shifting on him for days, and he had pulled off I-90 at Crow Agency to warp it down some. Although he had passed it many times, off in the blue distance, that day he had been drawn by the sight of it: a little cluster of white marble beneath a stone pillar on the side of a brown hill.

He stood awhile at the cairn and read the names of those men from Prague and Dublin and Naples and Aberdeen who had come to America and somehow found themselves in the cavalry, surrounded by all this open light and land, maybe stunned by it, or crazed, or hypnotized by it as it sometimes hypnotized Beau. They'd come all this way from some eastern hellhole or, beyond that, from some Silesian coal mine or a ghetto in Düsseldorf—all this way to die at Greasy Grass under a Dakota hatchet.

He had walked the five miles along the crest of the slopes to the bowl-shaped roundtop where Reno and Benteen had made their stand, feeling the sun on his shirt and the hard-packed clay under his boots.

Here and there in the coulees and the slopes, rising out of the dry grasses, white marble stones marked the places where troopers had died. Sometimes they had gone down in groups—McAllister could see them with their ponies down and their backs together, working away at their Sharps or their Henrys, cursing or crying in five different languages. But down they had gone, either alone or in a crowd.

Even in 1968, the battlefield looked exactly as it had in 1876. He stood there on the brown slope and watched the cloud shadows move across the valley all the way south to the Bighorn range and the Wyoming border. At the bottom of the long shallow hill, the Little Bighorn River wandered through stands of cottonwood trees and green grass, a ripple of sunlight on blue water, a slow hot wind ruffling its surface. A shimmer warped through the trees, and he could hear the cars and trucks like a dull seashell murmur as they worked their way up the shallow grade over on I-90. From Weir Point, a man could look north and east fifty miles, see a world of rolling brown hills as old as time, marked here and there with shadings of blue pine.

He was still a little saddened when he went into the bookstore to find some kind of souvenir. He found Alice Manyberries instead, an oval Crow face with high bones and a direct brown look and long-fingered delicate hands. He managed to have three years and one daughter with her before that propane tanker put an end to all that.

He used to think if he'd never come to the battlefield, then she'd still be working at Crow Agency in the heart of the Whistling Wind land and not lying dead in a field in Utah.

Well, then it was the army's fault, for not taking him when he asked. Or it was his own fault, for playing football back at Ukiah or later at Cal

State, because if he hadn't cooked his knees then, he would have been in Vietnam instead of driving up I-90 in Montana for Steiger Freightways.

And he wouldn't have Laurel Manyberries McAllister, now twenty-two, postgraduate in cultural anthropology. Laurel was working on a site down in Wyoming now. There had been enough of Alice in Laurel to keep Beau together when it was just the two of them after the funeral. Three months it had taken Alice to die. Beau and Laurel had taken a place in Billings to be near her. And the old man, Doc Hogeland, he'd become sort of a grandfather to Laurel and a solid friend to Beau. He'd been there at the bedside, sometimes, when Beau had come in to see her.

Back then, the doc had been the chief of surgery, and he did everything for her that there was to do. Grafts. Antibiotics.

And then one day it had been time for her to go, and she did. Doc Hogeland came looking for him at the Muzzleloader Lounge down on the Frontage Line. He talked to Beau a long time about what it was like to lose a wife. Hogeland had lost his wife after a six-year struggle with kidney failure. They'd been trying to get a transplant arranged when she went into a coma. She died a few days later. They'd been married thirty-six years.

Listening to the old man talk about his wife didn't help much, but it started a bond between them. It was the doc who had advised Beau to stay here in Billings, and it was the doc who got him the job with the Highway Patrol.

He went along with the suggestion more or less to keep Laurel near her clan rather than have her grow up an outcast breed in Provo, surrounded by Mormon real estate salesmen and cracker cowhand kids.

She had set aside her babyhood like a girl taking ribbons out of her hair. By seven, she had been cooking and cleaning and ordering him around, a little brown wand of graceful motion and a smile like a bright white flower, suddenly all grown and out of the house more than she was in it.

She had been sixteen when he brought Maureen home to meet her. Before that, he had kept his women away from the house, out of respect for Alice's memory and for Laurel as well.

But Maureen Sprague was pregnant by then and determined to marry Beau and make a home for him. Maureen was all streaked blond hair and angles and lanky East Coast lines. She played tennis and squash and jogged and wore headbands and little terry wristbands when she worked out. She drank vodka gimlets and watched *Brideshead Revisited* and *Upstairs Downstairs*. She read everything *The New York Times Book Review* told her to read. She was a nurse at the Julia Dwight Clinic when Beau met her. He saw her all the time, brought her the latest knifing victim, or a carload of bruised boys from a bar fight in Hardin, or a survivor of a pickup rollover. She had seemed funny and fresh and, he had to face this, as different from Alice as any woman could be. Alice had been all dark-skinned intensity and controlled passion, fierce in her own way, always probing Beau to find out his state of mind or his dreams or the contents of his soul.

Maureen Sprague was not like Alice. She liked it light and breezy and happy. Like most nurses, she had learned to make a joke out of tragedy, which fit neatly with McAllister's own instincts about the way to survive a career in law enforcement. Around her, Beau had been light and happy for longer and longer periods, until he realized he hadn't thought about Alice Manyberries for almost a week, and that had saddened and eased him at the same time.

Maureen had them in bed the first date, and she kept him there until he asked her to marry him. Maureen was an astonishing lover, delicate, powerful, inventive, slightly corrupt and dark in some of her needs. They had Roberta Lee five months after the wedding. And Maureen packed Laurel off to Montana State when she was eighteen.

Maureen's relationship with Laurel had always been friendly but careful, as if they both felt something might go bang if they hit it hard enough. Laurel had never spoken a word against Maureen, never made Beau feel guilty about marrying again, had always been sweet and gentle with Bobby Lee.

But she had been . . . dwindling. Getting spiritually smaller, was how it seemed to Beau. As if she were being bled nightly.

When she left for Bozeman and Montana State, they all drove her to the bus station. Maureen said she would miss her, but when she was gone, only Bobby Lee and Beau ever wrote to her.

A few years later, Beau too began to feel that he was being bled nightly, and he left as well. As soon as he was packed and out, Maureen had made Bobby Lee the battleground. Let a support payment be a day late, and Bobby Lee suddenly had the flu. Let a hard word be said at the door, and Bobby Lee would be "out" and Maureen would not know when she'd be back.

Or Bobby Lee was playing with friends.

Or Bobby Lee was too tired.

Or Bobby Lee had chicken pox, and no he couldn't come in and see her. She was quarantined.

She was at somebody's house.

She didn't want to see him.

Beau, Maureen would say, the sweet smile of reason stretched across a thin face shiny with hatred, Beau, we think it would be best for Bobby Lee if you didn't come around here anymore.

We?

Bobby Lee and I.

Let me hear her say that.

Why put her through that, Beau? Why not just go away?

Why not get the hell out of my way? he had said, and they had fought on the doorstep of his old house in Hardin, with the neighbors all out on their porches and Maureen shrieking at him, her muscular neck a bundle of tight cords, her mouth a twisted cut, her face flushed and bright.

Three days later, he had gotten the letter in the mail, a thick creamy bond paper with "Mallon, Brewer, Hogeland and Bright" in the upper left corner. The next three years had been an endless round of court actions, countersuits, legal warnings, scheduled visitations, postdated checks, and ulcerated feelings. Some of his friends had delicately suggested that he give it up and walk away, for Bobby Lee's sake. But the more clearly he saw Maureen for what she was—the cruelty and the ugliness in her, her readiness to make Bobby Lee a game piece—the less willing he was to leave his child entirely under her control.

A pain in his right jaw let him know how hard he was biting the stem of his pipe. A pain in his stomach let him know how it hurt to think about things like this when you had no way to fix them, short of murder.

And he had thought about that.

It was a fantasy of his, to put a round made of dry ice into his MacMillan and fire the dry-ice round at five hundred yards into the side of Maureen's head. The round would burn away in the air and blood. They'd never get a slug, have no ballistics.

No. They'd just have Beau McAllister, the victim's ex-husband, whose hatred for her was now a countywide legend.

It struck him as ironic, how he seemed to be tied up with the Hogeland family. He couldn't think about Alice Manyberries without thinking how much he owed Doc Darryl.

And he couldn't think about Maureen without wanting to beat the living hell out of the doc's kid. What was that old cop line, about stress. Stress is the feeling you get when you want to, but can't, choke the shit out of some asshole who desperately needs it. That summed up his feelings about Dwight Hogeland.

Screw this, he decided. He knocked the pipe bowl clean on the heel of his boot and put the pipe away in his shirt pocket, where the heat of it against his chest warmed him a little against the growing chill of the evening.

Five minutes later he was out on the interstate headed east toward Pompeys Pillar, into the rising night.

5

1930 Hours – June 14 – Los Angeles, California

Gabriel Picketwire was staring at Dr. Sifton's bald spot and trying not to scream when his cellular phone rang. They were in one of the crew tents, trying to patch up his knee; he'd cracked it hard on the side of the dumpster when he'd jumped. Dr. Sifton, the sawbones on the set, was a broken-down medic who was pretty liberal with the mood-altering chemicals and the Valium prescriptions. His ears stuck out at the sides as he bent over Gabriel's knee, poking at the cartilage. The phone sounded again, where it sat across the room on a card table full of explosives and electronic gear. It gave out a nasty peremptory burr, like a robot wasp.

"You gonna get that for me, Doc?"

"I look like a gofer to you, Chief?"

Sifton raised his heavy head like a buffalo disturbed at his grazing. His eyes were red and wet in a pink fleshy face. His hands still worked at Gabriel's knee. The phone burred again.

"Well, I can't get it. And don't call me Chief."

"It's probably your wife."

"I'm not married."

"Your boyfriend, then."

"Why are you such a miserable son of a bitch, Doc?"

"The world is tragedy for those who feel and comedy for those who think."

"Yeah? How about those who drink?"

"Bearable. I have to use the toilet anyway."

Gabriel lurched off the cot and hopped to the table. Dr. Sifton took the opportunity to shuffle into the Porta-Potty at the side of the crew tent. He left the door open. Gabriel could see him rolling up a sleeve. Under the hot downlight, the doctor's arm looked like a tube of pink sausage. In his right hand he held a hypodermic needle. A thin jet of fluid leaped from the glittering tip. Sifton smiled at Gabriel and closed the door.

"Hello?"

Background noise—trucks maybe. A highway.

"Blue Coat? Gabriel Blue Coat?" The voice was cramped and husky, but he knew it. Grief and some other emotion colored the timbre of it.

"Jubal . . . you'll have to speak louder. Where are you?"

"They killed him." Jubal's voice was old and wintry. Gabriel could hear frost in it, and dry branches.

"They what? Killed? Killed who?"

Gabriel balanced on one leg, stared out the flap of the tent at the crewmen walking by, and past them, out into the silky California dusk.

"Jubal, I don't understand. Where are you?"

"We are in . . . I should not say into this thing. They have machines. We should not say."

"Is everybody all right?"

"No. They plugged him. Plugged him good. He had no stomach. We shot at them but it did nothing. You must come."

"They shot Eddie?"

"They shot Eddie."

"Why? Why did they shoot Eddie?" He had a brief vision of a small boy chasing a scruffy black dog across a beach. Two women in linen skirts laughed into the wind, and the wind carried the sound up the beach toward him.

"Because they had guns and they can do that here. Will you come?"

"What happened to Eddie? Is he dead?"

"Yes, Blue Coat. But we have him."

Lately, Jubal had taken to calling him Blue Coat sarcastically. It was part of that whole obsession that had taken him over. Gabriel found it tiresome, but he tolerated it. Jubal had little else in the world, and now it seemed he had lost a great deal of that. A ragged lance of heat punched through his lower belly. It took him a time to recognize it as rage.

"How . . . what do you mean?"

"We took him back."

"Took him back? How?"

Dr. Sifton came out of the Porta-Potty and subsided into the cot, wheezing and groaning, working at the sleeve of his shirt. He looked past Gabriel, past the flap of the tent, at something out of sight in the deepening night.

"Back from them."

"Jesus . . . Jubal, is Earl there?"

"He is not Earl. He is Black Elk."

Gabriel drew a long breath and held it, feeling his lungs swell and the blood rise in his neck. He let it out slowly, looking at Dr. Sifton, who had settled back into the cot with one arm thrown across his eyes to protect him from the glare of the bulb. His mouth was open. His breathing slowed.

"Yes. Is Black Elk there?"

"No. He is going to steal us a car. Comes In Sight and the Sweetwater girl are talking to the men in the gray wagon."

"Are the men hurt? Did you hurt them?"

"Not yet. The young one is crying. I am here to tell you to come and help us with these people. They are not even going to let us ask any questions or look around. All they want is to rub us out."

"Where did this happen?"

"At the gas station."

"Was Bell there?"

"Yes. He was the one who shot first. Then the rest came, and they shot at Joe Bell, and we ran off up a big hill where we could watch them. We saw them put Eddie into a gray wagon. Then they all stood around taking pictures and putting yellow ribbon all over the place. Then the gray wagon men drove off. But they went to a bar not far away."

"The police came, and *they* shot Joe Bell?"

"That is what happened. I can't stand around here until the morning, Blue Coat. We have no truck and no clothes. They took them. We have the men who took away Eddie, and then we are going to do a sing for Eddie.

Then we will have a talk and think what to do about these people. We want you to come to this talk.''

"Why not just go in to the police there? Tell them about everything. They'll help you. Whatever you do, you can't hold on to those men. That's a federal offense. They'll turn everything they have loose on you. You gotta let them go.''

"They are looking for us now. The cars go around everywhere with big shotguns in the front. But they are too lazy to get out and walk around the country. They shine their lights up into the hills and the trees by the river here. You are a fool if you think they want to help us. Anyway, you come tomorrow and stay in the Holiday Inn in Billings. We will call you in your room.''

"Jubal—''

"I am Two Moon.''

Christ.

"Okay. Two Moon. I can't go there. We have three more days of shooting here. Maybe four. Then we have to go to Vancouver. Let me give you the name of a lawyer I know. He works for the federal Indian Affairs people in Helena. He'll—''

"You are a fool, Blue Coat. Good-bye.''

"Jubal, don't—''

He was gone. Gabriel threw the phone across the room. It hit the tent wall and fell down beside the doctor. Sifton moved his arm and turned his head to see what had landed. He pushed himself upright and slumped against the wall.

"Good news, Chief?''

"Not really. Is this leg gonna be okay?''

Sifton gestured toward his aluminum case.

"I have some Novocaine there—it'll ease the pain. You banged it up pretty good on that dumpster. You keep it wrapped, and I'll write up a prescription. A little pick-me-up.''

"Can I use this knee tomorrow?''

"You going to be here tomorrow, Chief?''

"Yes. Why wouldn't I?''

Sifton sighed and groaned and lurched to his feet. He put his hands in the pocket of his baggy linen pants and looked at Gabriel from under his fleshy lids.

"Your friend there sounds like he's in a serious situation. I guess I thought you'd be going to help him out.''

"You heard that? I hope you can keep it to yourself, Doc.''

"I am the very paradigm of discretion, Chief. In this business, doctors hear everything. Most of it would nauseate a dung beetle. I quite frankly have contrived to reduce my reactions to this sort of stimuli to a manageable level of contained amusement. And as you have observed, I have vices of my own. May I venture a question? Purely academic? Consider it part of my interest in contemporary anthropology.''

"Sure.''

"You *are* a Native American, are you not?''

"Yes.''

"Professional stunt person?''

"Yes.''

"And your background is Sioux?''

"Lakota. My band is Sans Arcs. You'd call us Teton Sioux.''

"Yes. Military service, too, I understand? A warrior?''

Gabriel stared at the paunchy man for a long time, thinking that a word excluded more than it included.

"Where'd you hear that?'' he said finally.

"You are talked about. The enigmatic Mr. Picketwire. Empirically, I observe that you have a familiarity with weapons. Also, you have a . . . directed quality that I have come to associate with men who have seen some sort of combat.''

"I served for a while in Southeast Asia.''

"Vietnam?''

"No, I was never in Vietnam. What's this all about, Doc? I gotta call a friend of mine.''

"The lawyer in Helena—well, that brings me to my question.''

"What question?''

"What's the Lakota word for lawyer?''

"In Lakota? There isn't one.''

"Ah. I didn't think there was.''

6

2245 Hours – June 14 – Pompeys Pillar, Montana

Bell's Oasis was an island of corpse-colored light at the far end of the darkened main street of Pompeys Pillar. The only other business up and running at this late hour was Fogarty's New York Bar, two blocks over on Custer Street. Beau could hear the music drifting through the still evening air as he rolled by on his way up to Bell's. "Evangeline" by Emmylou Harris.

There was a Mountain Bell van parked out in front of Bell's Oasis. The yellow crime ribbon was still stretched around three pump islands. More of it was roped around the chain link fence enclosure and the propane tank. No other cars were around.

Finch and Rowdy had checked out and gone home a few minutes back. Ron Thornton and Rita Sonnette were also off duty. Beau had gotten Patrolmen Pietrosante and Benitez—the Munchkin—away from their separate off-duty pleasures and out into the back country. Benitez had insisted on a cruiser, so Beau pulled one from the traffic pool.

They were calling in now and then over the CB-Communications patch. Nothing. No sign of the morgue wagon, no sign of Danny Burt or Peter Hinsdale anywhere.

Hinsdale's mother was getting pretty worked up about that. Hinsdale was a nineteen-year-old part-timer taking a course as an undertaker at Billings Vocational College. Actually, Hinsdale's mother had said he was "in the bereavement sciences course, specializing in grief management."

Bereavement sciences? Grief management?

Christ help us.

McAllister killed the cruiser lights and rolled to a stop beside the first pump bank.

"Five eleven."

"Five eleven?"

"Central, I'm gonna be out of the car here at Bell's Oasis for about fifteen minutes. I'll be OTA on the portable. Okay?"

"Ten-four, Sergeant."

"That you, Beth?"

"That's me, Beau."

"How come you're still on?"

"Overtime. The swing-shift girl isn't coming in tonight."

"Oh, right . . . the LT still there?"

"No. He's gone down to see Bill Garner. Big Horn County guys."

"Okay. Well, I'm ten-seven on the air."

"Bye-bye, Beau."

He got out and stood for a while, looking down at the blood patch on the pavement. It was funny about blood. Rain wouldn't wash it away. Gas wouldn't. That stain would be there for six months, until they salted the lot after the first winter snows. Salt would bleach it out. Somebody had once told Beau that blood was very similar to sea water. Salt water. Maybe this all meant something in a cosmic way, but probably not.

Beau walked over to the doorway of the main office. The snack-bar lights were on. He stepped sideways to the plate-glass window and looked in. He could see a man hunched over a toolbox on the floor, in front of a row of pay phones along the back wall by the washrooms. MOUNTAIN BELL was stitched across the back of his overalls. Beau tapped on the glass.

The man jumped up and swiveled, holding a screwdriver like a knife. Beau smiled at him.

"Sorry to frighten you. Sergeant McAllister, Highway Patrol. Who're you?"

The man was lean and young, very pink-skinned. A wispy red moustache rode on his upper lip like a pet caterpillar. He had pale blue, wet-looking eyes, the eyes of a man used to bad luck. He came over to the glass and peered out at Beau.

"You gotta badge?"

"It's on my shirt, son. Open up."

He stared at Beau's pocket for a minute, moving his lips.

Inbred, thought Beau. Bet he plays a hell of a banjo.

The stringy kid slouched over to the door, threw the bolt. "Yuh gotta be careful. This here's a crime scene, Sergeant."

"Yeah, I noticed. What're you doing here, son?"

He rolled his head on a boneless neck, indicating the bank of pay phones. "Service call."

Beau nodded. "You have some ID?"

The kid stared at Beau as if Beau had grown a third eye.

"Yuh kin see my uniform. I gotta truck."

"I see a uniform. I see a truck."

The kid rolled his eyes and let out a long sigh. He smelled of stale beer and peppermint gum. He dug around in his overalls and came up with a tattered card. As he handed it over, Beau could see patches of raw flesh and new scab on the fingertips of his right hand. He tried not to think what might have caused that. He was pretty sure he wouldn't like the answer.

HUBERT WOZCYLESKO. And a photograph of the kid without his pet caterpillar. It was Mountain Bell ID. Beau handed it back.

"Thanks, Hubert."

"Woz. People call me Woz."

"Okay, Woz. How come you're working this late?"

"Supposed to service 'em this morning. Couldn't. Hedda shoot-out here. Joe Bell killed some fuckin' Indian. I guess you heard?"

"I heard. Well, don't let me stop you. I'll just do a walkaround. See if everything's okay."

The kid shrugged, swiveled on a heel, and headed back to the phones. Beau walked past him and into the kitchen. The back door was bolted and barred. The alarm-box light flickered in the darkened corner, green like a one-eyed cat.

Hope Blasingame knows to feed the cats, thought Beau, strolling over to the doorway of Bell's office.

So. Is that packet still under the desk? Beau looked over his shoulder at Woz Wozcylesko from Mountain Bell. He had the casing off one of the pay phones and was picking away at the coin slot with something long and sharp, cursing softly to himself.

Meagher had been pretty clear about the issue. Leave it alone. Laws were laws and rights were rights. A lawman was a man of the law, or he was nothing but a lawyer with a permit to carry.

Meagher had once read an essay by somebody named Kant out loud to Beau over a bottle of Utah champagne, at the sleepy close of a retirement party for one of the Big Horn County cops. Meagher apparently kept the paper in his pocket because when he pulled it out it was so creased and worn, it almost fell apart.

The essay had been about how lying was *always* wrong because no matter how good your motivation for lying, you were somehow breaking down the—the *currency* of honest exchange, was how Meagher had put it. The *coin* of ideas and belief. So when you lied or did something deceitful, even if you were doing it to save a life or right some terrible wrong, it was still a lie, and a lie eroded the . . . tacit . . . understanding we all share about each other. About being able to trust in each other. In every other. And this went double for cops. Truth was what cops were all about, was Meagher's point.

Interesting thought, Eustace, Beau had told him. Anybody ever put this guy Kant to the test?

Not that Meagher had heard. What did that have to do with anything?

Well, you know. Like if Kant was trying to—if a young girl runs into Kant's apartment, her clothes are all ripped up and she's bleeding. Obvious victim of an attack. So then Kant is pouring her some tea or something, and suddenly there's this bang-bang at the door. So the girl jumps up and hides, like in Kant's closet. And Kant opens the door, and there's this huge outlaw biker asshole there, has his pants down around his ankles, loaded for bear, got a hard-on like pink steel, he's waving a knife, wants to know if Kant has seen this girl run by his door. Does Kant know where this girl is?

Yeah . . . ?

Yeah, so what does Kant do? Does he lie and save the girl, or does he tell the truth and get her killed?

Meagher wanted to know if Kant was armed.

Yeah. Let's say he is.

Well . . . I guess I gotta say he tells the guy the truth. Why do I get the idea this actually happened to you?

Yep.

So what did you do?

What you said Kant would do. I told him the truth.

You said she was there?

Yep.

Then what?

Then I shot him.

So what's your point?

The point is, trust in Allah, but tie up your camels.

What?

Tell the truth to people who have the truth in them.

That's not what Kant was saying.

I know, but Kant wasn't a cop.

Cops aren't all the law is. Cops are just the bouncers in the dance hall of the law.

So let me see if I get this. What are the lawyers?

They'd be the bartenders. Bar-tenders? Get it?

Yeah, I get it. And the judges?

They're the disc jockeys of justice.

Beau had laughed then. And what do they play?

Truth—the song of justice.

You really believe that, Eustace?

Well, said Meagher, reaching for the bottle. There you go.

Go where?

Go get another. This one's empty. Anyway, that argument's irrevelant.

Irrelevant. It doesn't address the principal tenets of the thesis. It's ad hoc.

Say what?

Ad hoc, Beau. *Ad hoc!*

Hey, Beau had said, getting up to look for some more champagne. That's a nasty cough you got there, Eustace.

He was looking at the television set on Bell's filing cabinet. There was a VCR underneath it, so it was probably what Bell used for his . . . diversions. Beau came around and flicked it on. What he got was a picture of the pump area out front, his cruiser, and the Mountain Bell truck glowing gray in the black-and-white image. There must be a camera mounted up on the roof, a cheap one from the look of the image, which was grainy and out of focus. Beau felt that kind of rare thrill a cop gets when something breaks his way in a case.

He bent down to study the VCR. It had a tape in it, and the illuminated panel said STOP. The tape had run through to the end.

Christ! Maybe he had the whole thing on tape!

He rewound the tape and hit the PLAY button.

The screen flickered and jumped, and then there was a blank screen with the TIME-DATE numbers running.

Today's date. Thirteen hundred hours this afternoon.

Yes!

Then the picture came up. It was just a fixed camera image, cars and trucks gliding in, people walking around, the normal business of a truck stop. There was no sound.

Beau hit FAST FORWARD and everybody jerked into high-speed motion. The day-date-hour indicator flickered forward. Beau kept the button pressed, watching the screen.

Trucks. Cars. People. Senseless motion.

The time indicator ran through 1600 hours.

It was getting close now. Beau took his finger off FAST FORWARD and watched the screen.

Bell was in the picture, leaning in a car window, talking to someone, the driver; there was a truck blocking the view. Bell stood up and slammed the roof of the car. It was a big car, black or brown or dark gray. Maybe blue. It looked like an old Caddy. Bell came back up the line of pumps, and the old Caddy pulled away. Bell watched it go, turned back, his face set and his mouth moving. He disappeared out of the camera line.

Beau hit the FREEZE-FRAME button.

Then he hit REVERSE and FREEZE again.

He leaned forward and looked at the old Cadillac for almost a full minute. The screen popped, and static arced and crackled across the image of the car, Bell leaning in the passenger window.

Beau shook his head and released the FREEZE button.

The car was—no, he thought. That's a different car. Anyway, the image quality sucks. That's another car entirely. He put the thought away and watched the video roll. Almost time.

Trucks were moving. Beau saw the J. B. Hunt tractor-trailer crossing the lot. More cars pulled away and—

The picture went blank—jumped—popped.

God-*damn*. Someone had shut the camera off.

Bell had shut it off.

Son of a *bitch*!

He ran the tape forward. Junk. Home movies. Some disconnected activities. Then a couple of women, naked, in a hot tub. This part in full color. Beau shut the machine off, and a terrible feeling washed over him.

He was already down on his hands and knees, feeling around under the drawers. He felt under there for a while, but it was just for something to do while he cursed himself out, cursed out Meagher and Joe Bell and the renegades and Vanessa Ballard and everybody else he had locked horns with today.

Because that packet was gone.

There was a sticky patch where the tape had been, and shreds of tape still stuck to the bottom of the drawer. But there was no package. Somebody had got to it. Somebody with the brass to walk through a police crime scene ribbon and take it.

Somebody with a uniform, maybe?

Somebody who knew where it was.

Oh, well, this is real irritating, isn't it? There sure as hell is something going on, and now if Bell comes back here to look for it and it's gone, the first thing he'll do is come to Beau and ask where the fuck it is. And when Beau doesn't know, he'll ask the LT, who sure as God made cold sores will come around and ask Beau what the hell *he* did with it.

And Beau couldn't even go back to Eustace right now and tell him that the thing was gone because then Eustace would want to know *how* he knew it was gone, and Beau would have to tell him that he knew it was gone because he was down here on his knees looking for it. And he'd have to tell Meagher about the tape, and when you looked at it, the tape wasn't really relevant. It might show that Bell deliberately shut the camera off, which *might* suggest that Bell knew something was about to happen. . . .

A lot of suppositions. Better to keep it simp—

"What're you looking for there, Sergeant?"

Beau jerked up and slammed his shoulder on the edge of the desk. That made it twice today somebody had snuck up on him while he was here in Bell's office.

"God-*damn it*, Hubert! Don't tippy-toe around like that. Whaddya want in here, anyway?"

Wozcylesko twisted his large mouth sideways, a man with a party-trick face. "Nothin'. I was just sayin' I gotta go now."

"You leaving? Fine. You get it done?"

"Nah. They're fucked good. Fucking truckers."

"Truckers—what'd they do?"

"Jokesters. Think they're funny as tits on a door."

"Why?"

"Always doing that stunt, fucking up the coin slots like that."

"Like how? They stick a slug in one? Bubblegum?"

He shook his head vigorously. Beau could almost hear his brain rattling around inside like a dried-up pea in a box.

"Nah . . . they put that Krazy Glue in 'em. You know, into the coin slots."

Beau got to his feet and walked across to the phone banks. There were ten phones in a row, three of them electronic ones set up to take credit cards, the other seven coin-operated phones. The kid followed him over and was now putting his tools away in the box.

"How many were vandalized?"

"Just a couple. They're junk now."

"And you say the truckers do this? They do it all the time?"

"Yeah . . . well, not here. But—you know. I heard about this shit. It happens. Kids do it. Truckers. Tourists sometimes."

"But not *here* before. Not that you know?"

"Well, no. Not here. This's my route. But I seen it other places. Really."

"These the only phones?"

"Nah. There's three out by the diesel pumps."

"And?"

"And what?"

"You check them?"

"Nah. Not on my sheet."

"When'd you get the call?"

"To fix these things? Call came in this afternoon. So I hear a whole bunch of people got shot to shit here?"

"Nobody got shot to shit except one young kid. Come outside for a second?"

The kid flinched and twisted his mouth again. "What're you gonna do? I didn't do nothin' wrong. I'm supposed to be here."

"You go into Joe Bell's office here?"

"Yeah, once. I hadda call in."

"You look under his desk?"

"What the fuck'd I do that for?"

Beau stared hard at him. "Take the top off that toolbox."

"What for?"

"Just do it!"

"Okay . . . okay . . . here."

He lifted the top tray off. Beau knelt down and sorted through needle-nose pliers, bits of wire, fuses, and connectors.

"Okay. First we're gonna go look through your truck. Then we're gonna check out those other three phones."

"You haveta have a warrant."

"For what?"

"That's a Mountain Bell truck. That's a public utility, belongs to the government. I can't let no civilian in there."

Beau reached out and gently, very gently, took hold of the kid's cat-erpillar moustache. The kid backed away and winced as the moustache stayed where it was, pinched in Beau's fingers.

"Hubert. Woz. You gotta help me here. I'm being as civil as I can be."

The kid started to squeal. Beau let him go, and he lurched back. Beau caught him by the arm and led him out toward the gas pumps. The kid was silent. He radiated sulk. Something else Beau would hear about next week.

Beau spent ten minutes rooting through the junk in the back of the Mountain Bell van. He found nothing. The van smelled strongly of solvent. It burned the nostrils and made his eyes run. And under that, another scent, spicy, like incense or . . .

Beau opened the glove compartment. The kid yelped at him, but he held up a hand to quiet him. He stepped back out and looked at the foil-wrapped package in the light of an arc lamp.

"What've we got here, son?"

The kid looked like he was going to wet himself. He backed away a couple of steps, absolute terror in his eyes.

Heartbeat ruffling, thinking maybe he had found Bell's package, Beau ripped the tinfoil cover. The musky scent rose up out of his palm. Buds and dark-brown leaves rolled in the foil.

Suddenly Beau felt ashamed of himself. Why was he taking all this out on poor Hubert Wozcylesko? All the kid was trying to do was get away with his stash.

"Hey," he said, putting his hands up, trying on his friendliest smile. "Relax, kid. I was looking for something else."

The kid's face went through a number of changes, settling on relief. "I didn't mean nothing, Sergeant."

"Son, I'll never understand why we go to so much trouble to ban something that grows by the side of the road. Might as well ban wildflowers or dandelions, right?"

"Yeah . . . say, you're chilly. You're okay, Sarge."

"Sure I am. Chilly as penguin shit. And we forget about our little snit-fit in there, too, right, Woz?"

"Oh, sure. All forgotten . . . say, . . . aahh?"

"Hope you're not going to ask for your dope back, kid."

"Oh, no, sir. No, sir! In no way, sir!"

"Kid, your truck smells of kerosene or solvent. You got a leak or something?"

Woz swallowed and looked a little startled, but his voice was steady when he answered. "No. That's fixer for fiberglass. I'm doing some body-work on my car, and I got a can of the fixer in the back there."

"You not into sniffing or anything, Woz?"

Woz rose up in righteousness. "*No, sir!* I seen what that shit does to you. Some of those poor Crow kids, they get into that. Fries their brains! That stuff is poison. I'll get that can outta there soon's I get back to the yard!"

"Good. Now let's see about those phones."

They were fine. It troubled Beau that the kid was out here, rooting around in a crime scene, and it troubled him even more that the kid *might* be leaving with that disk from under Bell's desk.

Beau felt a new wave of fatigue. He had been a cop for a very long time, and the more he saw of people, the more he disliked them. Anybody who wanted to be a cop ought to be required to spend a few days cleaning up in the monkey house. He'd learn all he ever had to know about human beings while he was working in a monkey house. There were only three reasons a monkey did anything! Food. Fuck. Or fight.

In human terms, that'd be money, sex, or revenge. Beau had never seen a crime that didn't come down to one or the other, or sometimes two out of three.

Maybe the kid was just a kid, and the phones had nothing to do with anything. He thought for a long while about calling Ident to get some prints off the pay phones but finally decided against it. He could hear Vanessa Ballard taking that one apart in a prelim.

"Now, let me get this straight, Sergeant McAllister. You found fingerprints belonging to Joe Bell on these pay phones?"

"Yes, ma'am."

"These pay phones that actually belong to Joe Bell?"

"Ah—er, . . . well, not to him technically."

"Pay phones placed on or around his legal business?"

"Yes, ma'am."

"And you suggest that you found it suspicious that these pay phones, which were placed on Mr. Bell's property, actually had Mr. Bell's prints on them?''

"Along with others, ma'am.''

"What others?''

"Well, we haven't been able to determine that yet.''

"Haven't been able—Sergeant McAllister, I submit to you—''

God, he hated it when Ballard submitted to him.

Well, actually, if you put it *that* way . . .

Putting it *that* way, it was clearly time for a beer.

7

2315 Hours – June 14 – Pompeys Pillar, Montana

He saw the kid off in his Mountain Bell truck, did a final walkaround to secure the premises, and climbed back into the cruiser. It was now close to midnight, and he had been on duty since six that morning. Close to eighteen hours in the saddle. Time to call it a night. Whatever the hell else was going to happen, it could happen without Beau's help. He thought about the sound of Emmylou Harris coming from Fogarty's New York Bar. There'd be enough time to drop in for a couple of cold beers, see how Fogarty was doing.

"Five eleven to Central. You there, Beth?"

"Hi, Beau."

"Anything on that wagon?"

"Not a peep. Heard from Tony Pietrosante a while back. Said he was on his third tank, and that you could . . . that you'd know what you could do with this search.''

Beau laughed. ''He's got that right. Anything from Trooper Benitez?''

''Trooper Benitez seems to have gotten his vehicle stuck in a coulee somewhere off the Ballantine side road, Beau.''

Shit.

''Somewhere? *Somewhere?* Benitez doesn't know his ten-twenty?''

''That seems to be the sitrep, Beau.''

''*Sitrep?* Jeez, Beth. We got anybody out looking for him?''

''Negative, Beau.''

''You gonna talk like that, Beth, you gotta say nega*tory*!''

''Negatory, Beau. All the Charlie cars are either doing patrol around Twilly's or along the interstate. We have no one to clear for him at this time.''

''What about traffic?''

''No cars at this time. Benitez has one. The others are on a RADD program down the line.''

''You hearing from him?''

''Ten-four, Beau. Last time was ten minutes ago. Says he's up to his ax-holes.''

Beau could feel that smile stretch his tired skin all the way to his sideburns. ''Up to his ax-holes, Beth?''

''Actually, he said he was 'stock up to my focking ax-holes in theez focking ay-*roy*-oh!' Beau.''

''Yeah? Well, Beth, my dove, I am looking at eighteen hours in the saddle, and I feel like somebody put kitty litter in my boxer shorts. I propose that I reconnoiter in the vicinity of Fogarty's New York Bar to see if I can identify any undesirable elements such as might be contemplating the violent overthrow of the sovereign State of Montana and the tugging down of the pants and garters of our appointed representatives. I will be OTA should Trooper Benitez manage to clarify his locationary *die*-lemma. Five eleven is OTA, my darling.''

''Ten-four, Beau. Have one for me.''

Fogarty's New York Bar was tucked away in a reconstructed blacksmith shop two blocks off the main street of Pompeys Pillar. It was lined in faded gray barnboard, dark and full of the smell of pipe smoke, whisky, cigarettes, and the wood fire that Fogarty always liked to keep burning in the old forge.

A long and battered mahogany bar ran the length of the big taproom, at least forty feet. The footrail was supported by brass elephant heads. A huge bull-buffalo head towered over the centerboard.

Fogarty had raided an old pool hall in Butte and come away with three classic green felt pool tables, solid slate, and a truckload of green-glass-and-brass hanging lamps.

The ceiling rafters were cluttered with New York State licenses, pictures of New York cops and detectives, Fiorello La Guardia in his fedora and dandy's collar, replica badges, and hats and nightsticks. There was even a model of the Brooklyn Bridge in a glass case.

Fogarty had made it clear that he'd personally shoot dead any cowhand or truck driver who managed to knock it over in a fight. Since Fogarty had actually shot and killed a man eleven years back during an attempted robbery, shot him twice in the chest with an old army .45 that he kept in the buffalo's mouth, the customers took him seriously. Everybody who just *had* to fight, fought outside like gentlemen.

Fogarty himself was a soft-spoken and easy-going man of no particular size or weight, but there was something in his eyes and the lines around his mouth, something in the huge white handlebar moustache and the precise way he had of talking, almost too low to hear, that kept the bar quiet and peaceful.

Maybe part of the charm was that you had to know where it was to find it. Fogarty didn't like signs, and it was two blocks off the highway. So in the end, only his friends and their friends and friends of those friends found their way there on a weekend evening. The place was full of people, older retired ranchers and their ladies, some cowhands from the government spreads, even a table full of Japanese cowboys from a big beef ranch being operated by a Kyoto company a few miles west of Billings. Actually, it was Ingomar's old spread. What was the name? Fargo? Far . . . Farwest. Farwest Beef and Dairy—something like that, anyway.

Go figure the Japanese. Talk about the samurai, act like the world's most tightly wrapped obsessive-compulsive race. Then come out here and buy up everything that looks like Real America. Well, God bless them. Beau figured this was their year. The circle turns.

Fogarty and his daughter Colleen were walking the bar, serving up tap ale and draft and bottles of Lone Star and Coors. A few solitaries, wrapped in their own trials, stood at the bar. A couple of waitresses Beau didn't recognize were moving through the tables with trays of beer and plates of hot wings.

Fogarty saw him come through the door and reached under the bar. By the time Beau had settled down on a stool, Fogarty was just topping off his glass. He set the bottle of Beck's aside and wiped the spillage away with an old chamois. Fogarty took good care of this bartop.

"Patrick. Busy tonight."

Fogarty's eyes flicked around the room.

"Everybody's come to see the Japs."

Beau swiveled around in the stool. A couple of tables away, eight young Oriental men in denims and plaid shirts were leaning back in their chairs and talking in high, animated voices, arms waving, heads bobbing.

"How they doing?"

"Ahh, they're good kids. Couple of 'em not bad riders, either. That one with the black jacket there, he took a fifth in the amateur rodeo in Hardin last month."

"Yeah? Good for him. Anybody pissed about the size of their spread?"

"Nooh. People figure, Ingomar priced it up around the snowline, the greedy prick. Who *else* could buy it? Not the Japs' fault—they could afford it. Big market for Montana beef back in Japan now. Plus the Japs really love that cowboy stuff. Ranch is owned by some big corporation."

"Farwest Beef and Dairy?"

"That's it. Probably the same guys bought most of Manhattan last year. Anyway, these guys try hard to be good neighbors, too. Gave a lotta help last year when those kids got lost up in the Bulls. Plus Doc Darryl got them to cough up a big check for the hospital. They're okay."

"Hogeland's a hell of a fund-raiser, isn't he?"

"Yep. Got himself a whole new—what do you call it? For babies who are born too early?"

"Neonatal?"

"Yeah. Neonatal unit. So how's Bobby Lee? She like her party?"

"Well, that party there, it didn't actually get right down to happening."

Fogarty nodded, looked up the bar and down again, and polished a mark with his chamois.

"Anything you want to talk about?"

"Not really. How's Colleen doing?"

Fogarty swelled a little around the edges.

"Now, she's a downy bird, she is. I had a couple more like her, I'd retire. She does more work around here than all three of my boys. . . . Heard about the shooting over at Joe Bell's."

"Hard to miss."

"That it was. Heard it was Bell did the killing, too."

"That he did. Almost killed us all."

"Shooting away at that propane tank, I hear."

"Yeah—where'd you hear that?"

"Talk of the town, Beau. It true you shoot him in the . . . ?"

"In the ass? Yeah, that's true."

"That cold enough there?"

Beau drained the beer, set the glass down, and watched while Fogarty capped another Beck's and slowly filled the glass again.

"Just about right. Yeah, it was a bad thing all round."

"Too bad about the youngster. Nice-looking kid, too."

Beau just nodded his head, feeling the cold beer working on him, feeling the sadness at the outer edge of everything tonight. He was thinking that if he got drunk enough, he might get up the nerve to go over to Hardin, climb up the back porch to Bobby Lee's room, wake her up, and give her her presents. Nice as it would be to see Bobby Lee, it would be just as sweet to do that and think about how Maureen would feel when she came into Bobby Lee's room the next morning and found the kid surrounded by balloons and stuffed teddies and that new Ninja Turtle skateboard.

Kids . . .

Youngsters . . .

"Patrick—what'd you say there?"

"I said the kid was nice-looking."

"Which kid?"

"The kid was shot."

"How'd you know that? Were you out there?"

"No. Been here since noon. But I saw him in the back of the wagon."

"What wagon?"

"Bob Gentile's wagon. Danny Burt was in here for a coupla hours. He took a bunch of us out there, showed us the body."

Christ.

"Did Finch Hyam or Rowdy Klein come in here?"

"Not today. What's the matter?"

"Anybody from our guys? Any law at all?"

"Not a soul. Too early for them."

"When did Danny Burt get here?"

"I don't know. Little after six."

"Was anybody with him?"

"Yeah, some young punk. Sat over there and drank French water. Irritating little snot. Burt hates him."

"What time'd they leave?"

"Don't really know. Burt only stayed to piss the kid off. You ever hear of something called grief managers? Something like that? If that ain't the stupidest—''

"But you didn't see them leave?"

"I saw them outside later. They was giving a guy they were talking to a lift."

"A lift? They went off with someone from here?"

"They drove off maybe around seven-thirty. Dark guy. Long black hair, mid-forties. An Indian.''

Seven-thirty. Almost five hours ago. Beau pushed the stool back.

"Going already?"

"Yeah. That wagon's been missing for five hours. It never got to Billings. Put this on my tab.''

"You don't have a tab, Beau.''

"I do now.''

Beau got back to the cruiser and called Central.

"Five eleven? Hi, Beau?"

"Beth, you hear from Benitez yet?"

"Not for maybe a half-hour, Beau.''

"Try to raise him, will you?"

"Okay, Beau. . . . Four six three, this is Central. Come back?"

The air crackled and popped. Beau drummed his fingers on the wheel. Come *on*, Munchkin.

"Four six three, do you read? 463? Trooper Benitez, are you reading? . . . 463 . . . 463?"

"Beth?"

"Beau, I can't get him up. Maybe he's got his radio off.''

Not the Munchkin. The radio was his lifeline. Besides, Benitez *loved* all that cop-tech stuff.

"Beth, here's what I'm thinking. I just got out of Fogarty's here; he says Danny Burt and the Hinsdale kid were in here for a couple of hours, says they left with an Indian sitting up front in the wagon with them. Looks like those peckerwoods and their big goddamned search started on the far side of Fogarty's bar and just plain missed them. Now, where'd Benitez say he was?"

"Just a minute.'' Beau knew she was scanning her Post-it Notes. She stuck them all over her computer monitor. Worked better than a floppy, and when the power went down or the system crashed, Beth always had her notes handy.

"Yeah. Somewhere on the Ballantine side road. Said he was maybe at mile fifteen. Stuck in a coulee.''

"Beth, raise Sugar if you can. Tell him to get me a couple of backup cars. I'm gonna do a pass down there. Thing is, there's no other side road between Pompeys Pillar and Huntley, and nobody west of Ballantine saw that wagon all evening. Also, the Ballantine side road splits near Arrow Creek. That's the only county road runs anywhere near a sandy section or anything Benitez might call an arroyo. I'm going to do the circle, coming in from the north. You get onto those backup cars."

"You think Benitez might have stumbled on them?"

"Beth, if anyone was gonna stumble on something, it'd be 463."

He found the cruiser at mile marker twenty-five of the Arrow Creek branch of the Ballantine side road. Doors wide open, engine still running, brights on full. The left rear wheel was buried to the fender in soft white sand and clay. A long rooster-tail of black sand and burned rubber marked the dirt for ten feet behind the wheel well. The Ithaca twelve-gauge was missing from the dashboard mount. Trooper Benitez was nowhere around.

Beau killed his own lights. Away from the white spots of 463's headlights, the darkness was absolute, as deep as the well of souls. A few pale stars rode above the black bulk of a hillside. Lizardskin was maybe ten miles away over that hill.

"Beth, I'm at mile marker two five, the Arrow Creek fork. I've found 463. Trooper Benitez is not visible. Where is my backup?"

"Beau, they'll be there in seventeen minutes."

"Beth, you tell them to crank it. Tell 'em to kill their lights at mile marker two three. Tell 'em no sirens."

"What're you gonna do, Beau?"

God-*damn* that trooper. He might be lying in a ditch. He might be drunk in a tree. Or he might have attracted some attention.

He keyed the radio and spoke in a low tone. The darkness seemed to slide in close and press against the window glass.

"I guess I'm gonna go look for him."

"Why not wait for backup?"

Seventeen minutes. Too long. Too much could happen.

"Hey, Beth. I *am* backup."

She started to say something, but Beau turned the volume down. The cross-talk would carry a long way. He popped the clamp on the shotgun rack and tugged it out, thinking what every cop thinks when he has to get out of the car alone in a bad place.

If it comes down to you or me, it's gonna be you.

8

2355 Hours – June 14 – Arrow Creek, Montana

T he night wind had a strange scent of pine and eucalyptus trees and something sharp. The moon was still back in the east somewhere, shining for other people. The Milky Way showed through the thin cloud cover like sparks through silk. Beau felt the chill of the high plains night on his cheeks and the backs of his hands. The shotgun was a heavy bar of cold iron. Under his boots, the sand gave way and made it hard to walk. The silence closed up around him like a pool of rising water as his breath scraped in his throat. It seemed to take him a year to walk twenty feet over to Charlie Four car, sitting in the middle of a penumbra of hard white light, the twin shafts from the high beams canted up into the sky, pillars of white marble eroding into an infinity of stars.

As he leaned into the driver's side door to shut off the lights, the muscles of his back and shoulder blades coiled up and grew cold. He was listening so hard, he could hear his own blood in his ears, listening for that snap and the thrum of a shaft coming in from the dark. It struck him then that this was a very old experience in this territory—a man alone in the dark, waiting for an arrow to come whistling in from somewhere beyond the light, perhaps to indicate the direction of eternity.

The coulee seemed suddenly alive with ghosts and whispers. His hand shook as he flicked the lever, and the pillars of white light disappeared. It was standard in police cars to disconnect the door switch for the dome light, so he left the door open. He didn't want to make any unnecessary noise. The key was still in the ignition. Whatever had distracted Benitez had happened fast enough to make him forget about locking up the cruiser and taking the keys.

Benitez had taken his portable radio. Beau thought about calling him on the radio, but then thought better of it. He'd had plenty of time to respond when Beth was calling him. In this silence, the sound of a police radio would carry a long way. He had a feeling that Benitez would have answered if he could.

Beau tried to place the land around this part of Arrow Creek. Low hills and valleys covered with prairie grass, getting sandy down the slope that led to Arrow Creek. The creek itself was a wide shallow meandering collection of pools and channels under a scattering of cottonwoods and chamiso bushes. The banks on this side were low and dry, hidden from the Ballantine side road by a series of shallow hills.

Benitez had gotten himself stuck trying to turn around in a narrow road. He had backed off the pavement and gotten his wheels into the coarse white sand along the shoulders. Then he had rocked it a bit, misjudged it, and slipped even farther into this low sandy trough—actually, you *could* call it an arroyo, just as Benitez had named it.

The arroyo led through a gap in the chain of hills, west toward Arrow Creek. This arroyo had probably been part of the river at one time, but sand and wind and the ways of water never like to repeat themselves.

Beau had an old army flashlight, a bent-neck affair with a red glass lens. He liked to use it on alarm calls, when he was clearing rooms in a warehouse or a private home. The red light didn't carry far. It left you a chance for surprise.

In its red glow, Beau could see the sign of heavy boots. And up there a couple of yards, a clear palmprint in harder dirt. Benitez had fallen here, stopped himself with his left hand. He was likely carrying that shotgun in his right. And *that* meant he was hunting someone.

There was a freshening wind down here in the arroyo, strong enough to move the sand. So Benitez must have gone through here only a short time ago. The edges of his tracks were only slightly rounded, and the palmprint was very clear.

What had he heard? Or seen?

There were no tire tracks in the area. Just the Munchkin's footprints.

Beau stood awhile with his eyes closed, rushing his night vision, inhaling the cold air, and listening hard.

A silky hiss off to his left. Sand falling down the slope of the arroyo. The wind in the long grass at the top of the hill to his right. It carried the smell of water from the Arrow Creek a few hundred feet away.

And that strange sharp scent, under the pine smell. The smell of smoke. A fire . . . somewhere up the coulee. In this night wind, the smell of a fire could carry for miles. But it smelled too strong for that. Benitez would have smelled it, sitting in the sand and swearing at his cruiser, he would have taken a breath and smelled that. Even Benitez would have been cop enough to wonder who would be camping out on Arrow Creek tonight. And stupid enough to think he could go find out all by himself.

The Munchkin's tracks led off up the arroyo, a straight line of bootmarks going away to the bend in the channel. Beau decided to climb up the slope a bit and stay in the grass. If Benitez had walked into something, it would be stupid to follow along like a pull-toy.

He did it as quietly as he could, but he was huffing a bit by the time he reached the top of the low hill. He tried not to think about rattlesnakes in the long grass as he worked his way along the ridge toward the river. The night was chilly enough to slow them down, but a foot in the wrong place would be too irritating to let pass.

He knew that there was one more low basin, then another rise of the land. It dropped away after that, down to the banks of Arrow Creek. It stood to reason that anyone camping around here would set up by the river.

And the smell of smoke was getting stronger now. He stayed away from the crests, trying not to silhouette himself against the starlight. Now that his eyes were adjusting, he could see the faint silver light from the stars lying on the prairie grass like frest frost. The shadows were as black as a crack in the world.

He eased his way to the top of the last slope. The land fell away fifty or sixty feet down to the riverbank. He could hear the chirp and gurgle of shallow water running and, through the black tangle of the cottonwoods, could see the soft glimmering of starlight on the water.

The smoke-smell was stronger now, musty and thick. He came down the hillside as slowly as he could, moving from shadow to shadow, the shotgun braced.

There was something large and black out in the shallows of the creek. He reached the cottonwoods. Under his feet he could feel the wet gravel. The sound of the water drowned out everything else now, making Beau feel very exposed. He flicked on the red flashlight. A bloodred circle glinted off gray metal.

Bob Gentile's morgue wagon was out there in the middle of the creek. The water was running around the hubcaps. He shut the light off. The trouble with flashlights was, they told other people as much about you as they told you about them.

They must have driven the wagon up the creekbed from somewhere down the side road. Clever. It'd leave no tracks. The windows of the wagon were tinted black. Nothing moved, either in it or around it. Stepping carefully, leading with the muzzle of his shotgun, he followed a sandbar ridge out to the wagon.

The crossing took him a few minutes, waiting a heartbeat after every step, expecting a shot to flare out of the blackness around the morgue wagon.

The driver's door was unlocked. He popped it open as softly as he could, ramming the shotgun into the gap, ready to fire. Nothing. He used the shotgun barrel to smash the domelight. In the red glow of his flash, he could see that the CB radio had been pulled out of the dashboard. The police set was smashed in. Papers were scattered around the interior. There was a gray metal coffin sitting on stainless-steel rails in the rear.

Beau went around the back and opened the tailgate door. The coffin moved easily and silently on the stainless rails. He pulled it out far enough to reach the latches. The lid came up and breathed the scent of violets and lavender and stale urine at him. He shined the red flash into the black interior.

Two wide wet eyes stared up at him, blinking and wild in a thin childish face. The boy was whimpering, and he struggled to bring his hands up to protect his face. They were bound to his waist with thin cords. A rag had been stuffed into his mouth and strapped in place with a leather belt. Another leather strap had been pulled around his ankles. A wide dark patch around his crotch explained the smell of urine.

This had to be Peter Hinsdale, frightened near to collapse. All the kid could see was a red light in his eyes. Beau reached out and covered his mouth. The boy arched and cried out under the gag. The smell of urine was overpowering now. The kid had wet himself in fear. Or he had been in here so long that there had been little choice in the matter.

"Kid. You gotta be quiet. Quiet. It's okay. I'm a cop."

It took Hinsdale a minute or two, struggling against Beau's gloved hand on his mouth. Beau kept saying it, in a low whisper, until finally the kid believed him.

"Okay . . . you gonna be quiet now? They're still around here somewhere, so you gotta be very, very quiet. You understand?"

The boy closed his eyes. Tears ran sideways down into his hair. He opened his eyes again and nodded once.

"Okay. I'm gonna get this off you. You promise to be quiet?"

Another nod.

Beau slipped the belt buckle and tugged it out from under the boy's head. His mouth was stopped with an oily rag. He pulled it out, and the kid sucked in a long ragged gasp.

"You're a policeman?" His voice was raw and high.

"Sergeant McAllister, Montana Highway Patrol. Who're you?"

"I'm Peter . . . Hinsdale." He coughed, struggled upright. "I gotta call . . . my mom."

"You will. Just keep it down to a whisper. Let's get you out of there. Gotta be hard on the nerves, lyin' in a coffin."

He got the cords undone and helped the kid out of the coffin. As soon as he got his feet on the gravel of the riverbed, he staggered a few feet and sat down hard. Beau stepped over to him and crouched down beside him.

"Peter—Peter, you're gonna have to stop crying now. We're in a spot here, and I need your help."

Hinsdale's face was wet and full of childish outrage. "What kind of shit is this anyway? Just take me home! You gotta take me home."

"And I will. But right now I need to know how many there were. How many people, and what kind of weapons did they have?"

Hinsdale sobbed again and shook his head. He put his face in his hands and spoke around them.

"I don't know for sure. Four, I think. There was one at the bar. Danny gave him a ride. I told him not to, but Danny was drunk."

Hinsdale pulled his face out of his hands.

"He's a drunk, Danny is. This's his fault. I'm gonna sue his ass—"

Beau reached out and put a gloved hand over the kid's mouth.

Jesus. *Another* lawsuit? What the hell was the matter with this country? Something bad happened, all anybody could think of was making some money out of it.

"Kid, shut the fuck up. You hear me? Now I'm gonna ask you again. I gotta know how many and what kind of weapons."

As soon as Beau pulled his hand away, the kid flared up and started to raise his voice.

"That's abuse! I'm gonna sue you, too. You haveta take me out of here! I'm a victim! I'm gonna—"

Beau sighed and put his hand over the kid's mouth again. When the kid jerked his head back, Beau used his left hand to pull his head forward again.

"Now look, kid—you're making me sorry I got that gag out. We're out in the woods with big bad bears all around. You keep shooting your mouth off like that, somebody's gonna hear it, come back here, sew it shut for you. Are you getting this?"

He gave the kid's head a hard shake, feeling his temper running very thin. After a jerk or two, the kid nodded again.

"So you gonna keep it low?"

The kid nodded again.

"Promise?"

Another nod. Beau slowly relaxed his grip. The kid pulled in a deep breath and looked up at Beau. His eyes were wet and shiny in the starlight. He radiated an infantile rage.

"I'm a *citizen,*" he hissed at Beau. "I have rights."

"Kid, you have rights as soon as we get back to Billings. Right now you have me. How many?"

"I'm—there was one at the bar. He came in and started talking to Danny and asked for a ride. I told Danny it was against the rules, but he didn't pay any mind."

"What'd this guy look like?"

"An Indian. Big and mean-looking. Fifty maybe. Said his name was Earl and he was trying to get to Billings to see his old lady."

"And a weapon?"

The kid shivered again. "He had a knife. One of those big Rambo things with sawteeth. We were about a mile down the road when he pulled it out and stuck it up against Danny's neck. He reached across me to do it."

"Okay. Anybody else?"

"Two more men and a girl. All Indians. They were waiting in a grain barn at the end of the street. They made me ride in the back here. They had these weird bows and shit. Real high-tech, you know. Like fiberglass or something. Came apart and stored in these metal cases. Lots of arrows and some knives. This Earl guy made Danny drive off the road back near Ballantine. We came up this creek about ten miles. Then they made me get in the coffin."

He started to shake again. Beau put a hand on his shoulder.

"They say anything to you?"

"Nothing. Just 'move here' or 'get over there.' The old guy was sick. Coughing all the time, like he had lung cancer or something. He was the guy giving the orders. The other two were younger. Still old, but younger than him. Your age, maybe. Both of them real mean-looking, like bank robbers or something. And strong. When they took the body out the one guy did it like it was nothing."

"They say why they wanted the body?"

"Not to me. But the girl was all over it, crying and carrying on like it was her brother or something. She's as mean as the rest of them. I was tellin' them they better let me go or I'd get a lawyer on 'em, and she kicked me."

"What'd they do with it? The body?"

He shook his head. "I don't know. When we got this far in the river, they stopped and I got shoved into the coffin. I said I wouldn't, but they just tied me up and shoved me inside. I *am* gonna sue them, too."

Beau was getting real tired of this kid real fast.

"Okay. I'm gonna go up the river here, take a look around. You go across to those trees, find a nice dark place, and stay there until we come back."

"No way! I'm coming with you. What if they come back?"

"Listen, son, let me lay it out for you in simple terms. I'm going up the stream to see if I can effect the arrest of a bunch of lunatic Indians, and if I have to, I'll stick you back in the coffin to keep you out of the way. You follow?"

"You can't—"

"Okay, kid," he said, pulling him up by his shirt. "Let's—"

He heard a wet splash, and gravel moving. The kid screamed, and Beau went back down in a crouch, shoving him away and pivoting on his left foot, bracing, bringing the muzzle up as a dark figure slammed into him. He felt a blaze of heat across his ribs, and then a second higher up.

He rolled back and brought a knee up hard, feeling it connect with bone and muscle. He had a brief vision of long black hair flying against the stars, and an arm raised, and steel glinting. The arm came down. Beau twisted away, feeling wet gravel and cold water on his back, the shotgun coming up again in an arc. He felt the contact in his hands, and heard the grunt. The figure tumbled left into deeper water.

Beau was up on his feet. Blood pounded in his throat. The fight was happening in a terrifying silence. No curses or cries, just a rasping breath and a quiet dedication to murder.

He saw the reflection of stars on water shattered by black movement. He fired, and a shower of white foam exploded in red fire. Gravel and shot skipped across the creek. There was movement to his left. His ears rang from the shotgun round. Orange afterlights floated across his retinas, blinding him. The smell of gunpowder was everywhere, and the hills rolled with secondary thunder. Someone was running away across the creek.

The kid, or the one with the knife?

He swiveled to cover that sound but could not bring himself to fire, and something twisted right at his feet, rising up out of shallow water. He felt another cut across his right thigh. He stepped back and kicked straight out in front of him, catching the man full in the face, sending him back into the water.

Beau took two steps forward as the man hit the water. The man rolled and tried to come up again, but Beau was on him. He swung the shotgun by the muzzle and felt the shock all the way to his shoulders. There was a sickening crack, and the body racked sideways, stretched out, and splashed into the creek in that final boneless way. A second, smaller splash sounded a few feet to the right. That knife, flying out of his hand.

Beau moved the shotgun to his left hand, stuck the muzzle into the man's neck, and pulled him up with his right.

The body was very light. Under his hands he felt softness and flesh. The long black hair trailed back from a fine-boned skull like seaweed from a shell. One eye was open, and tiny points of white light glinted off the cornea. The smell of blood was thick in Beau's nostrils. He could hear breath coming from the open mouth, shallow and tentative.

He had just gunbutted a young girl. Maybe killed her.

He dragged her body out of the creek and set it down as gently as he could on a bed of prairie grass. He found the portable radio and flicked up the volume.

A burst of static and sound.

"—ister!! Where the hell are you? Five eleven!"

Eustace Meagher's voice.

"Meagher?"

"Beau! Where the fuck are you? We heard that shot."

"I'm just past the range here. Come up the coulee. I'm right at the creek, about five hundred feet due west. You find the cruisers?"

"I'm sitting in yours. Where the hell's the Munchkin?"

"Haven't found him yet. You bring some help?"

"Myron's here. And a couple of Big Horn guys. You hold your position."

"Who?"

"Greer and Harper."

Beau had to smile. Harper and Greer were just the people he wanted to see. "Look, I've got a civilian loose in the area. Peter Hinsdale. He's out there somewhere. I have one in custody. Got two adult male Indians, armed, and one older male, also armed. Older male possibly noncombatant but armed."

"What's the status of your prisoner?"

"Severe skull trauma. We need a Medevac out of Billings. Get 'em moving now."

"Ten-four, Beau. Wait there, we'll link up with—"

From the far side of the river Beau heard a sudden leathery thump, then a high cold shrill scream, the clear sound of ripping cloth, and the scream cut off in midflight.

Beau shut the radio off and scrambled away from the girl's body, backing up into the shadows under the cottonwoods.

A full minute went by. Clouds floated upriver, casting ghostly purple shadows on the glittering river. He could hear the ragged breath coming from the injured girl.

Down in his lizard-brain, Beau knew he was being hunted. Knew it in his belly and in the skin on the back of his hands and in his lungs. There was somebody out there who was thinking of him the way a cougar thinks of meat. The silence came back up around him, and he struggled to still the sound of his own breathing.

He smelled blood and gasoline and urine.

He heard water over stone and wind in tall grass.

He saw blackness drifting like clouds across his eyes and starlight like silver coins floating on gunmetal water. The universe was shades of silver, black and purple, and a darkness without form or substance or bottom. Cold patches moved over his body as his nerves fired and burned and adrenaline pumped through his muscles and his tissues.

Suddenly everything had dropped away, the towns and the cities and lawyers and paychecks, even Bobby Lee and Maureen, they all fell away and Beau was out there in the middle of the oldest place on the planet.

Thinking of how the shotgun had only tangled him up in the river fight, he set it down on a tuft of grasses and slid his Browning out of the holster. He flicked the safety off and pulled the hammer back with the fat tip of his right thumb, feeling the metal grooves on the hammer and the slick glide of silicon grease.

There'd be two at least. If the old man had a cough, they wouldn't want him out on a hunt. A cough would kill them all.

From far up the river he heard the sound of something crackling and popping. A pall of smoke came down on the dark wind. A glow showed above the cottonwoods upriver. A fire. A big fire.

Red sparks settled on the creek and hissed like little snakes.

Smoke began to move down the valley and glide out over the water. A wavering black shape seemed to move behind it.

Beau put the Browning on it and squeezed.

It kicked and flared. A blue-white flame and a solid boom.

He fired twice, as he'd been taught, letting his breath ease out, fighting the kick with his shoulder.

There was a snap and a whistle. Something slammed into the grass and buried itself in the dirt six inches from his right knee. He rolled left and crawled backward into the dark.

Two more snaps and two more rushing whistles. One so close to the other that they hit almost as one.

Beau backed away, pushing at the gravel, his belly tight as a drumhead, ready for another bolt, ready to see a hard metal shaft sticking out of his body. His fear of that was something deep and paralyzing.

Now there was nothing on the water but pale smoke and starlight. He thought about going back for the shotgun. At least it would give him a wider field of fire. No. Whoever was hunting him, it was his style to get in close and do it with a knife. The shotgun wouldn't help in close.

Two rounds gone. Twelve left. One extra magazine.

And every time he put out a round, he'd mark his own position with muzzle flare. He'd never see where the shaft was coming from. All things considered, for this kind of a fight, that bow was a pretty good weapon. These guys knew what they were doing.

He shifted his hips, and a little rattle of gravel tumbled down the bank. He heard the snap and the thrum, felt the hammer blow in his right leg, a numbing freezing impact that jarred him from his toes to his ribs. His leg was pinned to the dirt.

Christ—the thing was all the way through him.

His pulse hammering in his right ear, he felt around the shaft. It was buried in the muscle and flesh at the inside of his right thigh, inches from his groin. The head had come right through. He could feel the razorblade edge in the dirt. Beau tried not to throw up.

Grasping the metal shaft, he tried to pull it free. Then there was pain, electric and complete. He cried out, bit down, turned it into a low growling moan.

That'd bring him. There was nothing to do but shut up and wait for him to come in.

The creek ran and tumbled in the banks and lees. That cold night wind sighed through the cottonwoods. In the east a pale green light was shining over the horizon. The moon was coming. When it rose, it would be like day. He could see what was coming. And what was coming would see him.

He waited, fighting nausea.

The light began to change. Shadows that were black became gray. An arc of moonlight had touched the creek far up at the bend. It would reach him soon. Where the hell was Eustace Meagher? How long had he been waiting here? How long since the fight at the wagon? How much blood was he—?

He heard water swirl. A pebble slipped. A gray formless shape moved across the water, blotting out the starshine. Beau set his hands and pulled his leg free, rising with the arrow in him, bringing the Browning up, firing at the sound, seeing only the afterlight from his own blast, seeing red fire on the water, the Browning kicking in his hand, butting at his shoulder and his forearm. He squeezed off three sets of two rounds, the rhythm dulling his fear. Six rounds. Six dazzling blue-white billows. A sound like a fist against meat, repeated.

And a slow subsiding settlement, something heavy gliding into deeper water.

He lurched forward into the sound, into the smell of his own gunfire, through the gathering smoke across the water. Twenty feet in, he fell across a wet body, turning as he fell, the Browning under him.

He landed inches from a face with three black holes in it, two of them eyes and one a larger uneven wound full of black blood under the right eye. Something pulpy and gelatinous floated around the right ear, under a thick black braid. In the starlight the dark face showed nothing but death. He found a metal and fiberglass bow in the gravel a few feet beyond him.

Still sliding on his belly, the fletching of the shaft grating on stones, he moved, half-floated, downstream, trying to see through the dark and hear through the noise of the water. Something was moving, stopping and moving again, dragging a heavy weight. This was off to his left, on the riverbank.

He put his left hand down into the gravel and settled into a low pool as cold as winter. Cold fire flickered like gasoline over his chest and his right leg.

The current here was stronger. It tugged at him, an insistent clutching persuasion . . . come along, come along with the river.

It brought him a body from above the bend.

The body settled softly against him, a sailor home from the sea. It smelled of shit and cooked meat. Hamburgers. Blood.

Under the half-light something gray and loopy rose up from its belly. The thin petulant face had frozen into an openmouthed permanent complaint. Its dead eyes saw through the clouds, and the dead mind floated through the Milky Way. The education of Peter Hinsdale was now complete.

Through the gathering smoke, through the brightening night sky, from beyond the low black hills, Beau heard several cries and four deep percussive booms, like a storm in the high passes.

He crawled away from Hinsdale and rolled onto his back, half out of the water, the shaft in his leg scraping on bone. He set his head back in hard gravel and watched the stars turning above him. They moved in a slow magnificent arc, rising out of the black hills to his left, gliding in a glacier of time across the perfect blue silk of the night, falling like jeweled rain into the black hills on his right.

That dragging sound grew closer. He tried to care about that and found that he did not. A lazy langour was rising in him, infinitely sweet and deep. The pain in his ribs and in his right leg was there but not there, a memory of pain.

A face rose up over him, breathing heavily. A hand caught his shirt and pulled at him. Beau felt himself being dragged farther up the bank, out of the water. The shaft caught in the rocks and twisted in his muscle, and he sighed.

He felt hands on him, running down his body. They reached the arrow in his right thigh. He heard a short exhalation, a muttered curse. Over the hills a low throbbing sound, rhythmic and deep, carried on the wind. He could hear men's voices in the dark.

Light from the rising moon settled over them. Beau looked up to his left and saw who was holding him.

"Well, well. Hello there, Benitez."

"Sergeant. Hold still. I hear the chopper."

"No problem—none at all. You hurt?"

"Yes. He cut me up good. I walked right into him."

"Me too."

"You killed him."

"That's my theory."

"He cut me, I fell down into the river. Lost my gun, lost my radio—lost everything. Some cop."

"Hey, Benitez. . . . Fuck that. He's dead, you're not. That's the way—it's . . . supposed to go . . . okay?"

"Okay, Sergeant. I guess . . . we not in Kansas anymore, huh?"

Beau twisted to look at Benitez.

After a little while, Benitez smiled at him.

0800 Hours – June 15 – Logan Airport, Billings, Montana

Gabriel slept eight inches from the brink of space, thirty thousand feet above the curving blue arc, the sun a thin orange blade. Beside his right temple, on the far side of the skin of the United jet, the air was brittle with ice crystals. Hoarfrost etched the oval plastic window. His long-fingered blue-veined hands rested on the fold-out tabletop in front of him, over a carefully creased copy of *USA Today*. A white cup half full of coffee sat at the edge of the tray. The coffee moved in a tidal way as the plane rose on a fold of air or trembled in a thermal, like a ship carving a reach through a sea of violet glass.

Under the wings old mountains broke into the light out of black valleys, cloaked in drifting snow. Far to the south a single volcanic peak lifted a secret crater lake high above the plains.

Gabriel's chest moved in a slow rhythmic way, and his face had settled into rough-cut planes of bone and skin and muscle. His thin lips tightened and relaxed as his dream arced and crackled along the filaments of synapse and memory beneath his skull.

It is always the same dream. They are at thirty-eight thousand feet over the South China Sea. The Royal Thai 747 is as dim as a medieval chapel. They are flying east toward an elusive sunrise that seems always to be just visible as a line of pink light at the farthest curving of the globe. Under the wings he can see tiny islets of white light against the moonlit furrows of the sea, cargo ships bound for Singapore and Ujung Pandang, Zamboanga, and Bataan, through the Sulu Arch to Sarangani Bay, where the long green rollers of the Pacific hammer and shatter on the cliffs of Mindanao and Dinagat. Here the islands ride like birch canoes at the brink of the Mindanao Trench. And in the Trench, seven miles down beneath the moonlit waves, crystalline constellations of luminous life flicker and glide between vast gray hills of dreaming monsters.

The lights on the islands below are different from American lights, which glitter in blocks and units and squares, the geometry of rationality. In the East the lights follow riverbeds, coastal chains, and mountain crests, so that the islands look like electric leaves floating on a great salt pond, delicate traceries of lights marking the patterns of life below. Here and there, in the clustered cores of the larger towns, a sliver of flame from a cracking tower or a coal-fired generating plant glints red against the pale blue of the street lamps and shipping yards.

There are twelve other men in the first-class cabin: a Buddhist monk in a saffron robe, wearing executive-length socks under his heavy leather sandals, a Vuitton briefcase open on his spinnaker belly; seven Japanese businessmen asleep over lukewarm sake and productivity graphs; a Malaysian minister and his languorous nephew folded together into a Thai silk coverlet that shimmers scarlet and golden under the reading lamps, their hands seeking and touching in absolute breath-held silence; an Australian developer nodding over his laptop computer; and Gabriel's prisoner, the young Palestinian boy the section has been after for five months, still in his school clothes, thirteen on the Saturday just past, staring sightlessly out the porthole, drugged and dead in the eyes.

Beethoven's Seventh Symphony is playing in the cabin. It constructs an alabaster Parthenon in the mind, floating in the clouds over the Sulu Sea. The flight attendant, a delicate flame in Thai silk as she moves down the aisle, brings the knife on a carved wooden tray and, in Asian politesse, contrives to bring his attention to the time, Mr. Picketwire.

Behind her the door is open to the night sky, yet no wind tears at her *ao-dai* and her hair frames her still features like black onyx around an amber cameo. Thirty-eight thousand feet below, the freighters churn through the waves. The night wind moans past the curved plastic of the doorway.

He nods to her and takes the knife, a Kay-Bar. The Palestinian child stands up and walks ahead of him to the open door. The monk watches and asks as they pass him, what is this boy's errand?

He's a messenger, says Gabriel.

To whom?

To his father.

Please, Mr. Picketwire, says the Thai girl, pulling at his arm. Special clearance has been obtained.

They walk to the door and Gabriel puts his hand on the boy's shoulder, turning him. The boy's face turns up to him. His cheeks are waxy and blue. His eyes are liquid and bright in the hard white spotlight over the door.

You understand your father's work? What he does?

The boy nods. He has been told. It has been explained to him. Section felt it only fair. He seemed to understand.

You recognize the reasons for this? You lived in his home, ate his food. These sentiments are genetic. You are not innocent.

Innocere, says the boy. From the Latin *nocere,* to be hurtful. The innocent are not hurtful. But no one is innocent. No one does not hurt something. Everyone is in agreement on this.

Yes, says Gabriel, this is the truth. No one can say they were not aware of this. But it's also clear that something must now be done, that some steps must be taken to indicate our position. It's important that your people understand that we have taken a new position. There'll be no bargaining. Understand, we have no animosity for you personally. You personally have done nothing yet. None of us has hatred for you here. But you will indicate our new position to your father. I personally feel nothing in this matter. It's selection. Husbandry. My own people learned that. So will yours. People who think they are true children of a god should study the lives of sheep. Allah's intentions for you seem to be unclear. He has been oblique on the subject of destiny for your people.

That's true, says the boy, turning away to face the open door. Will there be pain?

Be more specific, says Gabriel, and he steps into him, using his left hand on the boy's chin, the Kay-Bar held flat and level in his right hand, his right forearm tensed but fluid. He pulls back hard on the boy's chin, smelling his hair, smelling the soap and the dry-grasses smell of young boys, and in the same motion drives the Kay-Bar through the blue wool of the blazer and the white shirt underneath, in through the elastic skin, into muscle and cartilage, feeling the tip slide along ribs, finding the gap there where it always is, as familiar as the steps of his own house, and up at forty-five degrees under the left shoulder blade two inches from the spine, to the hilt, once to the left, twisting with his wrist, once back to the right.

The boy's mouth opens, and fresh blood spills out over Gabriel's fingers, as hot as spilled coffee, over the back of his hand. Gabriel steps back, sets his bloody left hand palm-down against the boy's back, and pulls at the Kay-Bar. It resists, then slides free with a liquid sigh, followed by a brief bubble of air and pink foam.

The boy falls forward through the open door. He drops through the night sky, tumbling, a hawk falling, and Gabriel watches him until he loses him against the immensity of the moonlit ocean far below him. A cold wind cuts his cheek.

He turns away and walks back to his seat, and the Thai flight attendant closes the door. One of the Japanese men watches him and makes a note on a paper in front of him. The man's eyes are without content, wet stones in a muddy river. His hair is thick and blue-black and shines like polished iron. Heavy gold weighs on his wrists. An acid-green silk tie seems to glow against the snowdrift purity of his English shirt.

The Thai girl kneels in front of him, silk rustling against her thighs, a sepia hand resting on his knee, her perfect masklike face turned up into the light.

Can I get you anything, Mr. Picketwire? She uses a starched white napkin to dab at the blood on the back of his left hand, where it has matted the black hairs and seems already to be turning to rust against his sunburned skin. The blood smells of copper and ammonia. She carries a scent like an umbra, frangipani or hibiscus.

Yes, says Gabriel. An Evian, I think.

He woke as the United jet banked left, the huge right wing rising in the porthole, cutting off the russet and ochre hills that faded into smoky blue in the distance. Billings was a grid of wide streets and office towers and malls five thousand feet below. The interstate ran like a snaking cable through the center of the town, curving left, twisting again to the north, then west again out across the rounded hills and gentle valleys of central Montana, toward Big Timber, Bozeman, and Butte. Far in the south, the Bighorns emerged from blue haze, islands in a sea of grass. He looked to the left as they banked, trying to see the Powder River country in the Bighorn foothills. The rivers caught the slanting sun and burned like golden threads in a green carpet.

The flight attendant had seen him waking. She smiled at him and leaned forward, her cornsilk blond hair held back in a tortoiseshell barrette, her pale skin luminous in the hard yellow light from the rising sun.

"You slept for a while, Mr. Picketwire."

"Yes. What time is it?"

"Just after eight. We're stacked up here for a little while. We'll be landing at Logan International in twenty minutes. Can I get you anything?"

Evian, he thought. Or black coffee?

No, there was nothing she could bring him.

10

0730 Hours – June 15 – Billings, Montana

"Good morning, Mr. McAllister! Mr. McAllister!"

Beau came up from a wonderful dream that had something to do with a fireplace and a swing chair and a lady he hadn't thought about in years. He had known her in the old days in Provo. What was her name? She had been the night dispatcher for Steiger. Black hair and violet eyes. They'd spent a couple of weeks in his cabin down on the Yellowstone. In the dream she was sitting in front of him, the fire burning low, her hair a halo of amber light and her face in darkness. She was pulling a cashmere sweater up over her head and Beau was leaning forward . . . leaning forward, and then he was shaking—no, somebody was calling him.

"Mr. McAllister, you'll have to wake up now!"

He opened his eyes and met the large fleshy face of a creature who was more or less taking up all of his personal horizon. She was leaning over him, a huge, powdered moon face full of craters and heavy red lips, tiny black eyes staring at him while she whipped the sheet back to his toes, revealing a certain autonomous response to—*Irene!* That was the name of the woman he'd been dreaming about!

"Who the hell are you?"

The heavy face swiveled on a chicken-skin neck, and her starched white uniform crackled as she stared at something in his lap. "I'm Hanrahan! Are we feeling some bladder pressure?"

Beau looked down at himself. Captain Happy was wide awake. He reached down and tugged the sheet back up to his neck and moved away from this apparition above him.

"What the hell is a Hanrahan?"

She frowned and tapped her nameplate. "I'm the head nurse here. Are you confused?"

"Confused? No, I'm not confused. Back away a little there, willya? I'm getting a neck crick."

"Hhmmph! Have we had a bowel movement today?"

Beau thought about it.

"Well, Hanrahan, I can't actually tell by looking at you, but my guess'd be no."

"Funny. Perhaps we'll need an enema."

"Perhaps you'll have to go get some help."

"S'happened before, Mr. McAllister."

"I don't doubt it. You first. I'll watch."

She stepped back and pulled her glasses down off her forehead, where they settled into preset grooves in her cheeks and on her nose. Her tiny black eyes looked huge and wet behind the lenses. She pursed her thick lips and scowled at him.

"You'll need a bath, sir. You smell like a horse."

Beau inhaled. It hurt his belly. "Well, you look like a cow. Bath won't do a damned thing for you, either."

"Hostility. Sometimes indicates a toxic reaction to medication." She pulled up a clipboard at the end of the bed and looked at the sheet. "Perhaps we should cut down on our painkiller."

"Yeah. I'll switch to beer. You switch to hemlock."

"Hhmmph. Dr. Vlasic was by to see you."

"Vlasic! He's the coroner. Am I dead?"

"Not yet. But we're doing everything we can. You're on a liquid diet, so there'll be no lunch for you. Now get out of bed in ten minutes and walk around. Don't go so far you tear out that drain in your leg there. Tug on that, and it'll open up a whole new world of sensory experience for you. You'll have to stretch those muscles, or you'll be all bound up. And see to it you move your bowels, or we'll do it for you.''

"Hanrahan, I think you move me!''

Hanrahan gave him one last look over the top of her glasses and sailed out the door. Beau sang another two choruses of "Wild Thing," then trailed away into silence. Where the hell was Eustace!

Beau spent an undefined amount of time lying on his back, counting the holes in the ceiling tiles and trying to figure out what had happened to the guy behind the curtains in the next bed. Whatever it was, it had been massive. There was some kind of machine on a rollaway cart up against the far wall. Power cables snaked all around the linoleum and ran up the far wall to a bank of grounded plugs. It emitted a regular sound, kind of a cross between a belch and a sigh, and a bellows would descend in a plastic cylinder.

The guy himself was out of sight behind the curtain. The cables and pipes emerged from behind the curtain and ran into the machine. The machine had nothing to say. It had been there since Beau woke up this morning.

An accident, maybe? Or kidney dialysis?

Beau hated hospitals. When he had been courting Maureen, back when he was just another gentleman ranker in a pinto car, he had spent a lot of his time dragging cut-up or shot-up or banged-up kids into her clinic in Hardin. Most of them survived, but the main impression Beau took away was of thin-lipped nurses in white polyester using stainless-steel scissors on bloody jeans and scorched shirts, tearing away at underwear, opening up the victim like greedy kids ripping away at a Christmas present. The gift was always bloody meat. The nurses were cranky, combative, unpredictable.

So why had he fallen for Maureen?

Well—one thing, she was a tiger in the dark. Beau felt a certain kind of heat in his lower belly as he remembered that part of their relationship. He shifted his weight in the hospital bed and felt a sharp tug at his left wrist.

Just what the hell were they dripping into him anyway? These hanging bottle things always made him think of that injured airman in *Catch–22*, the guy all wrapped up like a mummy. The nurses would come in and change his bottles around twice a day.

He tugged the sheet back and looked down his body, half afraid to see a tube coming out of his essentials.

No. That part of him was okay. The rest was a mess.

He had a vague memory of Eustace Meagher standing in a cone of hard light as something huge floated overhead and a massive beating sound hammered the cottonwoods up on the bank. Then he was being lifted onto a board as the *hutt-hutt-hutt* boys shoved him inside the chopper. Meagher had been trying to tell him something, but the chopper blades were beating them both into the ground.

He had watched them working on Benitez until some kid who looked about thirteen stuck something in his arm and the rest was more than a little vague. One thing for sure, he figured Benitez had beaten that nickname.

Well, he was still alive. And they'd gotten the arrow out of him while he was unconscious. He appreciated that. His leg was wrapped in gauze and a yellow plastic tube stuck out of the mound, dripping pink fluid into something underneath the bed.

He felt like a gunny sack that used to have a man in it but they'd taken that out and filled it with broken glass.

The girl . . . not that she didn't deserve it. But still—and the kid—Christ what a slaughter. What a Friday. Edward Gall, the young boy Joe Bell shot. The girl Beau had gunbutted. The nameless man he had shot. Probably others.

Peter Hinsdale.

Cops, like some professional athletes, most combat soldiers, and half the civilians in America, were always trying to organize the terrible *randomness* of bad times into a predictable matrix. It was all delusion, of course, and they knew it, but that never stopped them from giving it a shot. Full-moon Fridays were going to be crazy. Four guys in a car is a hostile stop, even if they turn out to be seminarians going to a vasectomy clinic. Bad things come in threes. If you always put your gun on last, you'll never have to use it. Always get up on the same side of the bed every morning, or you'll be off balance all day. If things start to go sour in a neighborhood, they'll get a lot worse before they get better.

It seemed to Beau that something ugly had come to visit in Yellowstone County.

He spent some time trying to drag an insight up from the bottom of this pool of disconnected events. He had a stray feeling that there was a unifying theme here, but the only one he could come up with was the obvious one— all the events had involved some kind of collision with Indians. Mary Littlebasket, if he remembered the family correctly, was from the Whistling Wind clan, the same clan that Alice belonged to. So that was Crow.

Charlie Tallbull, the man who'd been driving the pickup that Mary Littlebasket was killed in, Beau knew from his patrol car days. The Tallbull clan held a grazing tract down on the Wyoming border, and they leased it out to local ranchers from a little office in Wyola. The Tallbulls were Crow as well, but they were mainly businessmen. In the middle of the sun-parched desolation of the southern reaches of the Crow Reserve, the Tallbull operation was actually making money for the tribal collective. He and Charlie Tallbull had known each other slightly when Beau was assigned to speed patrol along the stretch of I-90 that ran from Garryowen to Wyola. Charlie Tallbull was the one with bail money or fine money for the young bucks Beau would catch driving drunk or racing on the interstate; Beau's impression of Charlie Tallbull was a good one, a solid hard-handed older guy with a deliberation to him, a slow and steady balance, and a brilliant smile that he showed rarely. How Charlie Tallbull got himself involved in a police chase was a mystery to Beau. Now Charlie Tallbull was here in the same hospital.

Beau decided to get up in a minute and go look for him. And maybe when he got out of here, he'd go see Moses Harper and ask him a few questions too.

And now the Bell thing—Indians again.

Well, maybe it really was just a coincidence. After all, if you counted the Northern Cheyenne Reserve, which was just to the east of the Crow Reserve, there had to be close to six thousand Indians in southeastern Montana. It stood to reason that some weeks would bring you a high rate of Indian-related police calls.

But the *kind* of call—this was a little more violent than usual, wasn't it, Beau? But it had been getting more and more violent *everywhere* in America over the past couple of years. Why be surprised that trouble had come to Montana?

And where the hell was Eustace Meagher? Somebody ought to have the decency to drop by, tell him what the hell had happened to everybody.

Christ, that was a bad day. You go months half-asleep from boredom and monotony, and in one bloody shift you get enough terror and misery to last you the rest of your career.

Maybe it was time to think about getting out.

Well, let's see . . . we have, if memory serves, $793.60 in the account at Bank of Montana, another $1,445.86 in the Highway Patrol Credit Union. Twenty undeveloped and unserviced acres on the Yellowstone River outside of Brisbin, the Chevy wagon, the Harley—which needs a new clutch and a paint job—and the double-wide up in Lizardskin.

Against that, you have to put fifteen hundred dollars a month in support and maintenance for Maureen and Bobby Lee—by the way, Maureen's making noises about the roof, at the same time she's been flashing a new Gold Card and spending wheelbarrows of cash at the Hilltop Mall—but if he has to pay for a roof, that's another three grand.

Okay. Maybe it's *not* time to start thinking about getting out. But it was hard to avoid concluding that maybe he had pushed his luck for too long; under that, there was the feeling, as well, that he had misread everything yesterday, and the terrible suspicion that it could have gone differently for everyone. Like most career cops, Beau liked to avoid confrontations. Violence always made things worse. He'd tried to settle things at the Oasis in a reasonable way, but that had gone badly, and the Indians had gotten away while he tangled with Joe Bell.

Then they'd hijacked the wagon—who the hell would have anticipated *that*? So now—thanks to you, Beau—we have some dead and some wounded, and nobody connected to what happened here will ever be the same again.

Or maybe it *was* just a bad shift. Things like that came along, usually out of nowhere, a dumb domestic call, a drunk with a gun nobody thought to look for, or sometimes you just walked right into it, into something that was more complicated than it looked on the surface.

The simple fact was, there was no way to do the job and stay safe from all disasters. Disasters were part of the package, and every cop was going to get his share.

About the girl . . . Beau tried not to let it get to him. She'd made an heroic effort to perform radical liposurgery on his belly, and all was fair in that kind of fight. But she was an Indian girl, and Indian girls got at whatever softness there was in the flintier canyons of his nature. As soon as he found his clothes, he'd go look for her. Maybe Hanrahan would know.

He was looking for the call button when he heard rubber squeaking on polished tiles, and something short and black-haired hurtled across the room and jumped up on his belly.

"Daddy! Mommy says you got arrowed!"

He plucked her away from his throbbing leg and held her up in the light. Her blue eyes were huge in her round pink face, and her hair was tied up in two absurd ponytails that stuck out at the sides of her head. She was holding a tattered bunch of daffodils.

"Bobby Lee! Hey—happy birthday, six-year-old!"

She twisted and settled beside his chest on the sheet, sitting cross-legged and looking down at him with childish gravity.

"You got arrowed?"

"Who told you that, darling? No, I just fell down a bit."

She twisted her face up in massive disapproval and thumped his chest. Beau jumped, and she scowled at him. "Don't lie, Daddy. Uncle Dwight told me all about it."

When the Lord giveth, he fucketh not around. He was giving it to Beau real good. Uncle Dwight! Jesus, maybe Maureen could find work with the Inquisition—she had a real talent for the delicate refinements of ex-husband torture.

"Uncle Dwight, eh, kid? When'd you see him?"

"He brought me here. He's out in the hall with Mom. We brung you a bucket of flowers."

Oh, super. Maureen *and* Dwight. He kept his emotions off his face and smiled at Bobby Lee.

"A boo-kay of flowers."

"No, they're in a bucket."

"Okay. They're out in the hall?"

"Yeah. Where is it?"

"Where's what?"

"The arrow?"

"Why?"

"I wanna take it to school."

"Right—I'll see if I can get it for you."

"Well, it's yours, isn't it? It was stuck in you. That makes it yours. Anything you get stuck in you belongs to you."

"Words to live by, Bobby Lee."

He was staring at her. Every time he saw her, he was transfixed, by her coloring, the depth of blue in her round eyes, the sheen of her hair, her skin, the childish smell of sugar and sweat and soap. The strength of his feelings for her sometimes shook him down to the bone.

"How are you, baby? I'm sorry I didn't get to see you on your birthday."

"That's okay now, Daddy. You got stuck with a arrow. I wouldn't expect you to come to a party with a arrow stuck in you." She looked around theatrically and leaned forward to whisper, "Mommy's mad at you again."

"Yes. I know."

"Why's she always mad at you? It wasn't your fault you got stuck with a arrow."

"*An* arrow."

"A narrow?"

"*An* arrow. I got stuck with *an* arrow."

"*An* arrow. . . . You know what I think?"

"No, what do you think?"

"I think, if you said you were sorry to Mommy, she would let you come home."

Beau tried to keep his voice steady. Maybe the day would come when he wouldn't feel so desperate about Bobby Lee, so sick with worry and concern for her. It was crazy. Maureen wasn't evil. She was just . . . mean as a snake. How do you explain *that* to your baby? You don't. Beau had taken a vow never to say anything against Maureen to Bobby Lee, or within her hearing. It was too bad Maureen didn't share the feeling. It was one of the worst things about this situation; Maureen felt free to say anything at all about Beau, and Beau had no defense other than to try to be as sweet and fair to Bobby Lee as he could manage, and trust in her own clarity to see what was true and what was not.

"I know, honey. And I'm sorry, too. But right now your mommy is very . . . unhappy. And she's—"

"No, she's not."

"She's not what?"

"She's not unhappy. I heard her laughing last night."

"Last night?"

"Yes. Her and Uncle Dwight were laughing."

"Yeah? What were they laughing about?"

She made a mouth, sighed heavily. "How would I know, Daddy? I was in bed!"

Right—all Beau ever wanted out of religion was the promise that someday he'd get close enough to God to slap the cuffs on Him and boot the Cosmic Butt into the back of a cruiser. Possession of a Loaded Universe without a Permit. Careless Operation of a Galaxy in a Built-Up Area. Exceeding the Grief Limit.

"Did you get birthday stuff? I have some things for you in the car. I'll get one of the guys to bring them over."

"It's all right, Daddy. Are you gonna be okay? Can I have the narrow?"

"Yeah, honey. You can have the narrow. I'll get it for you."

There was a motion at the door. They looked up and saw Dwight Hogeland leaning on the jamb.

Eddie Bauered to his earlobes in pressed jeans and melton plaid, six foot three of genetic perfection and the rewards of regular exercise, Hogeland was holding a huge plastic bucket full of wildflowers and baby's breath. He was smiling a Mona Lisa smile that was full of forensic secrets. He moved in that special atmosphere, partly inherited money and partly the lampwick exhalations of burning wax and moldy paper that always seems to float around successful lawyers. His silky blond hair was slightly gelled and combed straight back in a graceful sweep from his beardless chiseled bones and deep-set gray eyes. He had one foot crossed over the other, striking a pose in a pair of dark blue lizardskin boots that must have gone for eight hundred dollars in Denver, where Hogeland's firm kept an office. Beau knew where Hogeland bought his boots because Maureen was always telling him about Hogeland—where he bought this, how much he paid for that, what his next deal was going to net out at.

"Sorry to intrude, Beau . . . ?"

"Dwight, what a treat. Where's Maureen?"

"She's—I suggested she wait in the hall. I wanted to—ahh . . . Look, I realize this is a difficult time. But we wanted Bobby Lee to see that you were all right. We have some business here, so I suggested—I mean, Bobby Lee was very anxious, as you can understand. May I come in?"

Beau took a second to sort through several versions of a snarl and settled on civility.

"Of course, Dwight. Ah, thanks for bringing Bobby Lee."

Hogeland strolled across the floor and lightly set the flowers down on a side table. Then he sat down in the armchair and crossed his legs. He winced a bit at the smell coming from the next bed and glanced at the machine against the far wall.

"What I wanted to say, before she comes in—I wanted you to know. About Maureen. I would never counsel her to . . . I feel she was a little harsh over last night's party. True, the agreement states the terms. But under the circumstances—I mean, you had no control over the events out at Bell's."

A nice thrust there. No control. Time to change the subject.

"How's Doc Darryl? Up in the shiny new Learjet?"

"Yes, as a matter of fact. He takes it to California all the time. He has some business out there, and he hates the public airlines. I worry. Dad's getting on, but he loves to fly that thing. Good at it, too. How's Lieutenant Meagher? Well? Dad asks about him frequently."

"Meagher's fine . . . really fine."

Bobby Lee was watching the two of them carefully. She was quite silent, but Beau could feel the restlessness in her.

"Bobby Lee, do you want to go back and see Mommy? I have to talk to—" He managed it: "To Uncle Dwight for a minute."

"Can I have a dollar? There's a candy machine down the hall."

Beau looked around for his clothes. Dwight reached into his shirt pocket and pulled out a bill. Bobby Lee slid off the bed, stopped, and turned back to climb up and put her arms around Beau's neck. She gave him a fast and brutal squeeze and kissed his cheek.

"Phoo! Beard hairs! Bye-bye, Daddy!"

Another lithe vault, and she was out the door. They could hear her shoes flip-flopping down the hall.

There was silence.

"How do you come to be playing at Daddy with Bobby Lee, Dwight?"

Dwight's fine-boned face was as still and composed as a man who has achieved the perfect blend of conceit and ignorance.

"Hardly . . . hardly relevant, Beau."

"She's my child."

"An insight that seems to have only intermittent real-time applications, in light of your behavior."

"We going to get into this?"

Dwight raised a hand, palm out, and ducked his head.

"Beau, we seem to grate on one another. I regret that. I've never had anything but the greatest . . . you are . . . aggressive, surely—unorthodox. But everyone agrees that you are one of the . . . highest-profile law enforcement officials we have in Yellowstone County. Dad has—he holds you in tremendous esteem. As I know, you reciprocate. He feels quite close to your family."

"Not as close as you're getting, Dwight."

"And I regret that—that it seems that Maureen and I have become friends. This has had certain repercussions. The fact is, I have transferred her file over to Ted Mallon. I feel that—under the circumstances—it would not be ethical for me to represent her interests in this divorce action."

"Damned fine reasoning, Dwight. Amazing what insights come to a man a few seconds after a good orgasm, eh?"

Dwight's face hardened enough to reveal a certain toughness beneath the easy manner. It made it easier to see how Mallon, Brewer, Hogeland and Bright had become such a force in eastern Montana over the last ten years. There had to be a capacity for ruthlessness in there somewhere, even if it was the hybrid courage of lawyers. They called themselves "gunslingers" and joked about hard combat in the courtroom. It was all so goddamned pretentious. Comparing the bicker and cross-chatter of a courtroom to genuine combat was demeaning to anyone who had ever actually faced incoming fire and seen real dying.

"The fact is, we are not intimate, and that is not to imply that you have any standing in the matter, regardless. And should our relationship ripen into anything more complex, I would never consider . . . I care for Roberta Lee as deeply in my own way as you contend that you care for her."

"I don't contend anything, Dwight. I just see I got you all over my life like a nasty rash. You do your level best, which is damned good, to staple my balls to the courthouse roof every time we get in front of a judge. Now you're Uncle Dwight to my kid and getting ready to park your Yuppie-floppy in my used-to-be wife. That's an explosive situation. I'm just telling you that there's a hell of a difference between what's legal and what's likely to happen.''

"What's that? A threat? Threatening is indictable, Beau.''

"That's exactly what I mean! You got your head shoved so far up the skirts of blind justice, you can't see a damned thing except legal briefs and diverting draperies.''

"Clever, Beau. I like that bit about legal briefs. That's real clever stuff. I'm not going to let you provoke a personal exchange. If you want to discuss problems with your access agreement, you should take them up with Ted Mallon. He's been fully briefed on the history.''

"It's not history yet, Dwight.''

"That's—that's all I can say on that matter. No—that's it. I do have some questions about . . . well, you may not be at liberty to say, but the radio reports this morning suggest that your department was able to . . . effect . . . the arrests of those fugitives from the Oasis robbery.''

"Effect the arrests? Yeah, I guess we e-ffected something.''

Hogeland shrugged, spread his long fingers. A watch Beau could not identify glinted in the downlight.

"I take it no depositions or informations have as yet been filed?''

"You take it right. At least, I didn't take any. I was a little tied up last night.''

"Well—the . . . violence, I'm assuming there was violent resistance? Your injuries would indicate—''

"I haven't heard from Eustace yet. I have personal knowledge of at least two deaths and two severe injuries.''

"Who would these be?''

"You have to know, ask Vanessa Ballard. She was catching yesterday. She's on duty all weekend. But why do you want to know?''

"I have an interest in the issue. As a citizen, of course, I have—''

"Dwight, I just woke up an hour ago. I feel like shit. I have a rather depressing hole in my leg, and I've just met my nurse, who looks like J. Edgar Hoover. I don't know much about anything right now. I'd say you could safely assume that there's a good chance that some of the individuals apprehended last night were in some way connected with the Oasis incident. You'll have to wait for the official report. I'm sure Eustace will call a press conference this afternoon. Other than that, I can't say anything.''

"You *won't* say anything, you mean. I don't like being dismissed, Beau. I'm an officer of the court, just as much as you."

That one redlined on Beau's Dork-O-Meter.

"Christ, Dwight—you're a goddamned corporate lawyer! Your idea of a battle is springing an unsprung precedent or cooking a half-baked tort. You think handball is combat. It's a big day for you when your backhand is just so. You're all a-tingle when your daddy spells your name right on a check. I'd say you have as much right to information about a police action as the goddamned Hezbollah!"

"You *can* say that your handling of the Oasis incident seems to have contributed to the deaths of several people. That seems to be a reasonable inference."

Beau sighed and looked at Dwight for a while. Dwight examined the room unnecessarily and recrossed his legs. He templed his fingers and stared back at Beau, inhaling through his nose.

"Jesus, Dwight—when the hell did your type get to Montana? It must have been real late in the year."

Dwight Hogeland seemed to expand slightly. His forehead and cheeks paled under his tan.

"My family had steers grazing on the Bitterroot when your people were still butt-fucking their nigras and picking lice off their ballgowns down in some Tularosa hellhole."

"Yeah, I heard. Bad beef and rusty rifles to the army. A lot of troopers got hung upside-down over a Pawnee cooking fire because they were holding a Hogeland Henry. The cavalry used to call your great-grandfather's rifles the Piecemakers 'cause as soon as you fired one, all you had was pieces."

Dwight came to his feet. "That's a damnable lie, McAllister! A slander! You repeat that when you're healthy, I'll—"

"Pout? Stamp your foot? Cut me dead at the club?"

"Fuck you!"

Beau smiled at him.

"Funny how the shine comes off cheap leather when you rub at it a bit. And that isn't a damnable lie, as you well know, kid. You go ask Pike Twilly—he's got one of your family's rebuilt rifles up behind the bar there. Lost a piece of cheekbone when he tried to fire it, too. And my family never had to personally butt-fuck a nigra. We had our lawyers do that."

There was a movement at the door. They both turned, startled.

Maureen Sprague was standing in the doorway, holding Bobby Lee's hand, her green eyes bright and her thin face shiny with anger. A red flush showed under her dark tan. She was dressed for riding—jeans and a jacket and boots. A heavy gold chain glimmered at her sinewy neck, and a pair of gold earrings sparkled against her short streaked hair. Beau stared at her, wondering how Maureen could be so pretty and yet so ugly all at the same time. And how the hell was she able to afford all that gold? Maybe Dwight had the answer, but Beau wasn't going to ask him.

"They can hear you in the hall, Beau. Nice talk."

"Maureen—always a delight."

Bobby Lee was staring up at them, her face solemn and pale.

"Maureen, maybe we should talk later?"

"I wasn't going to talk to you at all, until I heard you bellowing at Dwight. You're scaring Bobby Lee. Can't you see that?"

Beau pulled in a long breath, trying to get himself under control. Maureen was trying to get him to explode. Then she could say, see, Bobby Lee, see how your daddy is?

He smiled at Bobby Lee. "Honey, you let Mommy and me have a minute?"

Bobby Lee looked relieved. She let go of Maureen's hand—after a brief struggle—blew a kiss at him, and ran away down the hall. Maureen called after her.

"Go to the playroom, Bobby Lee! I'll be right there!"

Through all of this, Dwight was cooling rapidly. Now that Maureen was in the room, the lawyer in him came slowly back to the surface.

"Maureen, there's no reason for you to put up with this. Beau has a talent for the hurtful phrase."

He smiled at her, a possessive and condescending benediction, then he looked back at Beau.

"There's quite a bit of the sadist in you—in all your kind, isn't there? Someday a good psychoanalyst might take a look at the nasty little habits that people like you spend so much time compensating for."

That got a little razor-blade smile from Maureen. Dwight saw it and warmed to the job, seeing it all on the movie screen at the back of his skull: Dwight Finally Tells Him Off! Special Added Attraction: In Front Of His Ex-Wife!

"Why the hell do you think I take such pleasure in seeing you restrained by every legal means I can? Because I think you're dangerous—dangerous to yourself, dangerous to the civilians and the so-called criminals you harass, and dangerous to Maureen and Roberta Lee, people who depended on you. You are not the law. You are about to get a large lesson in what the law really is, Beau. And when it's over, if you have anything left, you'll be able to fit most of it in your back pocket."

Beau leaned back into his pillows and shook his head slowly.

"Well, I guess I've been told. You're a piece of work, kid. Now, why don't you piss off down the hall there? And Maureen, I want you to feel free to piss off with him. And by the way, thanks for the concern for my health, I'm fine, *really* enjoyed seeing you all, and love to Bobby Lee, and let's all pick this fight up next week when I'm outta here, okay?"

"You'll be too busy to pick fights next week, Beau," Maureen snapped at him.

Beau looked at her, and back at Dwight.

Dwight folded his arms and tried to stare him down.

"What's that supposed to mean, Dwight?"

"Enjoy the flowers."

Sweeping the room in one last dismissive glance, the lawyer sketched a sardonic salute, offered his arm to Maureen, and they walked out. Beau could hear Maureen's stainless-steel tone as she called for Bobby Lee, then the click of her bootheels as they faded down the hallway.

The strange machine huffed at him for a while. Finally, Beau pulled back the covers and dragged his legs across the linen. They had stuck him in one of those peek-a-boo gowns designed by the North Koreans to rob prisoners of their dignity. He looked down at his leg. It itched. He scratched it. That was not the right thing to do. After a while, he opened his eyes and let out a long uneven breath.

"Okay, Beau. Keep that in mind. Now, let's see if you can stand up."

He stood up on his left leg. His belly was bandaged, but the muscles beneath seemed to be okay. He could feel fresh stitches pulling under the pads. He smelled of formaldehyde and Lysol.

Leaning on the intravenous drip stand, he managed to get his right leg down to the floor. He put gradual pressure on it.

It hurt.

He felt a rip in the big muscles in his thigh. The thing had gone right through him. It gave him an atavistic tremor. Well, the guy had paid for the privilege.

He walked like a very old man across to the bucket of wildflowers. It'd be in there somewhere.

He rooted around in the tangle of buttercups and heather and clover. The scent reminded him of riding in the Bridger range, above Paradise Valley, and he thought again about his land down on the Yellowstone, about retiring while he was still in relatively good shape.

The envelope was wrapped in a plastic bag and set upright in a spray of baby's breath. It had the old familiar logo in the upper right-hand corner: Mallon, Brewer, Hogeland and Bright.

He opened the bag and ripped the edge off the thick cream bond envelope. The richer the paper, the nastier the news.

WITHOUT PREJUDICE

NOTIFICATION OF INTENTION TO PROCEED AT LAW

IN THE MATTER OF . . . BE ADVISED THAT . . . DID WITH MALICE . . .

Beau skimmed through the familiar prose. Joe Bell had kept his promise—and he'd gotten Dwight Hogeland to do it. Nice incestuous little circle jerk. Beau was named, along with the Montana Highway Patrol and the Yellowstone County Controller. Dwight must have stayed up all night working on this one. Hell, he'd just *shot* Bell yesterday!

He skipped a few pages until he found the bottom line.

Christ.

Sweet Jesus Christ.

Joe Bell must be a proud man. He apparently had the most valuable ass west of the Mississippi. Beau put one hole in it, and the man wanted five million dollars.

That was a lot of money for one man's butt—even one the size of Joe Bell's.

Now, there was a funny thing. Beau looked all through the list of people being sued, and sure as hell, there wasn't one Indian name on it. So it followed that you shoot at a man with a bow and arrow, it's free. But you shoot at him with a Browning, it'll cost you five million dollars.

Something to keep in mind.

"Well, this is a sorry sight."

Beau looked up from the lawsuit notice and saw Tom Blasingame in the doorway, grinning back at him.

Tom Blasingame was something of a celebrity in the surrounding counties. Easily in his late seventies, he looked exactly like what he was, a very old and very tough cowhand, constructed mostly of barbed wire and dried beef. His face was withered and sunken and tanned as dark as a rifle stock. He wore an old dome-peak Stetson, antique jeans, and knee-high boots that were worn down at the stirrup bar.

Tom had enough Taxco silver on his belt and at his throat to mark him as a man with some cash. He had, as he called it, "chased the wild bovine" for over sixty-five years. He could remember when Montana was still called the Territory. When he talked of where he had been—which was rarely but well—he talked about the rivers: down on the Del Norte as far as Chihuahua, along the Gila out by Santa Rita, maybe along the Cimarron Cut-Off over the Canadian River, up the Raton Pass and down to the Purgatoire and the Arkansas and north to the South Platte and the Missouri. When Ingomar sold the Buenavista spread to the Japanese, Tom had retired to Lizardskin, where he kept a string of Tennessee Walkers and sometimes acted as a guide for government surveyors or tourists from the East.

Tom spoke little, kept his teeth in a glass of rye whisky by his cot, carried an old Remington revolver wherever he damned well pleased, never shaved but somehow never grew a beard, and never spoke above a soft and diffident drawl. If Lizardskin had a mayor, it was old Tom Blasingame.

Most of the Lizardskin residents were scratch-farmers or day laborers who couldn't afford the rentals in Hardin or Billings. Then there were some retirees from Billings trying to stretch their pensions; a family of Crow Indians raising desert wheat and corn for a roadside stand down on I-90; and the random assortment of drifters who seem to gather like clusters of weeds and wildflowers in the lee sides of every long valley and dry wash in the Far West.

Beau always thought it was hard to tell the city dump from most of the Lizardskin housing. People tended to scatter their goods all over their lots. The place was a jumble of rusted trucks and broken wagons, a tumbledown chicken shack, a failed outhouse, a double-wide trailer with a bunch of add-ons in pickup lumber and plywood signs stolen—harvested—from the high-ways. It was all dust and windblown sand, bleaching white under the long Montana sundowns, a sad wind always in the cottonwoods like the memory of a choir singing.

In the alleys and backlots, pariah dogs with their ribs showing eyed the rattlesnakes drying in rows from sagging porches. Feral cats like quicksilver slipped through the fences or lay around like fattened queens on the front seats of ruined Buicks, and from somewhere, from everywhere, there came the sound of music, a jaunty reel on a fiddle or the chatter of a country music deejay in between old Merle Haggard songs, coming scratchily from some cheap radio sitting on a card table behind a lazily swaying gauze curtain. It was the True West, miles off the interstate, scruffy and half-dead, sleepy and rundown and ragged as an old dog, but blessedly, mercifully quiet, deep in the heart of soft brown hills and buttes rising up out of the hazy blue, the pink glimmer of the snow up in the Beartooth. The air was pure and full of sweetgrass perfume. A single breath seemed to run right to your head like sparkling wine.

Beau had taken a loan for a double-wide trailer on the outskirts, far enough from the interstate to get a good night's sleep. Tom Blasingame had come over the first morning after Beau moved in, a bottle of whisky under his arm. They'd been close ever since.

"Tom. How'd you know where I was?"

Blasingame strolled into the room, briefly eyeing the patient in the next bed.

"Saw that pup Hogeland in the parking lot. He was pushing Joe Bell in a wheelchair. Maureen and Bobby Lee were with them. How'd that happen?"

"Dwight's helping Bell sue me for yesterday. And he's playing Daddy with Bobby Lee, and I don't know what the hell he's doing with Maureen, and I'd be grateful if you didn't speculate on it for me, that's all right with you."

Tom's dark green eyes showed a small glint. "Dwight's a real convenient boy, isn't he?"

"Yeah, well, what're you gonna do?"

"Time for a lawyer, Beau. You're up to your ass in alligators, get a bigger alligator."

"Hate lawyers. And who has the money?"

"Well, of course, you're doing real well by yourself now."

"Let's drop this, Tom. I'm doing what I can."

Tom eased his bony frame into a chair and grinned through his shaggy moustache.

"Beau, you think, just by lying down and making no fuss, they'll go easy on Bobby Lee, stop poisoning her about you? These people don't think like that. You be *nice,* they'll think you're afraid of them. Stop trying to get them to *like* you, Beau. Start making them *afraid* of you!"

"How the hell I do that?"

Tom sighed and rubbed his mouth. "Jesus, Beau—half of Montana's afraid of you. The other half's got money on you. Why don't you stand up for yourself?"

Beau closed his eyes, and Tom decided to give it a rest.

"You see the piece in the *Gazette*?"

Beau winced. "About me?"

"So they say. Haven't seen it yet. I called about you. They tell me Meagher's gone over to Hardin to talk to the Big Horn County guys, see if they've got anything to add to the story. There's a big fuss building up about all this, I guess you'd know that?"

"Stands to reason. Anything on the news this morning?"

"Radio says big gunfight at Arrow Creek. Mentions you, here and there. And they bring up that accident last week in Hardin, killed the young Crow girl and her baby? Sorta suggesting that you cops are trying to finish what the U.S. Cavalry started."

Beau groaned again, and there was a silence that stretched out in a kind of calming, comfortable way.

After a few minutes, Blasingame got up and walked over to study the man in the next bed.

"Now there's a feller, got a hard road under him."

Beau nodded. "I've been wondering about him. That machine there, looks serious." He lowered his voice to match Blasingame's soft tones. "He conscious?"

"Not so's you'd notice," said Blasingame, stroking his handlebar moustache. "Got him on a respirator. I'd say it was a fire or something. He's blue as a trout, and there's hoses all over him."

"Christ! It's not Danny Burt or an Indian-looking guy, is it?"

Blasingame shook his head. "I know Danny. Just a minute."

He picked up the chart, flipped the steel cover back, and read down the sheet. "Nope. Truck fire, it says. There's a notation here from the cops, too."

"Which branch?" asked Beau.

"Billings City. 'Notify if conscious.' "

Beau sat up, some vague uneasiness stirring in his belly. "Let me see the chart, Tom?"

Blasingame handed it across.

Beau read through the half-legible scrawl and the feathery computer print. He found the name at the bottom of the sheet. He stared at it for a while, then looked up at Blasingame.

"Anybody seen my clothes?"

Blasingame smiled at him, reached down, and tossed him a big paper bag. It landed on his bed with a weighty thump. Beau pulled the top open. Jeans, boots, a fresh shirt. Deodorant, shave cream and razor, toothbrush and paste, socks, and underwear. And the Smith & Wesson .44 from beside his bed back in Lizardskin. And a belt holster. And a Speed-Loader spare.

"Jesus—no cats?"

"Feets and McAvity're at your trailer. I fed 'em both before I came over. Stonewall's staying with me till you're back. They're fine, Beau. What's the trouble?"

Beau rang the buzzer for Hanrahan. "There's something goin' on, and nobody's taking it seriously."

Blasingame was staring at the sheet. "I don't get it. You know this guy Bucky Blitzer?"

"No. But who does he work for?"

Blasingame searched the printout. "Mountain Bell? So what?"

"So somebody burned a Mountain Bell truck last night."

"Yeah? Well, actually, some truck burned, is all you can tell from this. Why does this—what's the problem with it?"

"Coincidences. I don't like 'em." Beau rang the call button again, hard and repeatedly. "I'm not waiting."

"Waiting for what? Christ, Beau, you gotta stay in bed. This makes no sense at all!"

"I know! I know. I just got a feeling. Something's going on, and nobody's paying attention. It's gone on long enough."

They all heard a brassy bellow from down the hall.

"Hold your water, Mr. McAllister! Others here worse'n you!"

"There you go," said Beau. "Anytime I want to commit suicide, I'm just gonna check into a hospital."

Tom Blasingame listened to the squeak and slap getting closer. A voice full of brimstone and methane boomed in the hall.

"I'm *coming,* Mr. McAllister! Don't get your testicles in a twist!"

Blasingame reached over the footrail and lifted the paper bag off the bed. Beau watched him do it.

"Now, look, Tom."

"Now nothing. Look at your leg, Beau."

He looked down at it. The plastic tube was dripping darker fluid now, and more of it, and faster.

"That's blood, Beau. That's supposed to be on the *in*-side."

Beau started to tug the tube free of his wound. The world went white in the middle and red around the edges. His skull filled with helium, and he began to drift across the room.

Blasingame caught him just as the Hanrahan chugged into the room. She took in the scene and seemed to rise up a few inches off the floor.

"Were we playing with our tube, McAllister?"

Beau had a nasty answer to that. He hoped he'd remember it if he ever regained consciousness.

11

2200 Hours – June 15 – Billings, Montana

There was a policeman sitting on a plastic chair, leaning back in it, bracing it on the wall beside a set of double doors marked:

INTENSIVE CARE UNIT

NO VISITORS

He was young and soft-looking under the dark blue uniform. The crest on his short-sleeved shirt said BILLINGS CITY POLICE, against an embroidered background of mountains and cacti. He was wearing a big stainless-steel Smith & Wesson .357 on his black webbed leather belt and holding a copy of the *Billings Gazette* in heavy hands, frowning over the comics. Gabriel Picketwire stepped back into the elevator and rode it back down to the lobby.

Well, he should have expected that.

The sensible thing to do was to go to the cops and ask them to look into the background. Tell them about Jubal's suspicions, tell them about the babies. If Jubal was right, the numbers would bear him out—at least enough to get their attention.

If Jubal was right.

And if he was wrong, or if the local cops were as aggressive as they looked so far, then he'd find himself in a small room answering unfriendly questions. Once they had his face and name, his ability to act independently would be finished. They'd tie him up with questions and probably put a man on him.

Well, he'd decide later.

Right now, see about Donna.

He stepped out into the lobby and walked over to the directory.

Sweetwater General Hospital was a big-city hospital, sprawling through several wings in the west end of Billings. The directory showed a you-are-here map and named the various wings: Terry Wing, Viral Research, Cardiovascular, Ob-Gyn, Hogeland Oncology Wing, Bridger Wing, ICU North, Pathology. The map was pretty detailed about the layout, and Gabriel stood there in the middle of the deserted lobby, listening to the waxer whining down one of the shiny terrazzo halls, studying it with his mind as empty and still as he could make it.

He had come in earlier in the afternoon to scout it out. The registry clerk had been unhelpful concerning his fictitious Uncle William Roan Horse.

They'd had seven Native Americans admitted in the past twenty-four hours, as far as she could tell from the names. Native Americans usually had a federal Medicare number, and the only ones that had been admitted with that kind of notation bore no similarity to this William Roan Horse.

She had shuffled rather perfunctorily through a computer menu full of names, glancing sidelong up at him through the glass screen that protected her from contamination by the actual public out there. Gabriel asked to see the list, see if he recognized any family members. She recoiled and shook her head. He pressed her. She got angry.

"Look, mister. There's no one here who sounds like your uncle. We had eight Native Americans in the past few days, none of them sound like your uncle. One young girl, a Jane Doe; one boy, fell off a tree limb chasing a cat; three for kidney dialysis; one Crow man, victim of an accident on the interstate, hit by a tractor-trailer; and two young Crow women having babies."

"A Jane Doe?"

She gave him a hard look. "Are you asking for her?"

"No—just curious."

"She was admitted last night at midnight. She's in intensive care. Head injuries. Anyone inquiring after her is asked to contact the Yellowstone County Sheriff or the Highway Patrol. Are you inquiring?"

"No," said Gabriel, shaking his head. He pestered her awhile longer, just to blur the issue a bit. His uncle was a drinker, he explained, and he'd been trying to reach him last night. Finally had to fly in, see if he was in the hospital. Sometimes he forgets his name, forgets to carry ID.

So try Detox. She gave him the address. Told him it was always full of Indians. She gave him a look that implied that he'd know all about Detox, know the color of the paint in the shower and the kind of soup they served on Tuesdays.

He thanked her and walked away. Sorry to bother you.

He felt her watching him as he walked across the expanse of pale marble toward the glass doors, seeing only a tall lean man limping away in a long black raincoat, black slacks and boots, his long shiny blue-black hair pulled back in a ponytail caught in a Navajo silver ring.

She'd remember him, certainly. He should have brought clothes that suited the region. He should have waited until his knee was better. He had to credit Dr. Sifton, though, for turning him around. When a man like that thinks poorly of you, you're sliding. If he looked West Coast to her, that was too bad. But if he moved fast enough, it wouldn't matter.

The evening air was soft and full of the smell of growing things. And gasoline and smog, like any city, like all the High Plains towns. They all looked as if they'd been put up last week. No old buildings that hadn't been turned into tourist snares. All the new buildings looking so new, your eye slid right over them. It was a characteristic of these places that sooner or later you found yourself looking away from them, up to the hills and the buttes, where you could still get a feeling of permanence and stability.

Billings was in a long low valley, cut by the Yellowstone ten thousand years ago. Ten thousand years ago, this land had belonged to no one. Maybe ten thousand years from now, things would get back to normal around here. Gabriel hoped so, although he didn't really believe it and didn't feel that it was something he had a part in.

Still, it felt good to have made a decision, to have resolved to act in this thing. Dr. Sifton was—there was more to him than you saw right away. The doc had fixed him up with some Percodan and some amphetamines and written him a note to show Nigel Hampton and the rest of the crew. He was on full pay but released for injury. The director had just been relieved that

Gabriel wasn't talking about a lawsuit. Sifton even drove him to LAX and saw him on the plane.

Well, he'd find Donna, see about a sing for her. She'd like that. It would help her to get better. He'd taken the sing from a record he'd found in the ethnology library at USC in Irvine. Some busybody scholar had traveled the plains taping the old sings.

He'd made a cassette of it and listened to it on the plane. The sonorous drone and the rise and fall of it were strangely comforting. It meant little to him, perhaps as little as the words of the old Latin Mass meant to modern Catholics; relics of a dead age, empty sound and ritual, something they did in memory of a god who had forgotten them before the planet had cooled.

Well, he'd give it to Donna. She could listen to it, try to make it work for her. Donna was a believer.

Head wound . . . intensive care . . .

He found a bar across the street and waited until the shifts changed. At ten, the place had filled up with off-duty nurses and interns, having a frantically good time at the tops of their lungs, drinking white wine and imported beers, and talking all at once about the day's disasters and intrigues. They reminded him of the film crew, chattering birds in bright colors, wild in the eyes and brainless, full of herky-jerky motion, driving their bosses wild with sloth and union arrogance.

Sitting in the midst of them, radiating a certain stillness, he knew they had given him a circle, staying away in a kind of atavistic recognition of the—oddness—of the man in the black linen slacks and the black shirt buttoned up to the collar, the Navajo silver at his neck and his waist.

Gabriel leaned forward onto his arms and studied his reflection in the long etched mirror behind the bar, seeing the shadows in his bony face and the darkness where his eyes were, the mahogany-skull look he never managed to soften. There was no point in trying to stay unnoticed. It never worked.

They looked soft and satisfied. Probably the night shift would be just as soft, and lazier. The visitors would be gone, too. He'd have the place to himself.

So he drank a bit and tried not to think about Jubal and Earl and James. They'd come to him, tried to get him to listen to their story. He had listened long enough to dismiss it as one more paranoid fantasy. And Gabriel was tired of all the old paranoias, the conspiracy horses the old men liked to ride, tired of every whining Indian complaint.

The Pinda-Lickoyee were responsible for every evil thing that had overtaken the Dakota? Tell *that* to the Crow or the Pawnee, the Ree or the Ute or the Flathead, all of whom had seen their villages burned and their young men flayed in the Kakeshya by the Santee and the Yankton and the Teton people for a hundred years before the Isanhanska soldiers had come. Slaughter had been the entertainment of the Great Plains.

The Arikara had butchered the Hidatsa and the Mandan, and the Assiniboine had slaughtered the Dakota, in the time before the beginnings, when the Assiniboine had come running from the Ojibway, who were running before the French in Canada, and they all fought each other for the forest lands around the Great Lakes and Minnesota. Even the Pinda-Lickoyee name for the Dakota, the Sioux, was taken from an Ojibway word, Nadouessioux.

Down in Texas and New Mexico and Oklahoma, the Comanche murdered the Wichita, the Arapaho made slaves of the Kansas, and the Apache slaughtered everyone they could catch, especially the Spanish.

Then the Spanish had Texas and New Mexico stolen from *them* by the Isantankah, and the Isantankah went after the Apaches—Gallantin's raiders pulling two hundred dollars for an Apache scalp on a countertop in Santa Fe—and then in his turn, Gallantin murdered by the Yuma, who got rubbed out by the Kiowa, who got pushed into reservations by the pony soldiers and the tall-black-hat people.

And the horse cults? The great myth of the Plains Dakota?

The Dakota time of the horse had been less than a hundred years— something *they* had learned to steal from the Comanche, who stole *their* horses from the conquistadores.

Yun! Even the dirt in Montana was red, as if it had been soaked in blood. That was the way of it. The land had not been forever. It was borrowed from time, and soon they had to give it back. Everyone imagined that their time of privilege was god-given and forever. No god gave anything forever. The gods gave you something so that they could watch you get killed for it. Look back over your shoulder as far as your farthest father, and you see your own future.

And his time with the Defense Intelligence Agency—that had been more of the same, but done in the dark with Deniability Assured and everyone taking an oath to Protect the Administration, everyone hand-picked from Section. They'd called themselves the Skull and Bones in honor of the boss, an inside joke at the firm. And everyone they had killed had earned it, if not by their own actions, then by their inheritances and the blood that had been spilled in the gaining of them. No one was innocent. No one was pure. Every people had sins on their foreheads and blood in their pockets.

Still, it was hard to think of them dead. He could see Eddie at his wedding, a full Lakota ceremony, Eddie in his best—and only—black suit, and Donna like a pale yellow flower, and Jubal and James Comes In Sight and Earl Black Elk. That had been at the Rosebud, in the summer of 1988. Later, he had brought Eddie out to the coast and got him a job with Offshore Films.

That was over with now.

Something had to be done about what had happened. Somebody ought to open the thing up, see what truth there had been in it. It would be nice to find some truth in the old men. Something to believe in, even this late in his life.

Because there was something real in Jubal's story. The proof of it was that someone had killed them all. He pulled the clipping out of his pocket and read it again, read that he had come to Billings too late.

FIVE DIE IN POLICE ACTION

POMPEYS PILLAR. An attempted armed robbery ended in death for one Native American youth at a local gas station here yesterday. An unidentified Indian male was killed while attempting to rob Bell's Oasis. The owner, Joseph Bell, resisted the attempt, shooting one of the robbers. Montana Highway Patrol attended the scene and assisted Mr. Bell. Bell was wounded in the action. Four other members of the gang exchanged fire with the police and managed to elude capture. An immediate search was initiated by the authorities.

Bell was taken to Sweetwater General Hospital, where his condition was described as good.

In a bizarre followup, the morgue wagon taking the deceased robber from the scene was hijacked en route, along with two attendants, Daniel Burt and Peter Hinsdale. It became the focus of a countywide search that culminated in a violent police action in the vicinity of Ar-row Creek, off the Ballantine side road, where a Montana Highway Patrol sergeant tracked the wagon and confronted the gang members at approximately 11:00 last night.

An exchange of fire ensued, including, according to police sources, bow-and-arrow fire. One gang member was shot and killed by the MHP sergeant, and another female gang member was seriously injured in the exchange. Officers answering the call came under fire while proceeding toward Arrow Creek and succeeded in killing another male gang member.

During the minutes following, officers discovered a large fire raging one half-mile up the creek. An elderly male was found dead at the scene, apparently of a self-inflicted knife wound. A macabre footnote emerged later, when it was discovered that the body of the gang member killed at Bell's Oasis was completely burned in the fire—which enveloped a scaffold-type burial platform—in what appears to have been a Native American funeral ritual.

MHP Lieutenant Eustace Meagher is in command of the investigation. Since crimes involving Native Americans fall under federal jurisdiction, Special Agent in Charge Frank Duffy of the FBI Helena office will oversee the case to determine if this action signals another outbreak of violence by Native American terrorist groups.

Tragically, one of the morgue attendants, teenager Peter Hinsdale, was brutally slain by his captors before the police could free him. His partner, Daniel Burt, was found unhurt, tied to a tree a few hundred yards from the site of the fire. Also wounded at the scene was Officer Illario Benitez of the MHP.

Lieutenant Meagher credits the finding and capture of the gang to Staff Sergeant Beauregard McAllister of the MHP, who sustained severe injuries during the fight. Sergeant McAllister is being treated for his wounds at Sweetwater General Hospital and is listed in stable condition. Sergeant McAllister is the police officer who was involved in the Hilltop Mall shooting last year, which resulted in the capture of an escaped armed robber and a controversial lawsuit. Sergeant McAllister, a nineteen-year veteran of the MHP, is that force's most highly decorated officer, having been involved in twenty-seven combat situations during his time on the MHP, as a patrol officer, and as a member of the Combined Strike Force,

which targeted armed professional criminals throughout the state.

The female gang member, whose identity has not been released, is also being treated at Sweetwater General. Her condition is listed as grave.

All told, three gang members are reported as killed in the related actions, and one dead of self-inflicted wounds. Their names are being withheld pending notification of next of kin.

Spokespersons for the Society for the Protection of Ethno-American Rights (SPEAR) have protested the shootings and the publicity surrounding them. The American Civil Liberties Union of Montana, acting for SPEAR, will apply to the courts for intervenor status. The ACLU promises that every aspect of this case will be carefully examined to insure that no violation of due process took place.

SPEAR Delegate Maya BlueStones cited last week's police-chase incident in Hardin, which resulted in the death of a Crow woman and her child and the serious injury of a Crow man. BlueStones suggested that these incidents show a pattern of "racial bias" and "institutional hostility toward Native Americans which must be exposed and addressed."

Assistant DA Vanessa Ballard has refused to comment at this time, saying only that the Hardin incident has no connection with the robbery attempt at Bell's Oasis, and that the investigation continues.

The investigation continues. Was that more tin-talk, or was there some kind of doubt in the minds of the officials? Gabriel had never heard of a police department being careful about releasing the names of criminals. They were the first thing out, like coup counts on the lodge pole. See who we caught? See who we killed for you?

See what fine killers we are?

Perhaps. And perhaps no one had properly tested their skills.

In the end he trusted in his experience and let the hour of the wolf do it all for him. It was the same in Billings as it had been in the Philippines and Belfast and Quito; it was in the hearts of people to drift and have bad visions at a certain time each night, between three and four in the morning. In the dead watch, his Section commander had called it. In the hour of the wolf, terrible dreams come to the sleeping and a great weight settles on the hearts of those who are awake. In hospitals, most of the dying do it between three and four. In the homes, it is always at three or four that the wife, who has been sitting dead-eyed and staring at her hands on the kitchen table since midnight, finally takes the knife and climbs up the stairs toward the bed in which her husband lies twisted in his sheets, breathing through his mouth, smelling of warm meat. Wars start at three, as it did in the Gulf, when the warplanes brought new thunder and a fresh point of view to the mullahs in Baghdad. Trust in the hour.

The lobby was empty as a train station, a wide underground cavern containing a lake of polished marble, dimly lit by hidden spotlights. The registry office was dark behind the plastic. The doors hushed closed behind him as he slipped across the floor, a tall black figure, his long coat billowing out behind him, going from light to shadow and back into light as he passed beneath the ceiling lamps far overhead.

He took the stairs and climbed, in silence, hearing his steps and his own breath and under that the slow mechanical exhalations of the hospital, of its buried machinery and the thousand little pumps and bellows and ser- vomotors that kept it running, kept the patients afloat in the endless crossings of a sickbed night.

The stool and the newspaper were still there, but the cop had gone. The long hallway that led to the double doors was dark. The smell of antiseptic and floor wax was strong in the air. The sound of a radio was coming from somewhere. Gabriel tried to place the song, a faint reedy whine echoing from a sideroom somewhere on the floor. It was "Dust in the Wind," by Kansas.

He covered the fifty feet like a crow flying over a pond, settling into the darkness by the doors, his breath slow and his mind quiet as he listened hard. Muted sounds. Intermittent electronic flutings, changing in rhythm as the patients rose and sank on the tides of their lives. The huff and discharge of air from pumps and valves. "Dust in the Wind" still, louder now. He placed his left hand on the door and eased it open six inches.

A long hallway with a nurses' station in the middle of it, about fifty feet down. One wall of the hallway was glass, and beyond the glass partition a row of beds, perhaps ten of them, each one surrounded by medical support machinery, monitors, video screens flickering with heartbeats and blood pressure readouts. At the station, he could just make out the top of a woman's head. She was seated, head slightly forward and down, apparently reading something behind the partition, out of his sight. He could see the motion of her shoulder as she turned the pages. The sound of the radio was coming from her desk.

Movement. Another nurse was standing by one of the patients on the far side of the glass wall, shaking a vial of liquid. She leaned forward over the mounded form on the bed and seemed to touch a cheek. The tenderness of the motion appealed to Gabriel, gave him a feeling for her. He stepped through the doors and glided across the hall to an open doorway.

The nurse at the station had not moved. The other one, beyond the glass wall, was moving from one bed to the next, straightening a sheet, changing a pillow, concentrated and isolated in her work.

From the new position, a few feet back in the darkened storeroom, he stood and watched the beds, searching for Donna's shape, for some quality that would reveal her. Under their hospital sheets and bound up in the machinery, each patient looked like food for spiders, waiting in their bindings. Tiny green lights pulsed and blinked and sketched glowing geometric figures against the dimness of the ward.

He waited until the nurse had finished her rounds. She stopped by the sealed doors and looked back over her shoulder at the line of beds, as a gardener might do leaving a greenhouse, seeing to the hothouse flowers, feeling their heat and the water in the air, feeling the dim life in each burning bed.

Under the overhead lamp, she looked young and very white, a source of light. She stepped through and closed the door softly behind her and walked to the station. She stood a minute, looking down at the seated nurse, who did not look up. She smiled, reached over the partition, and picked up a magazine. She walked around the station and came down the hall toward Gabriel, her rubber-soled shoes whispering on the terrazzo. She reached the doorway where Gabriel stood motionless in the darkness, stopped there, caught in a spotlight, her yellow hair as violent as fire, tiny blond hairs shining on the curve of her white neck, her face in a dark shadow.

Gabriel breathed slowly through his mouth, moved nothing, thought nothing, a darker darkness in the storeroom.

She folded the magazine, looked at her watch, looked into the storeroom, looked into Gabriel's face, still turning, turning around now to look back at the desk. She smiled again and walked away to the double doors. Gabriel heard them open, felt the rush of hallway air as she stepped outside, heard her short gasp, and then her voice, soft, a whisper.

"You're back—where'd you go?"

A man's voice, a baritone rumble, something he could not make out. The policeman was back.

He heard their voices cut off as the spring-loaded doors swept closed again. Gabriel stepped out of the storeroom and walked quickly toward the duty desk. A heavy-set older woman was nodding over her folded hands, in front of a row of television monitors and alarm lights. Gabriel leaned over the desk and touched her gently with his left hand, feeling for the little nodule behind her left ear, pressing that, then taking her weight as she slipped forward onto the desk, settling her onto her forearms, on one cheek, breathing more deeply now, through slackened lips.

In the long ward, he walked past the beds, past the gray ovals of faces, hearing their uneven breathing, listening to the beeps and chuffs and droning of the machines. In one bed he caught the wet oystershell glitter of open eyes turning as he passed, saw the head swivel as he glided by. He stopped at that bed and stared across the sheet at the man, who stared back at him, unblinking, tubes running into his nostrils.

Above his bed, a monitor glowed green. Gabriel watched the numbers. They did not change. He was an Indian man—he had been in some kind of fight or accident. He was bound up in bandages and his arm was held out in a brace. His ribcage was also in a plaster cast. The man made no sound, and the green letters did not change. His heart rate did not alter.

Of course. The Crow man who had been in the accident. A tractor-trailer accident. Gabriel remembered the receptionist talking about it, when he had asked about his missing uncle. And the article in the Billings paper.

Maybe the man was dreaming awake. After a while, the effort of seeing this black shadow was too much for him, and he closed his eyes again.

Gabriel found Donna Sweetwater Bent in the seventh bed.

He had to look for a long time before he recognized her. Her head was shaved and bound in a skullcap of white cloths. A bridged tracheal tube ran into her throat under her small chin. Her brown skin looked yellow in the half-light. Her cheekbone was huge, blue and swollen, an obscenity of broken bones and eruptions of raw skin. Stitches pierced her. One eye was open, blind as a cataract. The other was closed. Beside the bed, a machine on a rollaway cart was doing her breathing for her, as noisy as a steam-press as it forced life into her and then pulled it back out. The monitor above her bed showed traces of heartbeat, and the peaks and troughs of her brain waves were flattened and languid, like sand dunes in a soft wind.

He came around and stood by her bed, looking down at her.

He remembered her third birthday. She had worn her hair in pigtails and someone, her mother who died the following month, had given her pink sandals. Her smile was incandescent. Relatives came in trucks and old cars. The party was held in a dusty lot at the back of Jubal's farmhouse. The sky had been clear and blue. It seemed to soar above the mountains like a vast blue wave. If you looked up at it long enough, it would pull you up into it and carry you away over the low yellow hills and past the black mountains to a high snowbound crest, where you would die far from your people, far from everything that held you in one shape.

You would be like water poured from a bowl.

You would sink into the earth again and be as if you had never been. That had happened to many of them.

That had happened to him.

He pulled the tape player from his coat pocket and laid it down on the pillow by her head. He had some trouble getting the headphones to fit over the skullcap. Donna did not move. Her green numbers did not change. The machine pulled at her and pushed at her.

He pressed the PLAY button and stepped back. The batteries were new. The machine would play the song endlessly, over and over again, until the nurses found it or the power drained away. Under the steam-press sound of the machine, he heard the droning of the singer's voice, a tiny scratchy sound, like a wasp trapped in the sunroom of an empty house, beating itself to death in the heat and the dryness, unable to imagine what this hard nothing was that kept it shut in and trapped. Its wings buzzed again.

He was standing there for a long time, hearing the wasp sing in Donna's ears. He was remembering now. There was a lot to remember. It came back in a river of pictures and sounds. He felt it pull at him as a river pulls at you when you stand too close to the current.

He seemed to float far above Donna's face, to see her from a great height. He felt the wings of his black coat move around him. He felt a hawk inside him. He could hear its wings, and when he put a hand on his skin under the shirt, he could feel the wings beating.

Afterward, he could not judge how much time had passed. It was as if he had been picked up and carried to a strange country, yet when he opened his eyes again, he had not moved.

He leaned over and kissed Donna on her ruined cheek. She smelled of Novocaine and alcohol and dry cotton. She had no breath. Her lips looked as if they were stitched shut.

He went back to the duty station. The nurse had not moved. He stood beside her for a while, studying the computer screens in front of her. One showed a list of information files. A cursor blinked at him.

He moved it to ADMISSIONS and hit RETURN.

It asked him to type in a name.

He typed M C A L L I S T E R and hit RETURN again.

The screen went blank and the cursor blinked its idiot blink. Beside him the woman moved her head and said "later" in a little-girl voice. The screen shimmered and beeped.

MCALLISTER, June?

MCALLISTER, Beauregard?

MCALLISTER, Vernon?

He moved the cursor to MCALLISTER, Beauregard, and punched the RETURN key.

CONFIDENTIAL PLEASE KEY IDENT NUMBER

He thought about it for a moment. The nurse said "don't" and sighed again.

There was a purse sitting on the floor under her station. He picked it up and found the wallet. Inside the wallet he found her ID card. He typed in her number. The machine went blank.

A second later, it read:

MCALLISTER, Beauregard
663877/t404 MSP MEDIPLAN
DOB 27/07/46
Single Six Ranch
RR #3 Lizardskin MON
TERRY WING
ROOM 404 EAST
Dr. Malawala

Dr. Butkis D. Psych.
STABLE

DO YOU WISH HISTORY?
IF SO CURSOR TO D2

He studied it for twenty seconds. Then he cursored to ADMISSIONS again and typed in BELL, Joe. He hit RETURN.

Another wait. His senses were quivering now. He was taking far too long. That nurse would come back and step through the door and he'd have to do something about that, and about the cop behind her. That would be the end of his anonymity. Whatever he did would make the morning papers.

The screen flickered and filled up.

BELL, Joseph
66210/t509 VA MEDICAL
DOB 11/02/39
90114 South Wyatt Drive
Hardin MON
TERRY WING
ROOM 509 EAST
Dr. Zorn
OUTPATIENT REFERRAL

DO YOU WISH HISTORY?
IF SO CURSOR TO D2

He studied the screen again. Then he picked up a pencil and wrote both addresses down on a scrap of paper. He cursored to QUIT and hit ESCAPE.

Not a bad idea. The screen was blank again. He felt the woman's pulse at her carotid. She sighed and made room for his fingers under her jaw.

He smiled and patted her head and walked away. He could hear nothing at all through the doors. The silence was unnatural. If the cop was asleep, he would breathe, and if awake, he would breathe and turn pages and shuffle his feet.

Gabriel opened the door and stepped out into the darkened hallway. He heard the sound of low voices coming from a room down at the far end. He would have to pass the room to reach the stairway. He came forward at a glide, moving quickly, the big black coat billowing out behind him.

The door to the room was slightly ajar. He could see the broad blue back of the cop, leaning forward on a high stool. The nurse was hidden from him by the size of the cop's body. He saw a fan of blond hair and heard her laughing softly. The cop's hand was busy, his shoulder moving. The nurse's laugh changed, became a low sigh and a whispered word. Her head came up above the cop's shoulder, and she looked right at Gabriel for the second time.

He watched her eyes as they glittered unseeing in the bright overhead light. Her red mouth was open, and then her eyes closed and she leaned forward, resting her cheek on the cop's dark blue shirt. Her pale blond hair burned in the light.

Gabriel moved away to the stairway door. It opened with a soft hiss, and he went soundlessly into the stairwell.

0500 Hours – June 16 – Billings, Montana

B eau came up from a deep dreaming sleep with a gradual awareness that the light was changing in the room. Finally surfacing, eyes wide, he saw the patterned sound-tiles above as if they were the grids and mainlines of Billings, as if he were flying in through a heavy cloud. There was a kind of surreal hypersonic crack, and suddenly he knew where he was and why.

Something had changed. It took a few minutes to realize that the machine was gone from the far wall. He turned his head, carefully, as if a sudden move would explode it, and looked toward the other bed. The curtains were pulled back; a man was lying on his side, breathing deeply, whistling as he exhaled. The light from the window was pale blue and gray. Noises were coming from the hall, carts being pushed along and morning voices, full of fascist cheer. The nurses were up and about their business.

He pulled the sheet back and felt along his leg. The bandages were mounded over his wound, but that obscene tube was gone. The muscle was sore, but he could move the leg without fainting, a definite improvement. It took him a few minutes to get into a sitting position, and he was mapping out his next move when a young woman in crisp whites backed into the room, pulling a cart full of juices and magazines. She saw him sitting up at the side of the bed and flashed a luminous smile.

"Sergeant McAllister! Good morning!"

He grinned back. "Trudy, isn't it? How are we?"

She made a face and brought the cart close to the bedside. "I hate that, too," she said. "Orange, grapefruit, or tomato?"

"Orange. What do we hate?"

"We hate all that 'we' shit. How did you sleep?"

Beau took the plastic glass and lifted it cautiously to his lips. The juice was wonderful, a sensory flood. He noticed that he was off the intravenous, too. Suddenly, he was starving.

"Weird . . . I had a weird dream, too. Something—I think I dreamed that . . . like a black angel, and it was standing at the foot of the bed, and then there was this white light. Weird."

"Percodan will do that. You have real weird dreams. That sounds like an out-of-body dream. Once I was in the hospital for arthroscopy and they gave me Percodan, and I had this dream I was over at the mall, only I was naked. Can you imagine that? I was stark naked and walking around with my girlfriend, you know, like shopping and stuff. Only I was absolutely in the total nude. Then everybody was nude and we all were on *Wheel of Fortune,* but all the letters were really faces. How's Mr. Blitzer?"

Beau was still picturing Trudy naked in the mall, so when she asked him how Mr. Blitzer was he took it the wrong way and looked down to see if he was covered, but she was already over at the other bed, one hand softly shaking the patient, who groaned and rolled over. Her smile shone down upon him in a perky benediction. He croaked at her and raised his arm. She pulled him upright, and he swayed in the sheets.

"Christ . . . somebody kill that parrot."

"You have a bad taste, Mr. Blitzer?"

Beau turned on his bedlight. Blitzer winced and looked across at him. Bucky Blitzer was a small leathery man with a Marine brushcut and a tattoo of a bulldog on his left bicep. His teeth were out and his cheeks were sunken. Somehow he conveyed a kind of cranky competence, and his eyes, although deep-set and surrounded by lines and shadows, were clear and direct. He pulled in a long slow breath and moaned softly.

"Drink this, Mr. Blitzer."

He drained his cup and wiped his mouth with his hand.

He looked back at Beau and smiled weakly. "You're McAllister, right?"

Beau nodded carefully. His head stayed on. "Yeah. Beau's the name. You okay?"

He pulled in another breath. "Yeah. I think so. Chest feels like somebody filled it with sand."

"You've been on a respirator, Mr. Blitzer," said the nurse. "I'm Trudy. You'll feel tender for a few days. You had a narrow escape there."

He coughed, drank some more juice, and looked around the room. "Yeah. Anybody seen my teeth?"

Trudy bustled over to a cupboard and brought back a glass full of liquid. He fished his teeth out and slipped them in.

"Hell. That's better."

"Yeah," said Beau. "You're right."

Blitzer sent him a black look, then grinned again. "I know. I look like a guy swallowed his face. Trudy, I'm hungry. We eating soon?"

Trudy looked at her clipboard and shook her head. Her hair was up in a French braid, and she looked very young. Beau realized that he was getting to the age when everybody looked too young to drive, let alone be a nurse or a doctor.

"You're on liquids. Sergeant McAllister can have breakfast, but you'll have to see your therapist first. I'll be back in a few minutes. Do either of you want a bedpan?"

Blitzer and Beau looked at each other, and a silent agreement passed between them. They shook their heads in unison, and Trudy laughed at them.

"Okay. But I gave you a bed bath yesterday, Mr. Blitzer, so we have, like, no secrets. I really don't mind."

"Not at gunpoint, darling," said Blitzer, coughing. Trudy laughed again and pushed her cart out of the room.

"I'll help you across there, Mr. Blitzer," said Beau.

"Call me Bucky, and no thank you. Day I need help to the bathroom, I'll get in the tub and play with a power drill. Wish I'd been awake for that bed bath, though."

"What the hell happened, anyway?"

Blitzer looked at him a while, considering. "That's a hard question to answer, and I'm not sure I feel like trying. It was one of the worst things I ever hope to see. Your cop buddies fill you in yet?"

"Not completely. I'd like to hear your side of it. If you're up to it?"

"Up to it? Not likely I'll ever forget it. I haven't got it figured out myself, yet. I *do* know what happened to you."

"Yeah? What was that?"

"You got into that scrap over at Bell's Friday? And then down the side road later—I heard you and your friends talking, I guess it'd be yesterday now? What day's it?"

"Sunday, I think. They took my watch. I'd say Sunday."

Blitzer pulled the sheets back and slowly levered himself onto his feet. He pulled the robe around him.

"I'll use the facilities there, if you don't mind me going first?"

"Not at all. You can't remember about it, or you don't want to right now?"

Blitzer shuffled across the linoleum, talking over his shoulder as he walked. "I gotta tell the city bulls anyway, so I'll practice on you. Gimme a minute to drain Elmore here."

He closed the door and left Beau speculating on the habit men had of naming their nuptials, and did women have names for theirs, or was that just a male thing? Thinking about it, he'd never met a woman who called her nuptials by name. He'd named his Captain Happy years back, around the time he first discovered it had a variety of uses, some better than others. Bucky apparently called his Elmore. Eustace called his Champion, after Gene Autry's horse. Beau had it on good information, however, that Eustace's wife referred to it as Trigger, because it sometimes went off unexpectedly. Myron Sugar referred to *his* as Brutus, for reasons he would not disclose, and Finch Hyam had named his Willy because that was occasionally the question, Willy having a mind of his own sometimes.

There might be something in all of this, some profound insight about life, death, and the meaning of the universe. But he doubted it. Blitzer came back out of the bathroom and interrupted Beau's train of thought.

"Hey, Sergeant. You know the difference between consternation and panic?"

"Can't think of it."

Blitzer settled into the chair and bounced a fist off his chest, clearing his throat. He had better color now, although his breathing sounded like somebody pulling a boot out of a mud puddle.

"Consternation is the first time you can't get it up the second time. *Panic* . . . is the *second* time you can't get it up the *first* time."

Beau's laugh hurt his belly, and Bucky's ended in a gasping wheeze.

"Okay," said Beau. "This guy goes into a bar—"

"Oh, right. That's original."

"Guy goes into a bar, he's got this tiny little man sitting on his left shoulder, see?"

"Tiny little guy on his shoulder, yeah."

"Okay, so the bartender comes over, sees the little man sitting there, but, hey, he's a bartender, you know, he's too cool to say anything, so he asks the guy what he'll have. The guy says oh gimme a double bourbon and branch. So the bartender pours it out, brings it over, sets it down in front of the man. Boom, this little man gets up, runs down the guy's arm, kicks the drink over, laughs like a loon, and runs off down the bartop kicking over everybody's drinks, pissing in the peanuts, running wild. Now the bartender sees this, they both watch, and the bartender says to the man, hey, what the hell you hanging round with a little bastard like that for?"

"I think I heard this."

"Yeah? Well it's almost over. So the guy says to the bartender, I'm an archaeologist, you know, and I was on this dig in the Sahara, and I found this lamp—"

"And he rubs it—"

"And he rubs it, and the genie appears and tells him he has one wish, and he—"

"He wished for a ten-inch prick."

Beau looked at him.

"What kind of name is Elmore anyway?"

Bucky looked back at him.

"We go back for years. Elmore's my buddy."

"So do me and Captain Happy. . . . You hear the one, guy wants to tattoo his girlfriend's name on it, her name's Wilma?"

"Yeah. Welcome to Jamaica's the punchline. You hear the one, two lawyers are walking down Main Street, they see this magnificent woman, a real heart-attack blonde, and one lawyer turns to the other and says, 'Man, wouldn't you like to screw her!' And the other lawyer shrugs and says, 'Outta what?' "

Trudy was standing in the doorway, listening. "I have one for you. You hear about the miracle baby born here last week?"

They both stared at her. "Nope," said Beau.

Trudy brought the trays in and set them down.

"Well, it had a penis *and* a brain. What do you call a woman without an asshole? No? Divorced! One more?"

"Okay."

"What's twelve inches and white?"

"No idea," said Beau.

Trudy pulled the tray-table up and handed Beau a warm wet cloth. "Absolutely nothing. Who wants some oatmeal?"

After the trays had been cleared away and Beau had cleaned himself up in the bathroom, he managed to shuffle back to the bedside chair. He sat down in it and watched Bucky run over his cheeks with an old Schick.

"So . . . can we talk about this a little?"

Blitzer settled himself back into his pillows and switched off the razor. He sent Beau a sidelong look.

"I'm not really inclined to. You ever been in a situation, it gets to be a situation before you notice?"

"All the time."

"You ever been to the Mountain Bell truckyard?"

"I've been past it, in the cruiser."

"Okay. I'm the night man at the yard. Mechanical and maintenance. We got thirty-eight trucks, a coupla cherry-pickers for the lines, but mostly handivans and Vanagons. My job, I used to be a motor pool ramrod. I was motor pool chief at Da Nang from '66 to '68 for the Third Marines, and the 109th Tactical. You know 'em?"

"Heard of them."

"Yeah. You in?"

"No. I tried but they four-F'd me."

"Four-F'd you? Christ, and you a cop now?"

"Well, I used to play football. I was a pretty good middle-linebacker in Ukiah, and later I played at Cal State. Scouted by Notre Dame, too."

"No shit! What'd they say?"

"They said, what the hell *is* that boy doing?"

"Yeah. Tough. What was it, your knees?"

"The knees, yeah. I was at Fort Ord, the docs asked me to do a couple of things, stair tests. They could hear my knees clicking across the hall. Sounded like a jar full of nails, they said. That was the end of my military career."

"What I heard, you done your share right here at home. I never fired but one shot in anger, and that was during Tet. Tet, wasn't anybody could get to a piece who *wasn't* firing. Whole damned country went up like a frying pan fulla bees. Damned funny, I go through three tours and a whole buncha Veetnam hookers, and here I almost die in my own hometown."

"About the fire? How much do you remember?"

"It was a bad one. I'll never forget it. I'll dream about it. I'm working on this oil pan. One of the guys popped it up there on the Musselshell ridge, hit a rock, up there where they're blasting a new road outta Musselshell? God knows why.''

"I know it.''

"So most of the service vehicles are back. I'm down under in the pit, working up, got a burred bolt on the panhead. I hear this one last truck comin' in, I think, hey who's that? It's late, right? Most of the guys are in hours ago, so this one guy's working real late.''

"They have to sign in?''

"Well, technically they do. But mostly, they just park 'em and lock 'em unless they got a problem with the truck.''

"What time'd this be?''

"Late. I'm on at eight, this was after midnight. It was the last truck in, because he hadda park it way at the far end of the lot, the rest of the trucks got all the good spots—''

He suddenly snapped forward and began to cough, pulling a sheet up into his face.

"Damn . . . god . . . damn.''

Beau had a theory about where this was going, but he didn't want to lead a witness. He drank some juice and waited for Blitzer.

"Anyway—where was I? Whoo! Need to breathe, don't we? Stop a guy from breathing, you get his attention right away there!''

"Spoil his whole day. I like to breathe *all* the time.''

"So—I say, hey fuck it, go back to work. Ten minutes later, the smoke alarm goes off, and I come scuttling out from under the truck. There's smoke drifting in from the lot outside, and it sets off the alarm. If there hadn't been a wind, we'd have lost the whole yard. As it was, I got the can and went racing out there. You could see which truck it was from the windows, 'cause they were glowing. I saw—well, shit. Anyway, I get to the last truck there, I see the way it is, flames all over the forward section. I open the rear doors and . . . well, that wasn't the right thing to do. The air gets to it. Hottest part is halfway up the cab there. Front of the cab, well, there's nothing I can do. Not a thing. If I could, I would have. You—well, the flames are real bad now. And there's this gasoline smell.''

Beau held his peace and waited.

"I don't know. Like airplane glue. Solvent. Something like that. So I give it up, and I'm starting to close the doors, see if that'll slow it down, and wham! The thing just *blows up* in my face. Knocks me on my ass. I get up, race back to the phone, and call the fire department. Then I go back, and you can see the first truck's a goner, nothing I can do for anybody. So

I get in to the one beside it, it has the keys in, and I'm backing it out when—this gets a little fuzzy here—there's smoke all over the place now, and I'm thinking hell, if the tank goes and I'm too close . . . anyway, I stall the fucker.''

"I wouldn't even have *tried*."

"Maybe not. You—you ever seen anything like that?"

"Once. Before I was on the force."

"Well, it's a . . . and anyway, these trucks are mine. I take care of 'em. Know all about 'em. It's my job. It's gonna be on me, this whole fuckup. Been with Mountain Bell since my discharge. Anyway, I get it going again, get it out of the way. Smoke's real bad now. I'm going back for the next one, I get to it, get my hand on it, open the door, and next thing I know I'm lying on my back halfway across the lane and I can hear the sirens coming and the smoke is . . . black. You know. Covering me. Like water coming up. I try to crawl, and the next thing I'm really sure of is I'm in a bed and there's this cowboy standing by the bed looking down at me and saying no, he ain't dead, or something. And there's voices in the room, and I have this thing in my throat and I pass out again."

"That was Tom Blasingame. He's a friend of mine."

"Looks like a gunfighter, some old-time marshal?"

"Yeah. That's him. You okay now?"

"I'll do."

Beau was silent for a long time.

Blitzer studied him sidelong, wondering where this was going.

"The guy who died."

"Yeah?" said Blitzer.

"His name was Hubert Wozcylesko?"

"Yeah. We called him Woz. He was an asshole but what the hell. This mean something to you, Sergeant?"

"Yeah. It does."

13

1130 Hours—June 16—Billings, Montana

Everything went pretty smoothly until he got to the elevator. Trudy caught up with him there, pushing a wheelchair with a vase of flowers in it.

"This is really a phenomenally dumb idea, Beau. Look at you, you can hardly stand up. Dr. Malawala will bust a vein when he gets here!"

She jammed on the brake and swiveled the chair around, her braid flying like a whip, her bright eyes wide and full of professional disapproval. Beau liked her—she was the nicest nurse he'd met in years—but Beau had a limited tolerance for hospitals, and he had just reached it.

He pushed off from the wall and set a little weight on his leg. The muscle sent him an instant warning, strong enough to bring tears to his eyes and drain the blood from his face. Trudy reached out to hold him, but Beau caught her hand in his and held it softly.

"Trudy, am I up for physiotherapy?"

"Yes. Of course. You have about a week of it. That's another reason why you ought to get out of your clothes and back in this chair and go back to your—"

"So what'd they expect me to do in physiotherapy?"

"You'd practice walking at the balance bars. Do some stretches. Learn to use crutches for a while."

Beau leaned forward carefully and kissed her soft cheek. She smelled of baby powder and doughnuts, and he had a pang of feeling in his heart, sharp and sudden, saddening.

"So what am I doing? I'm walking. I'm stretching—no, never mind, honey. My mind's made up on this. Now I've signed out and I've made my bed and folded up my little nightie and I'm all dressed and I left Mr. Blitzer all my juice, and you can take him back those flowers there. A lawyer gave them to me, and I don't like lawyers."

He adjusted his jeans, making room for the big Smith at his belt. The elevator door opened. The Hanrahan rumbled out of it like a bull out of a barn. She took in the scene in a moment, and her thick white face seemed to blossom into patches of red and yellow. She wheeled on Trudy.

"What *are* we doing with this patient, Nurse Corson?"

Beau started to say something, but she raised an imperious hand, pointing a finger the size of a billy club at his head. "As for you, we'll just turn right around and—"

Beau stepped backward into the elevator, pulling Trudy and the wheelchair in with him. The Hanrahan clutched at the doors as they began to close, her coated lips stretching into a large gaping hole, baring a set of teeth as even and yellow as military tombstones. Beau reached up and gently but firmly detached her fingers from the doors. They began to close again.

"I'll call security! You are in no position to—"

"Hey, Hanrahan," said Beau, as the gap narrowed, "do the world a favor. Mutate now and avoid the rush. 'Bye!"

He wiggled his fingers at her as the doors closed. They could hear her voice booming down the shaft as they dropped away. Trudy looked up at the roof of the elevator and started to smile.

"Jesus, mutate now! She's gonna be so pissed!"

"Yeah, I liked it, too. The DA used it on me last Friday. How much trouble will she give you?"

"Hanrahan? Everybody hates her. But we're unionized, and they're short of nurses. I'll be okay."

"Is my credit good for a favor?"

"Yes. But you have to promise to call me. I want to see you again."

That was direct. Times were changing, thought Beau.

"I'm . . . a little old for you, don't you think?"

Trudy watched him for a couple of beats.

"God. I said I wanted to see you. I didn't say I wanted to move in and rearrange your pictures. Anyway, I know what you're going to say. You're old enough to be my father."

"Yes, so—"

"But the important thing is, you're not. If I wait for you to ask me, you'll dither and screw around thinking about it, and I'll be sitting at home for a year watching *Jeopardy*, and then I'll get mad and when you finally *do* call me, I'll tell you I'm busy and then I'll feel bad about that and try to call you back, and you'll have the phone off the hook. *And* I know you're not seeing anybody. I asked. You used to be married to Maureen Sprague, right?"

"Yes. 'Used to be' is the point to remember there."

"Well, no offense, okay, but anybody who couldn't stand her is okay with me. I used to work with her in the Julia Dwight Clinic. We all thought she was a first-class bitch. So we have something in common."

Beau considered it. Why the hell not? He was a good guy. She was safe with him.

"Yes. Okay. I'd like that."

"Good. Now what was the favor?"

"There's a Crow man in here. His name is Charlie Tallbull. Can you find out where he is?"

"Why is he in? Wait! He's the—that was a police chase, right?"

"Right."

"He's in the ICU. That's in the Hogeland Wing. I can take you there, if you want?"

"If he's in the ICU, will we be able to talk to him?"

"I can check."

"When are you off?"

"God, Beau. So soon?"

"No. I mean, will you still be around later today?"

"I get off at four." She handed him a handwritten note. "This is my number, and no, I don't run off copies for everybody."

Beau nodded, grinning.

"Why don't you call me later tonight? I'll tell you if we can see him."

"Okay. While you're at it, can you find out about the young woman—the Indian girl who was brought in by chopper last night?"

"They have her as a Jane Doe. She's in the ICU, too."

She saw something in Beau's face and touched his arm. "Beau . . . this is a good hospital. If there's anything that can be done, they're doing it."

"Thanks, Trudy. I'll call you tonight."

The doors slid back, and they walked out into the lobby. It was filled with visitors. A bright sun glittered on the windshields of the cars parked in the lot. A couple of Big Horn County cops were leaning against a cruiser beyond the glass doors. Moses Harper and Dell Greer.

"There's my ride." He reached down into the chair and handed her the vase of flowers. "You take these back to Bucky. Tell him I'm buying as soon as he gets out. Take care of him, okay?"

She looked up at him, frowning, holding the flowers to her chest. "Beau . . . who takes care of you?"

Beau stopped smiling. "How old are you, Trudy?"

"I'm twenty-eight. Don't change the subject."

Beau kissed her again, gravely, and stepped back, looking at her, swaying a bit on his legs.

"I'll be fine, Trudy. You get on back there before Hanrahan has a stroke."

"You didn't tell me who takes care of you."

"Saint Jude. You know who he is?"

She beamed at him. The elevator doors opened again. "He's the patron saint of lost causes. 'Bye, Beau. Will you be sure and call me?"

"As soon as I've seen the coroner."

"Buy me a drink on it? Promise?"

"Sure. Maybe a cherry soda."

She stuck out her tongue at him. "I drink black russians. I'll be waiting. Bye-bye, Beau!"

Beau watched the doors shut with an odd hybrid sensation of risk and sadness and anticipation. Exhaling, he turned to face the broad marble floor. He crossed it like a kid on new skates trying out the ice.

Moses Harper saw him coming and came through the doors to help him.

"Beau. You look like shit."

"Morning to you, too, Moses. Greer come with you?"

"Yeah. We don't have a lot to do right now. We're still on paid leave until the County sorts out what happened with that girl and her baby."

"Yeah. That was what I wanted to talk to you about."

"So the dispatcher said. Where you wanna go? The Muzzleloader? Or home?"

It was hot outside, and very still. The air smelled of ozone and copper. A blue haze screened the hills to the north. The sky was promising a storm, a promise it usually kept.

"Vlasic still at the morgue?"

"Last we heard."

"Okay. Take me there, willya? We'll talk on the way."

Dell Greer got out of the passenger seat as Beau hobbled around the back of the cruiser. He extended his hand and Beau shook it, sizing him up. Greer was solid and slow, with a broad Nordic face and a little caterpillar moustache even rattier than Hubert Wozcylesko's, but he had clear eyes and a good smile.

"Sergeant McAllister. How are you?"

"I'm fine, Greer. Why don't you call me Beau?"

Greer reddened a bit and smiled again. "Thank you, sir. The creek fight there, that was nasty. When we got to you, you looked pretty bad. We're kinda surprised to see you on your feet so soon."

"Hate hospitals. Thanks for coming over. I wanted to talk to you guys anyway, even before the thing."

Harper and Greer looked at each other.

"Garner said so. Look, you get in the front there. I'll ride in the back."

Beau managed to ease himself into the cruiser without yelping or passing out. Harper and Greer pretended to see nothing, but Harper went slowly over the speed bumps as he drove out of the parking lot. The sun was brilliant, glittering off the windows of the bank buildings and the courthouse tower downtown. They drove awhile in silence.

"Well, sir, what did you want to know?"

This was a tricky situation for Beau. He knew Moses Harper pretty well—they had been together on a couple of upgrade courses in Helena, and Harper had a brother-in-law on the Highway Patrol over in Bozeman. Harper was unmarried, but he showed up sometimes at Fogarty's with a teacher from Yellowstone Technical, and he sat in on some of the poker games with Danny Burt and some of the Highway guys. He played the blues harmonica very well, and anybody who had the nerve to get up in front of a barful of Montana cowboys on a Friday night and play Chicago blues had to have character. Harper had that steadiness about him that made for good sergeants. He'd do well in Big Horn County. Beau had seen him once on a domestic call down in Wyola, a chronic call at an isolated ranch out by Little Grass Creek. The father was a Blood Crow with a gas-sniffing habit. He'd broken his wife's collarbone once that year, and the call came from her seven-year-old daughter. Beau had come along as backup since the rest of the Big Horn cars were off on a bank alarm in Hardin.

Halfway up the dirt drive leading to the ranch house, the man—a boy really, no older than twenty-three, ragged and thin—stepped out onto the porch, weaving, red-eyed, stinking of gas and sweat and fear, holding a Winchester 30-30. As they got out of the cars, they could hear a child screaming in the house. The dispatcher had already told them that the child was talking about blood, and it was basically a very bad situation that showed every sign of getting a whole lot worse in about five seconds.

A lot of cops would have split right and left and shot the man down right there on the porch. It was a Big Horn call, so Beau just eased his Browning in his holster and waited for Moses to make a move.

Moses stood in the drive for a moment as the boy raised the Winchester and told them to get away. Then Moses stepped around to the back of his cruiser and opened the trunk. He reached inside and pulled out a large brown teddy bear with a red ribbon around the neck. He raised it over his head and told the guy they were just here to deliver a teddy bear to his daughter.

The guy let them walk right up to him with the teddy bear, and after a low soft talk with Moses, the man handed over the Winchester and they cuffed him and that was that.

As it turned out, the man had stomach cancer, and they got him into the hospital for treatment. He beat the cancer and he beat his addictions, and now he was working for Charlie Tallbull as a farrier and his wife was pregnant again. The little girl was in trade school up in Billings. She was going to be a dietitian for one of Hogeland's clinics.

After the call, Beau had asked Moses what the hell he was doing. Moses just laughed and said that there wasn't anybody in Montana wanted to go to Deer Lodge Prison and have to tell the rest of the guys that he'd shot a man for attacking him with a stuffed teddy. From that day on, Beau kept one in his own trunk, and he saw to it that everyone else on his watch did the same. It sounded stupid, but it was effective as hell—a cop coming up the driveway with a large pink rabbit just somehow changed the whole atmosphere in a domestic call.

Beau also made sure somebody else on the scene had the man in his sights. Just in case.

Greer he knew very slightly, but he had heard good things about him. Still, he was going to ask them about a car chase that had resulted in two deaths and one grave injury, with no evidence of a felony. *And* Harper and Greer were going to be appearing at the shooting board hearing—whenever *that* was—so there were a lot of potholes to be negotiated here. It was a sensitive inquiry, one that ought to be left to Bill Garner, the sheriff of Big Horn County.

"Okay, first, this is none of my business. I know that."

"So do we," said Greer, from the back seat. "How come you don't take this to Garner directly?"

He was watching the shoppers and the tourists on the streets, but he was listening hard and he was wary.

"Like I said, because this is none of my business. But there's something happening around the county, and I'd look real stupid trying to make this official. I just have a bad feeling."

"Look, Beau," said Moses. "Would you do us a favor? You tell us how it started at Arrow Creek, we'll tell you about Mary Littlebasket and Charlie Tallbull. And we never had this talk, okay?"

"Okay."

Beau took a deep breath and told them about what had happened at Bell's Oasis and his part of the fight down at Arrow Creek. He told it simply, but it took a while. He was telling it partly to make them understand what was on his mind, but as he was telling it, he also realized he wanted to hear another cop's reaction to the whole thing. Had he been right? Could it have gone another way?

The two Big Horn cops listened to him without any reaction but an occasional nod or a short question about a place or a time. Beau ended with the chopper coming down. They were stopped at a red light about a block from the Yellowstone County Courthouse and the morgue.

Dell Greer let out a long sigh. "Better you than me, Sergeant. It was hairy enough, watching Meagher take that one guy on. Next time, I'm staying home."

Moses was watching Beau carefully. "How are you taking this?"

Beau considered it. "I guess I'm ducking the whole thing. I mean, back in the Strike Force, we had a lot of gun calls—"

"Twenty-seven for you personally," said Greer.

"That many? And then that screwup at the Hilltop last year. After a while, you ask yourself, am I . . . *causing* some of this shit? You know what I mean, Moses. I'd never have come out of that trunk with a teddy bear."

"What're you supposed to do, Beau? Way I heard it, you never shot at anybody wasn't shooting or about to shoot."

"Yeah . . . Ballard says I provoked the Hilltop thing. If I'd just let it go, they'd have caught him on the interstate or taken him down someplace where there weren't so many citizens around."

"Or he'd have killed a few people in the mall, or taken a hostage. Anyway, you know there isn't a guy around who would have dodged a call like that. If you hadn't taken him, he might have killed some poor trooper who didn't have your experience. I admire Ballard. She talks rough, but she's a cop's DA. But she's not operational. Nobody's ever shot at her. She's never shot at anybody—"

"I wouldn't bet on that," said Greer.

"At least she's not admitting it. I think, what's getting to you is the girl."

Beau said nothing. This was getting a little out of hand.

"Hey, I know . . . I know you don't want to get into all this. But—way I see it, you'd have something to worry about if you *didn't* feel like this. That's the guy I worry about, the guy who never has any doubts, always charges right in there. Sometimes you gotta shoot, but the day you *like* it, that's a guy I don't want in my car."

Greer coughed and shifted, a creak of saddle leather.

"Anyway, there you go. What can we do, Sergeant. Beau."

"Thanks, Dell. I guess what I need to know is, what happened last week? How did it start?"

Greer had his notebook out. "Okay. We take the call at 0505—day—date—it's just a ten-seventy—Reason we're onto it is the clinic has had a lot of theft from the pharmacy. Ritalin, Valium, Percodan—the usual shit."

"Hell of a lot, actually," said Harper.

"Yeah. So, you know, you gotta jump when you hear it, even though you know it's probably gonna be nothing. So we're up the Whitman Coulee—near your place?"

"Yeah. And?"

"And we're rolling, you know, not burning it, just coming in for the paperwork, and we hear this gunshot."

"*Big* round, too," said Harper, pulling into the Yellowstone morgue lot. Vlasic's four-wheeler was parked at the rear doors. The muddy gray morgue wagon was in a compound, smudged with fingerprint dust and wreathed in crime-scene ribbon and CIB seals.

"Yeah, big round. So we know Bill Haugge—the Rent-a-Cop at the clinic? He has this Ruger, big as a toy truck. That makes it a little more urgent. We burn it in the Hardin road. Come around the corner. There's this brown pickup pulling away—"

"Rusty-red, it was," said Harper.

"Brown. It was a brown pickup."

"South Dakota plate?" asked Beau.

"Yeah. Why?"

"That's Charlie Tallbull's pickup. He keeps it registered in South Dakota because he gets a break on insurance."

"Yeah. I realized—while I was chasing him. All of a sudden I realized it was Charlie Tallbull's truck," said Harper. "If I had known who it was, I wouldn't have been chasing them. I would have driven over to Wyola and waited for him to show up."

"Why did they run?"

Harper and Greer thought it over.

Finally, Harper said, "I think they ran because that asshole Haugge was shooting at them."

"He fired *at* the pickup?"

Harper shook his head. "No—well, he *says* no. He says he fired to get her to stop running."

Beau was trying to keep it all straight. "Mary Littlebasket? Where was she when Haugge fired?"

"According to Bill, she was getting into this pickup."

"Why was he so heated up about it? So some patient checks out without asking. So what?"

"Haugge says he was told by one of the nurses that she—that Littlebasket was stealing—"

Greer interrupted. "I got here in my notes that the nurse told Haugge that Littlebasket was *taking* a baby."

Beau looked around at him. "Taking. *Not* stealing?"

"She says *taking*. The kid was hers."

"Where'd she take the kid from?"

"They have a neonatal and preemie unit. The kid was on a machine of some kind."

"Was the kid sick?"

"Yeah, according to the nurse. Very sick."

Beau looked back at Harper. "Who was the nurse?"

Harper shrugged, looked at Greer in the rearview. Greer coughed and fussed with his uniform collar.

"I get it," said Beau. "It was Maureen."

"Yeah. Maureen Sprague," said Greer. "That's your ex, right?"

"Right. What did Maureen say was wrong with the baby?"

Greer was silent, staring at his notebook.

"Okay . . . baby male . . . it was, I gotta spell this out for you, Beau. A N E N C E P H A L I C. An-en-see-fallic. That mean anything to you?"

"Something about the head. I'd have to ask Maureen. Why was Mary Littlebasket trying to take the kid out of the clinic?"

Harper looked out the side window. Greer drummed a bit on the seatback. Beau waited them out.

"Okay. Here's about the time that things got nasty. Your wife—excuse me, your ex—she's not a real big fan of Indians, is she?"

"No, she's not." Beau didn't feel like explaining about Alice Manyberries, or his daughter Laurel and the way Maureen had driven her out of the house. And Littlebasket was a Crow, too.

"Well, as far as we could get it out of Miss Sprague, the Littlebasket baby was very sick, but his mama wouldn't believe the doctors. I got the impression your—that Maureen Sprague, that she felt this broad—Littlebasket—was just too stupid, just another stupid Indian, like what could you expect, was her attitude. Anyway, Littlebasket wouldn't cooperate with them. She was always crying and saying that the doctors had done this. That they'd done something to her baby and now they were trying to steal it. Maureen said it was postpartum depression. That right?"

"Yeah," said Beau. "It happens sometimes, after delivery. The hormones are all screwed up and the mother can react badly. Especially if the kid turns out to be sick. What I don't get is why Charlie Tallbull would have helped her do something that stupid. He's a sensible guy, he knows the difficulties getting healthy babies out of the reserves. Charlie Tallbull was the one who talked Hogeland into expanding his clinics into Hardin in the first place. Now you tell me he was helping some hysterical girl take her sick kid out of the clinic. It just doesn't make any sense."

Greer handed his notebook over to Beau.

"See that, that drawing there?"

> > > = = = = = = = = = = = > < + > < = = = = = = = = = = = = < < <

"I see it. What about it?"

"It was on her mirror. Mary Littlebasket wrote it on her mirror in lipstick, just before she ran. Mean anything to you, Beau?"

Beau studied it for a while.

"Not offhand. Arrows usually mean protection. Or direction. What this thing in the middle is . . . who's doing the investigation for Big Horn? Garner?"

"Yeah. Bill got us to take shots of the mirror."

"Looks like a warning to me," said Harper, leaning over to examine the notebook page. "I saw that, I'd go the other way."

Beau shook his head, puzzled. "I don't know it. Maybe I can show it to Charlie. It might mean something to him. It's sure as hell Indian."

"I hear Charlie's gonna make it," said Greer.

Beau twisted around again, wincing at the pain in his leg. "Where'd you hear that?"

Greer shrugged. "The guys. One of the C Watch guys has a girlfriend in the ICU there."

"It'd be nice if she was right," said Harper, his face grave. "It'd be nice if something good happened in the middle of this. I never want to see another Kenworth as long as I live."

Beau popped the door and eased his right leg out. Greer and Harper got out and came around to stand beside him. Beau stood with one hand braced on the door latch, looking at Bob Gentile's morgue wagon, parked inside the evidence compound.

Greer and Harper watched him for a minute.

"You sure you ought to be outta the hospital, Beau?" said Harper. "You don't look too great."

"I'll be okay. Anybody hear how Peter Hinsdale's family is taking it?"

"About the way you'd expect."

Beau was seeing the kid's face, seeing the fear and the need in it. He had failed that kid.

Harper put a hand on Beau's shoulder. "It was rat-fuck, Beau. It wasn't your fault. You'll see. The shooting board'll clear you, no sweat."

Beau pushed himself off the door and eased his weight onto his right leg. He shifted his Smith and started to hobble toward the back door. Halfway there, he looked back at Greer and Harper.

"Moses. How did Charlie Tallbull manage to get out of the pickup? Was he thrown?"

Harper's face was grim. Greer answered for his partner.

"Moses got him out. He had to climb in under the Kenworth to do it. It was pretty bad. Moses had to leave the girl and her baby, they were all—"

"Beau's got the picture, Dell."

Beau nodded toward the two troopers. "You guys are on leave right now. That right?"

"Yep."

"If I need some help, can I call you?"

Harper and Greer looked at each other.

"Can we clear it with Garner?"

"I'll do that, if you like?"

"Okay, Beau. If Garner says so, we'll do what we can. But what the hell are we supposed to be doing?"

"Well, can you look into the fire at the Mountain Bell yard?"

Harper nodded. "I've got some buddies in the fire department. I'll get them to pull me a sheet. Are we looking for anything special?"

"Yeah," said Beau, turning. "But I'm damned if I know what it is yet. See you guys at the shooting board."

Marco Vlasic was bending over a stainless-steel sink, washing his forearms with yellow soap and talking into a hanging microphone when Beau shuffled into the pathology lab. He turned and stared at Beau, a gnomish young man with a perpetual crease of worried concentration scarring his pale forehead. Still talking into the mike, Vlasic smiled and held up a hand, three fingers spread out.

Beau nodded and walked away toward the row of steel tables. The room was lit by a bank of fluorescent lights that bleached out everything to pale green or pale purple or shiny steel and white, like an old film that has lost its colors.

There were nine bodies visible, lying on stainless-steel trays, covered with plastic sheets, translucent and cold-looking. The bodies looked as if they had been frozen in blocks of ice. The room smelled of Lysol, stale blood, and old meat. Beau walked around until he reached one that looked familiar. He pulled the plastic sheet away from the head. And winced.

Marco finished washing up and hit a switch on the wall, shutting off the tape. He came over and stood next to Beau, drying his hands on a paper towel.

"What a difference a day makes, eh, Beau? What the hell are you doing here? Meagher said you were out of it, on your back in the hospital."

"I got better."

"Yeah? You don't look it. You look like last year's roadkill in a plaid shirt. The hospital release you like this?"

"They weren't happy about it."

"I guess not. Maybe you oughta go back, Beau. They had plans for you."

"I had other plans. Skip it, Marco."

"Okay . . . anyway, you wanna see your guy? I got him over there, next to the door."

"In a minute. You have a guy in here, victim of a fire? Wozcylesko. Would have died in a van fire."

"Yeah, he was here. They took him over to Sweetwater General to do a toxicology run on him. Sweetwater has a contract with the state agencies. Anything accidental that affects a civil employee, it goes to Sweetwater for the insurance investigation. They just brought him in here for the coroner's ID."

"Mountain Bell's not a state agency."

"No, but the insurer is state-contracted, so it amounts to the same thing. What's the problem?"

"No problem. I was just curious, you know? You get a chance to look at him?"

"A once-over. Danny Burt was waiting for him, real impatient. Gentile's has the wagon contract for Sweetwater General, too. I was just supposed to sign the certificate."

"So what'd you sign him off on?"

"This a police matter, Beau?"

"I don't know. Hell, I don't know anything lately. I saw the kid earlier in the evening. He was at Bell's Oasis."

"That's supposed to be suspicious? What was he doing there?"

"Fixing the phones."

Vlasic clapped a palm to his forehead, bugged his eyes wide, and staggered backward a yard, weaving dramatically.

"*No!* Holy Connections, Batman! You mean, a Mountain Bell guy was actually *fixing a phone*? No wonder you were suspicious!"

Beau suppressed a cranky snarl. "Funny, Marco. Real amusing."

"Well, jeez, Beau. I've been through enough autopsies with you. Sometimes you see things, they aren't there. Anyway, the party line on Wozcylesko is accidental death. He was smoking in the van, van was full of flammable vapor from a can of solvent. Cause of death, terminal stupidity! Happens all the time."

"Whose party line?"

"What do you mean?"

"Who's saying it was accidental?"

Vlasic looked at Beau for a time, his hand resting on the tray, his eyes narrowed.

"Beau. Is something going on in town?"

"Christ. In *Billings*? Nothing ever goes on in Billings, Marco. People drive all the way to Coeur d'Alene just to blink. I don't know, Marco. Look around you. You ever been this full before?"

"Lots of times, Beau. How about last September? That eighteen-wheeler thing? Guy has a heart attack, slams into a rest stop. Life's a lottery, Beau."

"What was he smoking?"

"Who?"

"The kid—what was he smoking in the van?"

"Well, Beau. My guess'd be tobacco. Most people, you see them smoking, they're smoking tobacco. Hardly ever see anybody smoking turnips lately, and the whole asparagus craze is pretty well over. Now and then, you'll see a guy light up a hamster, but the little fuckers squeal like hell, plus they go out too easy and you can't keep the filters on 'em. Nope, my guess, I'm definitely going with tobacco."

"How about dope? Anybody find out exactly *what* he was smoking? Find a butt or a roach?"

"In *what*? The van was totaled."

"Who's doing it for the fire department?"

"I'll find out. Want me to get the form?"

"No. I think Moses Harper'll do that for me."

"Since when is Big Horn County working for Highway Patrol?"

"Meagher's getting Garner to do me a favor, lend me some guys. I needed somebody from another force who wasn't going to have to answer to the CIB."

"What is there you have to keep from the CIB? Or is it Howdy Klein? Finch Hyam's partner? Now *that's* a reason. Howdy is a depressingly stupid butthead with the forensic brilliance of a balpeen hammer. Which everybody but Klein knows already."

"It's coming down to, why the hell did I shoot Joe Bell instead of the people who were robbing him?"

"Sounds reasonable."

"Yeah. If it really *was* a robbery."

Beau stood in silence for a long time. Vlasic was used to Beau's ways and was at any rate a fairly self-contained and steady man, working as he did at the near shore of the Styx and in regular contact with the boatman. He waited patiently.

Sighing again, he gestured at the corpse in front of them. "What happened to this guy?"

"He got Meagherized. See this here?"

He put his fingers against the leathery cheek and pushed the head to the side, revealing a massive neck wound. The skin looked rubbery and pale, pulling back from the ruined muscle and cartilage beneath it. Pink slivers rode in the blue meat, and arteries showed like white worms in the exposed muscle at the neck.

"Buckshot?"

"Full bore. Meagherized unto death. Too bad the lieutenant got him in the head there. Would have made a nice mount. Put it up on the wall behind his desk. It'd look good with all his FBI stuff. One aboriginal male in his prime."

Vlasic pulled the plastic all the way down to the foot of the tray. The torso was thick and muscular. Two incisions started at the points of the shoulders and ran inward, where they met the major cut, which ran from the breastbone down to the pubic bone. The man's face was puffed and swollen, and the features had that imbalance that comes when the calvarium is removed and the skull-flap is peeled back over the face. The man's head stopped at his eyebrows. Long thick black hair was matted around the back of the neck. The rest of his skull was missing. Beau could see the interior of the skull, like the inside of a nautilus shell, the arches and supports for the absent brain, the basal roots, the white nub of the upper vertebrae. Vlasic lifted the heavy left arm, let it fall.

"Rigor was sudden and passed in a couple of hours. Mainly confined to the face and upper neck. What we had here was an aboriginal male, in middle age, no congenital malformations visible. The eyes and the conjunctiva were normal, although there was some sign of old trauma in the left orb. Nares patent. Teeth all fucked up. Can't have good teeth in America without cash. Hemorrhage in the canals consistent with ballistic trauma. See here, this entrance wound exposed the carotid, pulled back on the lines of cleavage. This discoloration is normal postmortem lividity *in situ*. No forensic significance. Hey, we're not looking for cause of death, anyway. You been to the shooting board yet?"

"Not yet. Probably sometime Monday."

"Who's gonna sit on it?"

"Hell—probably the usual. Meagher. Vanessa Ballard. Finch. Maybe Rowdy Klein."

"Klein? You're right to worry about him, Beau. He was in here earlier, taking pictures of everything. The CIB's got something unseemly planned for you, I'll bet. Anyway, how's Meagher gonna sit on a shooting board when he's one of the shootees? You better keep your back to the wall."

"I'll wear my chain-mail boxers, Marco. You were saying?"

"About the internal, we did the usual thoraco-abdominal incision. No hernias, domes were normal. So were the pleurals. Pericardium okay, contents normal. Mediastinum as well. Pharynx had clotted blood, same source. You want the whole thing? Lungs and lights?''

Beau shook his head. "Let's go straight to dessert, Marco.''

"Well—stomach showed some incipient ulceration. Blood in the mucosa. Liver had some signs of previous hepatitis, but no necrosis.''

"Drugs? Needle sharing?''

"No tracks. No signs. I'd say, more likely he caught it on a reservation. Doesn't look like a user to me. No, I wanted to show you something—give me a hand here, I want to turn him.''

Beau studied the Y-shaped incision. "Those stitches hold?''

Vlasic glanced down, grinned. "Like in that old *M.A.S.H.* movie, eh? Use big stitches, he's an enlisted man. Hell, Beau, he's not going to be hitting the beach anytime soon. He doesn't care if he looks neat. They'll hold. I'm a pathologist, not a seamstress.''

"That's for sure. He looks like you stapled him together.''

"Here, just help me lift him up there.''

"You lift him. I just had breakfast.''

"Wimp. There . . . whoof. See these?''

Vlasic had rolled the body onto its side, exposing the back. The skin was stained with red blotches where the blood had settled. But Beau could see a row of white circles, five of them, each the size of a quarter and shiny with scar tissue. Vlasic let the body drop back onto the tray. The left arm flipped out and hung down at the side. Vlasic raised it back to the tray and arranged the body in a more natural position.

"What do you make of those, Beau?''

"Bullet wounds. Automatic weapons. The guy took a burst in the back. I'd say a long time ago. Big rounds. And fast. Probably military.''

"I'd say so. There were three exit wounds in the lower abdomen, and the pelvic bone showed severe scoring. But old. And the rounds were spent, or they'd have blown him apart. Ran into an ambush, probably. I think we have a Vietnam vet here, unless he was a mercenary. Caught a burst in Rhodesia—Zimbabwe now—or in Angola.''

Beau studied the blunt brutal features. Vlasic had closed the man's eyes, but the movement had brought one lid up a bit, and the lower half of a cloudy black iris showed.

"Looks like a hard-handed man.''

Vlasic was wiping his hands on a cloth soaked in alcohol.

"Not anymore—now he's mulch. You want to see the one you popped?''

"Christ, Marco. You're such a sensitive guy."

"*Vita brevis*, Beau. Especially when you're on the case. Come over here, take a look at this."

Vlasic pulled the cover back over the body. Beau watched it come up with a feeling composed of two parts sadness at the waste of life and one part joy that he was standing up looking down. Better you than me, friend.

"Now this is shooting, Beau. Classic head shot. Picture perfect. Such a good shot, you must have been aiming at something else."

He was staring across the ruined flesh at Beau, a twist in his right cheek. The blue downlight gave him a sardonic shadowing. Beau took a long breath and came around.

The body lay on its back, naked, arms splayed out and slightly curled. One eye was closed, and one side of the dark and heavy-featured face seemed serene, at rest.

The other side of the face was gone. There was a ragged green and purple hole under the right eye. The orb itself was milky and protruded from the socket. Teeth and white bone showed in the crater that had been his cheek.

"And his wounds were all before him. Certainly wasn't running away when you fired. What the hell did you use on him, Beau? A LAWS rocket?"

Vlasic raised the head and turned it on the limp neck. A massive exit wound, star-shaped, gaped in the blue light.

"See that. Like the nine-fourteen from Doomsville. Took him in the cheekbone there, powered right through, no deviation, no deflection. Hell of a round. You using that big nine-mill?"

"Yeah, the nine-mill. Jesus, Marco, put him down, willya? This isn't a contest."

Vlasic's smile flickered off and then back on. He shook his head. "Yes, it was, Beau. That's exactly what it was. This guy's a killer. You can see it in him. You can smell it in him. Here's a guy, been handing out death for a long time. You remember that when Vanessa and the gang start snapping and snarling at you tomorrow. I see a lot of death, Beau. Most of the people I see didn't deserve it. But now and then, you see one like this, looks like it dropped in from the Jurassic period. A killer. The world's a better place without things like this walking around upright."

Beau stared down at the man for a long time.

There was a hell of a lot of dying going on around him, and none of it was making very much sense. This man had done his very best to kill Beau and had probably killed Peter Hinsdale as well. Maybe he deserved to die. But a lot of people who deserved to live were dead, and not everyone who died had died well or timely. He put out his hand and touched the shattered face. It felt damp and cool. A rough beard scraped against his fingertips.

There were two new scars above the man's nipples. Lateral scars, paired like a mathematical symbol. Parallels.

"What do you make of these marks?"

Vlasic studied them for a bit.

"I've been wondering about them. We have what's left of that Gall kid, the one these guys tried to steal? You don't wanna see him. He's pretty well toast. Shrunk down. Classic pugilist effect, you know, from the muscles contracting. Skin all baked off. But you could see there'd been—not incisions. They were into the pectoral muscles, just like here."

Beau remembered those marks, and Finch and Klein had been talking about them at Bell's Oasis.

"I saw them on the kid Bell shot. They were brand new, too. What do you figure made those marks? Animals? Some kind of machinery?"

"Hooks, maybe. Signs of tearing and pulling. Let me show you."

Vlasic selected a scalpel from a standing tray and leaned over the broad chest, placing his fingers in a fan over the scar. He drew a thin arc. The skin opened behind the knife, showing blue flesh underneath. Vlasic peeled the tissue back, exposing the pink complex of muscles and ribs.

"See here—that's tearing. Where the muscle has actually ripped. Somebody put a hook into this guy and pulled on it until the muscle ripped out. Ring a bell with you?"

"Not immediately."

"No? Think *Dances With Wolves. Little Big Man.*"

Then it came to Beau. He saw it complete, felt himself at the edge of illumination.

"Sun Dance? The ritual thing. Warriors used to do it—it was some kind of purification thing. Crazy Horse refused it. Sitting Bull went through it, just before the Custer battle. They have somebody pierce their chests with claws or something. The claws are attached to cords that go to the roof of the lodge, and they dance around the lodgepole, leaning back on the cords, putting their weight on it, until—"

Vlasic was nodding vigorously, bright with approval and enthusiasm.

"Until the cord breaks or the muscle tears. Try that the next time you're depressed. You're good, Beau. Didn't think you paid any attention to history."

"Marco, you can't cross a coulee or ford a bend of any river in this state, anywhere west of the Missouri, without thinking about the people who used to live here. The country's haunted."

"So what do you make of this?"

Beau and Vlasic studied the body in silence.

"Well," said Beau, finally, stepping back and drawing a long breath, "nobody's gonna do that for fun. Why not just get a tattoo? No, this guy, he meant business. He was getting ready for something big. Something that meant a lot to him."

Vlasic pushed the flesh into place and stepped back, reaching for an antiseptic tissue. He wiped his hands in an absent way, thinking about the puzzle.

"So the original beef was robbery, right?"

"That's the story," said Beau.

"But you don't buy it?"

Beau was quiet for a while.

"It's like this, Marco. Usually, when you're trying to figure out why something happened, something criminal, it's best to take the most obvious reason. Like, a wife gets killed, you take a hard look at the husband or the boyfriend. A bank gets taken for a major score, you look at the staff. There's a hit in a crack house, you look at the tenants or the dopers next block over. Life's pretty simple. But that Gall kid? He had close to seven hundred dollars in his pocket when he died. That doesn't fit a robbery."

"It would fit if it was part of an organized operation. Remember the Panthers, back in the sixties?"

"Organized for what, Marco?"

"Look at these wounds here. Can you imagine the pain involved, Beau? I cut myself shaving, it's all I can do to get up the nerve to put on aftershave. Call it my manhood test. Scream when I do it, too. Drives my wife crazy. How you figure this guy here got the nerve to go through something like a Sun Dance?"

Beau shifted on his leg. The pain seemed electric. He saw it in his mind, a jagged bolt of blue lightning racing up his arteries, slamming into his brain.

Beau breathed out slowly and put a hand out on the edge of the table. Marco stepped toward him, then stepped back.

"How do people firewalk, Marco? Even Yuppies, New Age loonies in Oregon, they walk across red-hot coals. How do they do that?"

"Pain's a mindless thing, Beau. Cut up these bodies, you can see the wiring. But it all runs to the brain, and the brain does what the mind tells it.''

"That's a little simplistic, Marco.''

"Sure it is. I'm talking to you, right?''

"Right. So you're saying, this guy was in a trance or something when this happened, when he went through this ritual?''

"Exactly. And what does that say about him?''

Suddenly, Beau felt very tired. His hand trembled on the stainless cart. "It says . . . belief. Fanatical belief.''

"Yeah. You know SPEAR's into this thing, don't you? You read about it in the *Gazette*?''

"Not yet. What's the story?''

"Wait here. No, better yet, go over there and sit down. I'll be right back.''

Marco led him over to a wooden chair at the end of a row of tables. Beau settled into it and put his head back against the wall. Vlasic looked at him for a second, then walked into his office.

Beau found himself staring at the top of a dead woman's head. Her hair was black and shiny, worn in two braids. Her skin was pale brown, and her young breasts rose up under the plastic.

Beau looked away, closed his eyes, and tried to will the pain away. It wouldn't go. He figured that was the price of being a lapsed Catholic. If he still believed, maybe he could rise above the pain on a cloud of religious ecstasy. Like Cochise over there, riding a steel tray all the way to Valhalla.

Vlasic came back, folding a newspaper flat against his green hospital overalls.

"Here we go. 'An attempted armed robbery ended in death' . . . wait a minute, it was farther on here. Yeah, here we are. 'Spokespersons for the Society for the Protection of Ethno-American Rights have protested the shootings and the publicity surrounding them. The American Civil Liberties Union—' ''

"Oh, fuck,'' said Beau, closing his eyes even tighter.

"Oh yeah. This shit's their bread and butter. They've applied for intervenor status—''

"They'll never get that.''

"No. But they'll get permission to audit. Have a lawyer at the hearings or whatever. Some BlueStones woman, she's trying to link the accident out in Hardin with this. She's talking about 'institutional hostility.' ''

"Man, the shit never stops, does it, Marco?''

"It's tidal, Beau. It comes up and goes down. Right now, you're in a high-water period, shit-wise. Anyway, my point is, you oughta be thinking cults. Terrorists. Remember those AIM guys? Russell Means? The guys who took over Wounded Knee?"

"Yeah, I remember. And I watched those Mohawks awhile back, at Oka. They killed a Quebec provincial cop. Took the Canadian Army to get them out of there."

"Right! I tell you, Beau, this native rights thing, it's building. It's politically correct. All the university assholes are into it. These guys could be the . . . I don't know."

"The fund-raisers?"

"Yeah!"

"You got the old man here?"

"Yeah, he's in a cooler. Wanna see him?"

"What killed him?"

"It was a race."

"A race?"

"He had emphysema and diabetes and renal dysfunction. Any one of them coulda taken him out."

"What did?"

"Cut his own throat. Neatly, too. One downstroke on the external jugular. Still had the knife in his hand when they brought him in here. Klein photographed it *in situ,* then bagged it for evidence."

"So out of the five people who showed up in Yellowstone County last Friday morning, we got one Edward Gall dead of shotgun wounds inflicted by Joe Bell, the old guy is probably Jubal Two Moon, that fits. What about the others? Did Klein have the IDs?"

"Not yet. He lifted prints from all of them except Gall, and we already know who he is. Sent the prints to the feds. He's onto Frank Duffy to get his guys in Quantico working on it. Head shots and prints to the army. But right now, we got them as John Does One and Two. They didn't find anything on the others. Not even labels. We do have Peter Hinsdale ID'd."

"Is he here?"

"Not now. Klein had him done first so Danny Burt could take him, along with the Wozcylesko kid. Had to get him cleaned up for his mother."

"What killed him?"

"He was disemboweled. Somebody opened him up from his belly to his sternum. One upward stroke with a big combat knife. When it went in, the hilts bruised his skin. We got a nice imprint of the hilt. Klein has a shot of it. Boy came in here with most of his intestines down around his knees. Had about a pint of blood left in him. Nasty.''

"Klein have the knife?''

"The knife?''

"Yeah. The one Klein says killed Hinsdale.''

Vlasic considered that. "Okay . . . now that you remind me, I'd say no. He didn't have it. Guess it'd be in the river somewhere?''

"Yeah. Guess it would be.''

Beau was silent, thinking that Peter Hinsdale was another one of *his* victims. If he'd left Hinsdale in the coffin, maybe the kid would still be alive. What a miserable performance. Maybe Dwight Hogeland was right about him—maybe he *was* a toxic cop.

"Hey, Beau . . . thinking like that will kill you. You didn't kill Hinsdale. You killed the guy who killed him. You're a good guy. These are the bad guys. You know that.''

"Most of the time. . . . So, out of the five people who drove a blue Ford pickup into Bell's Oasis last Friday, we have one dead of shotgun wounds, one dead of nine-mill, one Meagherized, one suicide, and a girl I gunbutted— that about right?''

"More or less. So what? Like I said, shit's tidal.''

"Not very efficient, are they?''

"Well . . . ''

"Can't raise a lot of cash when you're dead, can you?''

"No? Ask the Catholics. Their leader's been dead for two thousand years. You ever see the Vatican? Hell of a corporate headquarters. And their logo's a dead guy stapled to a tree.''

"So your theory—the bows, the arrows, the traditional wounds— all that means another native uprising? Maybe connected to SPEAR? And this . . . unit is part of that, and their job is to rob gas stations and banks and earn money for the uprising?''

"It fits everything, doesn't it, Beau?''

"It's a damned complicated explanation for it. And I don't like it.''

Marco was watching Beau's face. "Beau, you gonna faint?''

"Not immediately . . . I just feel tired. Think I'll go back home, see the cats. Get some sleep.''

"Can I drive you?''

"What about these guys?''

Marco swiveled on his heel, surveyed the room. "They'll still be dead tonight. Frank'll put them in the coolers. Come on, let me take you home.''

Beau got slowly to his feet.

"One more thing. You seen Danny Burt yet?"

"Yeah. When he took away Hinsdale and Wozcylesko yesterday."

"How was he?"

"Hell. You know Danny. He's like an old boot full of piss and hot peppers. Wrists a little marked-up from where he was tied. Madder than hell about the Indians making a fool of him. Pretty upset about the Hinsdale kid. Not that he liked him, but the kid was his responsibility."

"Where's he now?"

"Working. He's coming back later for another load."

"Another load? What's he taking?"

"Beau, look around. You think we should stack 'em up in the corner? Hang 'em by their heels in the window?"

"You're a sick person, Marco. I've always admired you for that. Can I have this copy of the paper?"

Vlasic handed it to him and took Beau's left arm in a surprisingly strong grip. Beau felt muscle and wire in the small man's shoulders and across his back as Vlasic helped him toward the door. Beau looked back toward the young woman under the sheet. A terrible suspicion rose up out of his belly and drove the blood from his face. He stopped Vlasic with a pressure on his shoulder.

"Marco—who's that under the sheet there?"

Vlasic looked back at the corpse. He realized the connection Beau had made.

"No, Beau, that's not her. Read it in the paper here. That girl, she's in Sweetwater General. In the ICU. This isn't her. Hell, Beau, somebody would have told you!"

"Nobody's been telling me anything, Vlasic. I haven't heard from Eustace, I haven't heard from any of the guys. Didn't even get a call from the Benevolent Association."

Vlasic shrugged. "This is somebody else here. Young Cheyenne girl, died in childbirth. Sad story."

"Anything I should know?"

Vlasic moved under Beau's arm. He was quiet for a moment.

"Not really. It's reservation stuff. She was a hooker, you know. Hospital does *pro bono* work through the clinic in Hardin. Guess you knew that?"

Beau did. Maureen worked at the Julia Dwight Clinic in Hardin. She had always told Beau horror stories about lives being wasted on the reservations. He nodded, and Vlasic started to walk them both toward the exit.

"So she's hooking around the county, and she must have forgotten her pills, or whatever. She gets knocked up."

"That's odd. A hooker has her kid? Most of them go to the Dwight Clinic or somewhere and get an abortion."

"Yeah. Well, somebody tried one on her. You can see the marks on the cervix. But it was pretty amateur. Anyway, she carried for another two months, then went into premature labor. Died from internal bleeding. She was admitted last Friday night. She'd already lost most of her blood. They did what they could."

"What about the kid?"

Vlasic looked away. "We got him here. You don't wanna see him. Take my word."

"Why?"

"Anencephalic. Premature. Deformed as well. By any definition, a gork. Lived a few minutes, but you don't try real hard for something like that. They put it on a tray in a storage closet and let it die. Christ, Beau! What's the matter?"

Beau was staring at the young girl. "Is Mary Littlebasket here?"

"Who's she?"

"She's the Crow girl who was killed in that accident last week, down in Hardin."

Vlasic was shaking his head. "No. They took her back to the clinic in Hardin. She was DOA. I think her family came to get her. That'd be the routine. We'd only get her if there was some kind of question about cause of death."

"I want to see this woman's baby."

"No, you don't. Anyway, I'm not sure we still have him. If the family doesn't want the baby—this girl's family doesn't even want *her* body—then we usually give it to the students."

"*Students?*"

"The interns. For research."

"Where?"

"Where d'you think? Sweetwater General's the catch-basin hospital for most of eastern Montana. It's a teaching hospital as well. So they'd want anything like that, an anomalous baby."

"Is a baby with that condition . . . "

"Anencephaly?"

"Anencephaly. Is a baby with anencephaly a rare thing?"

Vlasic shook his head. "Not these days. Happens a lot."

"What causes it?"

"Christ. What causes anything? Something goes wrong in the fertilization. Genetic material is damaged. There are millions of cells in a single developing fetus. It's amazing that any of them come out right. I'd say, poor nutrition has a lot to do with it. And drugs. The reserves are full of addicts, gas sniffers, glue sniffers, the gene pool's a mess because of inbreeding. Families in decay. It's a hell of a thing. Don't get me started on it."

"So the chances of there being two anencephalic babies in a couple of weeks, born to reservation women, that's not out of the ordinary?"

"Who's the other?"

"Mary Littlebasket. Her kid was anencephalic, too."

"Yeah. Well, I don't know. Sure, it might be pushing the odds. But I doubt it. Statistical regression, Beau."

"What does that mean?"

"Things even out. If it gets real good for a long time, it'll probably get real bad for a while. If you roll a chain of sevens at the crap table, you think it's luck. But it's just math. If you paid attention, you'd see the same dice roll out a string of random junk. It would all boil down to statistical averages. The only reason people believe in luck is because they don't keep accurate records. They see what they want to see. If the reserve had several months of healthy babies, then a month of preemies and deformed kids, the tribe would say, look, this is evil, there's something evil at work. They'd do something, have a sing, cast out someone they didn't trust. Around the same time, statistical regression would see to it that the births leveled out again. The tribe would say, look, the magic worked. But a scientist would know it was going to stop and turn around anyway. That's why there's so much superstition in the world, why people believe in curses and astrology and runs of good luck."

"So a couple of deformed babies, that's nothing out of the ordinary."

"Not if you take the long view, no. Poor bastards. They're having a hell of a time down there. Hookers and dead babies. Makes you think a bit about SPEAR, maybe. If these guys are part of some kind of new Indian movement, they might believe they have a case to make."

"Custer died for our sins, Marco."

Vlasic twisted his mouth. "There was a hell of a lot of dying going on around here before Custer showed up. You know that, Beau. Better than most."

Beau was looking at the young woman.

"Would there be records about the incidence of deformed births on the reserves?"

"Sure. Why not ask Doc Hogeland about it? He's a friend of yours."

"I will. What'll happen to her?"

Vlasic raised his hands, a gesture of helplessness. "Nobody claims her, she goes to the hospital."

"To the students?"

"That's right."

"How much to bury her?"

"Five, six hundred. Depends on the coffin. Are *you* going to spring for that?"

Beau hesitated a long time.

"No, no, I'm not. Goddamn it, I can't afford it."

Vlasic stared at Beau for a long time.

Finally he said, "Beau, let's get you home."

14

1800 Hours – June 16 – Lizardskin, Montana

Every road leads homeward, angel. If you're lucky.

Vlasic insisted on buying Beau a meal. They ate at the Muzzleloader and talked in careful generalities, settling on the Bobcats and their pennant chances while Beau toyed with a bowl of barley soup and a mug of Lone Star. By the time they reached the Lizardskin road, the sunset was casting yellow fire across the polished hood of Vlasic's Cherokee. Ahead of them the hardtop gave way to stones and the stones gave way to dirt, to the red dust and yellow earth of the Whitman Coulee.

In the Far West, shreds of cirrus and altostratus spread across a teal-blue sky. The hills crowded close, dark as buffalo bulls on either side of the road. The air smelled of rain and lightning and pine trees. The headlights swept around the hills, picking out a sweep of sage or a stand of cottonwoods. Overhead a few pale stars glittered through the gathering dark.

Beau drifted in and out of sleep on the way back home, his head coming forward, then jerking back as he woke. Vlasic said little once they turned off the interstate at Hardin and climbed north up the Lizardskin road toward the Pine Ridge range.

Vlasic was humming a nameless tune, and the car's motion rocked Beau gently. His face was still and set in hard lines in the light of the dying sun. He was trying to see his way through this thing.

Apart from a few years spent working with the Interagency Strike Force—something he had done to distract himself from the apparently bottomless pain of losing Alice—Beau's career had been a slow and, as far as he was concerned, seemly progression through the ranks. If he'd gone to war, he would have been a middle soldier, not on point and not on drag, just a trooper with the rest of the boys. Life was too short to get all fired up over promotions and corner offices. He did the job and cut no slack. Hooked them and booked them and never looked back. It was a steady and soothing rhythm, something he could depend on to give shape and structure to the formless reality of life. Nor would he engage in the thousand petty intrigues that make up the typical cop society anywhere in the world.

He longed for no one's job, he coveted no man's influence. Meagher could have the whole damned state. Run for governor, like old Doc Darryl had a few years back. He had even resisted a promotion to sergeant, but Meagher wouldn't leave it alone. It was Eustace who had signed him up for the sergeant's examination, and Meagher who had drilled him on the questions.

Nor was Beau inclined to run against the pack, especially if the pack was hunting for someone to blame. If the ACLU was getting involved, then you could kiss good-bye to any chance there might have been to find out what had really happened with Joe Bell anyway. All the ACLU ever wanted to accomplish was the crucifixion of as many police officers as possible in the time available. Meagher would fight that very hard, by any means, the best of which would be silence.

Anyway, did it really matter now? The dead were dead, and the dead had gone looking for death. Montana had simply obliged them, something Montana had been doing for a million years. Montana was soaked to the grass roots with blood and bitter outcomes. It was a wonder the well water didn't run red.

So it was just a matter of bookkeeping now, of writing up the sheets and filing the proper forms and stonewalling the ACLU. Nothing Beau did would bring back the dead or ease the living. As for Joe Bell—there was a man, sooner or later, who would get into something that would take him down. That Bell was involved in something illegal, or unnatural, or both, was obvious. So what?

Most of the business west of the Mississippi River was run by some buried clique or cadre of semilegal operators, trading favors and passing around inside information on the golf course or at the Cattleman's Club or in the hallways up at the capitol. That was the way of things ever since the Johnson County wars. The owners divvied up the oil or the copper or the cattle or the pine trees or the real estate. You played by their rules, or you left the territory, walking or carried, flying or buried. The only reason any of the western states had a capital was so you knew where to go to find somebody to bribe.

It was the American way, wasn't it?

If there was any message in the last decade, it had to be that money made the rules. Free enterprise, a level playing field—all that shit was a cover, like having the feds regulate the stock market in New York. Campeau bleeds Bloomingdale's, then splits to Europe to build a ten-million-dollar castle and moon the regulators. Icahn does the same to an entire airline. Keating and the rest find a way to personally screw practically every pensioner in the Southwest. Fuck it, was Beau's attitude. Why raise a sweat over it? It was a zero-sum game anyway; the rich got obscenely richer by screwing the poor, and the feds stood by with their hands out, waiting for a cut.

Beau was going to go into Billings someday, get that message tattooed on his chest, so he could rip his shirt open when somebody pressed some private grief or excess misery into his hands:

EXCUSE ME BUT YOU'VE OBVIOUSLY MISTAKEN ME
FOR SOMEONE WHO GIVES A SHIT

Yeah, that's the ticket. Go home, have a Percodan and a bath and call in the cats, get a good night's sleep.

That was the thing to do, okay.

Oh, Christ! And call Trudy. Be sure to call Trudy.

Or *not* to call Trudy?

No. Call Trudy. Try for a life, Beau. Show some backbone.

And forget about all this detective bullshit.

Yes sir.

So . . .

So what?

So, just for curiosity, what *was* that package under Bell's desk? Something so vile that even Joe Bell wanted to keep it hidden.

Christ, what would be vile enough to shame Joe Bell?

Something very vile.

Or something very valuable?

So valuable that he had gotten Hubert Wozcylesko to go back to the station and steal it for him?

Steal it? Why? It was Bell's place, after all.

Bell couldn't wait. Why?

Because the place was crawling with cops, and he wasn't around to keep an eye on where they looked.

So whatever it was, it was something so kinky that any cop who found it would start in asking rude questions right away.

So the Woz got in there and took it.

Then what happened?

Did somebody take it from the Woz?

And kill him doing it?

And what made Beau think he was going to be able to do anything at all about it?

And why did he care?

Perhaps that was why the road back to Lizardskin seemed different to him. Something had changed in him, some part of him had been altered by the last two days.

Vlasic was singing out loud now. He had a pretty good voice for a coroner.

What was different?

Vlasic was singing "Annie Laurie," in a high clear tenor voice, softly, to himself, his young face uplit by the green dashboard lights, staring out at the road, his hands strong on the leather-wrapped wheel. Now a few heavy drops of rain were striking the windshield, and Vlasic, still singing, leaned forward to turn on the wipers. "Annie Laurie" was a lonely song, a soldier's song really, from another time, another war.

"Marco."

"Hey, Beau. I thought you were sleeping."

"How recent is the word on how that girl's doing?"

"The one you—the survivor?"

"Yes."

"According to Klein, and this is a couple hours old, she's still in the ICU at Sweetwater."

"Klein say what her condition was?"

Vlasic looked across at Beau. The rain began to come down hard. It made a drumming noise on the tin roof and hissed against the glass.

"He says she—well, she has considerable skull trauma. She's been in a coma."

"Who's her doctor?"

"Doc Darryl was looking at her. I know he had Nate Seidelman take a look at her, too. Seidelman operated to relieve the subdural pressure. Her heart was steady and her lungs were good. The question is—you know. Head injuries."

"Yeah. I know."

"She's young, though. They figure no older than nineteen. Twenty. She's strong, too."

Beau knew that. Better than anyone. She had fought him in silence, the only sound her breathing and the grunt of muscular effort. She had done her best to slice him wide open.

So why did he feel what he was feeling?

Nobody fights like that for money. They fight like that for something stronger than money. Sometimes for freedom, to stay out of prison. Or for vengeance. To ease the pain of loss and extract a payment in kind. They fight out of belief. Out of fanaticism?

Lights were showing through the heavy rain, a scattered glimmer of smeared yellow lights in rectangles and circles. Windows and doors and the lamplights of Lizardskin.

Vlasic rolled the Jeep down the single main street past the outbuildings. Early lights were on at Tom Blasingame's house, and a thin ribbon of wood smoke showed in the yard light. Up and down the long wandering line, house lights and yard lights shone in the rainy twilight.

Beau's double-wide trailer was two miles up, at the far end of the street, in a little sheltered cleft hard up against the lee face of the ridge, out of the path of the winds that came down out of Canada in the winter.

Vlasic parked the Jeep close to the big canvas awning Beau had rigged over the doorway. The headlights lit up the garage, shining on his old green Chevy wagon and the brown tarpaulin he had tied over his Harley-Davidson.

Someone, probably Tom Blasingame, had retrieved his wagon from the police station lot, where he had left it to begin his Friday tour of duty.

Vlasic put the brake on and sat back, looking at Beau.

"You get some sleep, Beau."

"I will. Thanks for the ride out. You want to come in, have some coffee?"

Vlasic shook his head. "No, thanks. Jinny'll be wondering where I am. You gonna be okay?"

"Why's everybody I see asking me that?"

Vlasic grinned at him, a wolfish rictus in the dashboard light. Rain was now a low steady drumming on the roof of the Jeep. A low rumble of thunder slid down the hillside and a sheet of blue light snapped in the sky, freezing the cottonwoods in a flash of wet black leaves and threading tangled branches.

"You go in there, look in a mirror. That'll explain it. You have any pain-killers?"

"I have some Percodan. A nurse gave me some when I checked out. And I have some Heinekens in the fridge."

"Oh, that's great. Mix yourself a cocktail. I'll come back in the fall, bring you some moss for your north side."

Beau made a face and maneuvered his leg out the passenger door. When Vlasic opened his door to help, Beau held up his left hand, palm out.

"Stay there, Marco. I need a nurse, I know where there's one right now, waiting for me to call her. Say hello to Jinny for me. Thanks again."

Vlasic leaned across the seat to pull the door closed. Before he shut it, he looked up at Beau. "You talk to Meagher in the morning. Tell him what we talked about. SPEAR and all that. Get his take on it. He's a good cop. He'll know how to handle it."

"Sure, Marco. Drive safe."

Vlasic shut the door and backed down the laneway. His lights cut across Beau's body as he turned and drove off down the Lizardskin road. Beau stepped carefully up the porch to the door of the trailer. An empty cat dish sat by the screen door. The overhead light was on.

Something heavy dropped down out of the awning brace and landed on his shoulder. It snarled in his ear, and Beau felt claws sinking into his back.

He raised his left arm and let the cat walk out along it, like a tightrope walker. It was Stonewall, a massive Maine coon cat, striped and colored like a raccoon. By the time Stonewall reached Beau's elbow, Beau was bracing his left hand on the doorframe. Stonewall had gotten into this game six years back, when he was still a kitten. Now he was full grown and weighed almost twenty pounds, but he was in no way inclined to give up the greeting.

They had a kind of game Beau called Constant Vigilance. Stonewall would hunt Beau, sometimes taking an hour or more to set him up and close in. Or he'd lie in wait for Beau to come home and spring when he thought Beau was looking somewhere else. He'd done it a couple of times when

Beau was in bed with a woman, twenty pounds of crazed cat landing on Beau's bare back, usually at a critical moment. It had soured a couple of promising relationships, which was probably Stonewall's intention.

Beau stroked the big cat under his jawline and Stonewall stretched out, raised his rear, and sank his foreclaws into Beau's wrist.

"Hey, you're soaking wet. How come you're out, anyway?"

Stonewall dropped heavily to the porch and looked up at Beau, baring his teeth and growling softly.

Tom must have forgotten to let him back in. McAvity was probably over at his place now, cadging free food and lazing around on the wooden floor in front of Tom's fire. McAvity was a yellow tom, long-haired and lynxlike, with tufted ears and a big belly, lazy as a flatland river.

Stonewall was a hunter, a solitary. Perhaps that was why he wasn't inside with Feets. Feets was a small black-and-white ball of fluff and attitude, a female, whose idea of roughing it was a nap without her blanket. Feets never left the trailer unless she was dragged, and she'd head back for it as soon as she got some traction and a clear run. Feets was smart enough to know that out in the country here, a puffball like her was snack food without the cellophane. Feets would be inside the door right now, yowling and bitching about the lateness of the hour and the deplorable condition of the kitty litter.

Except she wasn't.

Feets had a very distinctive call, a short rising bleat, almost like a bark. The sound of it was as much a part of coming home for Beau as Stonewall's game. Beau wasn't hearing it.

Stonewall yowled some more. Then he got himself tangled up in Beau's legs, extricated himself, and stood up to sink his claws into Beau's leg wound. Beau yelped and brushed him off.

Stonewall snarled again, flattening his ears. Beau leaned down and picked him up, holding him in the downlight. His green eyes were huge. He swiped at Beau's head with a paw, claws retracted, and snarled again, a greeting in Stonewallese. He had blood in his paws and in the fur around his jaws.

"Jesus, Stonewall. What have you been into?"

Stonewall bared his fangs again, tried to get his rear paws into Beau's belly, and started to purr. His ears flattened back, and he twisted in Beau's big hands. Beau let him go.

"Feets? You in there?"

He reached for the screen door. Stonewall went back down the steps

and turned around to watch, both ears forward, his body very tense. Something chilly ran down the small of Beau's back.

He tugged out the old Smith and thumbed back the hammer.

Paranoia, he thought.

Beau carefully unlatched the screen door and pulled it open. It emitted
a rusty groan. He braced it with his shoulder, unlocked the main door. He
lurched in on the bad leg, ignored the pain, cut to the right, out of the light,
the Smith out and up.

Nothing. Not a breath. The dark masses in the living room looked the
same. The trailer smelled of soap and pipe tobacco.

He straightened up and switched on the room light.

Two old saddle-leather couches, part of his settlement with Maureen,
a big rented television, a couple of bookcases filled with paperback books,
a cowskin rug covered with Stonewall's fur, and on the far wall above the
picture window, his single-shot McMillan long-range rifle, still padlocked
into its steel rack.

He stepped softly down the narrow hall to the galley, past the galley to
the built-in bedrooms, and through them to the big double-bathroom with
the black Jacuzzi.

He went through the place with the gun out and his ears ringing with
the effort of listening.

He found nothing. The bed was untouched. The random selection of
family shots on the dresser, a big framed picture of Bobby Lee at her first
communion, tie tacks and cufflinks, and a coffee mug with a flamingo-shaped
handle, full of old pipes and kitchen matches. The drawers were as messy
as usual. The rest of the place was neat, just as he left it. There was some
tinned cat food out on the counter, and a bag of Pounce. There was no sign
of a search, no sign of any stranger in the place.

It just felt . . . wrong.

So he looked it over again.

Fifteen minutes later, he found Feets at the bottom of his bedroom
closet. She had stuffed herself into one of his cowboy boots, backward. It
was lying on its side at the back of the closet, with Feets crammed into it
as far as she could go. She let out a little bleat when Beau found her. He
picked the boot up and carried it over to the bed. Feets stared up at him out
of the bootleg, crying softly and watching him with her massive golden eyes.
Her mouth opened again, showing needle-point teeth, and she bleated up at
him.

"What the hell are you doing in there?"

Feets struggled a bit and put a forepaw out in front of her. Beau turned the boot upside down and dumped her out onto the bed. She flopped out like an old sock and immediately crawled up on his lap and settled into it. She was trembling. Something had frightened her. Beau had no idea what that could have been. Maybe an animal around the place. A coyote crying and sniffing around a little too close to the trailer. He *was* at the far end of the town. There was nothing past the ridge above the trailer but more hills and valleys, all the way west to Arrow Creek. There were a lot of animals out there, and Feets was right to think of herself as lunch.

He stroked her behind the ears. It took her a long time to settle down.

Later, he carried her asleep into the living room and laid her down on top of her blue blanket, in a corner of one of the leather couches. He went into the galley and dug out a pack of frozen fish sticks. He dumped all fourteen out onto a tray and slid the tray into the oven. While they were baking, he found the coldest Heineken in the fridge and poured it into a tall glass with the FBI Academy symbol on it, the sole survivor of a set that Eustace had bought him when he left Maureen.

He walked into the living room. Feets was snoring softly on her blanket. He sat down, giving her a stroke or two, and managed to dig the remote out from under her without waking her.

He spent the next half-hour watching *60 Minutes* and wondering why Mike Wallace colored his hair. And it wasn't the same without Harry Reasoner. Also, why did anybody ever talk to these guys? Man, first thing he'd do, his secretary is on the intercom saying, Beau, it's *60 Minutes* and they have a camera crew in the waiting room and they want to do an interview, Beau would say, keep them there while I comb my moustache.

Take the next plane for Chichicastenango or Ouagadougou.

Once the smell of the fishsticks got strong enough, he went back out to the galley and scraped them off onto a plate. He doused them with malt vinegar and ketchup, lots of both, salted and peppered them, got another Heineken out of the fridge, and walked back into the living room to eat it on the coffee table in front of the television. He was into the sixth fish stick when he heard McAvity scratching at the screen door.

The fish sticks always got to McAvity. He could smell them all the way over at Tom's house.

Beau let McAvity in. He was soaking wet. He scrambled in past Beau and jumped up on the coffee table. He snagged two sticks and ran into the galley with them, his ears flat, leaving wet pawprints in the hall.

McAvity liked them with regular vinegar better, but if there was enough ketchup, he'd eat them with malt vinegar, because that's the kind of cat he was—flexible. Not a picky cat. Feets was the picky cat. Feets wouldn't eat frozen fish sticks under any circumstances. Not in public, anyway. Feets liked canned cat food, the good stuff, and on Sundays baby shrimp in seafood sauce with a little lemon juice sprinkled on top.

Stonewall liked anything with fur on it and fight in it. And sometimes birds, if he could catch them. Stonewall's trouble was his size. And the stripes. His Maine coon cat colors were all wrong for daylight hunting in Montana, where everyone else was wearing pale tan or dusty brown and even the grass was the wrong color. It was okay at night, except the birds never flew at night, when Stonewall had a chance to catch them. Bats, he could catch. But who wanted them? Stonewall would kill bats if he could catch them, but he never ate them. He'd just dump them on the front steps so everyone would know he was on the job.

Stonewall had made his reputation in Lizardskin, not on Dead Dog Monday, when he'd disemboweled a dachshund at the end of a very long and tiresome vendetta that was the damn dog's own fault anyway, but a year before that, when he'd dragged a newly dead rattlesnake into Tom Blasingame's house and dropped it into a pot of chili.

Thinking about it wouldn't decide it. He leaned over, picked up the telephone.

"Hello?"

"Trudy?"

"No. I'm Chloe."

"Oh. Sorry. Is Trudy around?"

"Is this Beau?"

Beau was stopped for a second.

"Yes. Yes it is."

"Trudy said you might call. They stuck her with the late shift. She won't be off until four in the morning. She told me to tell you—just a minute—by the way, you should be sure and watch the eleven o'clock news. They've been saying all night, they're gonna do a big piece on . . . well, you know?"

"I can guess, Chloe. What was her message?"

"Charlie Tallbull is awake and talking. They have him listed as serious but stable. She said to tell you he's pretty banged up but that you could probably get in to see him for a few minutes tomorrow. Is that okay?"

"Yeah, that's fine. I guess we don't know each other, Chloe. I'm sorry I don't know your last name."

"Corson. I'm Trudy's sister."

"Hello, Miss Corson. I'm Beau McAllister."

"Everybody knows you, Sergeant McAllister. I used to work at the Sears at the Hilltop Mall."

Beau groaned softly. Chloe heard it. "Hey, no. I don't mean to—everybody thought you did the right thing. I—I hope I didn't say . . . Trudy was so excited about . . . oh, shit! I'm screwing it all up!"

"No, no, Chloe. Listen, you tell Trudy I'll be in to see Charlie Tallbull tomorrow and I'll call her after I've talked to him. What time does she usually get up after a late shift?"

"Are you really going to call her, Beau? If you don't, she'll strangle me!"

Beau had to laugh. "I'll call her. Chloe, you be sure to tell her I called, okay?"

"I'll pin it to her pillow, Beau. Hope I can meet you soon! Bye for now. Oh, be sure to watch the news, okay? Channel seven."

"I will Chloe. Good night."

"'Night, Beau."

Beau hung up with an odd feeling of connectedness, thinking how simple were some of life's satisfactions. Getting a soft good night from a young girl was one of them.

Warmed by that thought, he sat down to watch some television. After a while, he drifted into a light sleep.

It was close to eleven when he snapped awake. A talking haircut was telling all of eastern Montana and northern Wyoming about the Montana Highway Patrol's vendetta against innocent Native Americans and featuring the exploits of Sergeant Beauregard McAllister of District Four of the Highway Patrol.

It got worse.

At the end of the seven-minute feature, another hairdo with a deep voice and perfect diction interviewed "a local lawyer named Dwight Peerless Hogeland," who had accepted a brief from the American Civil Liberties Union to assist in a "rigorous inquiry" into the entire incident, with a view to establishing malicious intent and racial bias on the part of the MHP.

Beau held his head in one hand and rubbed his forehead.

Of course, Dwight looked very good on television. His blue eyes—*blue* eyes? Dwight had *gray* eyes!

Oh, great! Dwight had got himself some tinted contacts. Well, the blue translated nicely, and he had obviously practiced looking straight into the camera when he answered questions. He kept his hands folded on the desktop and seemed very serious and competent. Very . . . electable.

Oh, god. Dwight Hogeland was making his big move. There was a congressional spot coming up. The Democrats were hurting for talent to put up against the unstoppable Republican machine. And here was talent. Homegrown, an old family, and enough money to twist arms and line pockets all the way to Helena.

Beau poured another Heineken, drank that, and went for another. When he got back there was a tense moment when the haircut, in what could have been a fluke, asked a difficult question.

Wasn't it true that Mr. Hogeland was also representing Joseph Bell in a wrongful injury suit against Sergeant McAllister?

Yes, said Dwight, looking directly into the camera—which was perhaps a mistake this time, because the interviewer was sitting right next to him, and it might have looked less mannered if Dwight had thought to look at the person talking to him.

Yes, it is true that our firm, Mallon, Brewer, Hogeland and Bright, is representing Mr. Bell in an action against the Montana Highway Patrol.

Did Mr. Hogeland not see in this a possible conflict, since Joseph Bell was involved in the death of one of the Native Americans killed in the two police actions last Friday?

Well, said Dwight, putting on moral weight with every sententious syllable, the true facts of that incident have yet to emerge. *How*-ever, as one of Montana's leading law firms, we feel that it is our public duty, our *pro bono* obligation as corporate citizens of Montana, and as sworn officers of our justice system, to involve ourselves rigorously in—in the vital issues of our state. And in this case—ah . . . it is clear to all of us at the firm, as it is to the distinguished members of the ACLU for Montana, that there exists a grave possibility that some injustice, some serious violation of the Fourth Amendment, some grave constitutional affronts, have occurred and may be occurring in the Highway Patrol. May in fact be an endemic and pervasive— ah, dysfunction within that agency, and as our firm has a long history of . . . dealings with the state police and . . . while we are cognizant of our connection with Mr. Bell, who may in fact *not* be the person responsible—originally responsible, that is—well, we did feel that, when approached by representatives of the ACLU, we could do no other than accept the burden of liberty. Deaths, tragic deaths, possibly needless deaths, have resulted from recent police actions. It is my—our—it is no less than our duty, as officers of the court, to assist in an open and . . .

Rigorous, thought Beau.

. . . rigorous investigation into these actions. We are certain that the officials of the state police will cooperate in this process—

"Count on it, Dwight," said Beau, and he shut the damned thing off.

If you judged a man by the quality of his enemies, Beau was in a lot of trouble. Having Dwight Hogeland on your case was like being bitten to death by ducks.

He poured himself a very hot bath in the giant black Jacuzzi, added a whole packet of soap bubbles, except for the last little bit of soapy fluid, which he painstakingly and delicately applied to the rim of the tub all the way around its circumference.

Then he peeled off his bandages. He had some surgical wraps in the kitchen, borrowed from the County. He grimaced at the cuts, tightly stitched with nylon thread. He'd rewrap them with new bandages later. Right now, a bath, come hell or high water.

He lowered himself slowly into it, easing his way past his belly wounds and his leg wounds, until he was completely immersed in the steaming water. He lay on his back under the water, listening to his heart pound, letting it slow down, until he could hold his breath no longer. He surfaced, blowing and huffing, and picked up the Heineken from the side of the tub.

Stonewall and McAvity were sitting on the floor beside the tub. They always came in to watch Beau in the tub.

"Hey, boy!" said Beau, flicking some soap bubbles at Stonewall. Stonewall's eyes grew large, and he batted at a soap bubble, shattering it. Beau flicked more at the big cat. Stonewall flattened into his hunting position as the bubbles drifted down through the steamy air. A bubble settled onto the mat in front of Stonewall. He went straight up and came down on it—killed that bubble dead!

Stonewall looked back up at Beau, a crazy hunting fire in his green eyes.

McAvity stayed out of it.

Beau picked up some more bubbles and set them on the rim of the Jacuzzi.

Stonewall stared at them for a long time, eyes wild, head held low and flattened in line with his muscular body, his hind legs gathered and taut, thinking about it, gauging the distances, watching the bubbles as the light broke up on their surfaces and they popped and glistened in the silence.

Beau kept his eyes on Stonewall.

Suddenly, in a great explosion of fur and muscle, Stonewall leaped up, arced, pounced perfectly onto the soap bubbles.

He hit the soapy fluid Beau had laid down around the rim. His paws scrabbled and his tail flew up in an effort to counter the balance. Beau pulled way back and Stonewall fell into the tub, yowling and spitting.

In less than an instant, he surfaced like a submarine-launched missile, a soggy furred missile, bursting through the soap suds, straight back out of the tub. The last Beau saw of Stonewall for a while were the pink pads on the bottom of his rear paws as he raced out of the bathroom, snarling.

Constant Vigilance, said Beau, smiling down at McAvity, lifting the Heineken in a salute.

McAvity raised a paw and began to clean it. Beau would not have said that he saw a grin on McAvity's face, but the world is a complex and subtle place, and not all of its mysteries are cracked open and devoured.

A while later, when he was safely in bed, all three cats dry and warm— Stonewall never bore a grudge—all in their various nests around the king- size bed, he yawned mightily and stretched and in stretching felt something stiff and shiny under his pillow.

He brought it out and held it under the reading lamp.

It was a Polaroid photograph.

It seemed to have been taken late at night, with a very sensitive film. The colors were all wrong, the details blurred.

But it was clear enough for Beau.

It was a picture of a big man in a hospital bed, taken from the foot of the bed, apparently late at night. The hard-planed face was soft in sleep, middle-aged and vulnerable, one arm thrown across his chest, trailing an intravenous line.

It was a picture of Beau.

15

1130 Hours – June 17 – Big Horn County, Montana

9 0114 South Wyatt Drive turned out to be a long hogback road that ran northeast, for some white reason, even though it was called *South* Wyatt, along the valley of the Bighorn River toward the town of Custer. It sliced through the Crow Reservation, leaving it at a ridgeback slope called Arapooish. Then it snaked in and out and over the fragrant drying-grass hills and coulees, treeless and barren as Mars, with only a few small cottonwood stands in the bendings of the river to mark the changes. The road was gravel and changed to dirt after a few miles, and a mile after that, it declined to a couple of ruts in the tall grasses. Here and there Gabriel had seen antelope darting like pale brown flames across the hills, and now and then a hawk would soar and drop off to the right. As South Wyatt climbed, it narrowed,

until it mutated into a pair of wheel-ruts that curved and arced over the hills. It stopped at a Lundy fence that said, simply:

PRIVATE

NO HUNTING OR FISHING

J. BELL

He drove the Ford into a small arroyo and covered it with plucked prairie grass. He had picked out a light green car from the Budget lot, one of the new Sables without sharp edges. It hid nicely in the brush, where even its shape seemed to blend with the rounded contours of the land. As he walked away from it carrying his gear, he looked back now and then and marveled at how well it concealed itself.

It had taken him another hour to reach the bluffs overlooking the ranch-style house and the outbuildings where Joe Bell lived. Most of the way was marked by standing poles carrying power and phone lines. And on the nearest bluff, Bell had installed a huge white satellite receiver dish; it shouted his presence like a white flag or a pillar of smoke.

Gabriel wore tall boots with his jeans tucked inside, and he carried a stick to strike at the tall grass in front of him. He wanted to give the rattlesnakes plenty of time to hear him coming and slide away. Crickets leaped and fluttered out of his path, and now and then he stepped carefully over a fieldmouse nest. Still the crows chattered about him, and any man who was really of this land would have known he was coming.

But Bell was not that kind of man. He could not live with the wind and the silences out here; the dish said as much.

Gabriel found a good place in the bluffs and settled in to watch Bell for a while, and think about what should be done with him. Gabriel watched the man hobbling back and forth from the ranch house to the barn. The light kept changing as clouds flew in front of the sun, the shadows chilled him, and up here in the bluffs the wind was cold and cutting. He shifted on the boulder and read-justed the binoculars, moving them to full power. The ground seemed to jump, and suddenly he was floating in the air in front of the big man.

The white man was big and bent. He walked like an old bear, head forward, intent on his path, favoring his right leg. The sergeant had shot him on the right side. Too bad he hadn't killed him.

Through the glasses, Joe Bell's face was a bright red circle of fiery hair and shiny skin. The blood was thick in him, and like all men of his kind, he carried it close to his surface, like the visible stain of his temper. He looked like a man who was used to shouting and hitting.

Bell was carrying bales of hay from a stack under a ramshackle lean-to, bringing them into a stable. Gabriel could hear the horses, and the strong smell of manure came on the wind. Bell did not keep his horses clean. The ranch itself looked haphazard, as if it had more or less fallen into these arrangements on the day it was built and Bell had not bothered to organize it.

Gabriel watched him for a long time, thinking about the man and what should be done with him. Somehow a straight-ahead talk with the man did not seem possible. Gabriel did not believe that Jubal and his people had tried to rob Joe Bell's place. So Joe Bell had lied about everything. Therefore, Joe Bell had something to hide and was not likely to give this lie up freely.

There would have to be some sort of persuasion. A little threat, perhaps, in this isolated place.

Gabriel did not intend to hurt the man, but what had happened to Jubal and the rest, that was something that needed unraveling. So he must wait and see how the day went, see who came and who went, and get a feeling for the man.

Time passed. He saw only Joe Bell hobbling about, and the cloud shadows sliding across the scene, staining the bleached timber purple, then clearing it again when the sun came back. The wind here hissed and rustled in the tall grass. The grass smelled of sage and flowers, dust and spices, a good smell. He had missed that smell in Los Angeles, a city that smelled like rotting fruit and burning rubber.

By now, the sergeant would have found his picture.

It would give the man something to think about. If there had been a plan to kill Jubal, to silence him, then the sergeant was a part of it. He had done the actual killing.

So the picture would let the man know that it had not gone well, and there was a new element in the calculation.

He reached up and touched his shoulder, feeling the cuts that the cat had given him. That was some cat that sergeant had. A good cat. It said something for the sergeant that a cat like that would stay with him and fight for his house. Gabriel had held the big animal out at the end of his arms and thought about breaking it. Still the animal had asked for nothing. It tried to claw him with its hind legs, and it twisted in his hands, trying to get those jaws into him. Its eyes were bright with murder.

Too fine an animal to kill. Gabriel had locked it in the garage and gone back to the trailer. The little cat inside was different, a toy. It ran as soon as he stepped inside and hid itself in a closet.

Gabriel would go see the policeman, after he had talked to Bell here.

It was important to talk to Bell first, because once he had talked to the sergeant, they'd never let him get close to Bell.

Gabriel had looked at that rifle in its locked steel brace. An unusual rifle, the McMillan. A single-shot rifle designed for very long-range shooting, for marksmanship and control. It fired a .300 caliber Winchester Magnum and had a muzzle velocity of thirty-three hundred feet per second. It would hit very hard, even as far out as a thousand yards. The scope was a fine one, a powerful Leupold. The combination would have cost the man close to twenty-five hundred dollars. Taken in all, it was a strange weapon to find in a double-wide trailer in Montana. It was in excellent condition as well, which said something for the sergeant. Gabriel had used one of these weapons on a project in Costa Rica. Shooting from a boat, at night, about five hundred yards offshore, he had killed a woman sitting at a table on the balcony of her house, drilled her through the left temple. An uphill shot into bad lighting, with a cross wind and the boat tossing in the swells. It had been a very fine shot. He had regretted the need to drop the weapon over the side as they drifted away. McMillan also produced a single-shot rifle in .50 caliber, a thirty-pound beast that could send a massive round over two miles, but it was too heavy for his kind of work.

So the man had good taste in guns.

And cats.

Maybe he was someone who could be talked to, a man who had some sense.

And maybe not.

Maybe he was just another Pinda-Lickoyee who needed punishment, like this one down here.

Beau drove Meagher's dark blue Lincoln Town Car to the parking lot of Sweetwater General, timing his trip so that he'd be there before Vanessa Ballard arrived. They were scheduled to see Doc Hogeland, and then Beau was going to go down and look in on Charlie Tallbull. Beau had asked for Meagher's car because, tell the truth, he was more than a little shaken by the Polaroid he'd found under his pillow, and Meagher's car had a heavy tint on all the windows. It gave him a certain sense of cover. It also seemed like a good idea not to cruise around town in his regular patrol vehicle or the green Chevy wagon; whoever had entered his trailer knew too much about him already.

He'd spent most of the morning setting up a perimeter alarm system he'd gotten at the Sears in Billings, a combination of motion detectors and infrared photo cells. The cats would set it off every half-hour if he didn't position the sensors just right, so it took a long time. Tom Blasingame had come over and asked him about it. Beau told him the whole story. Tom agreed to keep an eye on the place. He suggested taking the cats over to his place, and Beau thanked him for it. If somebody planned to come back, Beau wanted as clear a field as he could get. He was half-afraid he'd get himself so wired that when the alarm triggered, he'd leap out of bed and blow a large porthole through one of his cats. Blasingame had been impressed with the Polaroid.

"Nervy son of a bitch, Beau. Why you figure he did it?"

Beau had been wondering that as well. "My guess? The guy's a games-player. Maybe a psychopath. You see some of that stuff, in some kinds of . . . ''

"Killers, Beau?''

"Criminals. Sometimes ex-husbands will do it, just to show the wife they have the power. It's intimidation. Control.''

"You intimidated, Beau?''

McAllister looked around the trailer, at the tangle of wires and sensors. Blasingame caught the look and grinned.

Beau had the photo in his pocket now, and he was also wearing his full Highway Patrol uniform, *including* his Kevlar vest.

Whatever was going on, he was taking it seriously.

He looked up at the glass window wall where old Doc had his offices, right on the top floor of Sweetwater General. It *had* been his intention to do this all alone, but Hogeland had asked him to bring Vanessa along. He'd been vague about the reasons, but firm in the request. As for Ballard, she was anxious to get Dr. Hogeland's reading on the survival chances of this Native American Jane Doe in the Sweetwater intensive care unit. If Hogeland and Seidelman thought she was likely to surface soon, she'd suspend the whole shooting inquiry until she could provide testimony.

If not, it was set for 2000 hours this same evening. With the ACLU and SPEAR snuffling around the perimeter, Beau and Meagher and Ballard had agreed that later was better than sooner. It all depended on this Jane Doe upstairs.

Beau was in the hospital parking lot a full half-hour before the appointment. He had gotten into the habit of reaching meeting places thirty or forty minutes before he had to be there when he was up in Helena at the FBI field training seminars. Until this weekend, he'd done it more or less out of habit.

It seemed like a good idea to take it more seriously now, even if he had learned it from the FBI. Deep in his heart, he firmly believed that most FBI people—with the exception of some operational guys and Lieutenant Eustace Meagher—were sententious drones with all the street smarts of gravel. What the FBI loved to do was give simple things complicated names.

For example, they called this tactic "sector preemption," a means of providing their "field agents" time to "assess tactical and terrain advantages" and to "determine the probabilities of counter-preemptive action" that might "adversely affect mission viability" and "negate conflict initiative capability." That was how the academy dinks liked to talk.

Beau had once listened with a straight face while a special agent in charge talked about a DEA raid in which a chopper had gone down in Belize. The agent said that the DEA chopper had been "vertically deployed into the terrain."

That meant it had crashed.

The men in the chopper were carried on the revised roster as "negative assets."

Translation: They were dead.

If there was a short way of saying something, they'd hunt it down and kill it. And take longer to tell you about it than it took to do it. The years after Helena had taught Beau that very little in the real world worked the way they thought it did in the FBI, but a few of the tricks were useful.

He sat in Meagher's Town Car listening to the radio chatter, reading the *Billings Gazette,* and feeling the weather roll around Billings as if there were monsters upstairs.

There had been a storm during the night, and now the sky looked bruised and used; ragged tatters of clouds blew crazily across a lemon-yellow sky. The Rimrock cliffs to the north were obscured by a drifting fog bank that never rose above the horizon line. Leaves and dust swirled in the parking lot. The wind blew warm and wet as breath, then cold as a corpse's cheek as it shifted around to the north and caught currents from the high plains. Down along the river, kids would be playing hookey and fishing for trout in the shallows. The next few weeks would be unpredictable.

There would be days when the sky would be blue and boundless, as full of bright promise as a hooker's smile, and then there'd be the other days, days when the front would pile up so high, you could see it a hundred miles away, a big black anvil of cloud and thunder. The street would be full of little devils of whirling dust, the sky would turn low and ugly, and suddenly the hammer would come down and lightning would crackle in the air like burning trees, and everything that could move would find cover and dig in.

Summer had come to Montana in its usual style, alternating patterns of sunlit mornings and thunderstruck nights.

He had just reached the editorial page and seen the headline:

TIME TO REIN IN OUR COWBOY COPS?

Fortunately for Beau's peace of mind, Vanessa Ballard arrived, a few minutes early, in her silver BMW 635 csi, wheeling it into the space beside Beau's Town Car like a Harrier pilot coming in for a night landing.

Beau folded the paper, got out slowly, and came around to watch her gather her papers and unwind herself from the car. Ballard had the best legs in the High Plains and knew it. She lit up Beau's face with a white phosporus smile, perfection in a gray silk suit that harmonized with her silver BMW. She shook her golden hair out in a flare that caught the sun and shattered it in a fan of bright light.

"You do that on purpose," said Beau, adjusting his uniform slacks and silently cursing his hormones. Ballard seemed not to notice her effect.

"Do what, Beau?"

"Never mind. You ready for this?"

"Did an hour on my Power-Step this morning. Then I had a long laze in the sauna, and a rubdown with eucalyptus leaves. Smell me. Do I smell like eucalyptus?"

She leaned forward into Beau and exposed the right side of her neck. A delicate dusting of fine blond hairs floated on top of her snowdrift skin like sunlight on a frozen lake.

"You know, Beau, you're really not all that repulsive, are you? For a fascist, I mean."

"I'm not a fascist. I'm a misdirected flower child. I took the wrong turning long ago. I need to be taken in hand. I need someone to lead me to self-actualization."

"You self-actualize any better, there's going to be no one left alive in this area code."

She swiveled gracefully and joined him as he walked, heavy-heeled, across the black tarmac toward the pale sandstone towers of the hospital.

"Why do you drive that Nazi car, Vanessa? Makes you look like one of those Yuppie stockbrokers. I hate those things!"

"Leave my Bimmer out of this. Besides, it's an excellent car. I'd put it up against that freighter you push around any day."

"You put it up against the Town Car, Vanessa, won't be anything left but a streak of sauerkraut in the middle of the road. Anyway, we're supposed to be buying American, aren't we?"

"I'll buy American when America builds good cars."

The Sweetwater lobby was crowded with arriving visitors and strolling patients. They took an elevator up with a group of Indians, silent and solid in jeans and cowboy shirts, the women broad and blunt as boulders, the men long-bodied and heavy-featured, with black braids and deep dark eyes. They stared at Beau's tan patrol uniform. The oldest, a big slope-shouldered man with gundog eyes and a bad complexion, spoke to Beau as the doors opened and they filed out.

He held the doors back with one massive horned hand.

"Hey, McAllister. You come out to the Rosebud one day. You tell them you want to see George Cut Arms. You tell your people Satanka-Witko come back now. We don't lose no more babies."

Beau looked at him awhile. "What are you talking about?"

The men watched each other for a full minute.

"Satanka-Witko."

George Cut Arms let the doors close. He never broke his eye-to-eye with Beau. The car seemed to reek of threat.

"What the hell was *that* all about, Beau?"

"Damned if I know."

"What was he saying? Santana something? Scary guy."

"Satanka. Satanka-Witko. That's the Lakota name for Crazy Horse."

Ballard looked troubled. "The Rosebud's Sioux, isn't it? Over in South Dakota? Near Mission?"

"Lakota. Sioux's a white name."

Ballard was watching his face. Beau could feel her questions unspoken, but all he had for an answer was another question. "That's three, isn't it?"

"Three what, Beau?"

"Everything comes in threes."

"What the hell are you talking about?"

"Indians, Vanessa. That's three times now, and each time, it was an Indian."

"I'm pretty sure I have no idea what you mean."

"I know," said Beau. "Neither do I."

Gabriel waited, watching Bell as the sun rode the blue curve of the sky. As the day passed, a freshening wind blew the clouds away. Now the sun came out, and suddenly the heat was on his shoulders and he could feel it warming the tears the cat had put in him. It felt good, and he took his shirt off to let it work on him.

He was vividly aware of the land around him and the sky above him; it seemed as if they breathed with him. The sounds and the smell of the land came into him complete, releasing the gathered tension of so many years spent in foreign places, listening to jagged foreign tongues, assaulted by sights and smells that were alien to him.

Maybe there had been a day, just like this one, a spring day in a forgotten year. Maybe a Lakota just like him had waited here and watched an enemy down in that bowl of bottom land. It would have been a good place for it, and the land had not changed at all. Only the people were gone from it now, as if the land were an empty house still echoing with the sounds of those who had lived there. The thought comforted him, although there was psychic vertigo in it, like looking at a long line of mirror images of himself, an infinite chain of Lakota men standing in this same place, with time the surface of the glass.

Then a strange feeling came over him, and it made him look suddenly to his right. It seemed to him that someone was standing there, in the tall grass, watching him.

There was nothing. The wind moved in the grass, and a last shadow of cloud passed over the bluff.

Yet he could *feel* it, as strongly as if it were true.

And now when he looked away, he thought he could see . . . something standing there. Tall and dark, like him, with black hair that blew in the soft wind. Its face was turned away from him, but it knew that Gabriel was there.

Then Gabriel turned again to look directly at it, and there was nothing but the grass and the sunlight and the sound of the wind. A chill shook him like a dog shakes a rat.

Now this, he knew, was what Jubal would have called a sign. And Gabriel wanted to let that feeling take hold of him, surrender to it. But he shook it off. Sink into your delusions, and you drown, as the Ghost Dancers did.

In 1890, in the Drying Grass Moon, Kicking Bear had come back from a Fish Eater camp in Nevada with a dance they had learned from a Fish Eater—a Paiute—named Wovoka.

Wovoka had told them that Jesus Christ had taught him this dance, and that it was a dance that would drive the white men off the land, that a great wave of new earth would come and all the Ghost Dancers would rise into the air as the wave passed underneath them, carrying away all the white men and their engines and buildings and soldiers, and then the ancestors would come back, and the buffalo, and it would be as if the whites had never come.

This dance was called the Ghost Dance, and they learned to dance it at Cheyenne River Agency and at Pine Ridge and Standing Rock. They danced it all through the Falling Leaves Moon and the moon that followed, danced it until even Sitting Bull was dancing it, and the federal men decided they had seen enough of this dance and they sent Bear Coat to see William Cody and ask him to come and get Sitting Bull and the others to stop this dance.

But Cody would not do that.

So in the Horn Shedding Moon, in December of that year, an Indian policeman named Bull Head came to Standing Rock and told Sitting Bull that he was under arrest for dancing the Ghost Dance. Catch-the-Bear got his rifle and fired it at Bull Head, and Bull Head, wounded, fired back as he was falling, and that bullet hit Sitting Bull, knocking him down.

Red Tomahawk had come with Bull Head to help him arrest Sitting Bull. So he shot Sitting Bull through the head and killed him. And when Big Foot heard that they had killed Sitting Bull, he started to take his own people to Pine Ridge, to see if Red Cloud could keep them safe from the federals. On the way, they ran into Major Samuel Whitside and four troops of the Seventh Cavalry. Big Foot was sick with tuberculosis, but Whitside made him march all the way to Chankpe Opi Wakpala in South Dakota. Because Crazy Horse was buried somewhere along this creek, the Hunkpapas and the Minneconjous—Teton, just like Gabriel—went along without trying to fight. And on the morning of December 29, a fight started. His father had told him that a soldier tried to take away a rifle from a young man, and the young man, who was deaf—his name was Black Coyote, a troublemaker who was not held in respect by his own clan—that young man fired his Winchester and then the Seventh Cavalry killed three hundred of them, shot them with rifles and Hotchkiss guns right on Chankpe Opi Wakpala, where Crazy Horse was buried, a place the federals called Wounded Knee, and that was the end of the Indian nations.

So much for mysticism. So much for the Ghost Dancers.

The white man will become like a mist on water and blow away.

The bluecoats will fall from their horses and sink into the grass like blue birds falling out of the sky into a deep lake.

And their forts will fade away.

And the *pa-sapa*, the Black Hills, will be free of them, as a bear can shake itself free of lice.

And the bighorns and the deer and the wolves and the buffalo will come back like a black tide returning. And the young girls will wear shells and beads, and the Crow and the Absaroke and the Flathead and the Pawnee will slip away to other lands. It will be as if no white ship had ever come to this land, no pony soldier ever marked it, no Terry nor Custer nor Sheridan had ever come to hunt us like antelope in our own country.

Gabriel grinned and threw a pebble at a circling crow. Down in the bowl, Joe Bell was sitting on his front porch, staring at the setting sun and drinking from a brown bottle. An old dog, maybe a setter, was lying on the patchy grass in front of the porch. A horse was neighing in the barn; Bell had not let them out to run, nor had he taken them hay or water. The wind was blowing up the slope toward Gabriel. He could smell the barn and the horses, a strong ugly scent of rotting hay and manure and moldy lumber.

If you took away the phone lines and the power poles, and the satellite dish on the hill behind him, it could be any year in the past.

It could be 1877, the year Crazy Horse was killed, bayoneted in the belly by a man named Private Gentles as Little Big Man and another held his arms. Bayoneted again through the back and into his kidney. He fell down on the red dirt then, and they wanted to stab him again.

"Let me be, my friends," said Crazy Horse. "You have got me hurt enough."

Touch The Clouds was there, seven feet tall, and he bent down and picked up Crazy Horse and carried him into a soldier's bed. "He was a great chief," said Touch The Clouds, "and he cannot be put into a prison."

That was at Camp Robinson, on September 6.

The soldiers watched through the window and knew that something important had happened here, thinking that they had killed a big man and would be big men because of it. But they were wrong. No longer would they be big men on a big land, but only drovers and tinsmiths and clerks who once had fought Crazy Horse, who was dead and would now live forever unchanging, while little deaths awaited each of them, and little sticks to mark them, and a big land to swallow them up beneath the long grass and never speak their names again.

That was the Lakota consolation. It had been a bitter consolation. Gabriel looked around at the rolling hills, at the softness and the light that lay everywhere around him, and then he looked down at the red-faced man hobbling back and forth on his dirty acre of ruin, and it seemed to him that the ugly little collection of brown buildings was like a bruise on the skin of the countryside.

Doc Hogeland's office was on the top floor of Sweetwater General, at the southern end of a long marble-floored hallway lined with Western art.

Just inside the double-glass doors that set off the administrative offices, a marble pillar supported a huge Remington bronze of four wild cowhands riding runaway broncos and firing pistols into the air. It looked like a bronze tornado of motion, as much an expression of torque as it was historical art.

Beyond the glass doors, the atmosphere had that indescribable scent created by a great deal of old money. A crystalline woman glided forward on oiled manners and intercepted them in the middle of a Navajo rug in pewter, ochre, and sage purple, colors that were reflected and subtly echoed in every feature of the office suites.

She led them down a passageway toward a set of carved Mexican doors. The handles were steer horns. Brass cartridges were hammered into the wood in a geometric pattern. She opened the doors and swept them with her into Doc Hogeland's private office.

It opened like a ride up a long slope to reveal a vista encompassing most of downtown Billings and extending all the way to the low blue bluffs on the south bank of the Yellowstone. The floor was a Navajo pattern of varicolored sandstone and baked clay. A bank of glass windows ran fifty feet from wall-to-wall and ceiling to floor. The room was filled with yellow light, and the sky outside seemed to press against the glass like a visible force. From somewhere off to the right a stereo murmured something graceful by Chopin. The floor seemed to rise gently to the massive oak desk, dark and battered. In the bright sunlight, it was almost impossible to see if anyone was in the chair. A shape rose up into the penumbra, and a barrel voice drummed out at them.

"*Mizz* Ballard! You destroy me! And Beau! You look like a bowling trophy with all that brass! Thank you, Mrs. Miles!"

Mrs. Miles inclined her head and dematerialized.

The shape gathered itself out of the glare and formed into a tall, big-bodied old man with a soldier's carriage, a ragged shock of white hair above a craggy rock of a face, weathered and windburned, forceful without belligerence, with brilliant blue eyes glittering out of the recesses of his skull. He came forward at a lope, like an old wolf, and enfolded one of Ballard's hands in both of his.

"Vanessa. Have you married that fellow from Helena yet?"

"No, Doc. I threw him out."

"Excellent! I won't have him shot, then. Unless he hurt you?"

"Don't have him shot yet."

"Come here, child, give an old man a memory!"

Ballard gave him a kiss on his seamed and scarred old cheek, standing on her toes to do it. Hogeland Senior rose above her like a butte, massive and blunt, full of force and gravity. His smile broke across that face like a shaft of sunlight striking a peak. She could feel herself being warmed by it, and her own rush of affection for him.

He was wearing an ancient plaid shirt buttoned to the neck, and jeans so old and faded they looked like Japanese paper. His face was scored and carved in fissures and lines and creases, his skin as dark red as Montana earth.

Hogeland put an arm like a tree limb across Ballard's shoulders, resting it lightly on her, and extended his right hand to Beau.

Beau took it at the full extent of his arm, shaking it solidly and smiling at Dr. Hogeland, suppressing the urge to say "sir."

"Beau! How is Bobby Lee? Six now, am I right? I got her a little something. Just a minute—it's around here somewhere . . . yes."

He reached down behind his desk and brought up a small square packet, wrapped in navy blue paper with silver stars, bound up in a silver ribbon. He handed it to Beau and enjoyed watching Beau's discomfort. As usual, the old man had him off-balance.

"Hell, Doc. That wasn't necessary!"

The doctor shook his massive head, raised his heavy hand. "Presents are *never* necessary. That's why they call them presents. If they were necessary, we'd call them *taxes,* and nobody'd ever get any. It's just a little thing. I remember she loved horses. I found a little carving in Los Angeles last week. It's a copy of one of those Chinese pieces. *The Flying Pony.* I think she'll like it."

Beau hefted the package. The "little thing" weighed ten pounds, and it was probably brutally expensive.

"Will you bring her around someday? I could show her the—well, I guess a hospital isn't a little girl's idea of amusing. Would you let me take her for a spin in the plane? You could come, too!"

The last thing Beau was going to do was to let the old man fly him *anywhere* in that cruise missile.

"Not for me, Doc. But Bobby Lee would love it. I'll talk to Maureen about it."

When he mentioned Maureen's name, the old man's face changed. Then he grinned and slapped his hands together.

"Well! May I offer you something? It's too early for liquor, but I have Evian—terrible stuff—and coffee?"

They agreed on coffee. Dr. Hogeland served it himself, the delicate porcelain cups like eggshells in his big hard hands. He settled them all down on a battered old leather couch and chair grouping beside the window, Hogeland in the big chair, Ballard and Beau with their backs to the window, facing him. He raised the cup to his lips, sipping carefully, watching them over the rim as they tasted the brew.

"Good? Excellent. Had it in from Coeur d'Alene, special mail order. Montana's a fine country, but so God-cursed dull about food and drink, it might as well be Connecticut."

They set their cups down on the table. "So, Beau. How's that leg? I had Malawala up here in an absolute snit."

"It's fine. Hurts a bit. I'll live."

"Dangerous work, I hear. A tragedy, however you look at it. So many lives cut off."

"Yes. I wish it had—I wish there could have been some way to avoid it."

"I know you do, Beau. Back on duty already?"

Ballard cut in. "Well, we have the shooting board tonight. He can't be back on active until the board sits on it. Which brings us to the point—"

Dr. Hogeland raised his hand, palm out, his long supple fingers spread in a fan.

"In a moment, my dear. While I have you and Beau here, I want to clear up a small matter that I find . . . troubling."

Ballard and Beau looked at each other.

Ballard shrugged. "Certainly, if we can discuss it. It doesn't have any evidentiary connection with the . . . incident?"

Dr. Hogeland's face softened as he watched her talk. He took a clear aesthetic delight in observing such a beautiful creature living and breathing in his presence.

"You may wish to judge this for yourself. I merely wish to apprise you of certain . . . oh, damn! My son's here, in the next office! He's got something to say, and I wanted him to say it in front of—to say it to Beau's face."

Beau tensed visibly. He cleared his throat and let out a long breath. "Dwight is here?"

"Yes, Beau. I have no other son."

He seemed to wait in quietude, without expectations, as complete inside himself as a carved totem, beyond the passions and anxieties of younger lives. Ballard was literally squirming.

"I'm not sure I'm ready to discuss this case with him, Doc. He's taken a brief with the ACLU for these Indian rights people. There'll very likely be—we're sort of in opposition, Doc."

"I'm fully aware. This is another matter, and I'd like you to hear Dwight on the issue personally. I believe that listening to Dwight now will . . . will help, rather than render a complex situation even more convoluted."

Ballard looked at Beau, shrugged. Dr. Hogeland saw the signal and smiled at them. "Thank you. I take it as a personal favor."

He reached out and touched a fingertip to a brass plate next to the chair. In a brief moment, Mrs. Miles floated through the door and hovered at his shoulder.

"Ask my son to step in here, would you, Mrs. Miles?"

Gabriel felt a pain in his chest and realized that he had been holding his breath. A pulse thumped at his carotid, and his hands were sweating. That was what happened to you when you dragged out all the old miseries and fingered them over and over. Living in the past had killed his friends.

Mysticism and fanatical belief.

This landscape seemed to hypnotize a man. Too much light and space. There was a kind of narcotic here. So this thing that had come to watch him here, to stand beside him as he looked down at Joe Bell, was just what it appeared to be. Only a wind in the dry grass, and perhaps something of a dream or a wish or a need for company, and partly a trick of the light. Or of the shadow. Something that breathed itself out of the ground when Gabriel walked across its grave. A curved place in Gabriel's mind where life had worn his thoughts away and the nothingness showed through the way a mirror wears away and you see the clear glass of which it is made.

Still, he wished it would go away, because it distracted him. He tried hard to think in such a way that his mind would not present him with these distractions. He spent a long time trying to do this, as the sun began to ride down the blue slope of the sky and the living things in the hills around him became used to his presence. The crows went back to hunting, and the hawks went back to the sky, and the snakes moved the dry grasses again. And the thing would not go away. It came no closer and did not try to speak. It would not be seen direct but stayed just at the edges of Gabriel's vision. So after a long time he accepted that it was here, a product of fatigue and stress, maybe the drugs Dr. Sifton had given him, and of thinking about the past too much, about history and dreams and the ability of a people to delude themselves to death.

•   •   •

Beau and Ballard made careful small talk with Doc Hogeland for a few minutes. Then Hogeland's secretary returned, Dwight Hogeland following as a tender trails a sloop.

Dwight was in full Wall Street today, an Ermenegildo Zegna double-breasted blue pinstripe, shirt as white as the Ku Klux Klan, and an acid-green power tie with little blue ducks all over it, Dwight's concession to zaniness. He seemed scalded and avoided looking directly at either Beau or Vanessa.

"Dwight! Thank you for waiting. I know this is a busy day for you. We'll make this as brief as possible."

"Thank you, Dad."

Dwight sat down in a bone and leather chair, setting his briefcase at his toes. He leaned back, overbalanced, and caught himself with a hand on the chair arm. They all pretended not to notice it.

"Well, Dwight," said his father, his face a mask and his voice free of paternal inflection. "Perhaps you should begin this."

"Certainly, Dad."

He collected himself with a clear effort and now made direct eye contact with Vanessa Ballard. Beau realized with a shock that Dwight's eyes were gray again. He must have taken the contacts out. It unnerved him, and he missed Dwight's first few phrases. Gradually, Dwight's message developed through the murk of his circumlocution like a black-and-white photograph in a tray. A crime scene shot.

" . . . and in this climate of heightened awareness of abuse, it is vital to retain reservations. Nevertheless, we all must, in a sense we are compelled to . . . exercise personal vigilance . . . of wrongdoing. Of course I am mindful of the implications and the immediate judicial consequences of such an allegation. However it is not *safe* simply to disregard them if they are brought to our attention—"

Ballard set her cup down hard. "Christ, Dwight! Spit it out! Disregard *what*?"

Dwight straightened at her tone, sitting upright in his chair.

"This is an informal meeting. I am under no compulsion to provide this information to you! I think you should be—"

"Son, if you can't say it in ten words, go lie down till you can."

Dwight looked at his father, his face a pool of varied emotional currents. He looked back at Ballard, his face an aggressive jut of chin bone and frowns.

"I spoke—I had a long consultation with Beau's ex-wife on Sunday night. She has—detected signs of—there's been some blood spotting, and Maureen is a nurse, and she's convinced that—Maureen McAllister intends to have Bobby Lee examined by a specialist to determine whether Bobby Lee has been the victim of some kind of sexual assault!''

The air in the room crackled with unspoken rage.

"Does my ex-wife have a theory about who might be doing this to Bobby Lee?"

Dwight turned and looked directly at Beau, his face white and tight. It came to Beau in a burst of pale cold light that he was looking at a man who, for some reason beyond Beau's understanding, hated him intensely. And he knew in that same terrible moment that Dwight was going to name *him*. He tasted his own vomit at the back of his throat.

Beau put his cup aside delicately, stood up, stepped across to Dwight, gathered the front of his shirt and his Ermenegildo Zegna suit into his left fist, dragged the man to his feet, and cuffed him hard with a flat right hand sideways over his left ear. Dwight let out a sound between a bleat and a yelp.

Bracing as Dwight stumbled, Beau supported him and straightened him back up again, and held him steady long enough to hit him again, backhand, across the right cheek. His Highway Patrol ring drew blood on Dwight's cheek, raking the skin open under Dwight's right eye. A ribbon of shiny scarlet began to descend from Dwight's nose. Beau watched it swelling with a certain kind of scientific detachment while Dwight struck at him, twisting, trying to bring a knee up into Beau's belly, but Beau was in too close and it was happening too suddenly; you could see the shock—the *disbelief*— that there would be physical consequences to a legal assault. Dwight's world was cracking open—Beau could see these emotions flickering over Dwight's face.

As an afterthought, he drew his right fist back—now he could hear Vanessa shouting at him, but it was a long way away—and he turned his fist vertically and thumped Dwight twice—very, very hard—right on the bridge of his nose. He watched with a feeling of clinical satisfaction as Dwight's eyes reddened with pain and his mouth opened and shut like a gaffed trout. Someone was pulling on his upper arm now, and he let go of Dwight's suit jacket, and Dwight dropped back into the chair. Now the nose was blossoming like a spring rose, and red veins stood out on his cheeks.

Explain *that* on your next television appearance, kid.

Beau found himself unable to look at Vanessa, although he could feel the heat of her stare sizzling on his right cheek.

Dwight stayed in his chair, looking up at Beau, breathing hard, blood on his cheek and running from his nose. His nose looked like a brake light.

Ballard walked over and stood in front of Dwight, facing Beau.

"You touch him again and you go to jail."

Beau was silent. He nodded once at her, and walked away toward the window. He looked out at the skyline of Billings and tried to imagine how he was going to survive without a paycheck. His meager savings would not cover his alimony and Bobby Lee's maintenance and pay the mortgage on the double-wide. Well, the Harley was going, and probably the land on the Yellowstone.

It had been nice being a cop.

Maybe he could go back with Steiger?

He felt the back of his neck burning.

Nice move, you unbelievable asshole.

Doc Hogeland was sitting back in his leather chair and sipping his coffee. Dwight's hair hung in his face and blood pulsed from his swollen nose. His eye was blackening as he watched it.

He caught his breath, coughed, and tried to say something vicious that came out as "Yer godda be id jail id ad our, you fugging cogsugger!"

His father looked up, his face darkening. "Dwight! Shut up!"

"You sday oud of dis, you old fool!"

Hogeland Senior stood up and seemed to cast a shadow over everyone in the room.

"*Dwight!* You have a streak of coarseness in you I find absolutely repellent. Since it is obvious that you are unwilling to defend yourself physically, it seems the better part of valor to shut the hell up and put something on your nose."

He leaned over and tapped the brass plate again.

Mrs. Miles was suddenly among them, impassively observant. She glanced once at Dwight's condition.

"Shall I bring the bowl, sir?"

"If you would, Mrs. Miles."

She was back in less than thirty seconds with a wide aluminum bowl, some swabs, and a packet of sterile bandages.

Hogeland knelt before Dwight and wiped the blood off his son's face, talking softly to him, making concerned and paternal noises. Beau and Ballard waited, standing, until the doctor saw them.

"Please, Vanessa, Beau. Please sit down."

Ballard was shaking with controlled temper. Beau, although far from calm, decided to accept the fact that he had done it and could not take it back. He was at peace with himself. He'd do it again, and again. He'd kill the guy if it went that far. Then go bowling. He could always find work.

He'd have to find it in Billings or Bozeman. He wasn't going to move very far from Bobby Lee.

The doctor worked expertly at his son's face for a few minutes. He felt the bridge of his nose, eyes down.

"Not broken, Dwight."

He slapped his son on the right knee and sat back. Dwight's face was now half-hidden by a broad bandage across the nose. The bleeding had stopped. His eyes were red, and his suit jacket was covered with blood.

Beau looked as if he had just stepped down out of a group photo, starched and unmarked.

Ballard was only slightly less furious than Dwight, but she had by now gathered that something more was happening here than was immediately obvious. She struggled to remain still and attentive, her hands folded in her lap, her left leg crossed beneath her right, her ankles entwined gracefully, her mind racing.

"Now," said Hogeland, reclining luxuriously into the chair after his exertions. "That was very stimulating. Perhaps now we can begin to make some sense of all of this."

Dwight squirmed upright. He spat blood into the bowl and coughed twice. When he spoke, his voice was thick, and he could not quite achieve his consonants.

He coughed and tried again. "There's liddle to dizcuzz. I wad the bolice called. I wad—I want—this ban id jail."

"Son, hear me out, please, because I'm only going to tell you once. You two listen as well. This young fool here is clearly thinking with his pecker again, as seems to be a habit of his. Now Dwight, I can see that this is all a bit much for you, but you better just sit there and listen. And Vanessa—please try to relax child, you look like a leg-hold trap—Vanessa, first, this business about child molestation."

There was a sudden exhalation of air, almost a snort. No one looked at Beau, and Hogeland went on as if nothing had happened.

"I've been an old country doc for fifty years, and this sort of thing gets brought up now and then. Did even back in the old days, before we had all the magazines and TV to get everybody stirred up. Nowadays, when there's a nasty divorce going on, and you get a young lawyer with his brains in his pants there—just hold your fire, Dwight, I won't tell you again—like my son here, I'd be damned surprised if sooner or later the wife, sometimes one of her family, wasn't gonna go and run that sorry old signal up the lodgepole. What'd happen, Vanessa, if Maureen went to the—I guess it'd be the Big Horn County office?"

Ballard considered the question, her face closed and set, thinly controlled.

"If a complainant brings such a charge to the attention of a law enforcement agency, under Montana Criminal Procedure Law, the DA has no choice but to proceed in the interests of the child. A social services worker and a police officer would attend the scene. If the accused person was living in the house, he would be removed and held pending the results of an inquiry."

"And this inquiry—how would that go?"

"The child would be examined by a physician competent to detect the visible signs of sexual abuse. And a psychologist would conduct an interview with the child."

"Yes. I've seen these interviews. Usually, you see a professional who is already convinced that the child has been abused, trying to persuade the child that it's true."

"I bisagree, Bab. Ad thad's nod—"

"Quiet, Dwight. You've caused enough trouble already. Vanessa, I think we've all seen how Beau feels about this kind of an allegation. How does it strike you?"

"In certain divorces, where there's a lot of emotion, a lot of resentments, you come to expect something like this. It happens fairly often, more so these days since there's a lot of publicity about child molestation. Tactically, it's like using a shotgun on a butterfly, but the court has to take it seriously."

"How would you handle it? If it were placed in front of you?"

"I'd have no choice but to proceed."

"And what would be the outcome?"

"There'd be several. First, I have no doubt Beau would be completely exonerated. Eventually. But even the *fact* of the charges and the inquiry . . . many times you'll see that the courts like to bring the charge in order to try the matter thoroughly. It's one of the few criminal charges where you'll proceed on shaky testimony, and they do it because the crime itself is so offensive to the community. And there's a belief that a trial is the best way to exonerate the accused in a public way, *if* he's innocent. That's the theory, anyway. So Beau would be arrested, fingerprinted, held overnight, released on his own recognizance, all in a whirlwind of press. Considering Beau's high profile right now, and the presence of the SPEAR people and the ACLU—frankly, he'd find himself in the middle of the biggest media hurricane we've ever had in eastern Montana. When it was over, he'd be disgraced, arguably destroyed. He'd lose friends, maybe his job. He'd be tainted forever. He'd have to leave the state."

"Not ever," said Beau.

"You'd do what you could, Beau," said Hogeland. "But you know how it works. Meagher would never fire you, but I know you'd quit. That's how you are."

"Maybe."

Hogeland Senior slapped both hands on his knees and stood up.

"Yes. Well, it's a nasty business. And I intend it to stop right here, Dwight."

Dwight stared up at his father over his swollen nose and the bloody bandages.

"You cad idderfere, Bab!"

"Son, I can and I have. Now, I have no desire to know who first thought up this vile stunt. I'd like to think it was that little viper you're plowing— I'm sorry, Beau, but she *is* a bad piece of work—and not any blood of mine. I cling to that hope. But however it developed, you *will* return to your sweaty sheets and use your best efforts to dissuade this woman from continuing on this course."

Dwight blew his nose into a cloth, examined the results, groaned, and pulled in a long breath.

"Bab . . . wad if id's true?"

"Son, look at me."

Dwight struggled with his dignity and raised his head.

"Good. Son—you're a good lawyer. A great corporate lawyer, and a hell of a litigator. How much experience do you have in criminal law?"

"I ardiggled with Spellban Sterlig."

"And Spellman Sterling's a fine criminal lawyer with whom you served for *one* year. I want you to search the contents of your heart, son, and consider the ways in which you have contrived a range of ugly consequences for Maureen's ex-husband."

"Dose are legitibate and subbortable—"

The doctor held up his hand and counted off on his fingers. "One, you have done your very best to prevent him from seeing his daughter, Roberta Lee, of whom he is extremely fond. Two—and this I find particularly galling, since it took place in my own hospital—you took the trouble to visit him in his sickbed and leave a vase of flowers there and concealed—*concealed*— within the flowers there was a notice of suit in behalf of Joseph Bell. In a sick man's room, Dwight—such a cheap and shoddy trick—don't bother. This is my hospital, and I know what goes on in it. Regardless of your defenses, it was—at least I *hope* it was—beneath you. And three, you, as an officer of the court, to use your own tiresome locution—you *allow* a cruel and brutal slander to go forth concerning a man and a father who has, in spite of your best efforts, conducted himself with admirable restraint and has done so *clearly* in the interests of his daughter. If he were the hound you maintain, he'd have thrashed you months ago.''

Dwight's face was set and his breathing shallow. He had found something of surpassing interest in the vista beyond the glass.

''I hope you're listening, son.''

Dwight's eyes moved to his father's face. There was pain in them, and something close to hatred. Hogeland regarded it without reaction. Ballard and Beau watched the struggle and felt slightly sickened by it.

''Good. Now, here's what will happen. You will ensure that this slander against Beau McAllister ends here, in this room. You will inform Maureen Sprague McAllister, in whatever setting you consider to be appropriate, that should she continue in this course, I will have no choice but to sever her relationship with my clinic in Hardin. Nor will she be able to find employment in our Rosebud facility, nor in Red Lodge, nor in any other of my medical operations in Montana, Wyoming, and South Dakota.''

Ballard sat forward. ''Doc, I'm not sure you can do that. It's probably unconstitutional.''

''Perhaps. I'll get Dwight to defend me. Further, you will use your best efforts to persuade Joseph Bell to drop this absurd lawsuit against Beau and against Yellowstone County.''

Dwight stood up, staggered, and sat back down again, his hands supporting his face. Ballard finally spoke.

''We have no problem with that lawsuit, Doc. We are quite ready to contest it. Beau did what he had to do. He saved half the town doing it.''

''I've heard the circumstances. I agree you'd win. I find the whole thing—it's a shabby display. If your mother were still alive, Dwight, she'd be furious with you. I won't have the Hogeland name connected with this thing.''

He leaned forward and pulled Dwight's hands away from his face. He held Dwight's jaw in his big hand and spoke quietly to him, as he would soothe a horse or calm a child.

''Now Dwight, I hated to see this happen today. But you have been running wild lately, and it's beginning to affect my business. There are a lot of people in town asking me when I'm going to rein you in. I can't rein you in. You're a full-grown male. But this vendetta against Beau has to stop. You see to it. No more of Maureen's shrewish behavior. It's ugly to watch, and it poisons the air for all of us. And I must tell you that, although I am the chief administrator for this hospital, I am under some pressure from other members of the board to . . . reassess the wisdom of our standing contract with Mallon, Brewer, Hogeland and Bright. Some of the members feel that we ought to diversify our legal connections. I would not wish that to happen, son. I know how much our business means to your firm. But it might be taken out of my hands. Do you follow, son?''

It was clear from the pallor on Dwight's face that he followed very well.

''And''—he gently shook Dwight's head by the jaw—''and put an end to Joe Bell's lawsuit, son. Today.''

''I'b dod sure I cab, Dab.''

''Go to his house. Use your skills. Persuade him that it is not in his best interests to continue. Tell him, if you need to, that he has land development interests that need the cooperation of local businessmen. And these local businessmen do not wish to see law and order in Montana degraded by silly-ass lawsuits. Are we clear on this, Dwight?''

Dwight sat back and let out a long slow breath. A curious kind of intimacy bound them all. It held an undercurrent that Beau could not quite identify, although he knew the effect of it was making him slightly nauseous.

''Are we, Dwight?''

''We are.''

His father beamed at him and rose to his feet. He offered his son his right hand.

''Okay, Dwight. We have a couple of things to discuss here. I know you'll want to go home and get cleaned up. Will you shake hands with your old dad? No hard feelings?''

Dwight hesitated, then took the hand. His father pulled him to his feet, gathered him in, and hugged him fiercely.

''Good! Now Beau, will you shake Dwight's hand?''

''No, sir,'' said Beau, quietly, almost a whisper. ''I'd like to make you happy, Doc. But I can't do that.''

''That's all right, Beau. Perhaps I shouldn't have asked. I always push things a little too far. Now Dwight, you'll want to get along home. You'll take care of all this, won't you?''

Beau and Ballard could feel the sheer irresistible pressure of the old man's will. He was a force of nature, thought Beau. Something like him comes along perhaps once or twice in a man's life. If the man is lucky, he gets out of its way.

Dwight let out an uneven breath, half snarl and half cry, and turned away toward the door.

• • •

Hogeland spoke quietly to him for a moment, his voice a bass rumble in the hall, then he came back into the room. He was carrying a plastic bag with what looked like a cassette player inside it. He set it down on the table in front of them and poured himself a coffee. His hands were steady and his breathing even.

"Well," he said, "that was a nasty bit of business. I'm sorry for it, Beau . . . Vanessa. I hope you'll forgive me."

Ballard did not return his smile. "Did you know what Dwight was going to say?"

"Of course. He told me last night."

"And when Beau asked for this meeting, you insisted that he bring me along."

"I did, child."

"And you knew how Beau would react?"

"I was prepared to let events take their course."

"Including having a bowl and some bandages standing by, Doc?"

He gave her a wolfish grin. "Observant as ever, child. How like your mother you are. We all miss her terribly, you know. She was a good friend to my wife in her last weeks. Julia loved Bonnie. She was so vivid."

Ballard ignored this. "I have to tell you, Doc, that was one of the most terrifying uses of power I have ever seen. I feel sickened by it."

"I'm sure you do, Vanessa. Power is an ugly thing. So is surgery. But good things often come of both. And you'll admit that this abomination had to be stopped."

"Your methods—"

"Are my own, child. Dwight is my only child, and he suffered greatly during his mother's illness. As Julia wasted away on the dialysis machine, jaundiced and in ceaseless pain—Dwight watched all of it. He never left her. And when she died, he saw it as his failure. Her renal system was terribly degenerated. Dwight was always given to intense affections and passions. He sees things simplistically, as he saw Julia's death. Black and white. He needs to be seasoned. Life will do that, I'm sure, but I intend to assist the process, and my means are my own. When you marry and have children of your own, Vanessa, I'll be delighted to accept instruction from you in the matter." His tone shifted, and he grew businesslike. He lifted the plastic bag and handed it to Beau.

"That was found by Nate's intern yesterday afternoon."

"Yes?" said Beau, turning it in his hands.

"It was found on the person of our Jane Doe. The headphones were on her head, and the machine was resting on her breast."

Beau and Ballard considered it.

"I take it, Doc, that no nurse did this?" she asked.

"No, Vanessa. And the patient was under police guard, as Beau will confirm. Someone from the outside brought it in."

Beau was aware of the Polaroid photo in his shirt. "I had a visitor in my hospital room on Saturday night," he told them.

"Who was it?" asked Hogeland.

Beau pulled out the photo and handed it to the doctor. "I have no idea. But he was there."

"He left this?" said Ballard.

"Not in the hospital room. I found it under my pillow back at my house. He—whoever—had also been in my trailer."

Finally, Ballard said, "Why? Why do something like that?"

"Why steal a morgue wagon? Why the fanatical resistance at Arrow Creek? Why attack Joe Bell?"

The doctor shook his head slowly. "I have no answers for those questions. I have another question. Rather, a fact. We have a nurse complaining of a sore neck. She has a small but intense bruise on her upper mastoidal process. She was one of the two nurses attending to the intensive care unit on the night this machine made its magical appearance."

"Has she washed?" Beau wanted to know, thinking of latent prints.

"Yes, I suspect so. It didn't seem important. We thought she had fallen asleep with her neck in a strained position. It wasn't until this device was found that any of us thought to make any more of it. Not that it is at all clear that any connection exists."

"And this machine—who's handled it?"

"The intern. I'm having his prints brought around from records. We always fingerprint our staff for their ID cards—too many drug thefts from the pharmacy. The intern handed it to Nate Seidelman, who was smart enough *not* to touch it. I'm getting you his prints anyway. He put it in a Baggie and brought it to me. He thought, since there was a police connection, the machine might be relevant."

Vanessa looked at it. "Has anyone played it?"

"The batteries are dead. It must have been running continually. Do you wish to hear the tape? I have a player here."

"Yes," said Beau. "Do you have any forceps or pliers around?"

"Mrs. Miles will have some."

They managed to get the tape out and into Hogeland's stereo player without smearing any possible fingerprints. They pressed the key and listened to the eerie sonorous drone rising and falling.

"What is that?" asked Ballard. The doctor answered before Beau.

"It's a song, I think a healing song. I've heard it on the Rosebud."

"Then it's Lakota," said Beau, moved by the hypnotic chant. Hogeland looked at him with a certain amount of surprise.

"The Rosebud's Lakota territory," Beau said.

"That it is, Beau."

"Doc, do you know a Lakota named—Vanessa?"

"George Cut Arms?"

"Cut Arms? That's a Sioux name for a Cheyenne brave. But there are some Cut Arms on the Rosebud. Why? Is there a connection?"

"I don't know, Doc."

Hogeland looked at him closely, as if trying to read his mind.

"Well, our Jane Doe's not going to be seeing visitors for a long while. Her prognosis is poor."

Ballard spoke up. "She can't talk or communicate at all?"

"Not at all, child. She's very badly hurt. Still in a coma."

"This sing here—you called it a healing sing, Doc?"

"I believe so, Beau. They sometimes sing a song very like it in the clinic. Usually it's only the elders, because only the elders still believe. The youngsters are wasting away, really. It's a tragedy. The reason I'm as informally dressed as I am is because I was leaving today for the Rosebud. I do *pro bono* work there myself. I like to keep my . . . touch. They need so much help, and it keeps me grounded. I weep for that fine race."

"Yeah. Doc, are they losing babies up there?"

Hogeland's craggy face darkened. He nodded.

"Yes. So many. They won't come in for prenatal care. They're so young, many of the mothers. Many of them are prostitutes, and they are careless about birth control. Poor nutrition adds to it. And glue sniffing. Fetal alcohol syndrome. Anencephaly. Botched abortions at home or in the back of a pickup. What we have allowed to happen to the Sioux, to the Crow and the Cheyenne—we have much to answer for. I do what I can to— I do penance."

"Doc, you remember that highway crash last week?"

"Yes. Mary Littlebasket was a patient in my Hardin clinic."

"She had a baby. It was . . . "

"Anencephalic? Yes. A sad thing. She was inconsolable. She became convinced that there was some sort of conspiracy. It's not an unusual reaction.

Actually, Maureen was the senior RN on the case. She was treating the girl for postpartum depression, but apparently she was hiding the sedatives.''

Beau nodded. ''Look, Doc, I know this is going to sound stupid, but what the hell *is* anencephaly?''

''It's a fatal birth defect. It occurs at the beginning of organo-genesis—''

''Doc.''

''Okay, that is when the cells that make up the fertilized egg first begin to separate into the shapes and qualities that will ultimately become functioning internal organs. What you get is an improper formation of the neural tube—that's what will eventually form the brain and spinal column. The neural tube doesn't close properly, and as a consequence the brain doesn't develop.''

''You mean, the kid is born without a brain? How the hell can it *live* without a brain?''

''Well, circulation and respiration are usually maintained by lower brain-stem operations. Even in massive head injuries, you quite frequently see autonomic systems continue, although there's no higher cerebral activity.''

''Is the baby alive?''

''It breathes. It seems to sleep. Digestion and waste elimination go on. The body can survive for a while. Death comes, at most, in a few days. But there's no brain-wave activity, because there's no actual brain. The skull is usually grossly deformed as well—truncated, flattened. It's a terrible thing to see.''

''Doc, do you keep—does *anybody* keep records of the incidence of anencephaly on the reserves?''

Hogeland's eyes widened. ''I imagine—well, we of course are compiling a record of various birth problems. I suppose I could get Records to cross-index for anencephaly.''

''Can you get figures for Wyoming and South Dakota as well?''

''I can. May I know *why*?''

Beau looked at his hands. ''I'm not sure why. If I could see the figures, it would at least eliminate a couple of possibilities.''

''Are you talking about—is it something environmental? Is someone suggesting that there's a toxic source for these defects? Are *you* thinking that?''

Beau hadn't been, up until that point.

''Is it possible, Doc?''

Hogeland was silent for a while.

''It would have to be a very controlled study. And there'd have to be some test for iatrogenesis. And a control group. . . . But what the hell would it be? There's nothing out there in the reserves but grass and rattlesnakes. The water's checked by the EPA. They grow a lot of their own food, and the agricultural systems are the same statewide. They live in the same air, eat the same food. Even if there *was* some kind of short-term blip in the defect rate, that's no reason to imagine an environmental cause. Hell, the principle of regression alone would account for any short-term increase.''

"Statistical regression, you mean?''

The old man raised his head and cocked an eyebrow. "You've been *studying* this, Beau! You surprise me. The thing is, Beau, we have to go very carefully here. You can't just race around the countryside shouting about toxic dumps and infant mortality. You could start a statewide panic.''

"I don't want that either, Doc. How do we do this?''

"Well, I can pull the figures for you. To be honest, I haven't seen *anything* to support this theory, but then, I haven't really *looked,* either. Will you leave it with me? Do nothing rash, say nothing about this, until I can get something solid in our hands.''

"Please. Take it and run with it.''

"What are you going to do now?''

"If I can, I'd like to go down and see if I can get some time with Charlie Tallbull.''

"Certainly. I'll call the ICU. But—again—why?''

"This is going to sound pretty wild, Doc.''

"Wilder than what you've just said?''

Beau considered the old man and thought about waiting until Vanessa was gone.

No, he might as well get the reality-check now.

He told them about Vlasic's observations of the Sun Dance wounds, and his inferences about a developing Indian movement in the state, about the SPEAR connection.

They listened to his story in silence. When he was finished, Hogeland leaned back in his chair. "Hell of a tale there, Beau.''

Ballard was writing in a notebook. She finished and looked up at Beau. "I want to bring in the attorney general. This might be a federal concern.''

"*What* might be, Vanessa?'' said Beau, getting to his feet. "All we have right now is some arrows and a Polaroid. Let me talk to Meagher, let's *both* talk to him. But for God's sake, let's not get the feds in here.''

"I think Beau's right, Vanessa. At least wait until I can get some figures and see if there's anything to any of this. Frankly, I doubt there's any increase in infant mortality other than a minor one that would be in line with statistical probability. Let Beau dig around, and we'll see what surfaces. Will you keep me informed, Beau?''

"If Vanessa will let me." He looked at her. She nodded.

"Of course, Doc. If it's a matter of public health, you're the state surgeon general, anyway.''

Hogeland got to his feet slowly and walked them to the door, an arm on each of their shoulders.

Beau stopped at the doorway and looked at the old man. "Doc, I'm sorry I hit Dwight.''

"No, you're not. You're just sorry I *saw* you hit him.''

"Somebody had to," said Ballard.

They both stared at her. She kissed Hogeland on the cheek, smiled at Beau.

"Board's at eight. Let's talk first.''

When she was gone, Hogeland inhaled deeply. "Interesting woman, that. I knew her daddy. Did you ever meet him?''

"No, but I've heard.''

"Yep. One miserable old bastard. One good thing to say about him, though.''

"What's that, Doc?''

"He's dead. You keep me informed, Beau.''

Gabriel shook himself and stretched his legs out in front of him, rustling the grasses, yawning.

The time had come to go down there and talk things over with this man. Bell had been in one of the outbuildings for a while, working on some piece of machinery. Now and then, Gabriel had heard the irregular staccato burble of a gasoline engine, and the ranch house lights would flicker and brighten. Bell was trying to fix a generator. Good. He'd be distracted, and the noise would let Gabriel surprise him. He stood up and pulled in a long breath as he looked up at the infinite blue sky.

There was an early moon, transparent, hallucinatory. It floated in the curve of twilight like a shining disk of pink pearl. There was a symmetry in the hills around him and in the division of earth and sky. Beyond the darkening blue, the stars moved in their timeless arcs, droplets of water caught in a spider's web, trapped like everything in the world was trapped, bound in the web of the rule.

In the red earth under him, broken constellations of bone and skull waited for the turning of the ground. In the east, beyond the blue hills, there was a long night coming, the dark side of the planet turning as a monster in the deep turns in a dream, sensing the moon above it.

Beau found Charlie Tallbull at the far end of the ICU ward, trussed and suspended in a stainless-steel matrix of bars and pulleys, an oxygen tube cutting into his face, his left arm held out rigidly in a brace set into a rib-cast. Tallbull's body—what was not covered by bandages and plaster—was mottled and purple and dark red. His heavy face was dulled by pain and painkillers, but one eye was open and uncovered and alert as he watched McAllister make his way down the row of chambers.

Beau stopped in front of the bed where Jane Doe lay, her blue-black hair brushed and shining, a blue ribbon around her skull-wrapping, her face as still as stone.

He stood there for a while, looking down at her, noticing the fine-boned hands on the pink coverlet, listening to the machines humming and churning around him, watching the rise and fall of her chest. So damned young.

When he felt he had suffered enough for the moment, Beau came the rest of the way down. Charlie Tallbull tried to raise a hand, failed, grimaced, and said, "McAllister—who is she?"

Beau looked back up at the other bed. "She's one of the people who were involved in a robbery at Joe Bell's place."

Charlie Tallbull croaked and moved his right hand weakly on his chest. "I...know...that. Do you...know who she is? Her clan?"

"No. We haven't got an ID yet. She had no ID with her. We weren't able to find any at the creek. We're still looking."

"She has a Lakota look. A man came to see her."

Beau stiffened. "A man, Charlie? What did he look like?"

Tallbull wheezed and raised his head. A sharp short cough racked his big frame, and Beau could see the pain go through him like sheet lightning.

"They...drug you here. Hard to think. I saw a tall black man."

"Black, like an African black?"

"No, a tall man wearing black."

Beau thought about the dream he had had, the night his picture was taken, the dream about a dark angel.

"When did he come?"

"It was...the day before yesterday. It's hard to tell the time here. They won't tell you, and my watch is gone."

"Saturday night?"

"Yes."

"What did he do?"

"He . . . stood at the end of that girl's bed. He just . . . stood there. He didn't move for so long, I thought maybe he wasn't there. But I—he put something on her head. And then I heard a noise. Like a fly buzzing, and I listened to it for a long time, because it sounded like something I heard . . . but the machines make so much noise."

"Can you tell me anything about how he looked?"

"He was not big, but tall. Your height, maybe a little shorter, and not so big. No moustache. They . . . make it so dark here at night and there's no window. . . . What time is it?"

"It's seven o'clock. It's Monday."

"Morning or night?"

"Evening."

"What's the day like?"

"Sunny. We had some clouds, but they blew over. It's getting warmer. Are you going to be okay? Is there anything I can do for you, for Ella or the boys?"

"Ella has . . . the boys." A second flicker of pain passed over the man's leathery face. "Mary died, they tell me."

"Yes."

"And her baby?"

"Yes."

There was a silence.

"I'm sorry, Charlie."

"No matter . . . it was not your fault. I should not have tried to drive away. When that man fired at us, I guess I got scared. Mary was—very afraid, and she wanted me to get us away."

"Why, Charlie? What was she afraid of?"

Tallbull was silent for several moments. "She was afraid of the nurse."

"The nurse? Which one?"

Tallbull said nothing.

"Maureen?"

"She used to be your wife, they said."

"Yes. Why was Mary afraid of her?"

Tallbull was quiet for so long, his eyes shut and his breathing uneven and raspy, that Beau had a sudden flash of fear. Then Charlie spoke again.

"Do you know anything about the Shirt Wearers?"

"Yes. It was a kind of a brotherhood clan. Lakota, a lot of the other tribes—they had warrior societies. Cheyenne Dog Soldier. Shirt Wearers were Teton, I think."

"Teton, Yankton—Santee, too. They are back."

"Back? You mean, some of the men?"

"I mean, many of the young men think . . . no, it is more like a wish or a dream. Like some of you people think the stars tell you about the future . . . or numbers . . . or that you can talk to dead people with a piece of wood."

"What do the young men think?"

"They hear things. Everybody is talking."

Charlie Tallbull had three grown sons. Willy, Philip Joe, and Little Charlie.

"Charlie, does this have anything to do with your boys?"

Tallbull shook his head, but he looked somewhere else.

"Do they think that Crazy Horse is coming back?"

Beau could see the effect on Tallbull. He stared at Beau for a long time.

"Yes. Satanka-Witko. They think he's here now."

"Why? Why did he come back?"

Tallbull gave Beau a pitying look. "You think we don't need something to help us?"

"Yes, you do. But what do the Crow have to do with something like the Shirt Wearers? And Crazy Horse hunted the Crow as much as he hunted whites. He was a Crow enemy. He tried to take the Powder River country. He killed Bloody Knife and a lot of other Crow men."

"The enemy of . . . my enemy . . . is my friend."

"Charlie, what was Mary running from?"

"Mary was afraid they would take her baby away."

"But her baby was dying."

"I saw him."

"Then you know there was no hope for that baby."

"Then why were they trying to keep it alive?"

That stopped Beau.

"That's what they do. They have to do everything they can."

"Mary knew the baby would die, McAllister. She wanted the baby to die away from the clinic. Mary went to Billings to school, you know. She was going to learn how to keep records and do the banking for some of our people. She knew what was wrong with Russel. But she watched the nurses, and she didn't like what they were doing."

"She thought they'd hurt the baby?"

"Mary was afraid of them, of what they might want with the baby."

"What would they want with her baby? Other than to keep it alive, to give it as much care as they could?"

Tallbull closed his eyes and seemed to sink into himself. Beau waited, watching him.

He opened his eyes again. ''You people, you think different about the dead. You treat them like . . . they were broken, and you take them apart to see . . . what went wrong. To a Crow this is . . . bad.''

''It's medicine, Charlie.''

''I know it's medicine. It's not our medicine. The black man, when he left, I heard the fly buzzing and buzzing . . . and finally I remembered where I heard it.''

''It was a sing.''

''Yes, a Lakota sing.''

''A healing sing.''

''No. Not a healing sing. It's a sing for purification. To drive away a Walking Wolf.''

''What's a Walking Wolf?''

''It's a man with a bad heart. An evil man.''

''You mean the black man?''

''No.''

''Who do you mean?''

Tallbull was silent, his eyes tired and pained.

''Look, Mary wrote something on the mirror before she left,'' Beau said.

Tallbull's mouth tightened. He looked at his hands.

Beau pulled out his notepad. He flipped through it until he got to his copy of the drawing Dell Greer had shown him. He handed the book to Tallbull.

''You see that drawing?''

> > > = = = = = = = = = = = >   < + >   < = = = = = = = = = = = < < <

Tallbull's face looked like a window with an iron gate coming down in front of it. It went from flesh to concrete in a half-second.

''Well . . . Charlie?''

''When you have trouble in the police, do you ask us to fix it for you?''

''That's not the same. If there's something going on, something you know about, tell me and I'll try to help.''

''We don't need you to help.''

Beau looked at Charlie Tallbull, at his broken frame and the pain in his face. ''You need someone, Charlie.''

''Maybe we have someone. Now go away. I need some sleep.''

He closed his eyes and said nothing else. After a few minutes, Beau walked away, passing the girl's bed. He stopped there and looked down at her. Her breathing was steady and slow. The side of her face was swollen and purple.

He thought about Saint Jude, the patron of lost causes. It wasn't really a prayer, but he held the thought for a while, until he felt better, and then he left.

Bell was bending over a Honda generator, wrenching at a pulley, his broad back wet with sweat. The generator was roaring and popping, almost deafening in the cramped room. The little outbuilding was a tool shed of some sort. A long bench was covered with oily rags, tools, and bits of machinery. As Gabriel paused in the door, Bell tugged at the pulley and the generator popped, stuttered, and settled into a steady muted rumble.

Bell straightened up from the machine and arched his back, one hand on his right hip, cursing softly under his breath.

Gabriel knocked twice on the doorframe.

Bell jumped and spun—very fast for a big man with a wound.

"Who the fuck are you?"

Gabriel smiled and stepped into the room. Bell stank of whisky and old sweat. His face was bright red, shiny with sweat and fear.

"The name is Picketwire. I'd like to talk to you."

"What about? There's no work here, Chief."

"I'd like to talk to you about Friday."

Bell stared at him, a number of changes passing over his face. "You with Indian Affairs?"

"No. Just an interested party."

Bell considered him for a moment. Gabriel saw his eyes flicker over Gabriel's clothes, trying to figure him out.

"How'd you find me?"

"I asked the County cops."

"They know you're here?"

"I guess so. Can we talk?"

"Just a minute, let me get cleaned up here."

Bell turned and walked over to the bench. He picked up a jar of cleaning cream and began to work it over his greasy hands. "What did you want to know, Chief?"

Gabriel was watching him carefully.

The generator muttered and rumbled in the corner.

And a sudden white light exploded in his mind. He saw the wooden floor coming up at him—turning as he fell—he saw a tall man, a blurred shape, saw something like a pistol in the man's right hand.

Gabriel hit the floor and tried to roll, his vision red at the edges and dimming, and a large brown leather boot came at him—at his face—it hit him and his head snapped backward and he hit the floor hard, and there was a momentary flaring of bright white light and then there was a heavy black weight on him and he went down under it, trying to understand where the man had come from and how he could have missed him—feeling fear and confusion and a fleeting sense of professional embarrassment—and he heard someone say "asshole" and then there was nothing at all.

"Now what the hell do we do?" said the tall man.

"How'd you know he was here?" asked Joe Bell.

The tall man reached into his jacket and pulled out a compact disk case. "I was bringing this up. I saw something in the wash there, by your gate? I looked. It was a car, under some pulled-up grass. So I figured, maybe you had somebody sneaking around. I decided to come in quiet. I saw this guy here come down the slope and walk in on you. That generator—shut it off, will you?—it was making so much noise, I guess he never heard me. You recognize him at all?"

Bell shook his head, his face greasy and pale under the red beard. "No idea. Never seen him around."

"He's Indian. That tell you anything?"

"Yeah."

There was a long pause.

"Okay," said Bell. "Gimme a hand here."

They picked Gabriel up and carried him out into the yard. Bell looked around the ranch and up into the hills.

"Up there."

They looked up the long hillside.

"Shit."

They reached the crest of the slope fifteen minutes later. Bell's chest was heaving, and his shirt was wet with sweat. The big man had taken off his suit jacket, revealing a shoulder holster with a large semiauto pistol in it. They threw Gabriel to the ground and stood over him, chests heaving, mouths open, looking at each other. Something final passed between them.

Gabriel rolled over and tried to push himself up to a sitting position. The big man pulled out the pistol—it was a big Colt Delta. He and Bell watched Gabriel sit up shakily. The right side of his face was bleeding and one eye was blackening, the cheekbone swelling.

"Who the hell are you?" said Bell.

Gabriel looked at the two men, then at the hills around them. He'd come to his death, he could see that. It was funny, really, after all that he had seen and done—he was going to die like some effengee, cold-cocked and kicked senseless by a couple of redneck ranchers. It was funny as hell. That was what you got for lying around in the long grass, daydreaming about the past and conjuring up ghosts. The goddamned countryside had killed him after all. If they ever heard about it, the guys in Skull and Bones and the rest of Section, they'd put up a picture of him in the mess hall: Putz Death of the Year. He started to laugh.

Bell stepped up and started a kick. Gabriel caught his boot in his right hand and froze Bell there, wavering on one leg, huffing and sweating. The other man raised the Colt.

"Let him go." His voice was raspy and flat. Gabriel couldn't see his face. The man was just a large shape outlined by a soft mist of early starlight. The evening sky was a radiant screen of turquoise and tourmaline. The broken circle of the moon floated above his left shoulder.

"Tell him to stop kicking me."

"Back off there, Joe."

Gabriel let go of the man's foot, and Bell hopped backward out of reach.

"Now one more time. Who are you?"

"My name's Picketwire."

The tall shape was silent, but Gabriel felt a kind of grim humor in the man's voice.

"Nice to meet you, Mr. Picketwire. Who you with?"

Gabriel laughed again, looking around for the half-shadow, the man-shaped wind, the trick of the dark that had been keeping him company during the day. Nowhere around. See? What did he expect?

"I'm not with anybody."

"Bullshit," said Bell. "What are you, Indian Affairs? FBI?"

"No Indians in the FBI," said the tall man. "You with the reservation cops?"

"I'm not a cop at all."

"Then why were you staking out my place?" said Bell.

"I'm just out walking."

"Just a tourist? That your story?" The tall man's voice was thickening, the humor evaporating. Gabriel could sense the aggression in the man. The muzzle of the Colt was rock-steady, and he was a good fifteen feet away. There was nothing to do but die politely.

"He wanted to talk about last Friday?" the tall man asked Joe Bell.

"Yeah. What you want with that, Mr. Picketwire? I thought you were a tourist."

Gabriel said nothing. He had handled it stupidly, and now he was going to die for it. It wasn't a big surprise. He was overdue for it.

"Why did you hide your car down at the gate?"

"I didn't want it stolen."

The big man was silent for a long time. Finally, he spoke. "Joe, you got a shovel?"

"Yep."

"Go get it, will you?"

Bell hobbled off down the long slope of the hill. Gabriel and the tall man watched him until he reached the shed at the bottom of the slope. His red setter ambled out of the main house and followed Bell inside. Minutes passed. The dusk was deepening. The wind was soft and warm, laden with sweet scent and pollen. The tall man watched Gabriel carefully.

"You don't seem too worried, Mr. Picketwire."

"Nothing I can do."

"This situation doesn't bother you?"

"Sure it does. But you're too far away to get to, and you don't seem like a man who can be talked out of his weapon."

Bell was coming back up the slope now, his setter trotting along behind him.

"You could just tell us who you're with. Maybe there's something we can work out."

Gabriel sat up a little straighter. His head felt like a cylinder full of helium, and he was losing the vision in his right eye.

"There's no deal to make. Why don't you just get it done?"

"And you got no idea what's going on? A goddamned Indian?"

"Not a clue. Anybody hungry? It's way past dinnertime."

The man stood up, sighing. "Get up."

Gabriel got to his feet slowly.

"Now what?"

"Now nothing," he said, raising the Colt.

Gabriel saw the muzzle come up. The big man was going to shoot him right in the face. He heard the setter barking, and Bell's boots rustling through the long grass. Think about your training, try to remember what they told you. What was there to do?

In this situation?

You died.

There was a blue-white flare—silence—a massive blow—cold as ice—
the night sky revolving—the stars a blurring wheel of brittle cold lights—
sound now, a distant rumbling falling away down the slopes—something
slammed him in the back, and the stars rained down in his eyes like a shower
of stainless-steel needles.

Blood filled his throat.

He had a picture in his mind—a bending of the light.

Now we'll see, he thought.

We'll see if

16

2000 Hours – June 17 – Billings, Montana

The Criminal Investigation Bureau shooting board convened at 2000 hours on Monday evening, in the boardroom of the Yellowstone County Courthouse. The largest thing in the big room was a twenty-foot-long redwood table that had once been part of the household of a cattleman-king. He had donated it to the County as part of a final burst of philanthropy, a desperate and unsuccessful attempt to propitiate the cancer god.

His portrait had a prominent place out in the hall: a rakehell's face with hunted eyes and a prodigious beak, the required black handlebar moustache, and a suit from Savile Row that he had been buried in a year after the picture was done.

The boardroom was lined in more redwood and had a row of leaded-glass windows that had also been looted from an old Montana establishment, an army whorehouse in Billings. The glass in the frames was so old that it had thickened at the bottom, and its yellow tint cast a suitably jaundiced light over the business of the courts.

Vanessa Ballard held the upper end of the table, her snakesin briefcase open beside her, her Pearlcorder and a little seed mike propped up on the briefcase.

Eustace Meagher sat at the opposite end of the table, a chart-board propped up on an easel behind him with a detailed map of the Ballantine side road and the relevant sections of Arrow Creek marked off in green ink. Meagher's garrison belt and service piece hung on the back of his chair, and he had his clip-tie off and the first two buttons of his tan patrol shirt open. A pile of computer fanfold paper lay at his elbow.

On Meagher's right, Finch Hyam slouched in a wrinkled beige sports jacket and dark brown trousers, his lanky frame limp and his lean face shiny with sweat.

"Howdy" Rowdy Klein, Hyam's partner in the Criminal Investigation Bureau, sat beside him, head down, lips set, writing something on a yellow legal pad, working hard to convey the impression of a man with heavy burdens that he would neither shirk nor share. Sweat stained his armpits and the hollows of his dark blue suit.

In the long wood-paneled hallway outside the boardroom, a large group of men and women sat or stood in various combinations, according to their moods and friendships.

Beneath the portrait of the dead cattle-king sat Dell Greer and Moses Harper, stiff and starched in blue County uniforms, their Stetsons on their knees, hands on the Stetsons. They looked like nervous bookends. They were here to tell their stories and, they sincerely hoped, offer support for Meagher's contention that he had no choice but to shoot the Indian male who had confronted them in the hills above the creek. And they hoped— even *more* sincerely—that there wasn't some kind of unexpected career-terminating bear-trap hidden inside Vanessa Ballard's briefcase.

Next to them, sitting up straight and looking around the hall with unconcealed fascination, his large black-booted feet barely reaching the hardwood floor, was Trooper Benitez—now blooded and proven—tightly wrapped in a torso bandage under his pressed tan uniform, bruised about the face and freshly scrubbed, his shiny black hair combed straight back from his blunt Indio features.

Standing next to Trooper Benitez, slouching bonelessly against the wall, Myron Sugar ran through the Friday-night action again and again, trying to see the traps and snares and get it all straight in his mind.

Sugar liked to stick to his desk, and he'd gone along with Meagher that night with his heart in his throat. Maybe it was punishment for ignoring the sabbath. Maybe if he'd been a better Jew, he wouldn't have been working that night at all and someone else would have had to go and get involved in an Indian war.

Rita Sonnette and Ron Thornton and a couple of other cops were slouching around fanning themselves with their hats and grousing about the time this was taking.

In a far corner of the hall Marla LeMay sat in a railchair, staring straight ahead, her hands in her lap. She was wearing her waitress uniform. Rita Sonnette had picked her up at Bell's Oasis, where she had been acting as the boss for Joe Bell until his wounds healed enough for him to come back to the station.

Next to her, but not with her, Danny Burt sat in a hardback chair, reading an old *Sports Illustrated*. He wore his usual morgue wagon uniform— a black suit, single breasted, over a pale gray shirt and a thin black tie. Black brogues carefully tied, and a gold ring on the third finger of his left hand.

Danny Burt was a large man with a hard little potbelly and thick hands covered with fine blond hair. His head was shiny with sweat in the stuffy room, and thinning blond hairs stuck to his scalp. His face was pale and blunt, and his eyes, which at first meeting might have been mistaken for friendly and warm, were actually cool and remote-looking, gray-blue and flecked with green, like mountain onyx. At his wrist a gold Rolex caught the light from the lamp next to him, illuminating his hard face and the roughness of his unshaven cheeks.

The wedding ring was less than it seemed; Burt said he wore it to keep the women in line. He wasn't married, although he maintained that he had been once, back in La Crosse, Wisconsin. His wrists were exposed as he held the magazine. Fresh bruises showed on them, red marks and raw skin where the ropes had held him. There was a purple bruise above his left eye, and a butterfly stitch held a section of his eyebrow together.

Normally he liked to mix it up with the cops, and he was always a welcome addition to any barside chat. Today he kept to himself and answered Ron Thornton's conversational leads with noncommittal grunts.

Ron assumed he didn't like official business, even less since it was Danny Burt's carelessness that had gotten the wagon hijacked in the first place and Peter Hinsdale killed.

Standing alone at the farthest reach of the hallway, leaning against a wooden railing that overlooked the lower rotunda and the front doors of the courthouse, a short fox-faced man in a dark brown suit and heavy brown shoes stood watching the other witnesses. Frank Duffy, special agent in charge, of the FBI's Montana liaison office in Helena.

Crimes involving possible interstate flight or federal installations were part of the FBI's jurisdiction. But even if they weren't part of this one, the arrival of SPEAR and the ACLU on the scene would have brought them into it. SPEAR was on a list of subversive organizations with possible terrorist connections. Had been ever since 1973, when Russell Means took over at Wounded Knee.

Duffy's brown hair was thinning into a blade shape, exposing a high sunburned forehead. His ears were huge and projected straight out from the side of his skull. He had a sharp nose and a narrow jawline. His skin seemed stretched over his skull, and Duffy projected a general air of guile and suspicion.

Beau McAllister, in a sense the star of the evening—the way an aristocrat is the star of the activities around a guillotine—was back in Lizardskin, packing a bag and talking to Tom Blasingame about his cats.

A large white wall clock at the end of the hall ticked loudly in the hush and murmur, tinny and relentless.

Vanessa Ballard poured herself some water from a silver pitcher. She drank it all and set it down, and something about the motion stopped the small talk between Finch Hyam and Rowdy Klein. Meagher waited with an expectant look on his face, his eyebrows cocked. He knew Vanessa was still angry about the scene in Doc Darryl's office. Beau had gone over the top and down the far side on that one. Meagher hoped his career could survive it. Yet Meagher felt that Beau had been set up to do that, aimed and fired like a 105. Why would the old man want his son worked over like that? It was ugly.

On the other hand, the kid needed a beating, and if he was going to get one, why not let Beau have the pleasure? The kid had caused him enough grief over the last couple of years.

Vanessa Ballard looked up from her notes.

"Fine, gentlemen. If we're all ready, we'll proceed."

She turned on her Pearlcorder, read the time and date, and started to name the officers present.

Rowdy Klein was looking increasingly worried. When she got to the end of her list, he leaned forward and raised his hand, waving it to get her attention.

"What is it, Sergeant Klein?"

"Ahh—ma'am, shouldn't we wait for Staff Sergeant McAllister?"

"He'll be along," said Meagher. "Relax, Rowdy. You'll get your chance at him."

Ballard looked at Klein over the tops of her glasses. "That okay with you, Sergeant?"

Klein flushed red and wiped his face with a large gingham handkerchief. He folded it and stuffed it into his breast pocket.

"No, ma'am. I mean, this'll be . . . if you think it's okay?"

"I do."

Klein had a mean streak in him, especially where Beau was involved. The ugly scene between them in the aftermath of the shooting at Bell's Oasis was just one of a long string of confrontations. Meagher figured that Klein was jealous of Beau's reputation. Or maybe Klein was just an asshole. If Klein had been directly under Meagher's command, he would have been looking at the world from behind the grill in evidence storage over in Bozeman. But he wasn't. The Criminal Investigation Bureau was a separate department of the state's Department of Justice, created to spread the scarce resources of the detective operation around the state. They had their HQ in Helena, where they played Hide the Bunny with the FBI and generally involved themselves in what the department liked to call Serious Crimes. Meagher was only nominally Klein's superior.

Ballard was up to speed now. She ran through the reported events of last Friday, including the shooting at Bell's Oasis, running down the events in simple, clear terms, providing the context for the shooting board and, not incidentally, also setting up her sightlines in the event that criminal charges might arise from the evidence to be presented today.

Meagher sighed and forced himself to focus.

Rita Sonnette came in, told her part in a slightly shaky voice. It was her first shooting board, and like all rookies, it worried her. But there was iron in her. Meagher thought she was shaping up nicely. She'd be a good trooper.

Ron Thornton came next, and everything he said about the Bell shooting corresponded neatly with Beau's report and with Rita Sonnette's.

Very neatly. Even some identical turns of phrase.

Obviously, Ron and Rita had taken the time to work out their stories, which was fine with Meagher as long as Vanessa didn't object. As Ron talked, his young face bright with radiant sincerity and earnest professionalism, Ballard kept her head down and made notes, looking up now and then to stare at Ron over her reading glasses.

When Ron was finished, Ballard sent Meagher a loaded glance and called for the next witness.

They came in no particular order. Vanessa Ballard liked to run it that way. It helped to keep the witnesses off-balance and interfered with their tendency to try to corroborate one another. It hadn't seemed to work with Thornton and Sonnette.

Marla LeMay told her story, unimpressed and cynical, neither a support for Bell nor an accuser. She told it straight and seemed not to give a damn what they thought of it. Meagher was attracted to that quality in people. The world was too stuffed with people, especially civilians, who wanted to impress you with how much they knew.

Joe Bell would have been called in next, but since he was suing the county, he would have needed legal representation, and that was a delicate area right now.

"Why?" asked Finch Hyam, intrigued, his antennae up.

"Let's just say the situation is fluid, Detective Hyam. We can proceed without Bell's information right now. We have plenty of witnesses."

Hyam let it pass, but his eyes were bright with interest, and he looked over at Meagher, raising an eyebrow. Meagher frowned at him and shook his head once.

Ballard called Finch next.

It was clear from Finch's tone and the way he stared solidly ahead as he answered Ballard's questions that he had no doubts about the rightness of Beau's actions, that he thought Joe Bell was a danger to himself and others, and that anybody who pulled a gun around a Montana Highway Patrol trooper had better expect to get himself shot. That included any demented Indian fanatics suicidal enough to lock horns with a cop. He finished and nodded to Rowdy Klein.

Rowdy Klein tied himself in knots trying to make his case that Beau McAllister had mishandled his part of the incident at Bell's Oasis, but he didn't have much in the way of evidence, unless sheer bad will was evidence.

Meagher interrupted him, his voice hard and clipped. "As McAllister's CO I want to get in the record that there had been an exchange of fire before the sergeant arrived on the scene, but we do not seem to have established who *initiated* the exchange. So it seems to me that he can't be accused of interfering with a citizen's right to self-defense and defense of property *until* it's been clearly shown that Bell was actually defending himself. All I hear so far is proof that some kind of hostilities were being engaged in, and that McAllister's arrival helped to prevent further exchange of fire. If Sergeant

Klein wants to bring formal charges against my sergeant, he's got the legal right to do so, but I'm not gonna sit here and listen to him talk about something that took place while he was off somewhere practicing his quick-draw. Due respect, ma'am.''

"Hell, Lieutenant," said Klein, "how can you say there was no robbery attempt? What *else* did it look like?"

"That's enough," said Ballard. "Thank you, Sergeant Klein."

The next witness was Dell Greer, followed by Moses Harper.

They both described the events leading up to the Arrow Creek confrontation as simply as they could, referring to their notes and reciting the details in a lockjaw singsong cops use when talking to DA's. The details corroborated other testimony, and they were both excused with thanks.

Out in the hall, they picked up their hats, waved to the rest of the witnesses, and split for the parking lot at a slow run. From there they went straight to the Muzzleloader and ordered a Coors and a Corona, which they downed in two takes.

Danny Burt was next.

Burt came into the room surrounded by dead air. He smiled briefly at Meagher and the two CIB men. They had all gotten swilled together more times than they could count, at Twilly's or Fogarty's New York Bar. But today was formal, and Burt seemed to know that one of the results of this hearing might be a contributory negligence charge against him. The first thing he said made his position clear.

"I just want to make a statement, ma'am?"

"Certainly, Mr. Burt."

"I give—I retained a lawyer this morning, and he's saying that if this meeting gets into anything about the hijacking and that, then I'm gonna clam up. Okay?"

Ballard looked at him for a moment, her face blank.

"To whom did you give the retainer?"

"Spellman Sterling."

Everyone around the table tried not to react to that information. Ballard's eyes were bright and amused. "Are we to assume by this that you intend not to answer questions in this matter?"

Burt's blunt face closed up and his brows came down.

"I'm not sayin' I won't say anything. I'm just sayin' that if it gets into blamin' me or stuff like that, then I'm outta here."

"You can be subpoenaed, Mr. Burt."

"Fire away. I haven't been summoned for this hearing. I'm giving my testimony freely and of my own good will. It's just I got no intention of being no scapegoat for a police fuckup.''

"Hey, Danny, come on, man,'' said Klein, looking hurt. Ballard raised a delicate, long-fingered hand and he snapped his mouth shut.

"Mr. Burt, these proceedings are not criminal. We are gathered here merely as a committee of inquiry, to examine in an orderly way the events surrounding the several deaths that took place this past Friday. I can assure you that, as assistant district attorney for Yellowstone County, I would be seriously remiss in my duties if I were to allow any development of evidence here that provided a *prima facie* basis for an indictment without first ensuring that you—that any person appearing here, any person who might be the subject of a criminal inquiry leading to an indictment—had been apprised of your rights under the law, including the right to counsel and the right not to make self-incriminatory statements. Now, if you have reason to believe that there is a material possibility that information will come forth at these informal hearings that might . . . incriminate you or create some inference of guilt or culpability, then I would most strongly advise you now to get up from this table and leave. Mr. Sterling and I have a long professional acquaintance, and I would be delighted to communicate with him in this regard and to have him present at any formal interrogation.''

Burt's face went through a number of changes. "I—I haven't done anything wrong.''

"And no one here thinks you have, Mr. Burt.'' Her tone softened. She shut off the recorder.

"Look, Danny. This is merely an administrative function here. Obviously, Spellman thinks so, too, or he'd be here with his moustache in flames. Nobody thinks you've done anything that could, or should, result in any charges at all. Now, I know how sorry you must be, and I know you feel that, in some way, you are responsible for Peter Hinsdale's death.''

"Hell, Ms. Ballard—I feel like shit about it! Can't get any sleep! Been pissed—been drinking all weekend! Poor little bastard. I mean, the kid was a pain in the butt, only—not even—I mean, I think the whole thing *sucks.* Ma'am.''

"So do we all, Danny. We all think it . . . sucks. Now that I've tried to reassure you, may we continue?''

Burt looked around the table.

"Sure, Ms. Ballard. I'm sorry for my language.''

She smiled and turned on the tape recorder again. "Now we have reached the time when, as it has been reported by other witnesses, you and

Peter Hinsdale arrived at the scene of the first shooting. Perhaps you could go on from there, in your own words?''

"Sure. Well, me and Pete, we had another call to make, over at Laurel. Mr. Gentile has a contract with Zweibeck's Nursing Home, so we were trying to get this done. The medical examiner had already been there, and Rowdy said—''

"Let the record show that Mr. Burt has made reference to Dr. Marco Vlasic, acting as coroner, and to Sergeant Rudolph Klein of the CIB.''

Klein refrained from mentioning to Ballard that he preferred to use the name Rowdy.

"Yeah, and Sergeant Klein told me that it was okay to take the sti—the client away. So me and Pete, we bagged him and filed him in the cooler.''

"Try to resist the idiom, Mr. Burt.''

"What?''

"Please speak in plain terms, Mr. Burt.''

"Oh. Okay. We placed the client in a body bag, and we put him in the tray, and we slid the tray into the wagon. Then we—well, I got on the CB and Bob—Mr. Gentile—says that the people at Zweibeck's called to say that the old far—the elderly client who died was Jewish, and since it was Friday and the guy was orthodox, it seems that he hadda be taken by his own family and they'd made arrangements with the synagogue to take charge of the body and get him buried within twenty-four hours. So we had nothing to do, and I figured, you know, it was hot as hell and we'd had a long day, and the kid was yarfing at me—I mean, Pete was whining and complaining about the shift. Kid complained a lot, ma'am, he was kind of a pain in the—well, so just to, I guess, crank him off, I decide to stop in at Fogarty's for a coupla brews.''

"Fogarty's being Fogarty's New York Bar in Pompeys Pillar?''

"Yes, ma'am. So I park the cooler and Pete starts in yarfing again, so I say I'm going in and he kin slide if he don't—doesn't—if he isn't thirsty.''

"And this would have been at what time, approximately?''

"It would be exactly six. Or seven. Maybe.''

"Exactly maybe or perhaps maybe?''

"Huh?''

"Never mind. Please go on.''

"Well, I had a coupla drinks with Fogarty and we talked about this and that. And then I get into talking with this Indian guy who came in.''

"Can you describe him for us?''

"Yeah. Long black hair, in braids. Not old, but he had a tough face.

Like he'd been around, you know. Big guy. But he was friendly and—well, one thing leads to another, and . . . ''

"Yes?"

"So, I know this is stupid, but I get to drinkin' and I say to Fogarty and this guy, I'm tellin' them about the shoot-out, you know, and here I got this kid in the cooler. So we just go out, you know, to take a look at him.''

"And who took part in this . . . expedition to view the corpse?''

"Me. Fogarty. This Indian guy, said his name was Earl. So we scope out the stiffie and everybody says, you know, like it was too bad. I was feeling kinda bad because it was a dead Indian and here I am showing the body to another Indian. Like it was a sensitive issue. Which I guess it was.''

"Was this Native American male someone you knew, even casually?''

"Nope. I know most everybody in the county. This guy was from nowhere around here. Real hardcase, too. Looked like he'd done time.''

"Thanks for the guesswork, Mr. Burt. If you'll just relate, in any words you like, just relate the events as you were in a position to observe them, we'll take care of the forensic inferences.''

Burt ducked his head, swallowed, and ran them through it. After a few more drinks, the Indian named Earl had paid for his beers and gotten up from the barstool just as Burt and Hinsdale were leaving. At the door, he asked Burt which way they were going. Burt said into Billings, and the man asked for a lift.

"And that was that. We get about a half-block away, and suddenly I got this machete at my throat and Pete is crying, and next thing I know we're out at the end of the street. Earl gets me to pull in behind the grain barn there, you know, Minnocks Feed Barn? And there's a whole gang of them there. A young girl, pretty thing, but not in any mood for talk. Another man they called James, an old guy whose name I didn't get, and Earl from the bar. They all get in, Earl in beside me and Pete, and the rest in the back with the stiff. Pull the curtains around, and boom, we're outta town.''

"Did you see any other weapons?''

"Oh yeah! Metal bows and arrows. Real modern stuff. Expensive. And knives. They didn't talk much. They were . . . scary.''

"Did they discuss the events at Joe Bell's gas station?''

"Not a lot. I got the idea that it was the kid they wanted. Like it was a religious thing. The girl was pretty strong on that point. I got the idea getting the body back had been her idea, and they were going along with it to please her. But the old guy, he was pretty pissed about it. He opened up the crate—the casket—and man, was he cranked about *that*! I thought, that's it. Good-night nurse. Touched the wound, rubbed the blood on his cheeks and his forehead. Total fruitbasket! But you got the idea he was running things, and that the other two guys were muscle.''

"Did you form any opinions regarding their intentions?''

"They were getting the hell outta town, ma'am.''

"Yes. I meant, what their intentions might have been in their initial approach to Bell's Oasis.''

"Intentions, ma'am? I'd say their intentions was to rob the shit outta the place. They had the bows, and they was sure as hell a gang. Had a boss and a plan and a skinfulla bad intentions. They went there to rob Joe Bell. I already been over this with Finch and Rowdy.''

"Were they specific about that? They named Joe Bell?''

"Yeah! Joe Bell, they said. They said they were going to get the man, get Joe Bell. They said they had gone after 'the old man,' and I took that to mean Joe Bell.''

"Their exact words were 'get the man. Get the old man'?''

"Yeah. I got the impression that's what they wanted. Like they had picked out Joe Bell's place, and the rest had just happened. They said something about the shotgun, about it being under his desk, and one of the younger guys, I think it was James, says, 'We should have taken him at the pumps,' and then the old man tells them all to shut up. I guess he was worried about them talking in front of us.''

"And it was your distinct impression that this group of people, one young woman and one young male, and two middle-age males whom you knew as Earl and James, and the elderly man—''

"Donna! They called her Donna! She was crying and carrying on, and the old man said something like 'Be still, Donna!' and she clammed right up. That old guy, yeah, he was definitely running things.''

"Thank you. That Earl and James and—Donna? And this 'old man'— it was your impression that they had initiated the contact with Joe Bell in order to carry out an armed robbery of the premises.''

"Yes, ma'am. They had the bows and shit. They were as pissed off as a buncha scorpions in a frying pan. They were all fired up. I figured, listening to them growling at each other, I figured I could just bend over, kiss my—''

"I'm sure. And what happened then?''

"Then? Then they get me to drive to the Ballantine road and off into the creek. That's one thing. It was like they knew the creek, you know? Knew that it was shallow enough to drive in. And we get a few miles up the creek—by now, I'm hearing on the CB from Mr. Gentile and from you guys''—he nodded at Finch Hyam and Rowdy Klein—''so I know, like, the search is on.''

"I understand, from other reports, that you were now separated from Peter Hinsdale."

"Yes, ma'am. They stopped up the creek there, by the big bend below the bluffs. They go around, open up the back. Take out the kid's body. That was when I figured we was dead, because the girl, she goes nuclear. Rangy! Crying and stuff. The men were just sort of solemn and sad, but she—I don't wanna run into *her,* she's got a gun or something.''

"I understand."

"So they take a look at us, and they tell Pete to get into the coffin. I tried to stop that, but the way it looked, I figured if they were gonna stick him into a coffin alive, then maybe they weren't going to kill him. So I got him calmed down, and they put him in there. He was crying a lot, and they just slammed the lid on him. It was hard. They were hard people. Then they took me some ways up the creek. I figure, this is it, say your prayers and kiss your butt good-bye. But they just tied me to a tree. Did a good job, too.''

He held up his wrists and pulled the sleeves of his suit jacket back.

"No screwing around there. I'm down on my knees in the gravel by the creek there, all I can see is the tree bark in front of my face. I'm thinkin', okay, one of them just reaches around, cuts me a new mouth, takes my scalp, and I'm tryin' not to whine, you know, to go out with a hard-on— shit, ma'am, my language—''

"Yes. It must have been terrible for you. Would you like a glass of water?''

"I'd fuck a bobcat for a brew, ma'am.''

Ballard looked across at Meagher, her thoughts clear. She asked Burt a few more questions, which soon became circular. Burt was earnest, but beyond his feelings about being tied to a tree all night, he had little to add. When she told him he was excused and thanked him, he let out a long sigh, like a deflating tire. It was all he could do not to run from the room.

"What do you think'll happen to Burt, Vanessa?''

She shut off the tape. "I think Bob Gentile will probably get sued by Hinsdale's mother, and she'll sure as hell include Burt in that. I can't see any criminal charges against him. He's a victim, same as Peter Hinsdale. If Spellman Sterling's defending him, he'll do okay. I just don't see how he can afford Sterling. I know he asks for at least a thousand as a retainer. I didn't think Burt had that sort of money. On the other hand, he could pawn that Rolex.''

"I saw that," said Meagher. "Think it's a fake?"

"No. It's real. Okay," said Ballard. "Let's wrap this up."

By the time they finished with the rest of the witnesses, everyone at the table could see that there was a pretty good basis for treating these shootings as justifiable use of force.

There had been an assault, an armed assault witnessed by Marla LeMay and others. Missiles had been fired with malicious intent. Regardless of the actual sequence of events, it was obvious that these Native Americans had arrived on the scene with weapons, that some kind of confrontation had ensued. They'd present those results to the SPEAR people. Maybe they'd go away.

Klein spoke up. "That's true, Ms. Ballard. But we haven't established whether Staff Sergeant McAllister had any call to shoot Joe Bell. And he did allow the Indians to escape. Seems to me we ought to suspend—"

Meagher sat forward and slapped his palm down hard on the table. Even Vanessa Ballard jumped.

"God-*damn it,* Howdy, will you get *off* that horse! You got corks in your ears or what? Haven't you heard a thing said here?"

Ballard stopped the exchange by making a display of turning the tape machine back on. Police officers hate tape recorders. They use them to tape snitches and criminals. Having to talk into one turns their world around, and they don't like it.

"Thank you. Perhaps someone will see if Sergeant McAllister is out in the hall?"

Finch Hyam got up and went out the door. In a few minutes, he was back, followed by Beau McAllister in civilian clothes, a two-piece blue suit, a shirt and tie. He smiled at everyone, including Rudy Klein, and took a seat at the end of the table.

"Sergeant, we feel the time has come for you to tell us, in your own words, in as much detail as you can recall, everything you can about the events subsequent to the apparent hijacking of the morgue wagon. Including and with a particular emphasis on the confrontation at Arrow Creek."

"All of it, ma'am?"

"Yes, Sergeant McAllister."

Beau reached for a glass of water, took a drink, and set the glass down.

"Okay, ma'am. Better put in a new tape."

•   •   •

Afterward, Lieutenant Meagher drove him out to Logan Airport in his blue Lincoln. They parked by the departures gate, and Meagher reached over to shake Beau's hand.

"Well, that went okay."

"Yeah. That Klein's a real pain in the ass."

"So he is. You got everything? Cash, cards. The tickets?"

Beau patted his suit pocket.

"Got your piece?"

"Yeah. You still willing to drive over to the Rosebud for me, see that George Cut Arms guy?"

"Yeah. And I'll talk to the Doc, see if he has those numbers for you."

"You think I'm crazy, right?"

Meagher smiled, a sudden glitter of white teeth against his blue-black skin. "There's something happening. Maybe it's got something to do with SPEAR and these Shirt Wearers that Charlie Tallbull was talking about. There's sure a lot of tension on the reserves these days. But an epidemic of birth defects, some kind of toxic dump in Montana, or a plague, or a secret federal plot to exterminate the Indians—bullshit."

"I don't think that either, Eustace."

"Good. You go out there, see if you can get anything on this Gall kid, see if there's anything that'll help us. I'll get out a composite of this dark guy Charlie saw. Guy like that, he'd stand out. You got the cellular?"

"Yeah. What're you, my mom?"

"You better thank your stars I'm not. I'd have drowned you."

"There's something else."

"Okay?"

"I think we ought to have somebody watching Maureen."

Meagher studied Beau for a moment.

"You think she's in danger?"

"I think she's involved. I don't know if she's in danger."

There was a long silence.

"Okay, Beau. I'll get somebody on that."

"Thanks, LT."

Two hours later Beau had checked into a hotel in Anaheim—a psychiatric convention had packed the downtown L.A. hotels.

From his room he saw a vast plain of low buildings and apartment towers and warehouse blocks, grids upon grids of them, floating in a lime-green sea of smog and fumes. Here and there a lonely spire rose up out of the green fumes, dark and hazy. In the distance, along the northern horizon, a low saw-toothed range ripped up the skyline.

He opened the window and smelled the air.

Christ. It smelled like a cathouse basement. From far below came the sound of sirens and traffic and car horns blatting, and under that the murmuring, roaring, rushing sound of an American city, like a huge machine running at the red line, pushing everything past the limits. And far away to the west, at the farthest edge of sight, past the smog and the low rectangles and the gray rising arcs of the freeways, a shimmer of golden light where the Pacific Ocean hid just below the horizon.

Welcome to Los Angeles, Sergeant McAllister.

Then he turned away from the view, back to the cool dark of his hotel room. There was a mini-bar by the television set.

First things first.

He poured a long cold Scotch and used it to chase a couple of aspirins down his throat. His leg throbbed and burned. He sat on the edge of the bed, looking at his watch. Oh hell, he hadn't called Trudy back.

He hadn't even *thought* about her until now.

"Nice, Beau," he said to the empty room.

He looked at the phone for a long time, and then he picked it up and dialed Trudy's number.

He listened to it ring for a while then set the receiver down again and finished his Scotch.

Then he poured another one.

17

1300 Hours – June 18 – Los Angeles, California

Beau's rearview mirror was filled to the edges with overheated iron and fly-specked grillwork. A tin bulldog with a cigar in his jaws and a riveter's helmet was bolted to the radiator behind him. Now and then, the driver would hit the airhorn and rattle Beau's windows. When he did this, Beau would jerk reflexively and his foot would come off the accelerator, and there'd be more of that ugly grille in his rearview, and the psychopath behind the wheel would tap his own brakes, and then he'd hit that airhorn again.

They were doing seventy miles an hour down the freeway, the tractor driver now inches from Beau's tailgate. Two feet ahead, a woman with radioactive hair was combing it with an ice pick and talking into the carphone, flying along in her purple Cobra. Behind him, a massive tractor-trailer was climbing up his tailpipe. There was nowhere for Beau to go, unless he wanted to run his rented Town Car off the road, or drive over the Martian in the purple Cobra.

It didn't seem to matter to the guy on his tail; crash and burn, or dematerialize, but get the *hell* out of his way.

Beau was giving some serious thought to dragging out his off-duty Smith and trying a few shots backward out the driver's window when the Motorola cellular phone that was bouncing around on the passenger seat started to shrill at him. He had a moment of panic when it went off because he didn't know where the hell the sound was coming from, maybe from his own throat, maybe a radar lock-on for a car-to-car Beau-seeking missile. Then the glowing green *call* light caught his eye.

He cursed, swerved, and snatched the phone up, pressing the SEND button with his thumb.

The guy in the tractor-trailer was coming around now, trying to pass on the left, his Kenworth filling up Beau's side mirror, that horn shaking the earth.

"Hello!"

"Jesus, Beau! Where the hell are you?" It sounded like Meagher. Beau tried to slow down, but another vehicle, a blue station wagon, fired up into the space being cleared by the tractor driver, and now *he* was right on Beau's tail.

"Eustace! How are you?"

"Why are you yelling at me? What the hell's going on? What's that noise?"

The tractor-trailer hurtled past him, a Great Wall of China of dusty iron and spinning black rubber. He cleared Beau's left fender and cut sharply in front. His brakelights flashed on, and Beau had to hit his own brakes. The blue wagon behind him jammed on his brakes, flashed his brights. Beau could see a hand in the forward arc of sunlight over the driver's wheel.

The guy was giving Beau the finger.

"God *damn*!"

"You in the car, Beau?"

"So far." The noise dropped to a muted roar. Maybe it was the end of the round.

"Yeah. Jesus, this town is insane!"

Meagher laughed, a short sharp snort.

"Better you than me," said Meagher. "How was the flight?"

"You go up real high, then later you come down. What kind of question is that? If it was a bad flight, I wouldn't be here talking to you. I'd be out in some farmer's field looking for my right arm."

"What's the matter with you?"

"I don't like this town."

"Where are you?"

"Now? I'm going east on the freeway with what looks like an international convention of suicidal lemmings on angel dust. There's a broad up ahead looks like she'd glow in the dark. And the town is neck-deep in some kinda vapor looks like Martian swamp gas. Can you die of culture shock?"

"I demobed outta there, in '69. Hated the place then."

"It hasn't improved, Eustace."

Beau looked to his right, at the low grimy buildings and the packed bungalows, the bitter bare lots and the scrub bush and the yellow weeds and vacant lots packed with dead cars. Here and there a scruffy palm tree rose up out of the industrial sprawl and the barrios like a cavalry flag, wilted in the damp and smothering heat. Far away to the east and the north, the San Gabriel and the San Bernardino Mountains looked like smoking slag heaps rising up out of the limitless greenish-yellow smog.

"Can you hear me okay?" Beau asked.

"Five by five. They cleared you, you know."

"The board? Damned decent of them. How's Vanessa?"

"She's okay. She's holding off on the feds."

"So what was the upshot?"

"The basic decision was to say, well, we aren't sure it was a robbery, but it sure as hell was felonious assault and reckless endangerment. Benitez was pretty solid behind you, Beau. I had a meet with the SPEAR people this morning. A real ball-buster named Maya BlueStones. They didn't buy it, but there's not much they can do. There's no question these guys had weapons and used them on police officers. It'll sort out."

"Did Harper give you what he got on that Wozcylesko boy from the phone company?"

"Yeah. I kicked it around with him. The report says the kid had lit up a joint and the fumes blew. They're saying it was an accident."

"You know I took an ounce off that kid, just a little bit before the Arrow Creek thing?"

"Nice to mention it, Beau."

Beau heard the sarcasm in his voice. "What's that for?"

"I cleaned out your cruiser after we got you to the hospital. I found a packet of weed in your glove compartment."

"You buy the accident thing?"

"I got a full plate, Beau. Billings Fire Department has an arson investigator on it. If they get anything, I'll know."

"When I took it from Hubert—the dope? When I confiscated it, I saw the kid had these little scabs all over his fingers. Like he'd torn his skin off?"

"So? Maybe he got his finger caught in his nose."

"Somebody used Krazy Glue on Bell's phones, right? You remember?"

"Yeah—oh, I get it! You get that stuff on your fingers, you're losing some skin. So you figure Hubert did the phones himself, just to cover his visit to the Oasis, get that package?"

"It's a possibility."

"So he was in on it? Whatever *it* was?"

"I think he took the package from under Bell's desk."

"And then somebody took it from Hubert?"

"It fits."

"And then *fried* him? Why?"

"Beats me. Maybe that part *was* an accident. Kid was stupid enough to light up with all that solvent around."

"Now I wish I'd let you take that package."

"What about the Fourth Amendment?"

" 'A foolish consistency is the hobgoblin of little minds,' " said Meagher. "Ralph Waldo Emerson."

A turnoff was coming up on his right side.

MARENGO STREET
CITY TERRACE

"Hey, hold on a second. Here's my street." He jigged the car hard right and slid past a wandering pickup full of Chicano laborers. They cursed him out in shrill machine-gun Spanish as he went past. Beau rocketed around the off-ramp and brought the car to a stop next to a rundown Helpy Selfy. A crowd of rough-looking Chicano teenagers were playing soccer in the sun-baked asphalt lot. They stopped the game as Beau pulled up and watched him the way coyotes watch chickens.

"Okay, I'm stopped. What have you got?"

"Got a pad?" Eustace said.

Beau reached over to the glove compartment, snapped it open, and pulled out a memo book in black vinyl with the gold shield of the Montana Highway Patrol on the front. He propped the Motorola phone under his chin, looked around at the neighborhood, and pressed the auto door lock.

"Okay, shoot."

"Where are you?"

Beau looked at the street signs. Around him the barrio streets wandered off into a crazy tangle of grubby homes and barred-up storefronts. Kids raced past on huge skateboards. Heavy-hipped women in polyester tees and too-tight jeans pushed rusted shopping carts around inside the Helpy Selfy. Garbage littered the crumbling pavement.

"I'm at Pomeroy and City Terrace."

"Bad part of town?"

"Kinda like Butte without the scenery."

"Why the hell you screwing around there?"

"Here's where I'm gonna find 1623 Vallejo Canyon Drive."

"I thought the kid lived in a good neighborhood. Had a Gold Card, didn't he?"

"They give those away with shipments of coke now. Times change, my son."

"Yeah? Okay, well, Duffy did some good work, for a change. He Fed Exed the prints from those guys you tangled with—"

"*We* tangled with, Eustace. When SPEAR comes looking for me, you're gonna be right there in the barrel with me."

"Yeah, anyway, somehow he got Washington to shift gears for us. The stuff on the Gall kid we got from the credit bureau in Los Angeles. The rest is from the army. Vlasic was right about the war vet angle. Take this down."

Beau looked around him. Four of the Chicano kids had left the soccer game and were now lined up against the Lundy fence, smoking homemade cigarettes and staring at him in flat Indio, hard black eyes and sullen twisted mouths. Beau shifted his weight and felt the Smith digging into him.

Meagher read out the information that Duffy had brought down from Helena. Beau's memo book filled up with his careful block printing.

JUBAL TWO MOON

D.O.B. 02-23-25 PARMELEE SOUTH DAKOTA

ROSEBUD INDIAN RESERVATION—MINNECONJOU SIOUX

SELF-EMPLOYED TRADE CARPENTER AND HANDYMAN

HEREDITARY COUNCIL CHIEF LAKOTA NATION

MILITARY SERVICE THIRD MARINES USMC

SERVICE IWO JIMA AND PHILIPPINES SILVER STAR

HONORABLE DISCHARGE 1946

LAST KNOWN ADDRESS 1623 VALLEJO CANYON DRIVE LOS

ANGELES CALIFORNIA

ONE COUNT DRUNK AND DISORDERLY ENTERED RAPID CITY

JUNE 25 1976 NO OTHER CRIMINAL RECORD
NO WANTS NO WARRANTS

EARL BLACK ELK
D.O.B. 10-11-46 PIERRE SOUTH DAKOTA
LOWER BRULE INDIAN RESERVATION—OGLALA SIOUX
EMPLOYMENT VARIOUS
COUNCIL SUBCHIEF LAKOTA NATION
MILITARY SERVICE NINETEENTH ARMY CORPS
TRANSFERRED AMERICAL DIVISION 1965
VIETNAM SERVICE AIRBORNE RANGER LONG RANGE RECONDO
ATTACHED SPECIAL FORCES PROVISIONAL ADVISORY MAAG
LAOS MACSOG PHOENIX PROGRAM
PURPLE HEART NATIONAL DEFENSE VIETNAM SERVICE
REPUBLIC OF VIETNAM CAMPAIGN BRONZE STAR (2)
SILVER STAR (2) CAMBODIA LAOS LANG VEI PEGASUS OP
HONORABLE DISCHARGE 1971
LAST KNOWN ADDRESS VIA DEPARTMENT OF ARMY PENSION
220 DITMAN LOS ANGELES CALIFORNIA
VARIOUS COUNTS AGGRAVATED ASSAULT COMMON ASSAULT
FELONY ASSAULT BREAK AND ENTER POSSESSION UNDER
EIGHTEEN MONTHS SAN PEDRO ISLAND CORRECTIONAL
CENTER PAROLED NO REPEAT OFFENSE DISCHARGED
NO CURRENT WANTS NO WARRANTS

EDWARD GALL
D.O.B. 04-07-1971 LOS ANGELES CALIFORNIA
PARENTS AUSTIN GALL AND FILOMENA SUAREZ BOTH
PARENTS DECEASED AUSTIN GALL HEREDITARY SUBCHIEF
UPPER BRULE SIOUX LAKOTA NATION
EDWARD GALL EDUCATED LOS CAAMANOS SCHOOL
EL CERRITO CALIFORNIA
TWO YEARS LOS ANGELES TRADE TECHNICAL
LAST KNOWN ADDRESS 1623 VALLEJO CANYON DRIVE LOS ANGELES
CALIFORNIA
EMPLOYMENT VARIOUS
LAST KNOWN EMPLOYER OFFSHORE FILM GROUP
1550 BALBOA BOULEVARD GRANADA HILLS CALIFORNIA
NCIC NEGATIVE WSIN NEGATIVE
MAGLOCEN NEGATIVE MOCIC NEGATIVE

NO WANTS NO WARRANTS
CREDIT RATING B NO JUDGMENTS NO ACTIONS

JAMES CHIEF COMES IN SIGHT
D.O.B. 06-25-1945 LAME DEER MONTANA
HEREDITARY CHIEF NORTHERN CHEYENNE
EMPLOYMENT VARIOUS
NORTHERN CHEYENNE SHIRT WEARER SOCIETY
MILITARY SERVICE AMERICAL DIVISION 1964
LRRP RECONDO MACSOG PHOENIX
IA DRANG A SHAU DMZ LAOS CAMBODIA
NATIONAL DEFENSE VIETNAM SERVICE
REPUBLIC OF VIETNAM CAMPAIGN PURPLE HEART (4)
BRONZE STAR (2) COMBAT INFANTRY (3)
HONORABLE DISCHARGE 1971
LAST KNOWN ADDRESS RR 21 LAME DEER MONTANA
NCIC NEGATIVE BUT RMIN VARIOUS FELONY ASSAULTS
BREAK AND ENTER POSSESSION UNDER WEAPONS OFFENSES
THREE YEARS DEER LODGE MONTANA
PAROLED DISCHARGED 1984 NO WANTS CURRENT

Beau read the words again in silence.

"You still there, Beau?"

"Yeah. Christ, Eustace. You remember what Charlie Tallbull said about the Shirt Wearers? This James guy was a member. And they were war heroes."

Meagher was quiet for a moment. Beau looked to his left and saw the teenagers staring at him. He guessed all they saw was a big old white man in a rented Lincoln. He didn't make the mistake of smiling at them.

"Well, it looks that way, Beau. The old guy was at Iwo. Lot of Indians in the services. They make real good combat troopers when there's a war on, but they're lousy at peacetime soldiering. Ran into some trouble, looks like. Just don't look like professional thieves. What the hell was going on, Beau?"

"Damned if I can tell you. What's all this stuff here? RECONDO. MACSOG. Phoenix. Sounds like spook shit."

"The Phoenix stuff is, for sure. I ran into a few of those guys when I was in-country. Usually, they were free-lancers pulled from their regular units and sent off on some kinda wet-work operation. Duffy dug out the spook listing. That kinda stuff is never on open-loop networks. It wasn't listed on the NCIC record, but Duffy has a buddy at Quantico and he confirmed it. RECONDO is Recon Commando. MACSOG means Military Assistance Command Special Operations Group, more Vietnam spook stuff. MACSOG replaced Phoenix after the Phoenix operations attracted too much press. Both these guys were hard core, Beau.''

"Yeah. How the hell I took one out is beyond me."

"Yeah. If I'd known the guy coming up the hill at me was a Recon vet, I'd have shot myself. We lucked out. But I guess we can shitcan the robbery angle, right?"

"We can shitcan robbery. But I wouldn't shitcan the SPEAR thing. This change your attitude about the Shirt Wearers?"

Meagher grunted. "Yeah. I don't like it."

"They *are* chiefs, all of them. Even this Gall kid, his father was Austin Gall. The Gall name goes back a long way in Lakota. There was a Gall, a real hard bastard, face like a fist, eyes like black stones, he was at Little Bighorn, helped carve up the Seventh Cavalry. You got Indian aristocracy here."

"So why start a fight at a gas station? I don't know. It sure doesn't fit the sheets. I mean, we *do* have some felony assaults here. But no previous on armed robbery—man, what do we call these guys? I can't say Chief Comes In Sight every time I wanna mention him. Take me a year just to do the reports."

"Call them Earl and James," said Beau.

"Okay. James here has some hits for assault, and he did time at Deer Lodge. Earl did eighteen months at San Pedro. But Jubal is clean—except for that drunk and disorderly beef, which you explained. And this Gall kid, hell, he had a regular job."

"And seven hundred bucks in his pocket when he died. Did American Express tell you anything?"

"Yeah," Eustace said. "The cardholder is actually the Offshore Film Group. The bills go to their address on Balboa. Card's current. The Gall kid was a subsidiary holder. An employee. And he's clean, as far as a sheet goes. We checked with Rocky Mountain Information Network, checked Mid-Atlantic-Great-Lakes network, checked with Western States Info—nothing."

"What about the stuff in Two Moon's blue pickup?" Beau asked.

"The stuff in the back was weird. Some of the usual—beans and canned beef. Flour and dried beef. Beer. A crate of Meals Ready to Eat, army issue. But get this! They also had gear for melting lead and a casting mold for .50-caliber shot. Two reproduction Hawken muzzle-loaders, and a whole lotta black powder. Percussion caps, several cans of those. Machine-milling gear. And another one of those combat bows. All of it bought in Pierre.''

"Like for an expedition?''

"Or a campaign. Why the nineteenth-century armaments?''

"My guess, you're gonna work against the law, don't use weapons the law can control. Black powder, you can make that out of carbon, saltpeter, and sulphur. Anybody can get lead for shot. Bows are quiet, and arrows are reusable.''

"How much damage can you do with some old muzzle-loader?''

"Ask the Narraganset or the Pequot,'' Beau replied.

"There aren't any.''

"There you go. All this full-auto shit, that's just a substitute for marksmanship. Any asshole can spray a couple hundred rounds into a target, be sure to kill something. Why you think that shit appeals to crack dealers and gang kids? Takes no control. Even a dropout can fire one. Takes a cool hand to do it with one round. I got that McMillan at home?''

"The heavy-barreled thing, over the window?''

"Yeah. That's a single-shot machine. I can punch the eye out of the Jack of Hearts at six hundred yards with that.''

"Then how come you can't hit your foot with the nine-mill?''

"Good question. I never thought of that.''

"Anyway, that rifle you have, that fires a .300 Magnum round, I remember correctly?''

"Yeah.''

"You're not gonna be clipping the eye out of any Jack with that round. That round'll come in like a runaway freight. Hit you so hard your *relatives* would die.''

"My point is, all this sounds like something planned. Like it was a . . . project. Got an ID on the girl yet?''

"No. Danny Burt says they were calling her Donna. It came out at the shooting board. We took her prints, but a blind search like that, we'd be lucky if the feds got back to us in a year. No reason to think she'd ever been printed. We have copies of those photos of her that you found in Gall's stuff. You have one?''

"Yeah. Got it with me. You could try showing them around in Rosebud and Lame Deer. Anything else come around on her?''

"Not a thing. Garner said you asked for Greer and Harper, for help with this. Why not leave it to Finch Hyam? He's a good cop, he'll get under this.''

"I like to have somebody on our side. Did Garner say we could have them?''

246 C a r s t e n   S t r o u d

"They're both on AL until Indian Affairs decides if there's a lawsuit coming. Garner says we can have them until then."

"Look, I was worrying about Bobby Lee. If this guy can find my place, he'll find my ex-wife."

"Yeah. You said that last night. Am I going to hear why you think Maureen's involved?"

"Her name keeps coming up in connection with these baby incidents."

"Well, I got Harper and Greer. One of them will keep an eye on both of them. That okay with you?"

"That's fine. Okay, well, I gotta go."

"Beau, let me call somebody in the LAPD. I know a guy in the detective division, he could walk around with you. Be another gun on your side."

"I'll call him, I need him. What's his name?"

"Rufus Calder."

"Rufus? *Rufus?* He one of your people? Can he dance?"

"You say that to him, Beau. He doesn't have my sense of humor. He's a good cop, though. You go see him."

"Yeah. I'll bring him some tap shoes."

"Very funny, Beau. Rufus'll love you. Anything else you need?"

"Just, if you could, talk to this Cut Arms guy. Run this Shirt Wearer thing past him, see if he blinks."

"Yeah. I'll drive out there, see what he has to say. He recognized you in the hospital elevator?"

"Yeah. I guess he'd seen me somewhere."

"You know him?" asked Meagher.

"Not at all. By the way, how's Dwight? I guess he's pretty pissed off at me?"

"Does Batman have homosexual panic? Why do you figure his dad was so interested in getting Dwight off your back?"

"Doc Darryl is a throwback. He's an Early."

"One of the first to come, you mean?"

"Yeah. Those guys, they have a kind of code. Frontier justice. Doc Hogeland's roots run real deep into Montana. They had land on the Bitterroot back when you had to fight a Flathead warrior every time you went outside to take a leak."

"Yeah," said Meagher. "Dwight's always bringing that up. So what now?"

"Now?" said Beau, suddenly back in the moment. He looked around at the rotting barrio, at the hard yellow light and the beaten ground.

"Now I get out of the car. Pray for me, Eustace."

1300 Hours – June 18 – Billings, Montana

Vanessa Ballard spent the better part of a long, humid Tuesday afternoon in a meeting with, among others, Dwight Hogeland, acting now for the ACLU and looking a little the worse for his dance lesson with Beau McAllister.

Also appearing was Joel Sherman, who was on the ACLU staff in Helena, and a Native American lawyer named Maya BlueStones, a full-blood Ojibway with puffy pockmarked cheeks, tiny hard-rock eyes the color of wet mud, short black hair, and a sulphurous temper that she seemed able to switch on and off at will. She radiated self-righteous fire and disrupted the talks at several points to deliver sententious orations that Ballard later, for the benefit of Eustace Meagher, broke down into two basic categories: Native American—good; Euro-American—dogshit.

Although Eustace Meagher had dodged the meeting, mumbling something about locating an L.A. cop named Rufus Calder, the FBI agent, Frank Duffy, also attended, so that made four besides herself—three too many for Vanessa Ballard.

In self-defense, she set the meeting with them in neutral territory, the lounge at the Berkely House, a private club for Montana businessmen and corporate lawyers in an old Victorian brick mansion that stood on a crest of land overlooking the Yellowstone and the rest of Billings, as befitted the Players and Movers and Men of Affairs who built it and stocked it and who were—*all together now!*—making Montana The State of the Nation.

Ballard's membership in this club was a bequest from her father and mother, who were remembered around the state as a collective proper noun usually rendered as *Bootsandbonnie*.

Boots' real name was Augustus, but he preferred to be called Boots because it harmonized with the frontier image he had always been careful to project in public, although in his business relations he advanced the causes and crusades of Ballard Holdings with classic eastern coldness and aggression.

The Great Con was how Vanessa always thought of her father. Their relationship had taken a negative turn around her eleventh birthday, when her father—a big rugged redwood of a man with thick white hair and a blunt red-tinted face—had developed an interest in her bathing habits. She once looked up from her shower stall, scrubbing away at the dirt she always managed to grind into her knees when she was out playing at gunfighters with her gang, and saw—it stole her breath and snapped her innocence in a nanosecond—saw the florid drunken face of Boots Ballard through the steamy mist on the bathroom window, staring at her with something carnivorous—something vile—in his blood-thickened face.

Vanessa never told anyone this story, not even her mother. It would have distressed Bonnie greatly, not because it was a terrible invasion and a sign of something rotten at the core of the redwood, but because it would have been so *vulgar* of Vanessa to bring it up. Instead, Vanessa put up draperies at her bathroom window and talked Reynardo the groundsman into installing a deadlock on her bedroom door.

Now and then she would lie in bed in the still dark of the night and listen to the knob being turned slowly, a tinny scratching noise, like a rat in the baseboards, then silence and another long watch of the night, while she sleeplessly waited for the sky outside her window to change from black to pale rose to bright blue, and then she would go down the stairs for another breakfast of cornbread cakes and the hypersonic silent shriek of suppressed truths and a day full of bright brittle conversation with Boots and Bonnie.

Bonnie Ballard's real name was Portia, a curse laid upon her by a mother with an obsession for the classics, but she had allowed their "set" to nickname her Bonnie because Boots and Bonnie were almost all the way to becoming that all-important collective noun by this time, and Bonnie was alliterative and, well, just so darn *cute*.

Their "set" was the merchant aristocracy of Montana, a collection of hard-eyed women and predatory men who had found a variety of ways to twist money out of the red earth and leathery hide of the country, and who along the way had cultivated the elemental coldness, the steely blindness required if the rich wish to grow richer.

Oh, but they were good to each other, to the other members of the set, provided it didn't cost too much in nondeductible expenses or billable time. Bonnie had met Doc Hogeland's wife Julia during a fund-raiser for the Hogeland Oncology Wing. Julia was beautiful and genuine, and her grace, her *reality*, had drawn Bonnie as it drew some of the other wives, women who had surrendered themselves to the venality and the sterility of their lives but who wished sometimes to warm their bloodless hearts by the glow of a living person, like vampires at a birthday party.

Doc Hogeland's memory of Bonnie Ballard's kindness toward his dying wife was slightly roseate, a trick of light and distance. Bonnie had visited Julia several times, but each visit had been shorter than the one before it as Julia's color changed and the sickroom smells became less and less polite.

Boots and Bonnie. . . . Well, in the fullness of—and arguably in the nick of—time, God, proceeding ex machina, gathered Augustus Sewell Ballard into the bosom of Eternal Forgiveness with the aid of a bar of ninety-nine-and-forty-four-one-hundredths-percent-pure Ivory Soap and a slickened tile floor in the master suite of the Absaroke, the family residence precariously balanced on a rocky outcropping of Red Lodge Mountain overlooking the Beartooth Highway, down by the Wyoming border. Boots was found, erection still firmly in a death-grip, on the flooded floor of the bathroom, the mighty oak fallen, with his noggin neatly punctuated by a solid-gold tap handle and a look of intense concentration furrowing his Hyperion brow. Vanessa liked to say, around the bar or over lunch with friends, that at least the Great Con had died hard. He would have wanted to be remembered that way.

Bonnie Ballard, now a truncated noun well on her way to becoming a metonymy—as in "she did a Bonnie Ballard"—wore black with an undertone of sourmash bourbon. Several hundred aggrieved creditors and a few delighted debtors saw Boots safely underground, positioned a large ornately carved marble rock and a couple tons of red dirt and sod on his chest to keep him there, and went back to the eagle's nest to divvy up the remainder of his estate while Bonnie sat out on the sweeping wooden deck with the magnificent vista of southern Montana and the Beartooth Range to gladden her heavy heart and drank herself into a sodden stupor. She died of a heart attack shortly afterward, in roughly the same location, after choking on a manzanilla olive.

Vanessa Ballard, now the heir and chatelaine of the Absaroke, arranged for her mother's requested cremation in spite of her private fears that it would take the undertakers three days to beat out the pale blue flames in Bonnie's bourbon-saturated liver.

Bonnie had requested that her ashes be scattered along the banks of the Yellowstone River, and Vanessa had done her best to comply, driving all the way over to the Paradise Valley in western Montana to do it, the silver box bouncing around in the seat of her rusting Buick Le Sabre. Unfortunately, just as Vanessa launched her mother's ashes into the quicksilver waters, in a lazy bend by a stand of greening cottonwoods, a sudden wind came up and blew most of the gray powder back into her face and all over her favorite cream linen suit.

So, as she later told it at Fogarty's, in a circle of her cronies, prosecutors, a few privileged street cops, and some grizzled old circuit judges, it came to pass that Bonnie Ballard's final resting place turned out to be Ziggy's Kwikky-Kleeners over on the Frontage Line, near the I-90 overpass, just to the south of the Cenex tankyard.

While she actually came to miss her mother, Vanessa Ballard considered the circumstances of Boots Ballard's death quite condign, in the sense that she herself had always found her father to be ninety-nine-and-forty-four-one-hundredths-percent bullshit. The fact that he had died in a steaming bathroom, in the nude, falling in his red marble shower stall, engaged in God-only-knew what onanistic contortion, so intent upon his Special Purpose that he wouldn't even let go of it to break his fall, well, it all seemed to argue for a universal code of justice.

That falseness in her father, combined with the self-reliance that some-times comes to children with unhappy childhoods, gave her a profound affection for truth and consequences.

She put herself through Dartmouth and Harvard Law, came back to Montana, and, in a move that stunned the locals and unsettled those who expected her to join private practice, joined the district attorney's office, where she took a deep breath and settled down to straighten the moral furniture in Yellowstone County.

One of the few vestiges left to her from the explosion and dissolution of Ballard Holdings was the crumbling edifice of the Absaroke. She put everything she had into maintaining it and spent as much time in the old redstone monstrosity as she could. She lived alone, except for a Crow woman named Mary Bright Water and a couple of mongrel mutts named Wittgenstein and Buster.

A few people, Eustace Meagher among them, knew that Vanessa Ballard had no intention of ever joining a private practice, but had set her heart on a job with the Department of Justice, in particular the position of special prosecutor with a brief to investigate corruption and antitrust violations throughout the Southwest.

She lived her professional life solidly in the here and now, even if the now part meant that Maya BlueStones of the Society for the Protection of Ethno-American Rights had drawn her deepest breath yet and seemed on the point of delivering a sulphurous polemic against Beau McAllister and Eustace Meagher of the Montana Highway Patrol.

Ballard looked away around the richly paneled room, at the portraits of The Great Men Who Made Montana What It Is Today, and spied the aged waiter sagging in a corner. She lifted her empty crystal glass and raised one delicately curved eyebrow while Maya BlueStones heated up her grievances to a cherry-red glow.

"We were told that we'd have a chance to cross—to question this sergeant personally. So where is he? I want him available, and I want that to happen *today*!"

She was zeroing in on Frank Duffy, who was leaning forward, his pale hands on his knees, his head down, turning his glass in his hands. Blue-Stones's voice was carrying, and full of raspy subharmonics. Around the lounge, old men in fine suits shook their papers and harrumphed their harrumphs.

"Ms. BlueStones"—Duffy managed to interrupt her with a sudden sharp movement of his head—"the Federal Bureau of Investigation and the Yellowstone County District Attorney's office *asked* for this meeting with you, and with your associates here." He nodded toward Dwight Hogeland and the other ACLU lawyer, Joel Sherman, who were sitting by in pained resignation, hoping Maya BlueStones would cool her jets a bit.

"With Mr. Hogeland and Mr. Sherman *exactly* because we *share* your concerns about these . . ."

Don't hesitate, thought Ballard.

Too late.

"Assassinations, Agent Duffy!" BlueStones finished for him.

See?

"Ma'am, these men came into Yellowstone County armed and dangerous. They showed every—"

"Stop! I drove in here from Sheridan, and I saw so many pickups with those gun-racks in the back, with white men driving and all those guns showing, and I did not see one sheriff or state trooper try to kill *them!* I see that when it is a Native American who has a weapon, then suddenly it is a threat and you people bring out every means to hunt them down and kill them like dogs in a ditch. We have compiled—"

She sent a hot look over at Joel Sherman, who began to scramble through his briefcase. He extracted a red file folder and handed it across to her. She plucked it from his hand and waved it under Duffy's nose.

"Compiled a *list* of the atrocities committed by this one cop you have here on the force." She lowered her voice and began to read from the papers. "Beauregard McAllister. Involved in twenty-seven incidents of violence involving firearms in only nineteen years on the force! Involved in literally *hundreds* of incidents of physical abuse of prisoners! A known racist, prejudiced against Native—"

That was too much for Vanessa Ballard.

"Ms. BlueStones, Sergeant McAllister was once married to a Native American woman, a Crow woman named Alice Manyberries."

"The fact that he once shacked up with some poor native girl and then deserted her is hardly a basis for—"

"He didn't desert her! She—"

"I heard you say 'once,' Ms. Ballard."

"She was killed in a road accident. As a matter of fact, an accident very much like the one Sergeant McAllister was trying to prevent when Joe Bell—and I stress that it was Joe Bell—shot Edward Gall."

BlueStones shook her head, her short shock of black hair flaring, her voice cutting through.

"*If* you'll *let* me *finish!*" she snapped, in a tone all too familiar to Ballard; the syncopated cadence of the true believer.

"*For* example, we *find* that on the *fifteenth* of August in 1979, this man without cause stopped and detained a car filled with young Native American males and used excessive force, as per a civilian complaint filed by—"

"Every cop gets complaints. And if you're talking about the Roan Horse boys, two of them are currently serving time in Deer Lodge for deliberate homicide and cocaine importation. So it seems to me that—"

"*Not* my point, *if* you can give me a moment! You said you were here to *listen* to our legitimate grievances, and as officials of this state you are *required* to answer for these actions of one of your employees, as I am sure I don't have to remind you. I want an answer to my basic question—"

"Then *ask* it, goddamn it!"

Everyone froze and stared at her. Ballard tried to get her temper under control, the effort as visible as her anger.

"Forgive me, Ms. BlueStones, but you really seem to be more interested in making political speeches than in listening to our findings. Heat is not light, Ms. BlueStones, nor is oratorical brilliance necessarily illuminating. You have the written report of our shooting board. It includes the depositions of all the officers involved in the shootings, as well as civilian witnesses and my own assessment. We considered carefully whether charges ought to be laid against any of the officers—"

"And decided not to. What a shock!"

"Based on the information at hand, and on our experienced assessment of the matter, not just my own but two trained investigators from the Criminal Bureau—"

"More cops! Cops investigating cops! Bullshit! As a *woman,* Ms. Ballard, as a *sister,* you might have been expected to have more insight into the *mechanics* of male oppression! I find it *regrettable* that you seem to have mislaid your spiritual obligations—"

"Ahh, Ms. BlueStones, if I can speak?" said Dwight, breaking into the conversation. His nose was covered with a stretch of surgical tape and his left eye was raw-looking, but he seemed to have recovered his consonants.

"Go ahead, Dwight."

"Yes, well. Joel and I—and Ms. BlueStones—speaking for the American Civil Liberties Union, we strongly feel that only an independent civilian review board, composed of—correct me on this, Joel, if I go wrong—composed of qualified lawyers, defense lawyers in order to ameliorate the natural bias of the prosecutorial function—and a representative from SPEAR—perhaps Ms. BlueStones—and a person from the Justice Department—not the local FBI people, but someone from Washington who has skills in these kinds of issues and inquiries . . . and someone from the Civil Liberties Union—Joel has provided some names . . . and the whole sitting under a retired jurist perhaps, charged with powers of subpoena—"

"Charming. Under a tricolor flag, perhaps? With a front row full of old crones knitting? Haywains packed with manacled coppers, trundling toward the guillotine while somebody tootles *La Marseillaise* on a tin flute? That's an ACLU wet dream!"

Sherman blanched and immediately reddened, glanced fearfully at Maya BlueStones. Dwight raised his voice.

"After all, Vanessa, surely we here, all of us, are united in our desire to see justice done and to prevent any possible repetition of the dynamics that lead to such terrible consequences. We are all of us here—and in this I intend no slight to you, Agent Duffy"—here Dwight nodded indulgently toward Frank Duffy, who, like many members of the FBI, had a law degree of his own, a fact that had eluded Dwight completely—"but we are all of us lawyers, members of the bar and dedicated to pursue clearly, without let or hindrance, to let slip the hounds of justice, so to speak—"

"And the bitches," added Vanessa, sweetly smiling.

"Sexist!" snorted Maya BlueStones.

"We *are* sworn to uphold the law as something higher and cleaner and—"

"Christ, Dwight. Stop before you blow a metaphor."

Dwight blushed under his bandage. His unblackened eye was bright with anger. "Oliver Wendell Holmes said that it is a lesser evil that some lives should be damaged than that the state should play an ignoble part! All we are trying to get you to do is make damn sure that your particular state, that Yellowstone County, hasn't allowed murders to be committed by men wearing the shield and carrying the name of justice."

"All you want to do, Dwight, is to fuck over a good cop."

Maya BlueStones took a deep breath and started to say something, but Vanessa rode over that, angry now, her voice low and steady but resonant and compelling.

"No, you look. You arrived here with your minds set in concrete and your ears stuffed with dried bullshit. All you're interested in is making political points with this issue. I don't think you, Ms. BlueStones, Ojibway or no, I don't think you give one high-pitched rat-fart what really caused these deaths. If you were successful in getting this review board set up, all you'd use it for is to grab some headlines and spout divisive jargon about the plight of the red man. You're as much of a racist pig as any Ku Kluxer, Ms. BlueStones, and perhaps more dangerous, because everybody *knows* what they are, while *you* walk around wrapped in your self-righteousness and use your obvious talents and intelligence to spread hatred and reduce everything to considerations of pigment and racial origin. If you're up on your *Rise and Fall*, lady, you'll remember that the last crowd of thugs who saw life only in those terms were the goddamned Nazis." Ballard stood up, shook her blond hair out, and smoothed her skirt. "As for Joel here, and you too Dwight, all you want is a ticket to glory on her skirts. So if you don't mind, I'm going into the bar there to drink a toast to absent friends and I'll remind you that this is a private club and none of you are members. Come along, Frank. The air's better in there, anyway.''

She smiled at them all, a bright smile full of sweetness.

She turned and stalked off toward the bar, Duffy following along behind her, looking back over his shoulder as he left.

"Well," said Joel Sherman. "What an extraordinary performance, Dwight. Where do we go from here?''

Maya BlueStones was standing apart from them, a short spiky bomb hissing at every rivet.

"We are going straight to the governor's office! And to the Bar Association! We are going to *nail* that little cunt!''

The word floated up into the air between them and hovered there. Dwight and Joel Sherman stared at the woman in stunned silence.

Finally, Dwight sighed and shook his head.

"*We?*" said Dwight. "As in, you and me? *We* don't go anywhere. I understand your anger, but Ms. Ballard is a respected prosecutor in this county, and you aren't giving her a chance to use her office to help us at—''

BlueStones cut him off. "*You* are on a retainer and under professional obligations, Mr. Hogeland.''

Dwight looked pained, struggling with conflicting emotions. BlueStones was right, but when all this had blown over, she'd be off on another crusade and Dwight would still have to work with the legal community in this town. He gathered himself.

"Ma'am, I'm afraid I'll have to return your retainer. Joel, I hope you'll understand. The level of acrimony here—it's entirely unreasonable. Ms. BlueStones is far too confrontational for my tastes.''

"Dwight!" bleated Joel Sherman. "This is an ACLU issue. There are more important matters at stake than a personality conflict.''

"Yeah," said Dwight, looking past them and out toward the bar, absently stroking his bruises. "I'm getting that idea myself.''

"Vanessa?''

Duffy had seen him coming and turned around on the barstool to confront him. Vanessa, who had seen him in the long, smoked mirror behind the oak bar, turned her empty glass upside down on the copper bartop and gestured to the silvery old man in the red jacket.

"You even fucked up the Holmes quote, Dwight.''

"I did not. May I sit down?"

"Depends on what you sit on. Duffy, you have a jackknife or an ice pick or something?"

"Look, both of you. I think we need to talk."

"Frank needs a drink. I need a drink. You need a high colonic."

The old bartender brought them their drinks. Dwight asked for a Laphroaig and branch water.

The barman drifted off. Dwight lowered himself onto a barstool and sighed loudly. "I'm a wreck, Vanessa. Ease up on me."

"Ease up on *you*? From where we sit, you have it far too easy."

"I wish I understood where all this enmity is coming from. Is this all over Beau and Maureen?"

Vanessa set her glass down hard. "Dwight. If you are trying to find a way to tell Frank here about what you tried to do yesterday morning, you should know that Frank would probably share my sentiments on the subject and you've only got one nose."

"I wasn't, Vanessa. I have some ethics. Besides, that's a dead issue. I have spoken to the principal, and she takes the point."

"What about Joe Bell?"

"I haven't been able to reach him yet. I think I'll have to drive out there."

"Bell's in for a very bad time, Dwight."

There was a silence.

"Where's Beau, Vanessa?"

"How should I know? I assume he's at home."

"No, he's not. Maureen tried to reach him there. Tom Blasingame answered the phone. He said Beau was out and didn't know when he'd be back."

"Then he's out. He's on a medical leave right now, anyway. Maybe he went for a drive on his bike."

"There are—there are things happening, aren't there? Things I don't know about."

"You ought to be used to that, Dwight."

"Will you tell me what they are?"

"You'll hear about it."

"Can I hear now?"

"No. Anything else?"

Dwight picked up his glass, drained it, and nodded to the bartender for a refill. "How did I screw up the Holmes quote?"

"It was in Olmstead *versus* the United States. Justice Holmes's actual

words were, 'I think it is a lesser evil that some criminals should escape
than that the government should play an ignoble part.' ''

"Oh, yes. I recall it now. But his point, the principle is a good one.
You need to talk to Beau about this. There are higher goals in the law than
simple enforcement concerns."

"Such as?"

"Such as the good of the state. The protection of liberty and freedom,
which is, after all, the ultimate goal of the legal system."

"The ultimate goal of the legal system, Dwight, is to expand. To get
more laws passed so that more lawyers can get jobs arguing about what the
laws mean."

"If you have no faith in the criminal justice—"

"I have as much faith in the criminal justice system as I do in any other
device built by men, which is to say that whenever I fire it up, I stand back
a bit to make sure it doesn't explode and get grease all over my alligator
pumps."

"The protection of innocence is the first calling of any society,
Vanessa."

"I'd say the first calling of any society is to survive, and it's not going
to survive long if it allows abstract legal niceties to overpower a clear and
crying need for arrest and swift punishment."

"That's a classic fascist argument. Even a murderer deserves every
protection under the law."

"And in the meantime, the relatives of his victims suffer terrible dreams
and their lives corrode with unresolved hatreds. Where's the justice for
them?"

"As Holmes said, it's a lesser evil."

"Okay, I get you. So in the end, the preservation of legal process
justifies the *means,* which include the damage to victims and the ruinous
delay of criminal trial?"

"Plainly, crudely put—yes."

"Do you think justice *is* equal in the real world?"

"Well . . . there are variables, Vanessa. Sometimes things go wrong.
It's a fallible system."

"So, in effect, people are being hurt and victims are going begging for
justice to protect our right to the *possibility* of a fair trial?"

"Yes. You'd have to say that."

"And you'd have to say that there is also the possibility of an *un*fair
trial?"

"Sure, that's a possibility."

"So what you're saying is that we are supposed to allow the courts to function as haphazardly as they do, to bog down in plea bargaining, to lose track of cases, to fuck up prosecutions, to favor the rich over the poor, to mismanage the prisons and parole dangerous sociopaths and generally screw up royally—for the right to make a personal gamble that we, as a single case in the court, that we have a *chance* at a fair trial?"

"Maybe. It's better than *no* chance at a fair trial, isn't it?"

"Why?"

"Why? That's a stupid question, Vanessa. We all want a fair trial, don't we?"

"Do we? I've prosecuted hundreds of people, and the only ones who wanted a fair trial were the ones I kind of thought might be innocent. Innocent people want a fair trial. It's the *guilty* bastards who want to plea bargain, who want to avail themselves of every evasion and delay they can get their lawyers to use. Because they know that in a *fair* trial, their ass is grass and their next full-time position is bum boy in the prison shower."

"These evasions, as you call them, are all perfectly legal. They *are* the law. Everyone has the right to use them."

"And in return, society promises to give us justice?"

"Yes, but—"

"And we've agreed that this justice is particularly important when we are dealing with *guilty* people?"

"In a sense, yes."

"The very same people who refuse to live by this social contract?"

"Perhaps. But that's the—"

"So to sum it up, the rest of us have to put up with all this bullshit in the justice system for the benefit, in practical terms, of the very people who are *making* our lives so miserable. Is that a fair way to put it?"

"What's your point?"

"The point is, people hate lawyers because we are the professional *liars* of modern life. We strangle truth for bucks! The last thing in the world we want is a court system where simple logic rules the day."

"What *do* you respect, Vanessa?"

"I respect personal integrity and the sanctity of innocence. I intend to protect the second by using the first, and I intend to speak the simple truth as often as I can. I believe that the purpose of the criminal justice system is to protect the innocent and punish—*punish,* mind you, not rehabilitate—to *punish* the guilty, and not the other way around."

"That's vengeance, Vanessa."

"Vengeance is an underrated concept."

Dwight rubbed his nose absently, then winced. "Do I have the right to vengeance, then? For the pounding I took?"

"It's questions like that that started the law in the first place. And in answer to your question, no, you don't."

"Am I going to be told what's going on around here?"

"When I know, you'll know."

19

1430 Hours – June 18 – Los Angeles, California

Sometimes integrity is as simple as mowing the lawn. Sometimes strength is shown in the grace notes. Beau could see it as he drove up to the little wood-frame bungalow. Whoever lived at 1623 Vallejo Canyon Drive showed that kind of integrity and that kind of strength.

The house was painted a creamy white, and the fence around it was so new, the wood hadn't been painted yet. Inside the fence, the yard was a careful arrangement of rocks and desert plants. No attempt had been made to grow an English lawn in the desert climate of Southern California. There are only two things that are naturally green in Los Angeles, money and envy. The people who lived at 1623 Vallejo Canyon Drive had tried very hard to keep things simple and honest.

The house itself was a low wood structure with a big front porch, sheltered by an overhanging roof. Up on the veranda, a swing chair, freshly painted but old-looking, sat in an arrangement of potted cacti and desert roses. The screen door was closed. The draperies were drawn. There was no car in front.

Vallejo Canyon Drive was a narrow rising lane that led into a low chain of hilly territory, a kind of barrow set in the middle of the tortilla flats of East L.A. By local standards, it was a decent part of town, although the signs of poverty were everywhere, the old cars and the aimless teenage boys on the front steps, the disrepair of the pavement and the walkways, and the general atmosphere of fatigue and crushing boredom.

Beau parked the Lincoln on the street in front of number 1623 and got out, reeling a little from the hot air and the brutal sunlight after the air-conditioned ease of the Town Car. He had brought a hat along, his best black Stetson, and he was wearing his only lightweight gray suit and his black cowboy boots. He needed the suit jacket to hide the big Smith in his shoulder holster. He put the Stetson on and looked at himself in the Lincoln's tinted-glass window.

Christ, what a battered mug. Ugly as Texas roadkill. Shoulda trimmed the moustache. Shoulda lost some weight. Woulda lost some weight if I'd trimmed that moustache.

He finished off the look with his state trooper sunglasses. Never hurts to look hard in a hard town. And from the stares he was getting around the block, from the old folks on the porches, and from the five Chicano hardcases fixing that diamond-blue Eldorado over there, this looked like a very hard block.

He walked in through the carefully tended fence and up the wooden steps. The screen door was locked. The inside door was glass and wood-framing, held with a Yale lock. The interior of the house was dark. He could see some furniture and, on the far side of the room, another door leading into a bedroom. Through the front door he could see a small brass-railed bed, and beyond that another door leading through to the backyard. A table and four chairs stood in the backyard, with a vase of dead flowers on it.

Beau recognized the style of the house. Down in Tularosa they'd called these railway-car houses shotgun shacks. The idea was, a husband who came home and found his wife in bed with another guy, he could just pull down the shotgun off the wall, stand in the front door, and get a clear shot right through the house at the guy going out the back door. And not hit the walls or the windows.

It looked and felt empty, but he knocked on the frame anyway.

The sound boomed in the leaden silence of the afternoon.

Nothing.

He could have popped the inside door with little effort, but he decided not to. Maybe he could get something from the neighbors. It was a good move, as it happened, because when he turned around, he saw most of the neighbors standing on the sidewalk, blocking his path. Five young men from across the street had stopped work on the Eldorado. They were lined up in the pathway, wearing head scarves and—God help us—hair nets. They had their arms folded across their bare chests, and their meanest faces on, drooping mustachios and bad skin.

And hair nets.

Beau sighed and walked back down the stairs. He decided not to open up the conversation by asking them where their husbands were and how come Chicanas grew such nice moustaches.

"*Buenas tardes, hombres. Soy policía. Hablan ustedes Ingles?*"

"Choo gotta batch?"

He dragged out his state trooper ID and flashed it around. Somehow, it didn't open up the gates of heaven for him. A slope-shouldered guy with a railroad scar that tore across his upper lip and right cheek, one of the guys with his long black hair in a net, sneered. It didn't help his looks at all.

"Don mean a focking thing aroun here, *pendejo*. Wha'choo wan with this place?"

Beau, who knew damned well what *pendejo* meant, gave himself some air and tried again. "I'm looking for the owners of this house here."

"Hey, choo go ass the Firs California Stay Bank. Dey own everything aroun here."

"You know if the people are home?"

"No, cowboy. They gone."

Beau reached into his side pocket. Everybody jumped a bit. Beau pulled out the picture of the young Indian girl, thinking maybe she wasn't Indian after all. Hair Net leaned over to look at it, his ruined face twisted in concentration. He smelled of garlic and sweat. He was a little terrier of a guy, no more than five five, but thick as Texas beef. He looked up at Beau, frowning.

"*Si*. We know her. Why you wan her? She's a nice lady. She don do nobody no harm."

Beau didn't feel that now was a good time to mention that he'd cracked her skull with a gun butt last Friday night.

"She was hurt in Montana last week. We're trying to find out who she is. She didn't carry any ID."

"Who hurt her?"

"We're working on that now. You can help me. If you know who she is, that'd be a start."

"Wha'choo gon do with this guy, choo catch him?"

"Break his arms. For a start." Never hurt to give them a little street theater. Although the truth may set you free, sometimes it gets you killed first.

Hair Net and the gang held a brief conference in blindingly quick Spanish. Beau looked around at the houses and tried to imagine living so close to other people. It would take a lot of personal grace. Hair Net tapped the picture again.

"Her name was Donna." He turned to one of his friends. They had another short staccato conference in high-speed Spanish.

"Donna Bent, that's her name. She lives with this kid, another Indian. His name is Edward Gall."

Beau noticed the man's accent was fading along with the threatening posture. "You know them at all?" he asked.

"Hey, you know. Jus to see aroun. Nice kids. They kep the place good. Took pride in themselves. Help out with all the kids aroun. You need a loan, or some help with the groceries, Eddie was good for it. We a tight crowd aroun here. Eddie, he's a chief back in Colorado or someplace. See how nice they kep the house. Thas a hard thin to do, you got no money. Eddie has a job up in Hollywood. Works for this big film company. Was gonna do a film 'bout us, too!"

Beau's face must have shown his doubt. Hair Net bristled like an electrocuted rooster.

"Hey, no shit, man! We the Falcons! You heard of us?"

"No. Sorry."

"Hey, you watch. *Hombres, vengamos!*"

And right there on the sidewalk, under the brutal sun, they sang, five voices beautifully blended. Beau knew the song. It was "Rogaciado," a traditional Mexican song. Beau had grown up with songs like that in the scented Mexican nights. It brought back wood smoke and *fajitas* hissing and crackling on hot iron, and yellow lights in the cantina window, and the river running under starlight. The Falcons sang "Rogaciado" well enough to bring his heart up in his chest. He listened in solemn silence.

Hair Net finished with a little bow and waited for Beau's reaction. Beau clapped and grinned at them.

"Jesus. *Magnífico!* I know that song. That was beautiful."

Hair Net seemed to rise up and float a little off the ground. "Yeah. We the Falcons. Choo remember that name!"

Beau said he would.

"Maybe you li' a beer?"

"Yes. Yes, I would."

Hair Net turned to one of his friends. *"Cervesas! Y mas fria, por todos. Por favor."*

Beau smiled and bowed a little bow. *"Gracias. Es muy caliente!"*

The beers came on the run. They cracked a few, and Beau raised his can in a toast. "Los Falcones!"

"Los Falcones!"

They drank to that in silence. Hair Net wiped his moustache.

"So wha you gonna do now?"

"I guess I'll go find his film company."

Hair Net looked around at his companions. "You a cop, right?"

"Right."

"So choo make us deputies."

"Yeah?"

"Yeah. An we deputies, we let you in the house."

"Can you do that?"

"Sure." He reached into his pocket and tugged out a chain full of keys. He flipped through them until he found a large brass one. He held it up for Beau to see.

"I got keys for all aroun here. We the Falcons, man. This is *our* turf. Donna give us the keys, ask us to water the plants and stuff. Come on, we look aroun."

Beau thought it over. "Okay. Thank you."

Hair Net held up his hand. "Firs choo gotta make us deputies."

Beau smiled. "Okay. Repeat after me."

They formed up and stiffened, chins in and chests out.

"We the Falcons . . . "

"We the Falcons—"

"Being of sound mind . . . "

"Been of soun mine—"

He took them through it, grinning. They grinned back, and when he was finished, he pronounced them duly sworn in as a posse.

"Now," said Hair Net, showing a set of brilliant teeth and two solid-gold canines. "How much this posse job payin?"

A hundred bucks lighter, Beau stepped into the cool dark of the little bungalow. Hair Net and the Falcons stayed outside, slapping each other on the backs and flashing their bills.

Beau figured it was a fair trade. They had some fun with him, and he was in the house.

Now that he was in it, he smelled death in it.

Not a body or anything mortal here. But it smelled the way places smelled when the lives that had been lived there were over forever. It lay like dust on the threadbare furniture and the old army cot in the corner of the living room, where a wool blanket hanging from a pole must have provided the old man, Jubal, with what little privacy there was to have in the house. It hung in the air and moved like dust motes in the dim shaft of street light that transected the room.

Beau felt a sudden heat in his throat, and his heart began to pound. It took him a moment to realize what he was feeling.

It was anger.

Joe Bell had broken this peaceful place, this small island of good lives in a wasteland of greed and stupidity. Beau couldn't prove it, but he knew it the way he knew his own life and the little victories he had won and the great losses he had survived. Standing there in the center of this small house, seeing the care that had been taken in the furniture, the way it had been scrubbed and painted and scraped and polished, Beau felt the sudden leaden weight of all his years and everything he had seen.

Up until then, this had been, for Beau, a hybrid case, partly constructed of self-interest, to show that Joe Bell had fired without cause and that his lawsuit was malicious, and partly simple curiosity, the cop's desire to see how things happened and why they happened the way they did.

Until now. In this room.

Looking at the wedding picture above the sofa, the young couple in their modern clothes, the lean brown girl in a yellow dress and the young man in his somber black suit, their faces clear as well water, their hands together. And around them, in a scattered grouping, heavy-bodied Indian men in jeans and cowboy shirts, holding drums and feathered robes and frowning into the camera, as became the gravity of the moment.

EDWARD PIZI GALL

AND

DONNA SWEETWATER BENT

MARRIED MAY 24, 1988

ROSEBUD RESERVE, SOUTH DAKOTA

AND FAMILY

Something had happened to all these people, and Beau was a part of it. Beau had helped to break the hoop of these people. There they stood in a brief moment of promise and peace, with their deaths laid out for them in the future, but hidden by the bright light of the moment. And Joe Bell had made it happen. Joe Bell and whoever was helping him. They knew how this circle had been broken.

Because they were all there in the picture: Jubal Two Moon, toothless and erect, his face drawn and leathery, but smiling and proud; Earl Black Elk, glowering and dark but solid as iron, with one rough hand on Donna's shoulder, a protective gesture; and James Chief Comes In Sight, the Cheyenne friend, his heavy oval face bright with sunlight, his hooded eyes and sunken cheeks the same face that Beau had seen, lit by a pale moon, a black hole in the right cheek, lying in blood and brains at Arrow Creek. And others, eleven of them in all, broad Indian faces and heavy hands, sunburned and as much a part of the Dakota earth around them as a cottonwood root.

And at the back, a tall lean man with his long black hair pulled back tightly, the sun hitting his hard skull-like face, his eyes hidden in shadow, dressed in black with Navajo silver at his wrists and on his belt. A good face, but too strong for beauty and too grim for the occasion. It wore a smile precariously, the way a man looks who stands too close to the edge of a building.

He was striking and memorable, that one. His clothing was different as well. He was dressed in black, but expensively, and under his linen shirt he looked hard and fit. His mouth was a thin cut, like a seam in a rock face.

Beau stared at him for a long time, feeling a faint tremor of memory or insight. He tried to wait for it, to keep still and let it come. And it did.

This was the man Charlie Tallbull had described. The "black man." This was probably the man who took the Polaroid of Beau in the hospital bed, the man who had gone out to Lizardskin to leave him the message. This was the hidden man, maybe the Shirt Wearer that Charlie Tallbull was talking about, the man his boys thought was Crazy Horse returned.

Who the hell was he?

He stood there, in that rapt stillness, so long that the wound in his right leg flared up in sudden pain and bent him over double. He staggered and hopped to a thin wooden chair by the low corduroy couch, sat down, and extended the leg. The muscle burned quietly under the flesh, like a fire in a coal seam. There was no blood coming through the bandage to mark the suit.

Just to remind you, Beau.

He looked up at the wedding picture. It was hard to connect these people with the fight at Arrow Creek. He could see a time when the three of them might have sat down at a table at Fogarty's and talked about the things they had seen, the glasses going round and maybe some music, something like "Rogaciado," or Roy Orbison singing "Only in Dreams." The picture made these people real to Beau, in a way that the grim carnality of their deaths had not.

They had lived hard lives. Beau had seen enough of the life on the Rosebud, on any Indian reserve, to know that. Yet they had made their marks, gone to Iwo Jima, or to Vietnam, the younger ones to Los Angeles to make a life, and the older men had come back with medals and the undying gratitude of the government, back to walk in the empty bleached-out streets or on the barren earth of South Dakota less than a hundred miles from the Powder River country and the Bighorns, where their ancestors had hunted and fought and died.

Where, finally, they, too, had died, in a short sharp brutal collision, in a space of a few hours. To die like that, after having gone so far out in the world, to fall back into the vortex of the old land, as if drawn by some terrible gravity, compelled by some natural velocity—there had to be a rhythm to it, some kind of inner balance.

To find that hidden thing, that buried magnetic force that had twisted and misshapen these lives, that had finally pulled them under the long yellow grass of their own land . . . that would mean something. That would force meaning into it.

Beau would do that.

Find the thing that was buried. Drag it into the light.

Make amends.

Because although he did not intend it, and in truth could have done nothing to change it, he had helped to shatter this picture.

He looked around the little house and let out a long breath. The pain was subsiding now. Soon he'd have the bandages off. He'd have a vicious scar in the meat of his upper thigh, and he'd always have to favor the leg. It would be with him forever.

There was justice in that. It satisfied him.

For now.

A pool of warm light was gliding over the hardwood floors like honey. Finally it reached his outstretched leg and poured up across his boot. Beau shook himself and checked his watch. Christ. It was a quarter past five. He'd been sitting in the house, lost in thought, for almost an hour and a half. He got to his feet and stretched, feeling the stiffness in his body. He'd been banged and thumped and punctured, and now it was catching up with him. He decided to cut down on the pain-killers. They'd mixed with the *cerveza* and sent him off in a daydream. He walked out the door and went to look for Hair Net.

It turned out his real name was Jorge Valenzuela-Bellargue, a hell of a name for a guy no more than five five, but Jorge wore it well. He made sure Beau got the spelling right, and the spelling of each of his *compadres*— Jacinto, Pascal, Coronal, and Vasco—and their business address, which was 1630 Vallejo Canyon Drive, and pressed a six-pack of frozen Miller High-Life into his hands as he got into the Lincoln. He rolled down the window to let the superheated air out, and Jorge leaned into the car.

"How come you taking that picture?"

Beau had the wedding picture in his hands. He looked down at it, his thoughts confused, feeling sad and angry.

"I need the faces, Jorge. I'll take care of it."

"Look—hey, okay I call you Beau?"

"Please. I'd be honored."

"Okay, look. This place you gonna go, down on Ditman Street? You be careful who you turn your back on down there. They got a gang there, Jamaicans. Use to be with the El Rukns—*negros malos!* They see you, kill you for somethin to do, so the day is not a total waste. *Comprende?* How about, we go with you?"

"Where's your show?"

Jorge rattled off an address in San Bernardino, which he called San Berdoo, pointing to it on Beau's street map.

"Okay, Jorge—tell you what. I gotta go alone. But I'll be there to see the show. How's that?"

"Okay! You come see Los Falcones tonight! I guarantee you one very fine time! *Salud!*"

He stepped back from the car and snapped off a razor-edge salute. Beau grinned at him, returned it, and started the car.

"You tay care, cowboy!"

Beau pulled away. The Falcons waved to him as he left, and they watched him until he turned the corner. Mexicans, he was thinking. Los Angeles was lucky to have them.

By the time he got something to eat and had made his way back to the freeway, the traffic was rock solid and unmoving. He sat in traffic for an hour, and it was after eight that evening by the time he got into the general territory. The streets got uglier and narrower as he made his way south, and the greenery faded. The sound of sirens was everywhere in the thickening air, and all the stores looked like armored bunkers. The people in the streets were furtive or loud, full of herky-jerky motion and sudden dashes. Now and then, a piece of fruit or a beer can would hit the windshield. The street-corner music from the boom boxes was rap—bragging and violent, coarse and brutal music, the chant of mindless threat.

Two-Twenty Ditman was in another part of the forest entirely.

20

2000 Hours – June 18 – East Los Angeles, California

D own in the flats, it gets dark early. The sun was well down in the western
sky, and long shadows made a zebra-striped landscape out of the warehouses and tenement blocks. Cars had their lights on early in the failing
light. A tall steel pylon held a billboard up out of the ruined neighborhood,
like a buoy marking a sunken ship, high enough for the traffic on the interstate
to read it. The billboard showed an arc of pink sand shading into a cobalt
sea dotted with white sails and a couple, barefoot in evening clothes, walking
along the shoreline.

BERMUDA . . . YOU DESERVE IT.

At the base of the pylon, in the shadow of the rotting bulk of the overpass,
down in the underworld, six small black children were eating pomegranates
and watching a barefoot black girl in a party frock using a long stick to shove

a flaming can of Sterno under the gas tank of an idling taxi. The driver, a skinny Chicano in a head scarf, was reading *Variety* and talking into a cellular phone. There was a pile of cigarette butts on the crumbling pavement under his window. The taxi was pink, an old Checker, and it had a large illuminated sign on the hood advertising THE YOUNG AND THE RESTLESS.

The roar from the overpass was not strong enough to drown out the music coming from the long line of crawling cars and trucks. They were bumper to bumper in the smoky twilight, cruising the lanes and talking deals with the languid black and Hispanic boys who leaned in the passenger windows, shaking packets of rock or weed. The streets reeked of rotting fruit and gasoline. The stores were fortified bunkers where nervous Iranians behind bulletproof plastic sold groceries or package liquor.

Above it all, the ghastly blue glow of the street lamps and the thunder and boom of the overpass. . . . Beau sat in the car and watched the action outside for another hour, fascinated by it.

Just another day in paradise, thought Beau, checking his grid map again by the maplight in the dash, his windows rolled up tight and the air conditioning on, his Smith on the passenger seat, his lights off, parked in an alley across the street from 220 Ditman, Earl Black Elk's last known address.

There was, however, a small problem.

The problem was, 220 Ditman was a blocklong warehouse, shuttered in steel and separated from the street by a high Lundy fence topped with razor wire. There was a gatehouse, dark and apparently empty, behind the locked gates, and a few tractor-trailers were parked well back from the fence, close to the building, under yellow lights. The loading dock ran the length of the warehouse, but there were several different company names above the huge doors:

POMODORO FOOD TRANSFER

KELLERMAN COLD HAULERS

UNITED FRUIT

FARWEST BEEF AND DAIRY

SUNKIST

ARMOUR MEATS

IDAHO FOOD CORPORATION

So 220 Ditman was a shipping center for produce and frozen beef from the Midwest. Beau had worked out of similar places in Provo and Ukiah. It was odd that the place was shut down like this. A lot of times, you had a driver coming in, redball, running on pills, off the interstate at three in the morning, you'd always find a guard on the gate to let him into the lockyard and sign for the trailer. Otherwise, you'd have a $200,000 load of produce sitting unguarded behind a Motel Six while the exhausted driver caught up on his sleep inside.

So there'd be a guard around somewhere, in spite of the deserted look to the place. Beau checked his watch—a little after nine. Maybe the guard was off on a break. Beau started up the Town Car and drove slowly past the rundown houses, feeling eyes on him, knowing he was made as a cop, wondering where the local vice cops had their observation van parked, filming the dealers, maybe running a street crew, doing stop-and-chokes on the hypes, taking down the license plate numbers of all the valley cars full of white teens. Maybe he should find them, or at least contact this Rufus Calder guy in the LAPD Detective Division.

Sure, and get the usual treatment city cops reserve for out-of-state troopers from cowboy country. Call you Tex and get your last name wrong. Screw that. If he ran into a vice guy, he'd tin him and work it out. Otherwise, it was easier just to work it alone.

Whatever *it* was.

Now why the hell was Earl Black Elk showing this place as his address?

He couldn't have been living here. Beau knew enough about shipping centers to know that no insurance company would let a company bunk someone in a commercial facility, because someone living in meant someone cooking in, and that meant fires, and anyway, things like that were a big security risk. They'd never let it happen.

Well, Earl had a military background. Maybe he was a guard here, using the work address as a mail drop because he was living rough in various flophouse hotels.

Beau pulled up by the locked gate. The street action was slower down here—most of the dealing and socializing was concentrated around the houses at the far end of Ditman. Down here by the warehouse, Ditman faded into a warren of storehouses and fenced-off lots and small-time commercial factories doing mill work or transmission repair or engine rebuilds.

He got out and walked up to the gate. There was a small sign wired to the fencing.

NIGHT MAN ON DUTY
RING FOR ENTRY

Okay. Where's the buzzer?

Beau found it up higher, about where a man driving a tractor-trailer would see it. He reached up and pressed the buzzer hard, holding it down long enough to wake up whoever was at the other end of the wire. He heard, faintly, the sound of a bell ringing inside the warehouse.

A light came on in the second floor, over the sign for United Fruit. A flashlight beam snapped on and jerked around until it found Beau and the white Town Car.

"Whatcherwan?" An old man's voice, thick with sleep.

Beau held up his tin. "Police. Open up."

The light flicked from Beau across to his rented Lincoln and back again. "Ain't no squad car there."

Christ.

"You see the badge, friend?"

"I see it."

"You want to argue this here, or do we come back with your boss and you can explain to him why the gatehouse is empty and you're up there sleeping on boxes?"

There was a silence. The light flicked off.

"Gimme a minute. I gotta get dressed."

Five minutes later, one of the loading-dock doors rolled up, sending a hard square of yellow light across the dark yard. A black silhouette of a man climbed down off the dock and walked over toward the gatehouse. As he came into the light at the gates, Beau could see he was carrying an Ithaca riot shotgun, the muzzle more or less directed at Beau's chest. The man carrying it was white, in his late sixties, in a rumpled Intertec Security uniform, white-haired, red-faced, his face in a permanent knot.

"Get that piece off my chest, friend."

The muzzle dropped away.

The old man reached the fence and said, "Let's see that badge again, buddy."

Beau held it up, but out of the man's reach.

"That's no LAPD badge."

"State troopers. Let's see your ID."

When on shaky ground, shake up the other guy. Cop rules.

The old man dug around in his breast pocket, found a plastic-coated card, held it up for Beau to see, a look of soured virtue spreading across his red face. "It's Drinaw. You can call me Jimmy."

"Okay—Jimmy. Open up the gate. I'm not leaving this car out here for the homies."

"You got that right. Fuckin' nigras, fuckin' greasers, oughta take the lot of them and send 'em—"

"The gates."

Jimmy went over to the gatehouse, opened the door, and leaned in to press a button. The big gates slid back on tracks, and Beau wheeled the Lincoln inside, driving it right up to the open loading dock. Jimmy shut the gates and trotted after him.

"What's the deal, sir?"

It was "sir" now. The guy was hiding some small hustle, or a bottle, or some minor sin in which Beau had no interest. Beau locked the car and pulled out his notebook. That always made the citizens nervous.

"Just a couple of questions, Jimmy. You're employed by Intertec, right?"

Jimmy looked at his uniform as if it had just materialized on his body. "Yes, sir. Nine years. Before that, I was on the city force up in Oxnard."

"Ex-cop, Jimmy?"

"Yeah. Well, auxiliary force."

"Okay. You worked this warehouse long?"

"Two years. Nights and weekends."

"How come it's all closed down?"

"Recession. Most of the place is empty. Don't get much in here now. United's using the place to store sugar. Most of the others are pulling out. Neighborhood's too iffy, you know?"

"Yeah. Who's in here now? Other than United Fruit."

"You got Pomodoro. They do olive oil, canned stuff. And Kellerman Cold Haulers. They use the refrigerated section. So does Farwest. Armour emptied out about six months ago, and Idaho's into frozen stuff now—they keep that out in San Pedro, by the tracks there. This whole thing'll be shut down in a year, maybe less."

"Mind if I look around, Jimmy?"

He needed an invitation inside, just to cover the search rules. Jimmy seemed surprised by the request—not that Beau wanted to go inside, but that he'd bothered to ask.

"No, sir. Go on ahead. Not much going on anyway. I gotta go with you, though."

"Sure. Come on."

The loading door led into a vast darkened hall reeking of old fruit and mold. Steel pillars marched away into the surrounding darkness. On the far side of the vast hall, a few scattered boxes and crates gathered dust and cobwebs. To the right, a huge pile of boxes lay under plastic wrapping carrying the United Fruit pineapple. The floor was smooth cement marked with black streaks from the forklift trucks that now sat idle in a row fifty feet away. At the far end of the hall, a new-looking partition blocked off a section of the warehouse. There was a green light above the locked door, and the sound of a machine running came from somewhere in the darkened roof above it.

Jimmy had a little trouble getting back up onto the dock. Beau reached for his hand and lifted him up. Jimmy didn't like the show of strength. It ruffled his dignity.

"So whaddya wanna see?"

"You worked here for how long?"

"Two years."

"You get to know any of the day workers?"

"Nah. Coons and spics. Got no use for them. Spoiled Oxnard, those people."

"Yeah? How could you tell?"

"Huh?"

"Never mind. So they're all black or Chicano?"

"Yeah, like everywhere."

"You ever see an Indian?"

"A what?"

"An Indian. A Native American."

"You *sure* you're a cop?"

"Why?"

"You don't talk like one. Up in Oxnard, we don't call 'em no African-Americans or that shit. We call a spade a spade up in Oxnard. You one a them new lawyer-cops? Gotta degree and all that?"

"No, I'm not."

"Guess you gotta talk like that, eh? Polite, like. You don't haveta talk like that with me. I'm a cop, too."

"Yeah, Jimmy. I guess I forgot. So, no Indians?"

"None I can remember. Now, I don't see much of the day guys. I check in at six, see some of them off around nine or ten. Close up and patrol the grounds."

"Like tonight?"

"Well, got a bit of the flu there. Thought I'd just get a quick lie-down. Conserve my strength. Gotta be on your toes around this neighborhood."

They were walking now, Beau leading him down toward the big walled-off section. The partition was stainless steel, and it looked brand new. The door was made of heavy steel slats, locked with a sliding bar and a Magnum deadbolt.

"You ever see the employment lists?"

"Sure. Got a complete list in the gatehouse. You wanna see it?"

"Yeah, if you could do that."

"What're we after, anyway?"

No false statements here. Guy's on the stand next year at the trial—God knows *what* trial, but anyway—and Ballard says to him, So, Mr. Drinaw, just what *did* Sergeant McAllister say to you that convinced you he really was from the Central Intelligence Agency?

"Background work, in connection with a shooting."

"Anybody killed?"

"Yeah. Four people." Maybe five. Beau hoped she was still alive, holding on up there in Sweetwater General. Jimmy looked inflated, taking a vicarious hit of violence. "A gun call, eh? Sure, hold on. I'll be right back."

Jimmy hustled off toward the loading dock, his oversize black shoes making earnest little slapping sounds on the cement floor. Beau walked up to the stainless-steel wall and put his hand on it. He felt a deep resonating murmur, and warmth. He went up the short flight of steps and looked at the door. There was a sign on it, in three languages.

ENTRÉE INTERDIT

NO ENTRY

EINGANG VERBOTEN

The sign carried no other marking and offered no clues about the activities behind the wall.

Odd sign, too.

No Spanish. And French where you couldn't find a true Frenchman in a thousand yards, unless it was a headwaiter in a borrowed Porsche trying to score some coke for a favored customer back uptown.

Nothing significant there. Just . . . odd.

The Magnum deadbolt looked as solid as Meagher's skull. Maybe thicker. Only way Beau was going through that was with a key. Maybe Jimmy had one.

Beau walked down into the darkness away from the doorway, looking for some other hole in the defenses. The wall ran almost up to the roof of the warehouse. The whole construction looked as if it were a complete enclosure *inside* the warehouse. It was riveted and welded and looked like a strongbox.

Jimmy said that two companies were using part of the warehouse for cold storage. The machine on the roof sounded like a compressor, and the warm walls could mean good insulation and an efficient refrigeration unit.

Farwest Beef and Dairy, and Kellerman Cold Haulers.

Never heard of them.

Or had he?

Farwest Beef and Dairy sounded familiar. God knew why. Hell, he was getting to that age when *everything* sounded familiar, every face looked like someone he had seen before, and every story sounded like every other story. He heard footsteps and scuffling and came back up to the light. Jimmy was making his way across the hall, carrying a clipboard.

"You're supposed to stay where I leave you, sir. Can't have any unescorted people around the place. Insurance, you know?"

"Yeah, Jimmy. Sorry. You get the sheet?"

He nodded and handed it to Beau.

The corporation that owned the warehouse was called Merced Industries, with an address in Visalia, California. Under the letterhead, there was a computer printout of the seven companies that had leased space in the facility at 220 Ditman. No addresses were shown for the companies, just a list of their regular employees and other people allowed access to their leased areas.

Pomodoro had eight people, most of them truckers, and one fork-truck operator. No names rang any bells with Beau. Kellerman Cold Haulers and Farwest listed their employees jointly. A total of eleven people, six men and five women. Not one familiar name. No Earl Black Elk.

United Fruit showed one man, a driver, who apparently carried his own key and hadn't shown up since last month.

Sunkist, the Idaho Food Corporation, and Armour Meats had no one regularly employed at 220 Ditman.

"See, I told you," said Jimmy. "Place is dead now."

"How often is this list updated?"

"Anytime the people change. I gotta have an up-to-date list. Intertec'd have my nuts if anybody got in here who wasn't supposed to."

"Why?"

Jimmy went blank, his pale blue eyes squinting. "Why what?"

"Why would Intertec have your nuts? There's nothing here but sugar, and the only fully occupied bay has Fort Knox in it."

"That's the cold-storage unit. Belongs to Farwest. Anyway, they hired me to keep this place tight, and that's what I do."

"Intertec pretty strict about security here?"

"They got me here, don't they?"

"Yeah," said Beau. "I see what you mean. You have a key for this cooler here?"

"Nah. Farwest leased the whole section, built this cold room themselves. All I do, I see that nobody gets inside the warehouse. The cold room—that's their problem. Opens up to the outside there, anyway. Bay nine, down by the hydro transformer."

"So you can't get in here?"

"What for? I seen dead cows before. You want in?"

"No, that's okay. What about Kellerman Cold Haulers?"

"What about 'em?"

"I thought they had space in this section, too."

"They do. They sublease it from Farwest Beef."

"You ever see their trucks?"

"Who? Farwest?"

"Yeah."

"Now and then. Farwest is phasing out of here, too. They get a truck in here, maybe once, twice a month."

"You ever see the drivers?"

"Oh, yeah. All the time."

"Why is that? I thought you only worked nights and weekends?"

"I do. Only, that's usually when they come. Farwest Beef. They got a beautiful stainless rig, a Freightliner, real honey. Makes a run about twice a month."

"Loading or unloading?"

"Both. They run the rig right up to bay nine there. Banging and slamming around."

"What's the driver like?"

"Hell of a nice guy. Always got a joke for you. Always a couple of cold beers. I'll tell you, Farwest must pay real well, too. Rig's spotless, kept right up. Real top-notch stuff. No rust, no dirt."

"Why do you think they pay so well? The driver tell you?"

"No. Won't say much about that. Talk to you about anything else, though. But I can tell. You keep forgetting—I used to be a cop."

"You can tell what?"

"That the company pays real well. This driver, he must be raking it in."

"Why?"

Jimmy looked at Beau with an air of genuine pity, the old-timer getting one-up on the new man.

"Well, he's got a Rolex, doesn't he? Don't get that in Lucky Elephant popcorn."

"A Rolex?"

"Yeah. One of those—what you call 'em? Presidents."

"A President? That's solid gold."

"Thirty thousand easy. See what I mean?"

"What's this guy's name?"

"Hank something. It's on the list there."

Beau looked down the sheet. Under Farwest, he found the name Starbuck, Henry D.

"This the guy? Starbuck, Henry D?"

"Yeah. Hank's short for Henry, isn't it?"

"Describe this guy for me."

"Jeez, let's see. Big guy, big as you. Blond hair. Going a little bald. Got real big hands. Kinda heavy, but hard-looking. Clean shaven. Dresses nice. A lady's man. Wears a wedding ring, but he isn't married."

"How do you know that?"

"Well, if he is, he's got a real casual idea about it. I come around once, he was unloading these carts into the cold room, he and this other guy, and he's got his ring off—you know, so he won't catch it in the door. All drivers take off their rings and stuff when they're loading. Too easy to catch a finger."

"Yeah. And?"

"And I see he's got no white mark under the ring. That's how you can tell, you know. A guy who screws around, he'll take that ring off as soon as he gets out of the house. I asked him about it, but he just laughed, made some joke about how it was his life-ring, kept the sharks away. Say, you hear the one, these two lawyers are walking down a street, they see this great-looking broad, and one lawyer turns to—"

"What did you say?"

"It's a joke. So the lawyer says to his buddy, say, wouldn't you like to screw—hey, where you going?"

Beau was headed for the car, his head full of white noise. Jimmy caught up to him at the loading bay. He watched Beau jump down to the ground and unlock the Town Car.

"What's the matter, you don't like jokes?"

"I'll make you a bet, Jimmy. I'll bet Hank Starbuck told you that joke? Am I right?"

"Yeah. That's what made me think of it! Talking about Hank!"

Beau reached in and picked up the cellular phone.

"When's the last time Farwest had a truck in here?"

"Got a time sheet in the shed. Pin me down on it, I'd say, oh, ten, fifteen days ago. This all mean something to you?"

"I don't know yet. You say Starbuck had a guy helping him?"

"Yeah."

Beau looked down at the Farwest list.

"Was his name on the list?"

"No. He was in the truck with Hank. Long as there's somebody on the list, no harm in bringing a friend to help with the load, is there?"

"Did you get his name?"

"Nah. Didn't speak any English. At least, not around me. Now that you say it, though, I guess he had to speak English."

"Why?"

"Because I'll bet my left lung Hank don't know any Jap."

"Jap? Japanese?"

"Yeah. Japanese. The other guy was a Jap. Wiry little guy, with those stupid round black glasses on."

Beau was dialing the cellular and checking his watch. Midnight. Christ, Meagher'd be in bed. He'd wake his wife.

"Hate those people," said Jimmy, staring out at the street.

"Who?"

"The Japs. They're gonna buy the whole country. I hate 'em."

"Yeah," said Beau. "I figured you might."

21

0030 Hours – June 19 – Los Angeles, California

Beau was back on the interstate headed for San Bernardino by the time he finally tracked Meagher down in the Holiday Inn at Rapid City. Beau was getting used to L.A. traffic now. The secret seemed to be to keep the pedal floored and your brights on, hit the horn a lot, and cut in front of anybody stupid enough to give you road room.

Beau figured that Los Falcones would run late and party long, and a plate of *fajitas* was looking pretty good right now. The phone in his hand was warm, and the sound of the line ringing down the airwaves added a nice surreal touch to the scene.

The ringing stopped.

There was a dull thud, and a crash, clearer now, something breakable breaking. The phone thumped again.

"Who the hell is this?"

"Eustace! Don't tell me I woke you up!"

"Oh no, McAllister. I hadda get up to answer the phone anyway. How the hell did you find me?"

"I called your wife."

"Oh man. You wake her?"

"Oh no, Eustace. I woke the guy beside her."

"Very funny. What the hell do you want?"

"Eustace, justice never sleeps, you know. Out here in the night, your loyal troopers are fighting the good fight, holding back the yellow hordes, the red peril—"

"I take it you found something? Other than your pecker?"

"I found something. What are you doing in Rapid City?"

"I'm on my way to see that Cut Arms guy. Remember?"

"Right! Sorry. Did the doc come up with those figures?"

"I called again today. But didn't he say he was going out to one of the clinics?"

"Yeah. As a matter of fact, I think he was going to the Rosebud. But he would have flown, I think."

"Maybe I'll run him down out there. We'll go fishing."

"Oh, well, that's okay then. For a minute there, I thought you were actually *working* or something. You know, like your loyal underlings out here on the coast, putting their hearts on the line, digging into the seamy underbelly of the bloated corpse of American civilization, cutting deep into the entrails of—"

"Beau, cut it out. What have you got?"

"What have I got? You have a pen?"

"Just a minute . . . okay. Shoot."

"First, there's a guy works for Mountain Bell, name of Bucky Blitzer? He was in the hospital with me. I've called him a couple of times, but the cellular won't work in these hills. Could you try him in the morning, ask him about this joke I heard?"

"Oh, what the hell is *that*?"

"No, I'm serious. It's the one about these two lawyers, they see this blonde on the street? Remember?"

"No . . . wait. Yeah. You told me that one."

"Right. I want you to ask Bucky who told it to him."

"What the hell for?"

"Because I wanna know. Ten bucks says he heard it from that kid, died in the truck fire. Hubert Wozcylesko."

"And if he did? Man, I can see taking this to Vanessa!"

"Also, I need you to find out who owns a couple of companies for me."

"Sure. Who?"

"Kellerman Cold Haulers. Don't know where they're based, but it'll be in the national register. Get Moses or Dell to call Sig Tarr at the *Gazette*. He's a friend, and maybe there's a story in it for him."

"I know Sig—he'll want something for his trouble. Charlie Tallbull's doing better, by the way. They're going to arrange for him to get his physio in Wyola."

"Eustace, you notice, any Indian gets put in the hospital around here, he gets out as soon as he can?"

"Yeah? So did you. What else can I do?"

"I have another name—sounds familiar to me. Farwest Beef and Dairy?"

"I don't have to ask about that one. Those are the people bought Ingomar's spread. Remember, the Japanese guys?"

Beau slapped the wheel. "Oh, for chrissake! Farwest Beef and Dairy. God, I hate being stupid. It really complicates your life!"

"Yeah, everything takes longer. You remember last year, when we were doing the big fund-raising thing, for Doc Darryl's cancer wing?"

"Yeah, the goddamned cancer wing. We raised money for that every year for ten years. And every time we did, I ate Kraft Dinner for a month."

"Well, these guys, they were right on the bandwagon, pulled in a hell of a lot of money for Doc Darryl. I got to know a couple of them. I liked them. They were all right. Farwest is a California corporation, but the parent outfit is in Kyoto. Montana Beef, it's real big in Tokyo, Osaka, the big cities. Japs are gonna be as sick and fat as we are, give 'em a few years."

"I think Danny Burt's into something with them. I talked to this guy who's the security guard out at 220 Ditman—you know, Earl Black Elk's last known address?"

"They got a guard there?"

"Oh, yeah. That's another thing. Two twenty Ditman isn't a house or an apartment. It's a warehouse. Huge place, right under the I-5 overpass, in a real rat's-ass part of town. Right out of *Night of the Living Dead*, Eustace. Two twenty Ditman's about a block long, mostly empty. But Farwest has a cold-storage room built in, real secure. Very high-tech. And the guard, his name is Jimmy Drinaw, tells me that he sees the Farwest truck come in maybe twice a month. And he describes the driver. I ask him, what's the name. He says Starbuck, Henry D. I say, can you describe this guy? Guess who he describes?''

"Danny Burt?"

"Danny Burt. Down to the ring thing. Listen, did you notice his watch at the board meeting?''

"Yeah, I did."

"Jimmy Drinaw noticed it, too."

"Okay. This adds a whole new dimension. What in the name of God is Burt doing running a Farwest truck to Los Angeles?''

"Can you talk Vanessa into a warrant?''

"Not with what you've got there. Where's the felony?''

"He's using an alias. False pretenses?''

"What value has he received? Who has he conned? No, not enough. But I can sure go talk to him, let him know we're asking questions. See if he gets nervous.''

"Okay, but be careful. There's another guy around, he's real wired into this. I have a vague idea it's somebody in a wedding picture I have.''

"A wedding picture?''

"Yeah. I found it in that house on Vallejo Canyon. They're all there, the Gall kid, the girl—her name's Donna Sweetwater Bent, by the way— make a note.''

"That's a fine old High Plains name.''

"And the rest—Jubal, Earl, that Cheyenne guy, Comes In Sight. And a couple of new faces I want you to look at. One guy here, he's got that look on him you're always talking about. The Hundred-Yard Glaze?''

Eustace snorted. "You mean, the Thousand-Yard Stare? Looks like a skull, and the eyes go all the way back to the bone.''

"That's the look. I'm gonna get some prints, see if anybody in Billings has seen him around. He's out there somewhere—he's the joker in all this. I want to talk to him.''

"You get anything on Earl Black Elk? Did he live there?''

Beau thought about it for a while. His headlights carved a blue-white tunnel out of the California dark. Eustace could hear the wind and the rush of tires.

"I'll tell you, you get Duffy to go to the army and ask them, who sent in the 220 Ditman address, and when. I'll bet you, Duffy finds out it was sent in by Earl Black Elk less than a month ago. He never lived there.''

"So why send in that address? That's where his pension checks were gonna go. He'd need that money.''

"Yeah. But what if he thought something was gonna happen to him, and he wanted to leave a trace, leave it where no one could get at it, wipe it out?''

''Spooky stuff, Beau, that's out there next to Pluto. Christ, he *was* a spook, wasn't he?''

''MACSOG, you said? And Phoenix? That their kind of thing?''

''Absolutely! Only who was the message *for*? Not us. Duffy had to sell his firstborn to get it out of Quantico.''

''Off the top of my head, I'd say it was put there for someone who could get it. Someone who *did* have access.''

''Like another spook—another Vietnam vet, maybe?''

''We can run this wedding picture by the army. See if anybody recognizes the people.''

''Yeah. Like they'd tell *us,* Beau.''

''Yeah. Sounds pretty wild, right?''

''Maybe. Maybe not.''

''You get the feeling, Eustace, you get the idea, it's real dark in the mountains and there's this strange green light over the hill, and you and me are the old prospectors?''

''Beau, you've lost touch with the mother ship.''

''No, I mean, we're the two old prospectors—you know, it's the one where they see the green glow, and one guy says to the other, 'Well, Jebediah, let's go on over the hill and see what's going on,' and the other one says, 'I don't know, Jeremiah, that there's a pretty funny-looking green glow there.' Meanwhile, the credits are rolling up their backs, and we're hearing this weird electronic music.''

''Leave Los Angeles soon, Beau, before it's too late.''

''You'll call Bucky Blitzer?''

''Yeah. I'll do it all. So if I'm getting you, you figure this joke about the two lawyers, it ties into this somehow?''

''Nothing you can take to court. But jokes, you know, they go by word of mouth. So I'm thinking, suppose Bucky gets it from Hubert, both of them at Mountain Bell, and suppose Hubert—''

''Got it from Danny Burt. Yeah. I see it. Anything else I can do? I mean, since I'm up already?''

''How tight are you with Rufus Calder?''

''We humped the sixty together in Eye Corps.''

''That means something?''

''It means we're tight. What do you need?''

''Do you think you can get him to scoop Jimmy Drinaw?''

''On what?''

"Well, he's got an Ithaca riot gun. Last time I looked, they weren't legal for security guards. That do?"

"For a start. It won't keep him long."

"It'll keep him alive until we can roll this up. It'll keep him from tipping Danny Burt."

"Okay, I'll try. Maybe I can get him to put some surveillance on 220 Ditman. See who comes and goes."

"He'll want to know why."

"I'll tell him what I know."

"And what's that, Eustace?"

"Not much. Maybe Farwest and Danny Burt are into some kind of contraband operation. Maybe drugs, you think?"

"Yeah, that would cover it." Beau was struggling with his next request. No matter how it went, he was going to look bad to his boss, but he hated to keep things from Meagher.

And something had to be settled.

"One other thing. I don't know if I ever got around to telling you, but Bell had a videotape in his VCR, hooked up to a roof camera, and—"

Meagher cut in, his voice rising. "Are you going to tell me you had a videotape of the robbery, the whole action, and you *forgot* about it?"

"No—no no no. It—I think Bell came in and shut the thing off, a few minutes before the whole thing happened. There was nothing on it, at least I didn't think there was—"

"Why the hell didn't you bring it up at the board? Ballard would *love* that. It would show intent!"

"Has anybody heard from Bell yet about the lawsuit?"

"Not yet."

"Nobody's heard from him at all?"

"Not a word since Monday. He doesn't have many friends. I'll send a car out there. I'll send Moses Harper. You haven't answered my question about the videotape."

Beau said nothing, looking for a way to explain it that Meagher would accept. "I didn't think it was important."

"Maybe next time you could let me in on your thinking, Beau. It would help me preserve my illusions about being the CO. Now you *do* think it's important?"

"Bell was in the tape talking to somebody in a big old Caddy. Can't say what color, and I couldn't see the plates. But I know the year, give or take. It'd be between 1975 and 1979. Black or dark brown or dark blue."

"The driver?"

"Nope. But Bell was real pissed when he walked away from the car, and it was right after that he shut off the tape. Maybe there's a connection."

"So what do you want? You want me to get Motor Vehicles to run off a list of Cadillacs in eastern Montana, see if the RO's ring a bell?"

"Would you?"

"I don't see the point. So Bell was pissed at a guy in a Caddy. So what?"

"I think it would be good to talk to the driver."

Meagher groaned, yawned. "Sure, okay. We'll give it a shot. Look, I've still got room on my page here, Beau. Anything else I can do for you? Laundry? Boil your cats? Tell you the weather?"

"Yeah. How's the weather?"

"Actually, it sucks. I hear we got a *big* front coming in, a real howler. You should see it on the TV. Looks like black doom in a '59 Roadmaster. You better get back here before it hits. Get your cats indoors."

"Yeah, I will. Are we still keeping an eye on Bobby Lee and Maureen?"

"She's okay. So far, nothing. She goes to work, she comes home. She's having the house remodeled. Spending a lot of money."

"Tell me about it. She came along with Dwight when I was in the hospital. Gold chain, earrings. I know she doesn't *have* a lot of money. Maybe it's Dwight's."

"Well, she's spending *someone's* cash. We have some Big Horn cars in the area, and Dell Greer stays around when he can. Bobby Lee likes him. By the way, I stopped in there, and she gave me a letter for you. Wait a minute."

The traffic had thinned out. Beau was running in the dark through low black hills and stunted green bushes. The artificial lushness of the place, the flowers and the twisted vines, the heavy dark of the night sky without stars, the rotten smell of the city—it weighed him down and made him hungry for endless grasses and a horizon without limits or hard edges.

"Beau?"

"Yeah?" There was a sudden trilling bleat in his ear. He held the phone away and looked at it. It was flashing LOW BATT at him.

"You better hurry, Eustace. My battery's going."

"Okay. Jeez—she says 'Dear Daddykins'—*Daddykins?*"

"Come on, Eustace. You can do it."

"The things I do for you. 'Dear Daddykins, I got new shoes I am six now we have our own policeman his name is Dell can I have a gun for my seventh birthday are there goldfish bowls in hell I love you'—" Meagher's voice cut off in a shrill beep.

"Tell her hello," said Beau, into the dead phone.

Up ahead the road ran down a long decline toward a grid of lights and neon. San Berdoo. City of Dreams.

Why hadn't he told Meagher about the old Cadillac before now?

He had stared at the tape for a while, trying to get around a terrible insight. He'd pushed it down and covered it over, but it was still there. He kicked some earth over the idea and put it out of his mind. He'd go to the hockey arena, see Los Falcones, have a good time. All work and no play. . . .

Anyway, he was wrong about the tape.

He was tired and overworked, and his leg burned and ached.

Meagher would get Motor Vehicles onto it.

They'd find the driver, whoever he was, and it would be someone else entirely. They'd ask him what Bell had been saying to him. He'd have some explanation that would either help them or turn out to be nothing at all—some stupid argument over an unpaid bill or a set of faulty plugs.

And Beau wouldn't have named . . . anyone.

He slowed as he entered the San Bernardino turnoff.

That was as far as he could go.

22

0415 Hours – June 19 – Big Horn County, Montana

Cold.

And pain.

There was a weight on his chest. It was crushing the breath out of him. His mouth was full of . . . something. He tried to spit it out but could not, tried to brush it away and his hands wouldn't move. He turned his head, and a red sheet of searing agony flashed through his mind, convulsed his body, shook him violently and he tried to scream but his mouth was full of earth . . . something was close . . .

. . . he could hear something . . .

. . . scratching . . .

. . . pulling and scratching . . . the noise was close, but he couldn't see because something was in his eyes . . .

... in his mouth ...

... something ... was earth ... he was covered with wet earth and then he remembered, and the fear crawled into his mind and began to eat ... death but not dead ... buried but not dead ...

... and the scratching ... closer ... he moved his head again ... moved it through the sheeting red pain ... and the earth fell away from his eyes, and he blinked up at a black sheet with thousands of tiny holes in ... no ... it was the sky ... it was the night sky ... he had known the names ... Orion ... Cassiopeia ... something growled and bit at him and he felt warm breath and suddenly there were teeth—*teeth*—sinking into his shoulder, and he was being pulled ... he twisted ... the earth fell away from his chest ... more pain, but still he moved and he felt the teeth, and now he smelled hot fetid breath and his body was being pulled by the cloth of his shirt ... he arched and twisted again, and a hand came free, and he clawed at the earth in his face and his eyes and the ground seemed to open up and he was suddenly *released,* and he spilled out onto cold wet grasses—spiky against his cheek— he heard an animal growling and grunting and he felt the pull again ... and the pain—shattering, it was a living thing that coiled in his mind and chewed on the inside of his skull, he could feel its teeth raking against the pink wet bone inside his skull ... his face was a red mask ... and the animal let go and came in again—he saw it against the stars, a blackness that frightened him to his core ... every primitive fear ... every dark thing that had ever slithered across the floor of his imagination, and he tried to bring his hands up, and then the animal was on his chest and digging—scratching—whim- pering and tugging at his shirt and in the middle of his pain and his panic, the thought came to him like a soft warm light turned on in a childhood room.

This was Joe Bell's dog.

His Irish setter.

The animal pushed against him and snarled again, and bent down to bite his shirt ... Joe Bell's dog had found him ...

... in his grave ...

... and dug him up ...

Gabriel rolled to his left, spilling the dog off his chest, and he threw up on the grass, heaving and spitting until his throat felt like an open wound. Then he rolled onto his back and—carefully, like a man touching a glass flower—felt his face, his mind full of images of wounded men he had seen— terrible disfiguring wounds—teeth bare—jaws hanging and smashed—men opened to the backs of their throats—eyes burst and crushed and cheekbones blown away—he'd killed a man once, a friend, in a little clearing of the jungle growth ten miles from the Peruvian border—the man had tripped a perimeter mine and it had taken his face, and the terrible obscenity was that he could have lived and Gabriel did the only kind thing with a length of wire . . .

He felt his face and gradually, delicately, he measured the damage. The round had hit him in the mouth, just under his left nostril and it had turned there—in the freakish way of lead shot in the human body—deflected by the jawbone—perhaps he had turned his face at the last second—the round had carved a path around his upper gumline—the jaw was cracked—he knew that from the pain and the deafness—and then it had torn out of his body under his left ear. He could almost follow the path. The exit wound was raw and he could not bring himself to touch it.

If he lived, his face would be disfigured for the rest of his life. The pain was growing sharper. The shock was passing.

The Irish setter was panting now, a black shape under the soft starlight. Gabriel managed to sit upright. The dog came over and tried to lick his face. Gabriel stopped him and ran a bloody hand through the dog's ruff. He had no idea why the dog had persisted in his digging—whether the dog was looking for something to eat or someone to love, but Gabriel would see to it that this dog lived a long and happy life.

He tried to speak to the dog but could not move his face without cracking the bone, and the pain of it was almost enough to make him pass out.

The light was changing as he watched. The stars were paling and receding, and a luminous wash of violet and pale pink began to bleed upward into the night sky. He pulled his shirt-sleeve up and was surprised to see that he still had his watch, and even more surprised to see that it was still running.

Now, there's an endorsement possibility for you. A watch for Christ himself. Don't be late for your next resurrection.

He twisted his arm until he could get some starlight on the face. The motion sent another jagged blue bolt of agony up the side of his skull, and the image blurred. He fought to stay conscious, to concentrate on the dial, on the faintly glowing numbers.

If he had come down from the hill on Monday evening . . . and then it had gone badly . . . if this was right, he had been in the . . . grave. Call it that. That's what it was. For a full day and most of the following night.

For thirty-three, perhaps thirty-four hours.

And the thought came to him, slammed into his mind, left him trembling in its wake, that there was nothing miraculous about his resurrection, because it hadn't happened.

The bullet that should have killed him *did* kill him.

Was killing him now.

Maybe he was dying now . . . in the moment when the round struck him and all of this was just a few fleeting seconds of hallucinatory intensity, the last flaring of light and heat in a disintegrating brain. Maybe he was still falling through the air and the ground was rushing up at him . . . he felt his mind slipping, felt the thin cord of continuity and remembrance that binds the fragmentary images and disconnected moments of a man's life begin to fray and twist. He could hear the thin high shriek as the silver wire stretched and snapped, and every glittering image, every memory and incident that had composed the life and times of Gabriel Picketwire went spinning off into a deep blue immensity. Weakness went through his arms and legs, and he fell backward onto the grass and watched the shards and splinters of his life shattering, like a mirror, into the night. They burned and turned, a fiery radiance that shimmered, dimmed, flared, and sparkled and faded.

A rising wind stirred the grasses, hissing and rustling, feathering across his shattered cheek. The dog got up and trotted away down the slope toward the lights of Joe Bell's cabin. He looked back and whimpered.

Gabriel sat up.

Pain.

The pain was very real.

Gabriel managed to get to his feet.

The sky wheeled and steadied. He could see the warm yellow lights of the main house, bright against the purple hills under the pearl and opal sky.

He took a step, staggered, caught his balance. The dog moved a little farther off, and waited.

Gabriel pulled in a breath. His face felt like a mask of cracked ice and blood.

He also felt hunger.

If this was a kind of death, there were rules to it.

He could still remember the black bulk of the gun and the dark shape of the other man against the evening sky, and Joe Bell with a shovel in his hand.

The dog had been watching him, and now, seeing him moving, it ran a few yards down the slope, careless and buoyant. Gabriel came down behind it, his boots cutting a dark green trail through the silver grasses.

As he reached the bottom land, he remembered that there had been a sensation—it seemed a year or more in the past, a part of someone else's memory—of something beside him, of a bending in the daylight. It was gone now, he knew, gone back into the sea-green grassy hills that had carried him like a drowning man, that had taken him down beneath them and held him in the darkness and the silences and then raised him up again into the world of changing light and scented breezes.

He smiled—the pain cut at him, and the ruined fragments of teeth and jawbone grated against his wound.

Well, home is the sailor, home from the sea.

And the hunter home from the hill.

23

0830 Hours – June 19 – Los Angeles, California

Beau ate an early breakfast in the hotel coffee shop, watching the tourist buses fill up with old men and women in lurid pastel combinations, dragging themselves up into the darkened interior of the bus, looking oddly like children in their shorts and flowered shirts, children zapped with an age ray on their way to a birthday party.

The windows of the coffee shop were tinted dark gray, and the room was chilly with recycled air.

A fiftysomething waitress in a Snow White costume plowed through the tables toward Beau, leather-faced under her heavy makeup. She pulled a pen out of her Snow White hair-ribbon.

"That'll be it for you, Tex?"

"You know, I never trusted that prince."

"Huh?" Snow White's pen stopped on the notepad.

"Your prince. He took off, left you with the palace and the bills?"

She sighed and looked down at her costume. "Disneyland's down the road. The tourists like it."

"Listen, the Seven Dwarfs are visiting the Vatican, right?"

She cocked her hip and leaned against the banquette. "Okay. The Seven Dwarfs are visiting the Vatican."

"And they're there for a few days, you know, seeing the city, looking at St. Peter's, doing the tour, and finally on the third day, they get an audience with the Pope."

"You gonna have anything else?"

"No, that's it. So each of the dwarfs gets to ask the Pope one question."

"One question." She had her head down, writing.

"Yeah. And it comes round to Dopey, he wants to know, does the Pope have any midget nuns?"

"Yeah?"

"And the Pope says, no, no midget nuns. So Dopey says, okay, you have any *dwarf* nuns? The Pope says no. So Dopey starts to look really worried, and he says, do you have any real real *short* nuns? Again, the Pope says no. And from the back of the line, Grumpy yells out—*'Dopey screwed a penguin!'* "

She grinned at him, her teeth too bright and even, Hollywood teeth. She dropped the bill on his table.

"Yeah? Well, Dopey was always like that. Have a nice day."

Eustace Meagher watched the pickup truck work its way over the landscape toward him. It was like watching a bug crawl across a tabletop. Meagher took another pull from his Thermos and wiped the back of his neck. The wind out here was as steady as a river, smelling of dust and clay and grass. In the far southwest sky, a low bank of black clouds shimmered in the heat haze. Heavy weather back in Montana.

He looked around him. Parmelee, South Dakota. An outpost of peeling cement-block stores lined up like tombstones on a rotting asphalt street. Treeless and flat, South Dakota stretched away in every direction until it faded into a blue horizon of heat and wind. A few miles to the south, Nebraska offered more of the same.

In the town, a few old Sioux men sat under the shade of a sheet-metal porch and rocked and talked in low thick voices. Meagher figured he was the most exciting thing to happen in Parmelee since the end of the Indian wars. A buffalo soldier in a tan uniform, driving a blue Lincoln with Montana plates.

They'd talk about it for weeks.

He looked back up the highway. The pickup was closer now, maybe only a mile away. George Cut Arms and his people.

Or a scalping party?

Meagher wiped the sweat off his bald head.

Well, he was safe, anyway.

Moses Harper leaned back in the oak swivel chair and threw a ball of waxed paper at a framed picture of Henry Kissinger. Kissinger was smiling. Someone had drawn a tiny pen-wiper moustache on his lip. He looked a lot like Hitler's older brother.

Harper had his gun off, and his harness was hanging from the back of the chair. The Highway Patrol squad room was nearly empty this morning. It was close to ten, and the shift change was over. The six-to-six night shift had gone home, and the overlap units were wandering around in the yard outside, cleaning out their squad cars and eyeing the storm building up in the southwest. Sergeant Sugar was off this morning, and Meagher's office was empty, the door locked. Somehow, his chair seemed to radiate authority even without Meagher in it. It was strange for Harper, sitting around with all these state boys. There was a friendly rivalry between the two units, but deep in their hearts the Big Horn guys always felt a little like poor cousins next to the well-funded state troopers. Now here he was, one-third of a three-man task force. Served him right for volunteering.

Moses went back to his paperwork.

Farwest Beef and Dairy.

Kellerman Cold Haulers.

Merced Industries.

And Danny Burt.

They'd put out a bulletin on Danny Burt. He wasn't anywhere around. Bob Gentile hadn't seen him for a week, but he wasn't surprised. Danny had taken a week off after the Arrow Creek thing, saying he was too nervous to work. Gentile figured that was fair. Anyway, Gentile was having enough trouble without having Danny around asking stupid questions. Gentile was being sued by Peter Hinsdale's mother, *and* he wanted his goddamned morgue wagon back from evidence storage.

So far, nobody knew where Danny Burt was. The cars were out, and he'd turn up sooner or later.

Harper dialed the number of the *Billings Gazette* again and sat back listening to it ring. Kissinger leered at him. Out in the hall, somebody laughed out loud, and another male voice said *shit,* and then something dropped on the terrazzo floor. Through the plate-glass window, Harper could see the two female dispatchers in their computer stations—headsets on, screens blinking—leaning back in their chairs and talking to each other.

One of them was Beth Gollanz. Harper had once spent a week in Freeport with Beth. She was a nice lady, but she wasn't going to marry a cop. Sleep with one, maybe, but no marriage.

"Hello?"

Harper leaned forward and picked up the papers in front of him. "Can I talk to Sig Tarr?"

"This is Tarr. What can I do for you?"

"Mr. Tarr, my name is Moses Harper. I'm with the Highway Patrol."

"I wanna lawyer."

Harper laughed. "You don't need a lawyer, sir. I'm calling for Sergeant McAllister."

"That bastard! What's he need? Bail?"

"No, no, sir. Actually, he wanted you to do something for him."

"Oh, jeez," said Tarr, chuckling. "Hide the virgins!"

Balboa Boulevard paralleled Sepulveda, climbing into the Santa Susana Mountains. Beau could see the bowl of L.A. in his rearview, a Jurassic swamp of yellow fog and freeways. Granada Hills was in a better part of town, close to the entertainment offices and the lush neighborhoods of Glendale and Mission Hills. 1550 Balboa Boulevard was a bunker of rose-colored granite and tinted windows, retreating from the busy street in a series of rectangular recessions softened with expensive greenery and royal palms. A small brass plaque on the wall by the door read:

> HOLOGRAM PRODUCTIONS
> OFFSHORE FILMS
> RIGID ROOSTER STUDIOS

Rigid Rooster?

Beau pulled the heavy glass doors back and walked into a cool sepulcher of polished stone. A Persian rug in vivid reds and blues ran all the way down the long hall toward a glass-block desk where a young man in a silk shirt was answering a bank of beeping phones.

As Beau came toward the reception desk, the hall widened into a waiting area where a couple of boys in punker outfits were lounging on a gray leather couch, perfecting their chill. They watched Beau walk up to the desk from behind their acid-blue sunglasses. One of them popped his gum at Beau and said "cop" in the kind of tone you use when you've found half a cockroach in your grilled cheese sandwich.

The boy behind the counter looked up at Beau over his circular glasses. "May I help you, sir?"

Beau showed his badge.

One of the Lizard-Boys made a pig-snorting sound.

"I'm Sergeant McAllister. I need to see your personnel officer."

"Miss Haydon is busy right now, sir. May I tell her what it concerns?"

Beau set his file folder down and extracted the wedding picture. He held it up for the boy to see.

"This man here. His name is Edward Gall. He's an employee of Offshore Films. He's been in an accident, and I am investigating it. It's a police matter, and I'd like to see Miss Haydon right away."

"Is Eddie all right?" The boy seemed genuinely interested.

"You know him?"

"Of course. He's one of our people. He's in Montana scouting a film location. Is he all right? What happened to him?"

"I think I ought to tell it to Miss Haydon first. If you don't mind?"

The boy unhooked his headset and got up. "I'll go and tell her you're here." He punched a button on the phone bank and hurried away down the hall.

Lizard-Boy One made another pig-snuffle sound, and his friend laughed again, louder.

Beau turned to look at them. They began to laugh harder.

Beau walked over to them, leaned down, and took the sunglasses off Lizard-Boy One. The kid said "hey," but by that time Beau had pinched his nose between his thumb and index finger.

He shook it three times, back and forth, hard.

The kid's eyes teared up, and his face went bright red.

Beau let go of the kid's nose. "Is that better? You had a bad sniffle there."

The Lizard-Boys stared up at him. Lizard-Boy One had a nosebleed. Lizard-Boy Two looked like he was about to faint.

Beau handed Lizard-Boy One a Kleenex.

"There you go, son. That's a nasty cold you got there."

"Sergeant McAllister?"

Beau turned around. The receptionist was back. A young woman in jeans and an aquamarine blouse was standing behind the desk, staring at him.

"Yes, ma'am?"

"Is there a problem here?"

Beau looked at the Lizard-Boys. "Is there a problem, guys?"

They shook their heads in unison.

"Okay, then. You get that cold looked at, son."

The woman studied the scene in silence. She turned to the receptionist. "Dylan, see if the doctor has a moment."

She sent Beau a look freighted with warning.

Beau smiled at her, a gundog smile, full of innocent joy and good-heartedness.

"If you'll come this way, Sergeant?" Miss Haydon turned and walked down the hall.

Beau followed her, admiring her figure in the jeans, and grinning to himself. Sometimes this job was almost worth the trouble.

Beth Gollanz came into the squad room carrying a sheaf of computer paper. She dropped it on Harper's desk, in the middle of his papers and pens. It was about an inch thick.

"There it is. Took Motor Vehicles all morning to print this out. You should see the teletype. It's smoking!"

Harper stared down at the pile. "Oh, God. There can't be that many Cadillacs in Montana!"

Beth patted him on the shoulder. "They can't index them by year. They're not set up for that."

"Goddamn! Computers can tell you every credit card purchase made in Missoula by a left-handed Nicaraguan nanny named Filomena between three and three-fifteen on a Thursday, but they can't run off a year-by-year breakdown of Cadillacs!"

He hefted the pile and let it drop back on the desk. Then he looked up at Beth, and a slow sly smile spread across his tanned face. "Oh, no," said Beth, backing away. "Not on your life!"

"Dinner? Your choice?"

"No way!"

"And dancing? How about a weekend?"

Beth stopped and smiled at him. "Who's bribing who here, Moses?"

"Whom," said Harper. "Who's bribing *whom*."

•   •   •

Headband was doing lengths in the backyard pool. Bobby Lee was somewhere back in the kitchen, busy with her goldfish. Dell Greer was sitting in a lawn chair with his collar undone, trying not to let Maureen's body distract him. Half the sky was taken up with a huge storm front now. The sun was about a half-hour away from being eaten up by it.

Greer shifted his position in the chair and turned it away from the pool so he could see the yard and the door of the house. Maureen was swimming on her back now, the water sliding over her breasts and her belly.

Damn, thought Greer. I'm married.

And I don't even *like* her.

Why me? Why not Moses? Moses was no good at paperwork anyway. He'd just try to get someone else to do it for him.

He shifted again, trying to ease the strain in his pants.

Come *on,* he said to himself. Settle down there!

Show some taste.

Never have sex outside your own species.

Words to live by.

George Cut Arms set his beer down on the hood of the pick-up and grunted at Meagher. "That's just *this* year! And just from one clinic."

"How many of the women?"

"On the Rosebud? Maybe fifteen."

Meagher walked away and looked out at the flattened countryside. If God had really made this land, he'd done most of the work with a twenty-pound sledge.

"How can you be sure?"

"I asked them."

"And you believe them?"

"Why not?"

"Well . . . they're hookers, aren't they?"

George Cut Arms pushed himself off the truck and slid to the ground. His heavy body thumped the earth, and his boots scraped on the ground. "Look, buffalo soldier, you're a black man. Yes?"

"Last time I looked."

"And a cop?"

"Yes."

"So which part of you is the real part? The buffalo soldier or the cop or the black man?"

"All of it is."

"Yeah. Same with me. Same with the women."

"Don't they . . . take precautions?"

"Take precautions? Yeah—they don't work."

"Bullshit. They *have* to work. The girls are lying to you."

"*All* of them, soldier? All of these girls are lying? And what about the girls on Pine Ridge and up at Standing Rock? It's even happening to the Crow and the Shoshoni—"

One of the old men spat on the ground. Some things never ended, thought Meagher. A hundred years, and the old men still hate.

"—even to them. Charlie Tallbull will tell you. They killed his niece. His boys know—Willy and Philip Joe told us about it. They call them the Sleeping Ones. Mary Littlebasket had one, and they tried to take it. She left the medicine sign."

Christ. "What medicine sign?"

Cut Arms walked over and drew a few quick strokes in the dusty hood of the Lincoln.

> > > = = = = = = = = = = = >   < + >   < = = = = = = = = = = = < < <

"What does it mean?"

"It's a sign for protection from bad things. A warning sign. Whatever the arrows point at, we watch for. It is from that thing that the evil comes."

"And the cross? Is it a church? A priest?"

"That is our sign for your medicine. How many things is it going to take, how many people talking to you, before you believe us and do something? I will tell you, there are many of us who are not waiting for you to help us. The Crow boys have told us that a man has come into their country, into the Bighorn country, and they do not know who he is, but they say he is a great fighter who has a bad face."

"A bad face?"

"When Satanka-Witko was on the Red Cloud Agency, he was in love with Black Buffalo Woman. But she was the woman of No Water, and No Water came to the Powder River Country and took Bad Heart Bull's gun, and he shot Crazy Horse in the face. Crazy Horse tried to move away, but Little Big Man held his hands, thinking to stop a killing, and No Water's bullet hit Crazy Horse in the left cheek. "This man who is in the Crow country is a Lakota man, a great fighter who has been asleep but is now awake again, and this man has a bullet in his left cheek."

"But Crazy Horse is dead. He's buried on the Wounded Knee creek."

"I told your man, McAllister, back at Sweetwater Hospital, I told him Satanka-Witko had come into the world again. If I'm wrong, then who is this Lakota man? He was in the ground, and now he has come out of it. I have been told this even by the Crow boys, who have heard it from their old men."

"And how have the old Crow men heard it?"

"It has been in the wind, and in the long grass."

Meagher stared at the man, full of disbelief. "Oh, good. That's great. It was in the grass. That's all right, then. George, what the hell am I supposed to make of *that*? I mean, you're here, you *look* real. How can you buy this kind of thing?"

"Look around you. What else do we have? I go your way, I have nothing at all, I'm just a red nigger. You and me, we had other ways to look at things, but now the whites, they run things, and they don't believe in anything. I say, for me, for my clan, the old men know something, and if they tell me they heard it in the wind or in the tallgrass, then that's good enough for me. If you belonged someplace, had your own land back, you'd think like me, you'd let go of what the whites have been giving you. It's too much to carry. They give it to you to keep your hands busy, so you don't make trouble and start to listen to yourself. Me, I went that way, but now maybe I start to listen to these old men here. Maybe now, you should, too."

Meagher looked down at his hands. They were tightened into fists. He walked back to the Lincoln, conscious of all the Sioux on the streets of Parmelee now, in little groups and singly, in the shade and in the hard sunlight, looking at him as he talked with George Cut Arms.

He was thinking about the skull-faced man, the "black man" that Beau had seen in the wedding picture. Was he an ex-soldier, like the two men killed at Arrow Creek? But Beau had said nothing about a scar on his face.

But if he was a Sioux and a fighter, who was to say what was true and not true about it? Meagher had not been born here, but sometimes at night even he heard something in the wind and felt a living thing close at his shoulder and turned to see nothing but a bending in the light or a darker shadow in the hills. The Academy had had nothing to say to him about any of this.

"What are you gonna *do* about it, soldier?"

Meagher stared at the man, angry at him for no reason. George Cut Arms stared back, his thick dark face a blunt instrument, his heavy arms folded across his barrel chest. The wind whipped up a dust devil along the street, and the sky seemed to press down on them all. A man could go crazy out here. There'd be no horizon to keep his mind in his head. It would just spread out until the wind took it, and it would blow away into the blue horizon like smoke. There'd be nothing left of him but ashes.

He reached into the Lincoln and pulled out his car phone. The handset blinked at him.

NO SRV

Damn.

"Is there a phone around? Or do we send up a smoke signal?"

George Cut Arms raised his right hand, pointed at the shaded porch where the old men were sitting.

"In there."

Miss Haydon walked Beau out to the reception area after their interview. The receptionist swiveled in his chair and called to her. Beau stepped away to give them some privacy and studied the framed awards on the wall over the gray leather couch. The Lizard-Boys were gone, although there were several wadded-up, bloodied Kleenexes in the wastepaper basket next to the couch.

A door opened up to his left, and a large fat man came out into the reception area. He was wearing a baggy suit and a white shirt with no tie. His ears stood out from the side of his head, which he carried forward on his neck as if it were too heavy to lift. He looked at Beau, his face slack with age and weariness. He made Beau think of an old buffalo. He was drying his hands, and Beau realized that the door led to a washroom.

Miss Haydon came up to Beau and shook his hand. "Sergeant, I want to thank you for telling us this in person. It's a terrible tragedy, and we'll do anything we can to help your department. I had Dylan run this off for you."

She handed him a sheet of computer paper. "This is a staff list. We are actually three separate corporations, but there's a parent company and we do the employee accounting through this office here. This man, Gabriel Picketwire, is the one in your photograph. He's a stunt man. He works for a lot of film companies around town. He's an independent, but he belongs to SAG and also the stunt-men's organization. He lives on a boat in Newport Beach. It's a Cheoy Lee ketch called *Blue Coat*. But he's not there now. At least, he's not answering his phone and his service doesn't know where he is. Actually, no one seems to know. He has no family—"

Something in her face caught Beau's attention.

There had been something between Picketwire and this woman. It was gone now, but the traces of it lingered in the woman's eyes.

"He walked off a set last week after he was hurt in a fall. As a matter of fact, it was Dr. Sifton who—"

The old man came forward, and she turned to him. "Doctor, how's Gash?"

The old man shook his heavy head in a kind of apology. "He'll be fine, Paula. May I meet this man?"

"Of course! Excuse me! This is Sergeant Beauregard McAllister, of the Montana Highway Patrol. Sergeant McAllister, this is Dr. Sifton, our medical supervisor."

Beau shook his hand. It was damp and chilly. The man looked very sick. His eyes were wet and sunken, his lips pale as sand. "Sergeant McAllister, I've just been attending to the young boy with the nosebleed."

"Really? Is he all right?" Beau tried for a sincere tone.

"A little older. A little wiser. It seemed to be more of a psychosomatic affliction brought on by a personality disorder. Michael is a gifted talent, but a little uncontrolled."

He looked at Beau for a moment.

Beau held the look steadily, his face blank.

The doctor shrugged it off.

"Anyway, I'm sorry to meet you in these circumstances. What seems to be the trouble?"

"The sergeant is looking into—" She touched Dr. Sifton's arm. "Apparently Eddie Gall has been killed."

"Killed? In an accident, Sergeant?"

"No, sir. I'm afraid not."

"He was shot, Lucas."

The doctor studied Beau for a while, his heavy face unreadable. "I heard you mention Gabriel Picketwire, Julia. Is he involved?"

Beau cut her off. "Just a routine followup, sir. Nothing to worry about."

"I see. . . . Well, I'll leave you to it, then. I'm very sorry to hear about young Eddie. He was a fine boy. We all loved him."

"Yes," said Miss Haydon, her eyes filling up. "We all did."

Beau left them in the hall and walked back out into the glare of the midday sun. He was halfway to the car lot when he heard his name being called. He turned to see the old doctor making his way down the landscaped walkway. He stopped by the Lincoln and waited for him.

"Thank you, Sergeant. I wanted a word with you."

"Yes, sir. Is it about Edward Gall?"

"Well, in a sense. I wonder, do you have plans for the . . . well, of course you will."

"I have to go downtown. But I have time."

"Perhaps we could sit in your car, then. I'm rather an old fart, and the heat affects me."

Beau looked at the old man. He looked back unblinkingly, an old bull buffalo with a bad heart. "What's this about, sir?"

The man indicated Beau's file folder. It was open, and Beau's hard blue script was visible.

"You're asking about the Sonesta Clinic?"

"Yes. I'm going there now."

"I can short-cut some of this for you. I sent Edward Gall to the Sonesta Clinic. And about Picketwire—I had something to do with this."

Beau looked at the man for a while. "Let's get in the car. It's cooler."

Gabriel forced himself to look again.

It was as if Gabriel Picketwire had been erased. The eyes were perhaps the same, but the face—it was a ruin. It shook him to the core. His throat was thick and tight. He thought about the shotgun he had found in Bell's tool shed. He could hardly look worse, and at least he wouldn't be alive to spend the rest of his life behind a face like this.

But then, maybe he wasn't alive. Maybe he was a walking corpse, and if that were true—and in this narcotic land many things seemed possible—then it wasn't his life anyway.

So the first thing to do was to try and fix this ruined face, and to do it without a doctor or a nurse.

The nurse, however, would hear from him.

One of the people who would need to hear from him, if Bell had told the truth.

Naked, his legs shaking, he stood in the huge tiled space—Bell had spent a lot of money on his bathroom—and considered what he should do, how much morphine and how many Percodans he would need to do it.

He had a sharp knife on the countertop in front of him, along with some clear nylon thread and a sewing needle. And a bottle of hydrogen peroxide, clean towels, some cotton gauze, and a field dressing from his kitbag.

After . . . after he had finished with Bell, he had walked down the lane to retrieve his car. It had been a long walk, and the setter was still hiding from him. Of course, the dog would have known what had happened to Bell. At least, he must have heard it, since it went on inside the generator shed. And he would have smelled the blood, as the horses had.

Gabriel regretted frightening the dog. He would have to go find him. He couldn't stay here for much longer. Someone was sure to come back, looking for Bell. Maybe the tall man.

Maybe the police.

Gabriel could not be here when they found what was hanging in the tool shed.

He'd started his car somehow and driven it back up to the house. Now he had his field dressing and some sulfa powder and even a vial of morphine, a little plastic vial with a built-in needle. Army issue. He had used these things a hundred times, years ago. Once or twice, on himself.

Morphine first.

He looked up at his reflection in the mirror. It shook him, but he held the look, trying to see it as a corpsman would. First, something for the pain.

He raised the ampule and carefully injected half the vial into the vein in his left arm.

It burned.

Pain again, as familiar as breathing now.

He stood there, head down, and waited for it to recede. Then he lifted his swollen lip and examined the upper jawline. Six, maybe seven teeth gone, and a couple of ragged stumps of root showing through wrecked flesh. The jawbone still worked, but speech was nearly impossible. The exit wound was terrible. He'd covered the neck wound with his field dressing after the shower. He'd need something antiseptic to use as a mouthwash.

He'd use the hydrogen peroxide for that.

Now the morphine was kicking in, a warm burning in his veins. He rode that as well.

After a while, it passed. He sipped at the peroxide bottle, feeling the burn, feeling the bubbling foam in his wounds.

He spat red blood and pink foam out into the sink.

He looked up again, seeing the ruined face, the shattered image. He was looking at someone he did not know.

Somehow that made it easier, and he picked up the small shiny steel blade. He began to cut, and after a long time, he began to stitch himself together. This was a bright red passage arced with blue-white sheets of pain and nausea. Gabriel never knew how long it lasted, and after a few hours could not even remember it clearly.

When it was over and he could walk again, he tried to clean up the bathroom, and he washed his hands several times. Then he dressed in the clothes he'd worn from Los Angeles, the black jeans and the black shirt with the Mexican silver. The water running from Bell's gold tap was pure and bitterly cold. He swallowed three Percodans and an amphetamine caplet from his kitbag and walked out into the front room.

The red dog was sitting in the front yard. He got up as Gabriel came out onto the porch. The afternoon was almost gone, and it looked like a storm was coming up from the west. A huge front towered over the low hills, flat as an anvil and climbing up ten thousand feet into the purple sky. A lurid sun, like a bruise, lit up the belly of the cloud front.

He and the red dog climbed up the long hillside. The grave was still open, and the earth was caked with Gabriel's blood. He stood and looked down at it while the dog chased insects and played in the long grass.

He smiled, a death's-head grimace in his stitched and bandaged face. Bell had been sitting at a computer, staring at a list of shipping bills, when Gabriel had walked into the room.

The look on Joe Bell's face was something Gabriel would take with him to—he smiled again, ignoring the pain—to his grave.

He wondered for a while how the County would react when they found Bell's body. There would be a search. It would be hard for a man to move around the county. He'd need some help.

If what Bell had told him was the truth—and at the end, Bell would have told him anything at all just to stop the knife for a second—if what he had told him, about Danny Burt, the tall man who had shot him—and the nurses at the Julia Dwight Clinic—and the Rosebud, and Standing Rock—all the ones collecting their "finder's fee"—the one at Julia Dwight who had been the sergeant's wife, which explained the killings at Arrow Creek—if any of it was true, then he could go to these Tallbull people.

They would help him. The computer disk would also help. Bell had been looking at it when Gabriel took him.

A woman named Mary Littlebasket was on the disk. She was a Crow, and one of the women who had been . . . seeded? The shiny rainbow-colored disk had all the names, a record of a trade in human life. Bell and the tall man, Burt, they had taken the record to use against the people who were running this obscenity. Blackmail.

The Crow . . . were Crow. But all that was in the past, a hundred years gone. Lakota, Crow, what did any of that mean now? They were like cattle in a pen, raised for slaughter, with a wolf outside the fences. A Walking Wolf.

Even the Crow would want this Wolf killed. Mary Littlebasket was Crow, and she was dead, and her uncle was a Crow, Charlie Tallbull. Gabriel remembered a man in one of the ICU beds beside Donna, a big dark man wrapped in casts and braces—that was Charlie Tallbull. Even if a Lakota man came to them, they would have to believe him. They could call it a Walking Wolf, or a witch, or a criminal conspiracy, or an abomination. It didn't matter what you named it, as long as you stopped it. Jubal and the rest of the Shirt Wearers had been right all along, and now there was only Gabriel left to finish it.

The Percodans rolled through his blood like an amber flame, warming him, pushing the pain down below the level of thought. And the amphetamine bubbled and fizzed in their wake, like luminous foam in a subterranean river.

Gabriel kicked at the dirt piled up around his shallow grave. He reached down and picked up a handful of it and wrapped it in a white cloth. He tied it off and put it in his shirt pocket. The red dog watched him, unreadable and wary. The dog had seen and smelled some very bad things since he had dug Gabriel out of the ground. The door to the tool shed was closed, but there was wind enough to bring the dog some news about his last owner.

"We'll free the horses. Then we're going, okay? We'll go see this woman. You come with me?"

The setter listened without understanding, but the tone comforted him, and he followed the man down the long hill toward his green car.

In a few minutes, they had reached the gate to Bell's property. Gabriel got out to close it and stood a few minutes, looking up the winding track leading to 90114 South Wyatt Drive. It was a long time since he had come to this place, although his watch was telling him it was only two days. This was Wednesday afternoon. He had come here on Monday.

He would have to come back here, if he lived this second life long enough. After all, he was buried here. It wasn't often a man was given the chance to visit his own grave.

As he got back into the car, he saw the movement in the long grass by the wire fence, saw the thing standing there.

It was as if a man made of dust and smoke were standing there, dark and changing in the light. He was middle height, with long black hair, a solid muscular body, covered with ochre dust and reddish zigzag markings like lightning bolts. His face was marred. Broken. His left cheek was carved and furrowed, and his upper lip was scarred, twisted into a kind of shattered smile. The wind moved in his long hair as he stood in the tall grass and watched Gabriel. His hands were empty, the palms turned outward at his sides. In his long hair a single feather hung suspended from a leather thong. It was a hawk's feather.

Gabriel knew him, knew that if he walked up to him, he would see that the man had a small pebble tied behind his ear and another under his arm. No picture of him had ever been taken, but Gabriel knew him, and a fearful coldness came over him as he tried to make himself believe that this was only a twist of light and shadow, and he watched the figure turning, moving now—seeing it as brighter air in the glowing afternoon sun, its ruined face turning away from him, and it passed away up the green slope, a bending of the grasses, a dry rustle, a cloud-shadow. It moved soundlessly up the long hillside toward the crest, stood for one moment against the sky, and drifted into nothing.

Gabriel closed the door on it, no longer sure that it had ever been. In another portion of his heart, he was quietly, deeply afraid to find out who was staying here and what was leaving.

Beth Gollanz sat up and arched her back, twisting to the left. Harper looked away from her blouse, trying to keep his mind on the work. It wasn't easy.

Motor Vehicles had kicked out a total of 3,673 registered Cadillacs in the Eastern Montana Regional Records Division. He had split the records with Beth, and they were sitting on opposite sides of the lunchroom table, papers and coffee cups scattered around, running down the sheets with highlighter pens, underlining every listed Cadillac that fit McAllister's description.

Maybe fifteen years old.

Dark blue or dark brown or black.

Harper had tried to narrow the terms a bit by suggesting that they look for owners who lived close enough to Pompeys Pillar to get their gas at Bell's Oasis, but Beth had pointed out, regretfully, that Bell's Oasis was just off the interstate, so it was possible that the Cadillac driver they were looking for lived a long way from Pompeys Pillar.

"Christ," said Harper. "He could come from anywhere!"

"True," said Beth. "Even out of state."

"Hell, this is ridiculous. We don't even know what we're looking for! Look at this—some of them are owned by corporations or leasing companies. *Anybody* could have access to the car we're looking for. Didn't Beau get any *part* of a license number?"

"Not that he told us about, Moses."

"Listen, maybe I oughta go see Joe Bell myself. Put some heat on him. He *saw* the goddamned guy. Let *him* tell us!"

"He's suing the department. He's not going to tell you a damn thing! You're just trying to slip off, leave me with the whole job!"

Harper leaned over the papers, put a hand on her cheek, and kissed her on the lips.

"You know, Beth, when you're right, you're right! Welcome to the wonderful world of law enforcement!"

Dell Greer was taking a walk around the front of Maureen Sprague's house, partly for security reasons and partly just to give his hormones a break from Maureen.

The storm front was ten thousand feet high, blue-black and ugly as sin, a hundred miles wide. It had been coming on all night. It had just kicked hell out of Idaho and Utah, and it looked like Montana was next on the agenda.

There was a peculiar intensity to the daylight. The colors seemed to glow. Greer pulled in a long breath.

The air reeked of ozone and heat, the smell of twisters.

He heard a small voice from the porch. Bobby Lee was out there, hands on her hips, in jeans and a pink cowgirl shirt, heavy concern showing on her face.

"Uncle Dell!"

Greer came up the walk, grinning. "Yessirree, ma'am. What's on your mind?"

"Where's Uncle Moses?"

"He has to look up something for your daddy. He'll be along this afternoon. See that cloud there?"

Bobby Lee came down the steps onto the lawn, shading her eyes. "Why is it colored like that?"

"Well, that's partly the sun shining on it, and partly all the rain it's carrying, honey."

"Does Daddy have his cats inside?"

"Oh yes, you relax about them. Those cats, they'll be inside under your daddy's bed, rolled up in a big ball."

"Where's Daddy now?"

Greer ruffled her blond hair and stood up as another car turned the corner at the bottom of the hill and started up the long curving street. Another Volvo station wagon. There were more Volvo station wagons in this neighborhood than there were in Oslo. Or was it Stockholm?

"Well, I'd say your daddy's working. Has he called you?"

"Mommy got it. She said I was playing, but I wasn't. I was right there. Mommy's real mad at Daddy."

She sat down on the step and cradled her chin in both hands, propping her elbows on her knees. They both watched the Volvo cruise by. A little girl waved at Bobby Lee through the back window, but Bobby Lee didn't wave back.

She looked sideways at Greer, the clarity in her blue eyes shining through him. In the strange storm-changed light, she looked as if she were cut from alabaster. Luminous.

"Uncle Dell, how hot is hell?"

Greer rocked back and squatted down to get eye-to-eye with her. God, the blue in those eyes. It was hard to concentrate on what she was saying, her eyes were so bright and blue. He tried hard to take her seriously, because he knew that children were very quick at sensing condescension. You had to talk right across to them, because like it or not, there was a real person in there, just as real as any grown-up.

"Well, now, Bobby Lee, I'm not real sure there *is* a hell."

Risky talk, that. Greer had to work hard to keep the rest of the guys on the Big Horn force from finding out he didn't really believe in God. Not their brand anyway, a hard-handed man sitting in the clouds, dealing out thunderbolts and grief for technical infractions while terrible men did vicious things without any punishment at all.

Bobby Lee considered his statement quietly.

"Mom says there *is* a hell and that Daddy is going to go there. Do you think Daddy is going to go to hell?"

Greer sighed and felt a kind of sadness for the sheer mean-mindedness of saying such a thing to a little girl.

"No, honey. I don't think your daddy is going to hell. If you wanna know what I think, I think your daddy is a real fine man, and I'm proud to have him as my friend."

Bobby Lee was watching the storm front now. "Will there be lightning?"

Goddamn that Sprague bitch anyway.

"Uncle Dell, are you listening?"

Greer looked around at the storm system. Christ, bigger and blacker by the minute. "Oh yeah, I'd say so. Are you afraid of lightning?"

"No. Lightning is when God lights His pipe."

"Your daddy smokes a pipe, too."

"Yes. Mommy says it smells like a outhouse. What's a outhouse?"

The screen door slammed open. Maureen was standing there, her shiny tanned skin flushing pink, her green eyes wide, and her mouth torqued in an angry twist. She was wearing a tiny G-string bikini in some shiny green material that matched her headband. Her hard little body glistened with suntan lotion and sweat. Her nipples showed like tiny bullets through the snakeskin fabric. Her breasts were hard and round, her stomach ridged and leathery. She had oven mitts on, and she was holding a goldfish bowl away from her face, out toward Bobby Lee and Moses.

The water was steaming. Bits of skin and flesh floated in a murky brown soup. The smell of fish and sewage drifted down the steps. Bobby Lee stood up and faced her mother, her mouth open and her eyes wide.

"*Bobby Lee!* I've told you never to play with the microwave!"

Greer stood up and backed away, trying to hide the grin.

"*Well?* Why did you put your goldfish in the microwave?"

Bobby Lee's face closed up defiantly. "You said Daddy's going to hell!"

"What does *that* have to do with it?"

"So I'm gonna go with him!"

"Don't be stupid, Roberta Lee!"

Bobby Lee's face was bright with childish anger. "And I'm gonna take Pete and Mikey with me!"

"I don't understand!"

"They have to *like* it there, don't they?"

The doctor's sleeves were pulled down to the edges of his palms, French cuffs, closed with gold and lapis lazuli cufflinks. His hands, broad and ridged with blue veins, rested in his lap like a pair of fat pink pets. Beau could see several puncture wounds on the backs of both hands.

Apparently Sifton was on some kind of intravenous medication. Beau looked back up at the doctor's face, seeing the gray in his skin and the pallor of his lips. Sifton was talking about Edward Gall.

"A very fine boy. Quite intense. He and his wife have a little house down in East Los Angeles. They had me down there once, for a dinner. Actually, it was to meet some singing group. I suppose Edward thought I might use my influence, get them something in the industry. Anyway, the point is, they were trying to have children, and there seemed to be something amiss."

The Lincoln was idling roughly. Beau blipped the pedal, and it smoothed out. He turned the air conditioning down, wondering why the doctor wore suits and long-sleeved shirts if the heat bothered him. Well, come to think of it, the doctor looked like a man who could use all the heat he could find.

"I take it this is where the Sonesta Clinic comes into it."

"Yes. I'm sure you know, modern times call for modern moralities. Wives work well into their late thirties, trying to put together the perfect life—the car, the beach house, the quintessential pale pink stucco Italianate in Sherman Oaks or Santa Barbara. It's the same across the country. The trouble comes when older couples—people who, in a saner world, would have had their children in their teens or twenties, when nature intended them to have them—well, now they approach the great divide between youth and decline. And suddenly, perhaps as a final act of denial, they want to have children, they want to live the youth they traded away for some chimerical illusion of career and professional accomplishment. Selfishness, really. I fear for all the young children who are being raised by middle-age work-obsessed parents who see the children in their lives as just another demonstration of their social skills, as additional trophies, or even—and this is worse—as small mirrors of themselves, to be dressed up like little mannequins in Oshkosh B'Gosh and Polo and paraded around as reflections of their own good taste and personal style. Rather vile, really."

"About the clinic?"

Sifton looked over at him.

"Yes, the Sonesta Clinic. That's certainly a part of all this. It started there, anyway. I'm not . . . my career is a sorry one, Sergeant. I have this position with Offshore, but you know what kind of doctors work for—maybe you don't. A doctor who works for a film company, his job is to keep the talent sober or stoned or whatever it takes to get the picture done. I'm considered safe because I have my own needs."

"Montana has its own share of ugly realities, Doctor. What's the Sonesta Clinic?"

"It's a fertility clinic. Very expensive. Clientele from the film industry, that sort of thing. I'm not on the staff, but I had some connections with a doctor there. I wanted to help Edward. Edward was—they were an attractive couple. How is she, anyway?"

"Donna's in an ICU ward in Billings. She has a severe skull trauma."

"How did she get it?"

"I gave it to her."

"Really. How sad for you."

"Yes, it is."

"I called the clinic and persuaded them to—the phrase is *pro bono,* isn't it? They resisted, naturally. The usual routine with young people is to send them off to try again. But Donna was—she's a forceful woman. She was convinced that there was a problem. So they relented, I think just to pacify her. But as it turned out, Edward did have a minor problem."

"That's what the Sonesta Clinic deals with?"

"It provides a variety of services in the field of fertility—dysfunctional obstetrics."

"A variety of services?"

"Yes. Hollywood provides an intriguing range of clientele for them. For example, a female celebrity, obsessed with fame, for whom heterosexuality offers no charms, but who nevertheless feels that the . . . illusion of normality requires that she conceive . . . also, she wishes to recreate herself, to achieve biological immortality. Well, they are in a position to assist her. To provide a suitable donor, with the proper genetic antecedents, in order that she might bear, might be *seen* to be bearing, a child. And it's achieved without the nasty physicality of coitus."

"Wonderful for the kids, I'll bet."

"That's how Hollywood breeds actors. Psychopaths, emotionally traumatized children, predators—Hollywood thrives on them. Trust me, I've seen them up close."

Man. Hollywood. Beau was leaving it tonight, if he could.

"And Gall? You said he had a problem. What was it?"

"Edward's sperm count was low. There were several treatments available. They had every chance of a normal conception."

"I saw the card he had, from the clinic."

"Yes. He was admitted in March, and they gave him the card because they were monitoring his sperm count, to see if it was responding to treatment."

"How does this connect with my case?"

"Well, the clinic is also funded for research. They have a wonderful range of talents and resources. The community here . . . there is a great deal of money. And a certain sense of dynastic obsession seems to develop here, in the film community and the older families as well. They place a lot of importance on continuing the line—and improving it."

"And the Sonesta Clinic helps them."

"That's their service. They're in a position, because of their independence from federal funds, to pursue lines of inquiry that are closed to more traditional organizations."

Beau considered the man carefully. "Why are you telling me this?"

The doctor's heavy face rose up on his neck, as if against a psychic resistance.

"I have a terminal condition. As do we all. I treat myself, and I prescribe certain palliatives that are not usually available to the general public."

"How long do you have?"

He shrugged. "When Edward was in for treatment, he—Edward was a very inquisitive boy. He wanted to do a documentary on this whole phenomenon of fertility treatments. I think his instincts were more journalistic than cinematic. Offshore has a documentary branch, Hologram. Edward became very interested in the research and development operations of the clinic."

"And he found something?"

"They acquire materials for their researches. I believe that Edward found something there that disturbed him."

"What do you think that was?"

"From what little he was prepared to say, I inferred that it was something on paper. A connection. It was something he found in a box containing research materials."

"What kind of materials?"

"I've told you all I can about them. You can't get to them anyway. Nobody can, not in this city."

"Where do they get these . . . materials?"

"They say they operate in conformity with 'industry ethics.' They say they are doing nothing illegal. But the public . . . there are understandable instinctual taboos."

"Against what?"

"These matters are far too complex to examine here. And you don't have the time, Sergeant."

"I can get real interested in this. A lot of very weird things are happening in Montana, and now you're telling me that it's connected to this clinic, and I know there's a clinic in Montana involved. So it looks like I could get the FBI *very* interested. So let's cut the bullshit and start straight here. You help me, and I'll help you."

"There's no help for me. And as far as the FBI is concerned, you wouldn't get past the district attorney. You'd be on a plane back to Montana by nightfall."

"I doubt that."

"You don't understand Los Angeles. Los Angeles lives on the surface of things. Any organization that provides prolonged health, or drug therapy, or the promise of offspring in the face of every biological obstruction, those institutions are the lifeblood of this city. The Sonesta Clinic is an intrinsic part of the community here. I doubt very much that the political infrastructure here would allow any indictment to go forward that would result in profoundly revealing disclosures about the community. There are forces here, much older and far more influential than the film community. Most people think of Los Angeles as an entertainment center. But before that, there was water, and land, and oil. And now there is a valuable technological base, weapons, aerospace, the software industries. This is a very rich and very powerful town.''

"Bullshit. If what I think is happening is *really* happening—we're talking about fetal tissue, about stealing dead babies for research. That's a situation . . . nothing could stop the law from running something like that down, no matter where it went."

Dr. Sifton shook his head slowly. "You still don't have the picture, Sergeant. And anyway, I wish merely to advise you as to what is possible and what is not, within the context of Los Angeles. As a police officer, you must have run into situations like this. Montana's not the moon. Power is still power."

"Did Edward tell *anyone*?"

"Yes. He told the old man who was living with them."

"Jubal Two Moon? Did Jubal believe him?"

"Obviously they took it seriously. You saw them."

"When's the last time you saw Edward?"

"About a month ago. I treated him for wounds. He had become mildly septic, and I gave him some antibiotics."

"Did you treat the wounds?"

"Of course. I recognized them for what they were."

"And what was that?"

"I think you know, Sergeant. A ritual, a kind of purification ceremony. Prior to battle or struggle. Many of the Plains tribes used it. It's called a Sun Dance."

There was a long silence in the car. The old man's breathing was short and labored. Beau realized that he was in pain.

"Doctor, why tell me all this?"

"I feel responsible."

"Why? Because you turned him on to the clinic?"

"No. The clinic does what is required of it by the real world. Power manifests itself and sees to its conclusions. No, I think a casual barb sometimes cuts very deep. I said something to a man last week, I think that man may have . . . I may have set something loose that was better restrained."

"Are you talking about Gabriel Picketwire?"

"Yes. He was injured. I was treating him for a small tortion. I was on the set, and he interested me. He's a very interesting man. There are few of his kind left in the world. Sometimes, under the influence of my injections, I develop a certain detachment. I wanted to see what this animal could do. Have you ever gone to see the big cats, at a zoo?"

"No, but I've seen them in the mountains."

"Free, then?"

"Yes."

"Then you wouldn't understand."

"Try me."

"I wanted to set it free."

"Why? Pity?"

"No, nothing so admirable."

"What then?"

The doctor heaved and relaxed again. His hands were locked together in his lap, the knuckles white. Beau could feel the pain in the old man, a cold chill consuming him cell by cell.

"I suppose . . . to look the animal in the face. To see it without the glass wall. To watch it in action."

"Watch it do what?"

Beau's cellular phone began to shrill. Beau picked it up as the doctor smiled and opened the car door. Heat and hard white light flowed over him. Silhouetted, his face in darkness, he waved a languid hand and stepped out of the car.

"Go back to Montana, Sergeant. See for yourself."

The door slammed shut. In the cold leather interior of the car, Beau felt the phone vibrate in his hands, and the shrilling bell hurt his ears. A massive tiredness settled over him. He keyed SEND and put the phone to his ear.

"McAllister."

"Beau. This is Eustace."

"Hello, Eustace. I don't like L.A. Can I come home now?"

"No, you can't. Listen, I talked to Bucky Blitzer. You were right. He *did* hear that joke from the Wozcylesko kid. I need to know where you are right now!"

"At Offshore Films. Why?"

"Get your ass down to 220 Ditman. Rufus Calder'll meet you."

"Okay, I'm going. What's the rush?"

"Rufus heard from his surveillance guys. There's a truck at bay nine right now. Looks like they're cleaning the place out. And guess who's doing it?''

"Danny Burt."

"Yeah, Beau. Go down there, nail his fat ass to the wall."

Beth looked up from the computer paper when she heard someone tapping on the glass window of the Communications room. Valerie Fromberg was rapping it with her knuckles. When she got Beth's attention, she pointed to her headset several times.

Beth picked up the desk phone and punched the COMMO key.

"Yes?"

"It's some guy named Tarr, a reporter. He's asking for Moses, and I can't raise him on the radio."

"Moses is out at Joe Bell's. Nobody's answering the phone out there, and Moses went to see if he's on another bender and not hearing his phone."

"Didn't he take a squad car?"

"No, they're all on the road."

"Can you talk to this guy? He's pretty excited."

"Okay. Have you got your tape on? Moses'll want to hear this."

"Yeah, I'll switch him."

The line clicked and beeped. "Hello?"

"Hello. Where's Harper?"

"Is this Mr. Tarr?"

"Yeah. Who're you?"

"I'm Beth Gollanz. Moses had to step out of the station for a bit. Can I help you?"

"Are you a cop?"

"No, I'm a civilian employee. But I'm helping Moses with a case. Maybe you can tell me, I can get the information to him."

"Where's Lieutenant Meagher?"

"Out of town."

"Where's McAllister?"

"He's not available right now. As I said, maybe I can—"

"For chrissake, lady, is *anybody* there with some brass on his shirt? Any management around at all?"

"They're all on the road, sir. I'd be glad to help—"

"Lady, you're not helping *me*. I'm helping *you*! And before I go down this road any further, I wanna talk to some brass and get some promises!"

"What kind of promises, sir?"

"Look, I'm doing McAllister a favor, okay? And suddenly I'm up to my ass in alligators. I wanna know why I'm looking at what I'm looking at, and I wanna know if I'm gonna get sued, and most of all, I wanna know, if I help you, I get the story *exclusively*! Just only me, right? Nobody else!"

"Sir, I can't make you that kind of promise. I'm only—"

"You find McAllister or Meagher. Tell 'em to call Sig Tarr at home in an hour. That's where I'm going. Tell 'em what I said and what I want. You have a nice day, honey!"

The line clicked off.

Valerie Fromberg came on the line. "What the hell was *that* all about?"

Goddamn that Moses. Where was he?

"Valerie, do you have the lieutenant's cellular number there?"

"Yes. I already tried it. He's on his way back from South Dakota, and he's not in a service zone. He's supposed to call in anytime, though."

"You have Beau's number?"

"He's not in the state, Beth."

"He has call-following. I put them all on call-following. Give me his number. And try Joe Bell's line again!"

"Okay. Here's Beau's number."

Beth wrote it down on one of the computer sheets.

Call me, Moses! Call in, you sneaky bastard!

The front swept down over southeastern Montana like a dam breaking in the sky. A thunderclap shattered the heavy air, and the sky fell on the hills and the grasses and the towns. On the interstate, the visibility dropped down to a few feet in ten seconds. The sky glowed green and purple, shot through with brilliant flashes of sheet lightning. Billboards bent in the rushing wind. A wall of brown dust a thousand feet high rolled on toward Hardin and Pompeys Pillar. The clouds came down from the sky and roared through the streets of Billings.

Maureen and Bobby Lee and Dell Greer ran for the back door, the first of the hard rain peppering their legs and rattling the fiberglass roof of the poolhouse. They could hear a hammering sound on the glass, and the front door was slamming and banging in the wind. Maureen raced from window to window, slamming them down against the rising storm. A thunderclap boomed above them, shaking the house.

Then another, and another.

Greer hustled through the house to the front door, tugged the screen door closed, struggling against the wind. He looked out at the street, where his cruiser was rocking in the wind. It was locked, and the windows were up. A green egg-shaped Sable was parked across the street. A red dog was sitting behind the wheel, staring up at the door.

Now *that's* what you call—what's the word?

Sur . . . something. When something is too weird for words.

Bobby Lee stood in the middle of the living room, shaking, her face white. Greer slammed the door. He knelt down and hugged her.

She looked past him, at something else.

"Who's *he*?" she said, raising her hand.

Greer, still on his knees, turning, reaching for his nine-mill, cursing at his stupidity, saw the windows fill with white light and felt the thunder slamming against his chest, still turning, saw the screen door open and nothing in the door but rain and white light, and the street beyond it. And then, turning still, searching, his nine-mill now out, he saw the pale green rug rise up and strike his cheek, and he realized he was lying on his face. He tried to get up, but his hands would not work. He felt cold. He saw his nine-mill in his right hand, huge and black. The red plastic inlay on the foresight seemed to glow. The gold class ring on his third finger was very intricately carved, and he wondered why he had never noticed how fine a piece of work it was. It was very very fine.

24

1745 Hours – June 19 – East Los Angeles, California

Like bad bars, whores, and overdue bills, Los Angeles looked worse in the daylight. Beau would have sailed right by Marengo if he hadn't seen that big billboard with the BERMUDA . . . YOU DESERVE IT ad sticking into the yellow sky above the crowded freeway lanes. The Marengo exit came up fast on his right, and he peeled out of the traffic and soared around the off-ramp, pushing the Town Car so hard, the tires shrieked and his cellular phone slammed into the passenger door and his papers flew all over the footwell. He hit the horn to move a Jeep stuffed with Chicano women out of his way, got a bouquet of middle fingers for his trouble, and accelerated up Ditman toward 220. He couldn't see any squad cars or flashing red lights. His respect for Rufus Calder went up a couple of notches.

The drug dealing was still going on, although it had kind of a Wednesday afternoon laziness to it—a few old cars, and a mixed crowd of women and kids and wolfish teens ambling up and down the street in front of the Iranian grocery store and the crumbling apartments. In the gritty yellow light of the Los Angeles sunshine, all the buildings looked ancient, their outlines softened, as if they were ruins of an earlier, and not particularly better, civilization. He slowed the white car as he neared 220, looking for an obvious cop car.

He found it, a dark green Ford LTD with two men inside, parked in the same alley where he had positioned himself last night. He rolled up alongside it, so that the two drivers' windows were side by side. The black man at the wheel rolled down his window, waited for Beau's to come down, and flashed him a huge brilliant grin.

"Now, you gotta be McAllister."

"You're Rufus Calder, then. Pleased to meet you." He extended his hand, and Calder shook it twice, hard, through the windows.

Calder was in his late forties, a thin angular man with eyes slanted slightly upward, surrounded by humor lines. An ugly pink scar twisted his right eyebrow into a jagged Z, dropping the lid slightly. He wore a pale beige suit in some light fabric, over a crisp white shirt and a yellow tie.

His partner was a young kid, brown-haired and brown-eyed, with a stylish blunt haircut and round-rimmed dark brown glasses. He was wearing an olive-green silk sports coat and dark brown baggy trousers. His shirt was collarless, in a burnt orange, and it looked like silk. Calder watched Beau as Beau checked out his partner.

"Sergeant, this is Detective Freg. Ain't he pretty? Luis, I want you to meet Staff Sergeant Beauregard McAllister, of the Montana Highway Patrol."

Freg nodded at him, without smiling.

"Your name is Luis Freg?"

The man smiled a little. "Yes. You know me?"

"I know *the* Luis Freg. The matador, got a *cornada* in his chest in Madrid, back in the thirties. You even look like him."

Freg loosened up to let some teeth show. They were very white against his tan. "I am named for him, but we are not related. How do you know of him?"

"I'm a Hemingway fan, and Hemingway wrote about him. I even went to see a fight, but that was in Mexico."

"They fight differently down there," Freg said, now smiling brilliantly.

Calder grinned at Beau, sharing Beau's reaction to Luis Freg, amused by it.

"Okay, McAllister, here's the thing. You see the yard there?"

Beau twisted in his seat. The truckyard at 220 Ditman was about half filled with vehicles of various sizes, parked here and there around the fenced-in lot. Drivers were sitting on their hoods or lounging around the dock while about twenty men and women scuttled around, dragging flats on power carts or running forklift trucks in and out of the loading doors.

At bay nine, a huge stainless-steel and maroon Freightliner with an unmarked stainless-steel trailer was parked right up against the bay doors. A gray tarpaulin was spread across the opening, effectively hiding the activity inside the door.

Beau shook his head. "How come it's so busy? It was empty last night."

"Yeah. Apparently the owner, Merced Industries, declared bankruptcy yesterday, and all the companies are trying to get their shit outta the building before the bailiffs lock it up. So this is gonna make things tricky."

"Yeah, I don't see any squad cars."

"We don't bring prowl cars down here unless we do it in fives. This area, in the summer like this, it'll blow up in a minute. We keep a low profile around here—hey, which reminds me, you gotta look at this. You'll like this, Sergeant."

He handed Beau a photograph. Black and white, taken with a telephoto lens at night, it showed Beau in his tan suit, standing at the gate of the warehouse, reaching up to press the entry button. Beau smiled and handed it back to Calder.

"I figured you'd have somebody around. Who was it? Vice?"

"No, Strike Force. They were zooming a possible AR and saw you cruising around. Took this for fun. I just wanted to show you we ain't asleep down here in Lotusland. . . . So the thing is, we got Jimmy Drinaw outta here at the end of his shift this morning. Man, he was pissed at *you*, McAllister. Anyway, he's bagged, and we got him on the Ithaca. He took that with him when he left the Oxnard force, so we can hang him up for stolen police property. You want us to?"

"No, I just wanted him out of the way. If we make a case, we'll need him for chain of evidence."

"So what now?"

"How much did Meagher tell you?"

"Not a lot. He says you maybe got a drug thing here, but not to bring the narcs into it. He wants me to keep it under my vest for a while, see what it comes up as."

"Can you do that?"

Calder reached into his suit pocket and flipped out a leather case. He showed Beau the badge, a bright gold badge and the engraved letters LIEUTENANT.

"I can do pretty much what I want, McAllister. I'm Two I C of the intelligence division. We own the town."

"Okay. First off, I don't think it's drugs, I think it's something else. But what I need is probable cause to pop a guy, says his name is Hank Starbuck—"

"That'd be the Danny Burt guy?"

"Yeah, and when I pop him, it's gotta be solid enough to enter bay nine, do a kick-in, maybe search and seizure. It's gotta stand up in Montana as well as L.A. County."

"What do you think is in there, McAllister?"

Beau wiped his face and took a long breath. "Man, I wish I knew. Tell you one thing, Lieutenant. It's gonna be nasty."

Calder's face stiffened a little. "Burt have a record?"

"Nothing connected to smuggling or drugs. Misdemeanors and minor assault charges. And we don't have anything on him for a warrant. Legally, we don't have shit on Danny."

"Okay, that's no good. We asked Jimmy about guns, he said he didn't see any, so we can't go with weapons dangerous."

"You run the Freightliner?"

"We did. It's registered in Visalia. Merced Industries owns it, leases it to Kellerman Cold Haulers."

"Merced owns the warehouse, doesn't it?"

"So far. Like I said, they went bankrupt yesterday."

"Convenient."

"Yeah."

"Look, if they filed bankruptcy, what's the position on them taking stuff outta that warehouse?"

Calder considered it. "Well, it happens all the time. Usually, the bailiffs get there, the place is a burned-out shell anyway. So they don't rush to lock up the assets. But technically—maybe we could use it."

"You think? Pop Kellerman Cold Haulers for violating the trustee rules? All I need is the excuse to walk across the street there, knock on the door."

"Well, if the Freightliner is owned by Merced, and Merced filed yesterday, and Kellerman Cold Haulers is using the truck—Luis, what's the law here about the Freightliner?"

Freg tapped his long-fingered hand on the dashboard.

"Luis is a lawyer, McAllister. Got a degree and the whole thing."

"Congratulations, Luis."

Freg nodded gravely. "Okay. I think, if Kellerman Cold Haulers has legally *leased* that Freightliner, and they're all paid up to date, then they have a legal right to run it, and in a sense, Merced is in a debtor relationship to Kellerman. I don't think you can pop the truck. *But*—"

Calder smiled at Beau.

"*But*, if Kellerman Cold Haulers is running the truck illegally—you know, in violation of any state law—then the lease is null and void because of the insurance violation."

"Yeah, and then it reverts to Merced, technically?"

"True, and then you'd have the right to go over there, ask the driver to prove that he has the legal right to remove his property using a vehicle that is technically under an act of impoundment according to section 337, paragraph 9 of the Civil Bankruptcy Act, wherein—"

Beau held up a hand. "Very nice, Freg, but what state law have they broken? You ran them. They're paid up, they have all the plates. What's the infraction?"

Calder was still smiling. Freg smiled, too.

"Well, they've got two broken headlights. That's a clear violation of the safety laws, and that would violate the terms of the lease, since it can't be legally leased unless it's insured, and it can't be insured without proper safety equipment."

Beau looked over at the big steel truck. "You know, maybe it's my arthritis, but I'm buggered if I can see anything busted on that truck." He opened his eyes very wide and looked innocently at the two L.A. cops.

Freg and Calder both laughed. Freg got out of the car and walked around to the front. He put on a pair of dark glasses and walked away toward the open freightyard. On the way across Ditman he picked up a chunk of rock.

"Vandals," said Calder, shaking his head sadly.

"Yeah," said Beau. "What's the world comin' to, huh?"

They both watched Luis Freg duck around a passing Chevy and scoot through the gate.

"Freg is not your average cop, Calder."

"He's a good kid. I first saw him, I figured him like you did. You know, suitrack with a gun. And this lawyer stuff, that always puts me off. But he's sharp, knows how to work the system. Our beefs hold up, and the juries *love* him. Listen, why'nt you park that boat there, hop inside with me. Soon as Luis gets done, we'll just roll in there, real casual and laid back, just cruising the yard, you know, me and a visiting trooper. We stop—*say,* isn't that a pair of broken lights on that Freightliner. Well, golly, we oughta stop and tell the guy!"

Beau rolled away to lock up the Lincoln Town Car. Then he came back and got inside with Calder.

Across the street, Luis Freg was strolling down the line of parked trucks, nonchalance in every stylish line.

"So Eustace says you guys humped the sixty in the war."

Calder put his head down and smiled to himself. "Yeah. You in?"

Beau told him about his knees.

"Well, you didn't miss shit."

"Meagher talked about a hill once, you called it the Lizard."

"Co Roc? He mentioned it, huh?"

"Yeah. Well, I thought it was a kind of a coincidence, the lizard thing."

"Yeah? How come?"

"Well, I live in a place called Lizardskin, up in the hills there."

Calder was looking at him blankly. "Yeah? And?"

"And—it just seemed, you know, like a coincidence. Both of us having a place named that. At the time, anyway."

Calder was grinning at him.

Beau started to laugh softly, at the absurdity of . . . everything.

"Well, there you go," said Beau.

"Yep," said Calder, watching Freg as he reached the front end of the big Freightliner. "There you go."

Freg moved, and there was a glitter, a tumbling of broken light. Calder started the green LTD.

"Okay—lock and load, boys."

The wind howled around the phone booth, rattling the glass and whipping at Meagher's pant legs. His ankles burned with flying sand and dirt. God-*damn* the cellular phone system.

The line was ringing.

"Hello?"

"Sig?"

"Meagher!" Tarr's voice boomed in the earpiece. Meagher pulled the headset away from his ear and winced.

"Yeah, keep it down."

"What's that noise?"

"It's the goddamned wind."

"No shit. Power's out in Hardin and Billings. Good thing it isn't dark yet."

"Yeah. Look, I called in and the dispatcher said you were real upset, wanted to talk to me or McAllister."

"You're damn right I do. Listen, what the fuck are you guys up to? This is some weird shit you got me into."

"What is it?"

"Oh no, you don't! I thought about this, and the first thing is, I did this work for you, and I want something for it."

"You want an exclusive. I can't do that. You know that."

"I know you can't gimme an exclusive. But you can gimme a jump on it. If this is hairy enough, we'll have the networks in, it'll be *huge,* Eustace. And I want the first quarter-mile."

"What have you got?"

"Promise me?"

"I promise. I just don't know what I'm into. What did you get? Anything on Merced and the others?"

"Oh, yes. I'd say so. Have you got a minute?"

"No, I gotta go for a bikini wax and get my toes oiled. Why the hell you think I'm calling you from a phone booth on the goddamn interstate?"

"Okay. I peeled most of this off the CompuServe system. They can boil the whole country down for you, pump out all the corporate histories. The rest I got from the Corporate Registry Service in Wilmington."

"I'm listening."

"First off, Merced Industries filed for bankruptcy yesterday, outta the headquarters in Visalia. They own that address at 220 Ditman, and a couple of other properties. Now, Merced also leases trucks and cars, and one of their customers is this Kellerman Cold Haulers, the same guys who have this sublease from Farwest Beef and Dairy."

"Okay. So what?"

"Well, first off, it looks like they didn't *have* to. It looks like they were bled white and dumped by whoever operates it. *And* Kellerman Cold Haulers is a subsidiary of Merced Industries, through a shell corporation in Delaware."

"Why do that? Taxes?"

"Maybe. That's what you're gonna tell *me* when this is all out in the open."

"Okay. What else?"

"Farwest Beef and Dairy looks legit. They're incorporated in California, at the Ditman address, got their headquarters in Kyoto, and they're also in Montana, through a subsidiary called Buenavista Ranch. That'd be Ingomar's old spread, the one these guys bought out last year. To raise beef?"

"Yeah."

"So what am I into?"

"Finish up first! Then I'll tell you."

"Well, all this stuff goes round and round, through a couple of shell corporations in Delaware."

"Why Delaware?"

"Delaware's like Liberia. You can get anything registered there. It's a trigger name. Anyway, it goes round and round, a couple of numbered corporations, until you get to a company called Oceanic Group."

"Oceanic? Who are they?"

"I can't tell you. The shareholders are based in Kyoto, and the Japanese don't file with CompuServe. You have to go to Japan, and even then you may not get it. They import and export stuff, and they have a subleased fleet to do the hauling. One of the subsidiary corporations is Merced, the same guys who just filed bankruptcy. Oceanic has a contract to ship beef for Farwest. They got Merced to lease the trucks to Kellerman Cold Haulers."

Meagher's forehead ached. "Man, sounds like a bag of snakes to me."

"Every snake has two ends, Eustace. One end bites, the other end doesn't."

"Hey, words of wisdom, Sig. Hold on, I'll get my needlepoint and do a wall hanging."

Tarr laughed. "I mean, it works out. Oceanic owns Merced, right? And Merced files for bankruptcy. So when one of your subsidiaries files for bankruptcy, the parent corporation has to file a petition for claims, just to get the tax write-off."

"Yeah. So what?"

"So when Oceanic did that, they had to do it through their lawyers. Through *a* lawyer, anyway."

"And?"

"And the lawyer has to give the U.S. reporting address of the firm. The reporting address is usually the place where the American papers of incorporation are. Usually, it's the lawyer's office."

"Where was this lawyer?"

"Address is on West 84th Street, in Denver."

"What's his name?"

"Charles Kellerman. The same guy who's on the shareholder's list of Kellerman Cold Haulers. But that's just white noise, I think. The point is, you recognize that address?"

"Should I?"

"It's the Denver branch of a local law firm."

Meagher's headache went away in a flood of cool light. "And—"

"And that local law firm is Mallon, Brewer, Hogeland and Bright."

"Jesus!"

"To cut to the chase, it turns out that Dwight Hogeland's firm also leased some vehicles from Merced, including family cars and a jet plane."

"What car?"

"Well, there's a 1975 Cadillac Fleetwood Brougham, a Porsche 911, a Cherokee, some others."

"Does it say who drives them?"

"No. Anyone connected with the leasee, I'd guess, depending on insurance restrictions. No way to tell. But that's not the really neat part. Guess what the plane is? The one they lease?"

"A Learjet?"

"Buy the man a cigar!"

"Jesus Christ!"

"My sentiments exactly, Eustace. And I'll tell you something *else*. I'm not the first guy been asking these questions. CompuServe has a query registry, part of their service to newspapers. You can punch it up, find out if anybody else is making the same kind of inquiry. See who's on to the same story? So, routine, I punch that up and I find out they did a one-time printout for a Visa customer, the whole package, and that Visa customer's name was Joseph Bell of South Wyatt Drive, Hardin, Montana."

"Look. I gotta tell you something else."

"Else? You haven't told me dick so far!"

"Who've you talked to about this?"

"Nobody. I came home, tried to reach you. Why?"

"Okay. I want you to stay put, and don't answer the door. Don't go out for beer, keep the lights off. You got a gun?"

"Yeah."

"Go get it, load it, and keep it in your hand. Don't put it down to pee, understand?"

"Eustace, you trying to make me nervous?"

"Yes! I sent a Big Horn County guy out to Joe Bell's place today. He found Joe Bell. At least, he's pretty sure it's Joe Bell."

There was a long silence while Meagher listened to Sig Tarr's breathing and the wind rattled the phone-booth glass.

"Bell's dead?"

"Unbelievably dead, Sig."

Calder angled the green LTD in front of the Freightliner, partially blocking the left fender. Luis Freg was waiting at the side of the trailer. They could hear carts rolling into the trailer, and footsteps. A portable radio sitting on the loading dock, beside the sealed tarp, was playing a Bob Dylan song.

It was "Knockin' on Heaven's Door."

Beau remembered the movie where he'd heard that song. It was a Peckinpah movie called *Pat Garrett and Billy the Kid.*

Beau figured it was a lucky thing he wasn't superstitious. He tugged out his big blue Smith. Calder saw that and pulled out a matte-finish steel Colt Python. Beau figured Luis Freg for a fancy nine-mill. He was kind of surprised when Freg tugged out an army .45.

Hey. A traditionalist.

Freg went around to the far side of the truck. A driver sitting on his Kenworth saw Freg walk around and said "shit" and slid off the hood. Freg smiled at him.

Beau nodded to Calder. Calder slapped the steel hull of the trailer. It boomed like a drum. The footsteps stopped, and a small Japanese man peered out of the folds of the tarp.

"Yes. What you want?"

Calder showed his badge, keeping the gun at his side.

"Police? What's the matta?"

"You have a broken headlight out here, sir. Can you come down, take a look at—"

They heard a voice from inside the trailer: "Who is it, Jenji?"

The man turned and looked inside the tarp. "It the police. They—"

Beau glanced up at the steel wall of the trailer, and maybe it was luck, but he happened to be looking at a panel where a line of rivets was showing a brown track of rust, and then there was a big star-shaped hole about two inches above the third rivet and a clap of thunder so loud, his ears were hurting, because something had slapped the side of his head *very* hard, and he could hardly hear for the ringing. A round slammed into the stake truck behind him—Calder was firing his Python, Beau saw him, his thin body crouched, the Python up and out, the cylinder working, the hammer going back, a sliver of blue fire from the muzzle. Beau fell back against the stake truck, felt it hitting him in the shoulder blade, and now he had the Smith up—the red bar was rock-steady, and then the gun bucked hard and another booming explosion hammered at his cheeks and ears and the red bar blurred into a haze of smoke and blue fire—he wondered what that was—then he saw his own wrist, the sleeve of his blue suit, and the Smith bucked again in his hand—he felt that in his wrist, it hurt and he knew he was firing. He straightened up, still firing, the concussions slamming around in between the

trucks—dust jumping from the seams and rivets—the noise almost continuous now—seeing the rounds punch in—seeing daylight on the far side—
more holes appearing like a conjurer's trick—one-two-three-four in a ragged
row—more rounds were coming out of the steel wall—he could hear them
humming by his body, hear the wooden stakes of the truck behind him
cracking, hear a tire squealing with escaping air—the trailer rang and rocked
and clanged and shuddered and over that the solid pounded-earth booming
explosions of weapons and someone was shouting a word and the word
sounded like *stop stop*. Beau was suddenly aware that his Smith—there was
something wrong with it—a dry metallic clicking, and then he knew it was
empty, and he heard one more solid gunshot like a punctuation point, and
he looked to his left where Calder was crouching, his mouth open, his right
arm out and rigid, the steel Python vibrating from the muscular tension in
the arm, and there was sunlight—*sunlight*—in yellow discs on Calder's face
and the material of his beige suit, and something caught Beau's eye, a glitter
of hard light, and he looked back up at the trailer and straight into a shaft
of sunlight shining through the body of the trailer, and then a wave of absolute
silence crashed in on both of them and they could hear each other breathing
and Beau could feel his heartbeat in several different places in his body—a
thumping under his left jaw and a hissing sound in his right ear and inside
his chest a deep continuous rolling tremor and under that the sound of
something wet dripping onto the crumbling asphalt.

Calder sat down on the ground hard and put his left hand on his forehead
and lowered his head. Beau watched him do that without feeling any need
to walk over or to say or do anything.

More fluid was running from the trailer now, milky white with a delicate
threading of pink and scarlet. It was pooling on the cratered asphalt, running
down through the holes at the base of the trailer.

Beau went down into a crouch and put a hand on the trailer—the metal
was hot and slick under his hand—and he looked under it. On the far side,
Luis Freg was on the ground, his olive-green jacket crumpled and disarrayed,
bright blood bubbling and frothing out his burnt-orange shirt. His .45 was
on the ground beside him, and he was turned slightly on his right side,
holding himself in tight, his soft brown eyes staring hard at Beau, tugging
at his belt where the black square of a portable radio was showing. Beau
scrambled under the trailer. Wetness dripped over his face, and he felt the
fluid under his hands.

He reached Freg and rolled him onto his back, and Freg got the radio
out. The wound in his shirt was frothy and bubbling, and Freg was trying

to speak. Beau eased him onto his back and ripped the shirt open and saw the wound in Freg's left side, a few inches below the collarbone. He took the radio from Freg.

"Ten-thirteen this is a ten-thirteen at two two zero Ditman the food warehouse at two two zero Ditman a ten-thirteen!"

"Identify yourself. This is an unauthorized use of an emergency system! Identify yourself!"

"Hey look, butthead! I'm Sergeant McAllister of the Montana Highway Patrol, and I'm down here at 220 Ditman, and there's been one hell of a gunfight down here, so get me some help, get me an ambulance and some paramedics, you've got an officer down with a sucking chest wound!"

"What's the location, sir?"

"Two two zero Ditman. The warehouse. Detective Freg is down, and Lieutenant Calder may be hurt, too."

"Yes, sir. Please don't break radio contact. We'll—"

"Fuck you, lady!" He set the radio down and got up onto his feet, looking for something he could use. He saw a crate of oranges sitting on the ground at the back of a pickup truck a few yards away. A man was lying on the ground beside it, staring at him. He got up and ran over to the crate. It was sealed with clear plastic. He ripped off the seal and ran back to Freg.

He wiped the blood away with his right hand until he had the skin exposed. The wound was ragged and filling with bright blood. It looked like a little well of red water in the man's chest.

Beau stretched the plastic over the wound and held it down. There was suction against it as Freg drew in a breath.

He pulled in another, and the plastic sheet held. Freg coughed and spat some blood, and pulled in more air.

His color got better.

Now they could hear sirens, and the people around were getting to their feet and dusting themselves off. Beau kept up his eye contact with Freg, his hand pressing down on the plastic, feeling the heat of Freg's blood and his body, the dreadful wreck of flesh under his palm. It sent an atavistic shudder through him, and he trembled. He felt a hand on his shoulder, and he jumped. He wouldn't look away from Freg, afraid that if he broke his connection with the man, he'd lose him.

He heard Rufus Calder's voice close beside him: "Luis, you hang on."

Freg tried to smile, and he reached up to hold Beau's wrist. His fingers were cold.

"Get me a tarp, a rug, something, Rufus. He's going into shock." Calder got up and went looking.

"You gotta hang on now, Luis. We Irish, we gotta stay together, okay?"

Freg tried twice and made it on the third breath.

"I'm not Irish . . . I'm Mexican."

"I guess you got your *cornada* in the chest there, Luis."

"*Si* . . . I hope this . . . don kill me."

And then Calder was back with a tarp, and the narrow space between the trucks was suddenly full of people in blue and white. Someone pulled Beau out of the way, and he realized the paramedics were here. He watched them surround Freg until he couldn't see anything of the man but his baggy brown slacks and his Italian loafers. He bent over and picked up the .45. It was empty, the slide cocked back.

Calder was standing beside him.

"Christ, McAllister. I haven't been in a firefight since I got outta Da Nang. Let's not do this again."

Beau nodded and looked around him at the trailer and the stake truck. "I think I'm gonna stay away from truckyards. This is the second time in a week I almost got shot in one."

Beau looked down again at his right hand. It was hot, and it was shaking as if it were alive. There was blood on it, and it seemed to Beau that he had pushed this line of work as far as it would take him.

"I guess we better go look inside," said Calder.

"Oh, right," said Beau. "I forgot."

They pushed their way through the crowd and walked back to the rear of the trailer. The tarp had been pulled back, and four uniform cops were standing inside the trailer at the back, staring into the interior of it. One of the cops, a sergeant with yellow stripes on his dark blue shirt, turned to watch Beau and Calder climb up onto the dock.

"Rufus—how's Luis?"

Calder shrugged, looking past the man into the trailer.

"Jesus," he said, and let out a long sigh.

The walls and roof of the trailer were full of holes, ugly star-shaped rips and punctures. The late afternoon sun was pouring in through the holes in one side, piercing the wreckage.

The Japanese man lay on his side, pressed up against the back of the trailer. He had taken at least one round in the back and another through the side of his skull. He was holding a furniture pad, and it looked as if he had been trying to pull it up over his head when the rounds came in. He was dead.

Farther inside the trailer, his back supported by a stainless-steel cart that was lashed securely into a wall brace, Danny Burt was sitting on the floor of the cart, in the middle of a spreading puddle of milky-white fluid and blood. Brass cartridge cases lay scattered around in the fluids. There was a large blued weapon on the floor in front of him, a semiauto pistol. The slide was racked back and the magazine was out. There was a second magazine in Danny's left hand, and it looked as if he had been trying to slide it into the receiver when the rounds finally found him. He was wearing a black suit and a white shirt. His gold Rolex glimmered on his left wrist. He had taken several rounds. The one that took away his left cheek and most of his forehead might not have been the round that killed him. The round that had blown away most of the inside of his right leg just below the crotch, that round would have opened his femoral artery for a good six inches. Given his excitement, the adrenaline pumping through him as the rounds came in and he fired blind through the walls, most of his heart's blood would have jetted out of that wound in a few seconds.

Well, whatever.

The point was, he was dead, and Beau walked over to look down at him, his boots squelching in the fluid on the floor.

A Colt Delta. A ten-mill.

That's not a handgun. That's artillery.

He thought about all the hours he'd spent drinking with Danny Burt, at Pike Twilly's or Fogarty's, Danny always in the middle of a crowd, leaning on the bartop, always a fresh frosty bottle in his big hands, delight and humor in every line of his face, telling some outrageous story about one of the stiffs, what they'd done with it, tricks they'd played on the other guys, or the latest joke from the morgue attendants. Or sitting rapt, just part of the crowd, while Beau, or Tom Blasingame, or Moses Harper told a war story, or one of the funny things that happened to them on the shift; bar talk, the smoke hanging heavy in the amber light, the music playing some cowboy honky-tonk got-tears-in-my-ears-from-lyin'-on-my-back-starin'-at-the-ceilin'-an'-cryin'-over-you, a chilly wind scraping at the frosted windows, and six feet of snow in the streets, a great muffled quiet lying over everything, like God's particular blessing.

And now here he was, good old Danny Burt, with his guts in his lap, and blood all over his Rolex, and all his secrets fading in his shattered skull.

Beau wondered how much he really knew about any of his friends, about Meagher or Finch Hyam or Fogarty. How much did he know, really *know*, about Maureen, even when she was soft and naked with him, or sitting curled up in his left arm eating popcorn and watching *White Cargo* where Hedy Lamarr steps out of a velvet-dark tropical night and says the line—they'd say it with her—"I am Tondelayo." God, he *must* have loved her, that *felt* like love.

And drinking with the guys, that had *felt* like friendship. And if it wasn't, if it could all go down like Danny here, in a puddle of his own piss and blood and white water, then you could lose everything and have nothing and never even *know* what was real and what was just life being gentle with you, leaving the flesh on the skull face of things.

He prodded Danny's leg with his boot.

Well, fuck all that.

Better you than me, Danny.

There were three carts in the trailer, three stainless-steel carts about four feet high by two feet wide and three feet long. They had hinged lids held down by six pressure clamps. They looked watertight. The pressure clamps were tied off by small silver wires, and the wires were clamped with tiny customs seals. Two of the carts had several punctures in them. This was where the white liquid was coming from. It dripped out of the holes and trickled down to the bottom of the carts, and dripped onto the wet wooden flooring of the trailer. One cart had a long gouge on the side but no puncture. Beau put a hand on it. He could feel heat and a low steady vibration. There was machinery inside, probably running on a battery. There was a label stuck on the lid.

The sign read:

OCEANIC FROZEN FOODS

CUSTOM CLEARED AND BONDED

PERISHABLE DO NOT BREAK SEAL

He put the barrel of the Smith into the silver wire of the customs seal and twisted it off. Then he unsnapped the pressure clamps and lifted the lid. The smell of chemicals was strong, and there was a lot of wet warmth coming from the interior.

Inside the cart, under a secondary lid of clear glass, misted with water and fluids, he saw a baby floating in a thick white fluid. Maybe it weighed a pound. Maybe two. Feeding tubes ran into its belly, and other tubes emerged from its lower intestinal tract.

This one was a baby girl. Her skin was pale yellow, and her hair was a delicate dusting of black lace.

Above her eyebrows, her skull seemed truncated and oddly shaped. The word came back to him.

Anencephalic.

Under her pale yellow skin, even through the thick milky fluid in which she floated, Beau could see the tiny flutter of movement in her chest. She was alive.

• • •

They used a forklift to take down the steel door inside the cold room. There they found six more carts. Inside each cart was a baby connected to some kind of life-support system. Two were dead. By this time, the yard was full of cops, and people were being questioned everywhere.

Beau had found a place to sit, out of the way of the officials and the uniform guys. He was thinking about how much money he had saved and what his life added up to now that he was getting older and fifty wasn't just a vague destination a long way down the line. Calder walked up to him and cleared his throat.

Beau looked up at him. "How's Luis?"

"I think he'll be okay. He's in the trauma ward now. But look, Beau, you gotta go back to Billings. They got a plane waiting for you out at LAX."

"What's the rush? Why am I leaving? Am I in trouble?"

Calder looked down at his hands and then up at Beau. "There's a Learjet waiting for you at the airport. They sent it all the way from Billings."

"Why? I have an open ticket. Anyway, this is my case. What're we gonna do about the babies here? We gotta save the ones we can save."

"That's for the medics. They got them now. Nothing we can do about that."

"Then we're going to the Sonesta Clinic."

"The Sonesta Clinic! Is this their shit?"

"Some of it. At least, they're involved."

"Then we're fucked. . . . Look, right now, you gotta go. Come on, I got a cruiser here. They'll run you right to LAX."

"You got some bad news for me, Rufus?"

The black man turned and faced Beau. Beau could see him steeling himself, pulling back from the emotion. It was something Beau did when he had to tell someone something very bad. He braced himself.

"Is it about my kid?"

"No, she's *fine*! She's just fine. It's your ex-wife. She's . . . some In- dians have called a press conference, and she's going to be the center of it. Meagher says to call him."

Calder looked back toward the trailer, at the obscenity it contained. Beau was blank-faced, shell-shocked.

"Is it about this?"

"That's what they're saying."

25

2005 Hours – June 19 – Los Angeles, California

The Learjet was parked far away from the main terminal and the big airliners, at the seaward edge of the airport.

In the cruiser, Beau shaded his eyes against the glare as the car wheeled through the security gate and accelerated across the runways. Overhead, a silver 747 rose into the deepening night on a trail of superheated air and kerosene smoke. In the east, the city lights were on. Sunlight burned in a thousand windows from the northern hills down to the beaches and the low brown slopes to the south. On the freeway the traffic had been a solid chain of red taillights. The sunlight glimmered off car windows and polished chrome. The air was full of noise and wind, and it reeked of burning oil, salt, melted rubber.

On the runway, the Lear had its turbines running. Beau saw a blast of heat from the exhausts twist the air into a crazy shimmer that curled and eddied behind the jet like water. There was an Exxon truck parked some distance away, and a long black hose had been pulled up to a wingtip. In the slanting light, the black figure of a man crouched on the wingtip.

As the squad car approached the jet, Beau could see that the lights were on inside the plane, a row of white lights along the slender fuselage. The port was open, the boarding ladder flipped out and down. In the yellow oval of the door, Beau saw a large man bending over, staring out at them as the squad car crossed the final runway. He stepped down the ladder and walked forward as the squad car came to a stop. He waited outside the window, his craggy face a stony gate slammed down over his emotions. He watched as Beau spoke into his cellular phone for almost five minutes.

Finally, Beau hit the END button and climbed out of the cruiser.

"Beau," said Doc Hogeland. "I'm so sorry about Maureen."

Beau slammed the cruiser door. The patrolman at the wheel leaned across the seat and raised his hand. Then he was rolling away, and Beau turned back to the jet. "I was talking to Meagher."

Hogeland nodded, impassive.

"You're refueling with the engines on?"

Doc Hogeland glanced up at the wing. The attendant was stepping off onto the ladder, wrestling with the avgas line. He waved at them and jumped to the ground.

"Fifteen hundred miles to Billings. Plane has a three-thousand-mile range, but she feels funny without a full load. Takes time to cool and restart. That's why I asked them to put me way out here. It's risky, but I've done it before. The nozzles are grounded and the intake port is lined with latex, and there's a ground wire to the truck tank. I used to do it on the carriers. It's a military procedure. Come on—we're going to miss our clearance."

Hogeland went ahead of Beau, lumbering up the steps, huge and bent, an old man in jeans and boots, but there was muscle in the frame. He wore a leather flight jacket, and his white hair was yellow in the cabin lights as he turned to look at Beau coming up behind him.

"We can be off the ground in five minutes. Shut that port—the button's the red one by the crank. It's automatic, so don't get your fingers in the way. Then come on up to the cockpit."

He stalked off up toward the controls. The interior of the Lear was like the inside of a sleek cabin cruiser, in various tones of deep blue tapestry and rosewood veneer. A salon next to the cockpit curved around a black ebony coffee table and connected with a low bar and two passenger seats with belts and headrests. Through the portholes, Los Angeles glimmered in the haze, a hectic grid of neon and reflected sunlight. Hogeland had something playing on the stereo. It sounded like Waylon Jennings.

Beau came forward to the cabin. Hogeland grunted at him.

The doc was speaking into the headset, the radio crackling. He had his right hand on the T-bars, and the turbines were winding up. The Lear was already rolling forward.

He nodded toward a headset. Beau put it on as the plane started to turn left toward a runway, following a line of amber lights. The city moved out of the picture as the nose came around to face a line of white lights that receded into a point. Beyond that was the ocean.

"This is Flight 55 private requesting clearance."

The control tower voice was clipped and raspy with static. "Roger, five five. Hold on six."

"Roger, tower. Five five holding."

There was a short pause.

"Roger, five five, you are clear for take-off."

"Roger, tower. Flight five five taking off."

Hogeland's big hand eased the throttle forward, and the little jet began to roll forward into the runway. The lights began to flicker past the wings, and Beau felt himself being pressed back into the seat. Then the jets were howling and the nose was coming up, and suddenly the lights were falling away to the left as Hogeland powered up and banked right and the broad flat plain of the ocean was under the wings. Hogeland held the bank and watched the altimeter, and now the land came around again, the city under them, a glittering horizon of lights and towers and beyond it the dark slopes of the mountains. They rose up through haze into a deeper blackness. Now stars filled the windshield.

Both men were silent through all of this until the jet reached thirty thousand feet.

"Tower, this is five five. We are at altitude."

"Roger, five five, you are at thirty-two thousand. Transponder functional. Your hand-off is coming up in thirteen minutes. Have a good flight."

"Roger, tower."

Hogeland steadied the plane, leaned forward to punch a code into a computer board. Beau felt hydraulics kick in, and a green light began to pulse in the control panel. Hogeland unstrapped his belt and rubbed his face with his hands.

Beau turned away to watch the city lights far below, sliding away under the wings. Up ahead the mountains rose toward them, and the night was a tilted horizon of stars.

"Why'd you come to get me? I could have taken a commercial flight."

Hogeland grunted again and looked sidelong at Beau from under his shaggy brows. "I guess I wanted the time alone with you. Maybe to talk, get things out on the table."

"You know they traced the Cadillac."

"Yes. Dwight called me after he heard from Meagher. The car was leased through his office in Denver."

There was a long silence. Finally, Hogeland said, "I wonder why Eustace let you fly with me, Beau. Considering."

"He didn't like it. But the only alternative was to pull you off the plane at LAX and cuff you, and Vanessa wouldn't come up with a warrant. She's waiting to hear from Maureen. Right now, there isn't sufficient evidence to charge you. I told Eustace, maybe I better stick with you, see you get home safe."

"You thought I'd fly away, try for Brazil or someplace? Come on, Beau. You know me better than that. I need a drink."

The old man slipped out of the belts and went back to the bar. Beau stayed in his seat. He could hear him at the bar, glass clinking. He came back and handed Beau a very cold bottle of Beck's beer. Hogeland held a crystal glass of pale Scotch. He climbed back into the pilot seat and raised his glass to Beau in a salute.

"So. . . . I gather that our Danny boy has gone on ahead."

"You could say that."

"I tried to calm him down. After Friday night, there was no holding him back. He was determined to take it all apart. I think Spellman Sterling spooked him. Danny didn't kill that boy, you know."

"Hinsdale?"

"Yes. Oh, true, he *was* worried about Peter. He thought the boy had heard everything. He was trying to talk his way out with Jubal and the others. Apparently, you interrupted that."

"Who did kill him?"

"No idea. Who do you think? You were there."

"I guess Earl, or one of the others. It wasn't the girl. She was busy with me. Does it all come down to Danny Burt, Doc?"

"Danny was mean and greedy. I needed him to transport the harvested fetuses. He wanted out. He and Bell were blackmailing me. Danny had taken a CD ROM disk. It had most of my data on it, stupid of me, but you see, I wasn't really doing anything illegal. And I wanted the project documented. The need is great, Beau. Eventually, we will have to face up to that. I did ground-breaking work. But Danny was in it for the money. He thought the boy had heard too much. And he saw only the profits."

"But not you, eh? Not the old country doc."

Hogeland signed. "Beau, I was hoping we could talk straight. I think, if you can try to understand, I feel there's not a lot of distance between us. You might be surprised."

"I've been everything else this last week. Go ahead, try me."

"How much have you figured out, Beau?"

"Fair amount. I'll stop you if I get confused."

The doctor grimaced and looked sideways at Beau, up from under his thick white eyebrows, his lined face tinted green from the cockpit lights. His eyes glittered with intelligence and a kind of cynical humor.

"You won't do anything too physical up here, will you, Beau? Unless you think you can land this thing?"

Beau pulled at his Beck's and felt the cold liquid burn through him. The doctor spoke again. "They didn't hurt Maureen, you know."

Beau suppressed the wave of rage and held on to the bottle, as if the bone-aching cold in it could reach his heart and lungs. "How about Bobby Lee, Doc?"

"He didn't hurt Bobby Lee at all. Of course, she was frightened. And the policeman seems to be stabilizing."

"I'm glad to see you're taking this so well, Doc."

"I'm doing what I can. I'm sorry about the policeman."

"His name is Dell Greer."

"Dell Greer. Some of this has to be laid at his door, Beau. He should have been doing his job. He was taken from behind, according to the report. He has a concussion and a severe subdural hematoma. Maureen was taken right away."

"Bobby Lee saw this?"

"Yes, but she's sedated. Moses Harper is with her, and your other daughter is coming in from Wyoming. The County sent a helicopter for her."

Beau was quiet for a while.

"You hear about Joe Bell, Doc?"

Dr. Hogeland looked bleak. "I heard some of it. I gather it was bad."

Beau looked at the old man, at his green-tinted face and the black holes where his eyes were, hidden in shadows. Finally, Hogeland had to ask him.

"Did Eustace describe . . . apparently your man went out there and found him."

"It was Moses, according to Eustace."

"Yes. He found Bell?"

"Most of him."

Hogeland winced. "Eustace wouldn't go into details."

"He was skinned."

"What do you mean, skinned?"

"Just what it sounds like. Moses figured he had been alive for most of it. The guy used Stretch 'N Seal, you know?"

"Stretch 'N Seal?" The old man thought it over. "Yes, that's clever of him. The wrapping would prevent immediate shock and heart failure. Very . . . ingenious."

"You get the idea this guy's done it before? He covered the parts he'd skinned with Saran Wrap, and that sort of held Joe together. Moses told Eustace he'd never buy beef in a Safeway again."

Hogeland wasn't listening. From the look on his face, he was trying to get his mind around what had happened to Joe Bell. Beau let him do it. He deserved it. Finally the doctor spoke. "Why was your man out there in the first place?"

"He was trying to trace the Caddy, figured he'd get Bell to give him a better description."

"Why the Caddy?"

"Bell had you on video, the day of the shooting at the Oasis. I ran across it that night, when I went back to look around. You could see him leaning in the window, yelling at someone."

"And you knew it was me?"

"No, but I knew the car. I mean, there are a lot of old Caddys in Montana, but I had a feeling it was yours. I've seen yours around, ridden in it twice."

"Why not say so? Instead of letting them go to all the trouble of chasing it down?"

Beau let the question hang for a while.

"Damned if I know, Doc. I guess I didn't want to drag you in. It might have been another car, might have had nothing to do with what happened. Hell, on the face of it, it didn't mean a thing anyway. So there was a blue Caddy at the scene. So you drive a blue Caddy. That's not a connection. But if it *was* you at Bell's Oasis that day, and you don't mention it later, then *that's* interesting. Why were you there, anyway?"

"Bell wanted me to meet with Jubal and the rest. Bell figured we could buy them off or scare them off. I told him he was an idiot, and he blew up at me."

"You could have done that over the phone. Why drive all the way out to Pompeys Pillar?"

"He said if I didn't come out there, he'd bring them in to the hospital, bring them right up to my office. I had to try to talk sense to him. But it was useless."

"So he decided to try and kill them?"

"Bell was a bad-tempered man. I know they were pressing him because he'd been asking questions around the reserves. He was known among the prostitutes. I think, when they confronted him in the office, he just went over the top."

Beau had figured it the same way. Hogeland spoke again.

"So what was the connection with the Caddy?"

"You're here, aren't you?"

Hogeland was staring at him. "You had nothing!"

"I had some suspicions. You've just confirmed them. Sig Tarr chased Oceanic down through the Merced bankruptcy. The law firm handling it was Dwight's. Meagher wanted to nail Dwight for all of it. He figured it all went back to him. But I was the one who saw your Caddy at Bell's. I didn't want to believe it, but when Dwight's name came up, I figured you had to be the one. Who else would have the medical connections, the money? So in a way, the Caddy did it, but only for me. And the jet, of course."

"Records, eh, Beau? Damnable records."

"Why take Merced into bankruptcy, Doc? It just drew attention."

"That was Charlie Kellerman. He panicked. He figured, if we took Merced into bankruptcy, we could close down the routes, hide it behind the trustee. Oceanic was well back. No one could get access to the shareholders' list."

"Maybe. But this plane, it stands out. Why the plane?"

Hogeland sighed and drank some more Scotch. The plane rose up and shuddered in an air pocket, dipped and rose again and leveled out. The green light blipped hypnotically, the reflection staining Hogeland's left cheek as he turned to look at Beau.

"You're young yet, Beau. You get old, you figure there's not a lot of time left, you better do some of the things you love. The grave's a fine and private place, as they say."

"No Learjets for the dead?"

"I flew Corsairs in the war. Not your war—the good war. We were the lords of the South China Sea. Mindanao, Subic Bay, Burma, Corregidor, Bataan. I was in the Battle of the Coral Sea. I flew at Midway. Those were great days, Beau. You've never been to war, have you, son?"

Beau shook his head, thinking that there were many wars and many ways to lose yourself in them.

"I have, Beau. I've seen a great deal of the world, seen the glory and the destruction in it. A man can see a lot in life, and even in the most horrible kinds of struggle, there are epiphanies, there are times when a man's life can seem . . . he can feel God at his side. A man can sense himself at the outer edge of life, like we are here, at the outermost reaches of existence. Out here, a man can see a long way into himself, into what it means to be alive, and what it means to approach the . . . infinite."

Beau was thinking that there wasn't a bad man he'd ever met, didn't like to put a nice shine on his crimes, work it out so he was really a good guy, like he really had no choice or it was all for the good of the nation. He said nothing.

"You know, Beau, I often wonder why men think that the next hill or the next ocean wave has the great mystery concealed behind it when all a man has to do is look up, fly a few miles, and he comes to the real frontier— not a thousand miles up the Amazon or three days' ride into the Bridger range or halfway up Kilimanjaro. There isn't a dull little town or a shopping mall or a bank or a gas station that isn't just a few short miles from the perfect silences of space. Just a delicate membrane of air. We could peel it back. . . . " He shuddered and slapped the controls.

"This machine will approach Mach One. I had it refitted according to military specs. I can even cut oxygen into the afterburners. It'll go up to fifty thousand feet. If I pushed it, maybe sixty thousand. That's as far as this plane goes. I could take us up in a climb, go to the afterburners, we could break out of the atmosphere and ride a perfect arc, like a slingshot rides the opposing forces of gravity and velocity. We could break through into the . . . immensity around us. *See* it, however briefly."

"What would happen if you did?"

Hogeland laughed, sipped some Scotch.

"Flame-out. You'd lose all power. No control. You'd wing over, go into an uncontrollable dive. We used to call it 'auger in.' "

"So it would be *damned* brief."

"Hell, Beau! Life is brief. We get up above the grasses, break out of the earth and glide for a while, we feel the sun and we see the wide world, and then we come back to the earth and sink into it. Why not go higher and fall farther? In the end, what's the cost?"

"So far? Seven people. Dell Greer almost died. God knows how many women who had their babies stolen. The babies themselves."

The doctor was shaking his head. "My intent was not to—"

"It happened. Your intentions have nothing to do with it."

"My intentions have *everything* to do with it. Did you understand anything of what I've been saying, Beau?"

"Yes."

"I know you did! I can sense it in you. You play the bull cop, but you don't have the flatness in your eyes, that wild boar look. You think and you *feel*, Beau. You try to keep it hidden, but it shows. I think you can understand where I was trying to go, where I was trying to take all of us."

"I know what I found in your truck, Doc. I saw where *that* was going."

"But *did* you? Really *see*?"

"Doc, I got it on my boots. That's real enough for me."

They flew awhile in silence. Outside the cabin the air was clear and ice-cold. The jets whistled softly behind them, and the wind flowed over the screen. The stars glittered like knives against the limitless black night.

Hogeland let out a long breath.

"Was I wrong, Beau?"

"It *looked* wrong."

"They weren't *alive*, Beau. Not like you and I are alive."

"I saw heartbeats. I saw a tiny human in that box."

"They had a kind of life, yes. But there was no *thought*! No memory. No awareness of their own existence. They're like seeds. They can *become* life. But life is a process of becoming. You're not suddenly *human,* suddenly *seeing* and *knowing*. That kind of awareness is what we call consciousness, and consciousness comes on us slowly, like coming up from a deep dreamless sleep. We are awake, and we know we are awake. Man is the animal who *knows*."

"How can you decide for them? How can you know whether or not they were alive that way?"

"But science is always making distinctions of that order. That's why even the most humane and enlightened doctor will resist an abortion after the first trimester, because he knows that life is not a switch thrown at the moment of orgasm, a life flicking on in a darkened room. It is a process of change, of becoming, and that *becoming* is exponential as the cells divide and subdivide. If the fundamentalists and the fanatics are right, then masturbation is murder."

"You went too far."

"And how far is too far?"

"These were individuals. Little people. Not a collection of cells or an egg."

"Tell me where the line is, then. Tell me at what point in the development of this organism does it become an individual, a person."

"I don't know."

"Nor do I, Beau. But I can make an educated guess, and that is what this is all about. Do you know what a blastocyst is?"

"What's the point, Doc? It isn't going to change anything."

"It's important to me that you understand why I know I *did nothing wrong*! I may have done nothing that was even *illegal*!"

"How about immoral? Or is science the last refuge of the scoundrel now?"

"If you understand the process, you'll understand my . . . what I tried to do. What I can *still* accomplish!"

"Try me."

Hogeland straightened in his seat. Beau could see the change come over him, see the man rebuilding himself in his mind, becoming the grand old man of medicine. He looked at his watch. They'd be closing in on Billings in about an hour. Hogeland's voice was rich and full of persuasion now that he had found familiar ground. The doctor wasn't used to being perceived as anything less than a monument to medicine and compassion.

"Two weeks after the sperm has fertilized the ovum, cell division has produced perhaps a hundred cells. Fluid has accumulated within the cellular mass to form a kind of irregular inner cavity. At around the same time, this cellular aggregate has arrived in the uterus and begins to attach itself to the uterine wall. Is it a person yet, Beau?"

"I don't know."

"Do we have funerals for miscarried eggs at two weeks?"

"No. The woman wouldn't even have known she was pregnant."

"Exactly. So we can say that there's no *soul* in there yet. Unless you're with the Catholics?"

"I am Catholic. But I . . . it's more complicated than that."

"Yes. That's the trouble, when you're Catholic and you like to think. It creates an existential tension. Now, when the blastocyst has reached this stage, the cells are . . . adherent. They stick together. Instead of just being like a bag of marbles, they are becoming connected. This is the first time that you can say there *is* a single entity, and not just a bundle of unconnected cells. Is it human now?"

"No."

"In this entity, there are two separate cellular groupings. There's an external layer, and a small cellular protrusion that extends into the inner cavity. This inner mass is the part of the blastocyst that actually becomes the human. The other mass, the exterior mass, ultimately becomes the placenta and the outer membranes. They're discarded at the birth. Is it human yet?''

"I'll tell you when I think so.''

"We call this stage 'primary embryonic organization.' This is the first time we can discern the beginning of the actual embryo. In this process, we see the basic structure begin, we see what we call the 'primitive streak.' This is an actual line, a thickening of the cells along the main body axes, front and back, left and right, head and tail. Now this is critical. If two streaks appear, you get twins. If three, you get triplets. Each streak is the— let's say almost the spine—of an actual individual. But it has no neurons, no cortical development. It can't feel or know anything. Am I boring you?''

"Just keep going, Doc. I'll stop you when I'm in too deep.''

"Now we have reached 'organogenesis.' This streak begins to fill out into the major regions and organs. We're headed out of developmental individuality and into *functional* individuality. This goes on until about the end of the eighth week.''

"When does it get a heart?''

"That's the first organ to become functional. It starts to beat around the fourth week after the egg is fertilized.''

"And when does it get a spinal column?''

"Now you're making the classic layman's error. You have to understand that the fetus—we're now at the stage where it's a fetus—may have the outward appearance of a human child, but internally it is still very far from having any kind of organized neuronal connectivity—''

"What?''

"From feeling or reacting to anything. Now, if we go back to the third week, we have seen a layer of cells in that streak start to form a neural plate, *but* the cells of that plate are not neurons. They *will* be, but not yet.''

"When does this baby start to *think*, Doc?''

"You're really asking, when does the fetus start to undergo some form of inner experience. Can it feel pain?''

"Or fear, Doc.''

"Precisely, and that's the vital question. You'll agree that pain and fear are internal sensations?''

"Yeah.''

"So if they're internal sensations, they have to pass along *sensory* conduits. Along neurons and into an organized thalamic—into a real brain?''

"Okay.''

"So if pain and fear depend on a significant degree of brain function, you're not going to see that in any truly valid way until the fetus is twenty-two weeks old. Because all the science, all the anatomical studies have invariably shown that these vital neuronal connections are not complete until the first fibers from the thalamus enter the cortex. Then we can say that the channel for feeling, for fear and pain, is now complete. But that only means that the *wires* are there. That doesn't mean the *current* is flowing. You don't see any kind of rhythmic organized electrical activity—such as you might see in the brain waves of a sleeping person—until the neural substrate is very well advanced, and you don't see *that* until the seventh *month* of pregnancy. That's when premature babies are easily viable, because they are developed enough to carry on the business of being alive on their own. But are they *conscious*? Are they humans yet?''

"Look, Doc. Boil it down. What's the minimum level of experience for you to say these babies were conscious?''

"I'd say the absolute minimum would be when they can *feel* pain and *know* it as pain.''

"And when does that happen?''

"As I said, probably around the time that the upper brain stem and the cerebral cortex begin to function. But let's be conservative. Say six months, to be on the safe side.''

"And how old were the—''

"Some of the donors you saw were fetuses in the area of five months. And the term babies, of course.''

"*And* the term babies! Yes, Doc, I saw them. They were full-term babies, born alive. Don't give me any horseshit about 'harvesting fetuses.' You were taking living babies.''

"Not always!''

"Oh, right. Only now and then. That makes it okay. How'd you get the short-term babies? The five- or six-month ones?''

Hogeland looked out the windshield and sighed. "Maybe we crossed the line there. I know I suffered for it, and there were nights when it wasn't as *clear* as it should have been. We made it a point to recommend early testing in cases where the mother had a history of alcohol or substance abuse. Occasionally, when the opportunity . . . when the mother seemed incapable of caring, we took babies that had no other purpose in life, babies that were doomed to a cycle of poverty and cruelty, many that weren't ever going to become human.''

"Why not?''

"You understood my point about pain and feeling being absolutely dependent upon higher cortical function?''

"I think so."

"And you're persuaded?"

"Yes . . . I guess so."

"Then, by your own standards, these . . . babies . . . were not *alive,* and could *never* be expected to feel pain or awareness, because they have—in the simplest terms, they have no brains to feel *with.*"

"Anencephalic. Is this where Maureen came in, Doc?"

"Your wife—I know she was a difficult woman to live with, but she had real compassion for the people we would see in our clinics."

"That's the source, isn't it?"

"If you mean, were the clinics the places where we were able to harvest these tragically deformed babies? Then I guess you're right."

"Just how did you do that, Doc?"

"There were deficiencies in the understanding of birth control. They were always getting pregnant. Many of these children were . . . Maureen saw a lot of anencephalic babies, and we—they can be *saved* you know. Many of them have a sufficiently developed brain function to keep most of the autonomic functions going—heart, lungs, kidney and liver, the renal systems. Life can be maintained, if a system for providing nutrients in a sterile environment can be applied."

"Your little carts in the truck?"

"Yes. Jenji provided those. He is a brilliant man and a courageous researcher."

"Not anymore, Doc."

The old man grimaced and looked sideways at Beau.

"A waste. A terrible waste."

"So where was the profit, Doc? Or was it just for the love of science?"

"This country is—we are burdened with a kind of yahoo mindset in America. We think with our stomachs if we think at all. The legislators curry favor. They don't have the heart to lead. There's no vision here."

"But there is in Kyoto? For a price."

"They recognize the potential for genetic research. For the transplant system. It would be possible to maintain these subjects, to allow them to grow. They could be a source of life when they reached maturity. Their organs would be harvested and distributed on a compassionate basis. There are also great implications for research. There's growing revulsion toward animal experimentation. That's not going to go away. My backers saw a way to address all these social issues. They were willing to pay for the whole project. We had made a great beginning."

"Pay for viable brainless babies, you mean?"

"Crudely put."

"It's a crude thing, Doc. How much? By the ounce? By the truckload? By the inch?"

"There were substantial funds available."

"Millions, Doc?"

"Easily."

"What was Maureen's cut?"

"It wasn't a 'cut.' As you said, she was paid a finder's fee. She wasn't the only one. There were some others, in South Dakota."

"I asked what her cut was, not how you planned to describe it to the IRS."

"Usually, depending on the viability, on the reliability of the donor, whether or not the donor was likely to create problems for the project, we'd pay around five or six thousand dollars."

Jesus.

"Did Dwight know about Maureen's part in this?"

"*No!* Dwight had no idea! Dwight was no part of any of it!"

"How could he miss it?"

Hogeland grimaced, shook his head. "Dwight has a . . . literal turn of mind. He thinks in black and white. Some of the . . . nuance . . . of events tend to pass him by."

"Maureen was spending a lot of cash. How'd he miss *that*?"

"I told him she was helping me in an expansion plan. I was paying her as a consultant. Some of it was true. We *did* have plans to expand the clinics. There are many reserves across the southwest. There's a tremendous need—"

"Christ! It's a good thing Bell fucked it up for you. What I don't get, when it started to go sour, why not come to me? We could have stopped a lot of it. We could have stopped Bell."

A flicker of uneasy hesitation showed in Hogeland's eyes.

"Bell had ambitions. He was pushing the Rancho Vista development. You know how it is with zoning boards. Money has its own momentum. It can roll over a lot of ethics. Sometimes a decision can go either way, and it goes where there's money or a political debt. Bell had paid a few of the members. Not me, but still . . . I knew about it. I let it happen. I was . . . distracted, let's say. Bell threatened to go to the papers. It seemed easier to . . . tolerate him. To go along."

"So you condoned bribery and corruption?"

"Come on, Beau. You know how business gets done. The board is open to . . . persuasion. There are vulnerable people, people of influence. Bell could cause a lot of grief.''

"Couldn't you see it falling apart?''

"It's not easy to accept . . . especially when you . . . when you're as deeply into the thing. It takes on a momentum of its own.

"I guess this is where your purity gave out, eh, Doc? Is this where you stopped harvesting and started planting?''

"So many wasted lives, Beau. Why not make something good come out of it?''

"How much money were you going to give back to the Lakota and the Crow and the Cheyenne?''

"We were providing free medical care. I was building better clinics. We had new ambulances. I was planning another wing at the hospital.''

"Couldn't get enough from our paychecks, right?''

"*Paying* the native peoples—it would have been vulgar, an affront to them. They would never *sell* their children.''

"No, Doc. They wouldn't. That's why you and Maureen and the rest of your people had to steal them.''

"It wasn't *stealing,* Beau! Can't you see? Our intentions were for the best. We could *still* do something great. We can change medicine—transform it. Isn't that a cause worth risking yourself for? Enough organs for all the sufferers, freedom for all the innocent animals now being slaughtered in labs. And you know the fetuses have no inner life. Many people would argue that we have no right to victimize other species for the sake of our own. At least my methods used our own kind. And they weren't babies, Beau. They were— they couldn't even be called sleepers. They were—''

"Spare parts, Doc? Never mind, I'm not the guy you're gonna have to convince.''

"Beau, you saw what happened to Julia—you saw how it was. If there had been a *system* then, an organized *program* for harvesting, for *cultivating* organs, Julia would be alive now. You lost a wife. I remember how it was for you. Can't you understand how I felt? After all, Julia and I had been together for thirty-six years. Something had to come of that!''

"Tell me, why'd you set Dwight up, that day in your office?''

"I was surprised by the intensity of your reaction. I wanted an opportunity to deflect my son's obsession with you.''

"Because you were afraid I'd start to dig around, find out more than you wanted me to?''

"Dwight was creating a climate of confrontation. I wished to dispel some of that, to provide breathing room.''

Far in the east, at the curving of the earth, they could see the gridlights of Logan Airport and the shimmering web of Billings and Laurel, amber and blue against the black density of the hills and valleys. Starlight glittered on the Yellowstone, a silvery scintillation that snaked and coiled through the city lights and on up the valley toward its distant connection with the Missouri. The Missouri would take you to the Mississippi, and the Mississippi would take you to the sea.

The jet rose on a crest of cold wind. They were both silent, watching the lights roll toward them on the great curve of the earth.

For the cop in Beau, it was very simple. Land at Logan, hand the man over to the FBI. Type it up, and go back to Lizardskin to sleep the whole thing off. Let the morning, and the mornings after that, wash it all away, as the river takes everything to the sea.

"Five five private, this is Logan Tower. Come in."

Hogeland picked up the radio. "Logan, this is five five private."

"Five five, you are directed to land runway niner four and proceed to the security hangar. Do you understand?"

Hogeland seemed to settle in the pilot's seat. "I guess that means Eustace has some people waiting for us. Is that right?"

Beau rubbed his face with his hands, fatigue draining him.

"The FBI came back to us about Gabriel Picketwire. The name rang *big* bells with the Defense Department. They sent a couple of men in, and the whole operation is going to be handled by the federal agencies—Indian Affairs and the Justice Department."

"What about Maureen?"

"SPEAR has Maureen. Charlie Tallbull's boys—they're Crow—are running that part of it. They want national coverage, and they're going to get it. She's going to be making a public statement. This BlueStones woman called a press conference. They're going to turn Maureen over to the FBI at the television station, in return for air time. Charlie Tallbull's boys have her right now, but she's apparently okay. This Picketwire guy, he turned her over to them."

"Why did he do that?"

Beau looked at the old man for a while.

"Come in five five! Do you read?"

Hogeland ignored the radio.

"He wanted to stay out of it, I imagine," Beau said.

"You mean, he got what he wanted? He got Joe Bell?"

"No, Doc. I'd say he wants you."

Hogeland was silent for a long time.

The radio burst into urgent chatter.

He leaned forward and shut it off.

"Has anyone talked to my son yet?"

"No. Eustace went to Vanessa Ballard, and she's waiting for Maureen to turn up, tell her story. Until then, Dwight's beside the point."

"Is there any way I could get some time with him? Try to explain? Before everything gets out of my hands?"

"That's up to the feds. Maybe Vanessa would have some say. I'd guess your chances were poor."

"What'll happen when we land?"

"It's up to the feds. You'll be well treated."

"There'll be a trial . . . public disgrace."

"Christ, Doc. You should have thought of that before you started all this!"

"They'll never understand what I was trying to do."

"No, Doc. They sure as hell won't."

"And Picketwire—he's still free? Still out there?"

"Count on it, Doc."

"How old are you, Beau?"

Suddenly, Beau's heart blipped, and he felt his belly tighten. A cold wind blew across his backbone.

He looked down at the wheeling earth ten thousand feet below.

"Too young to die in a blaze of someone else's glory, Doc. Let's get this over with, okay?"

Hogeland's seamed and leathery face was closed, his thoughts gone inward. "Don't fly, do you, Beau?"

There wasn't much to say. Beau watched the old man and tried to keep himself under control.

"I won't get the death penalty, will I, Beau?"

Beau considered it. "No. Criminal conspiracy. They'll call the baby trade 'kidnapping.' One thing sure, though, you'll do a fair stretch of prison."

"Deer Lodge?"

"That's the usual destination."

"A lot of Indians in Deer Lodge. A lot of Crow and Lakota."

Beau saw the point. "They could sequester you, or your counsel could argue for transfer to an out-of-state prison."

"That might take care of my fellow prisoners. But what about this man?"

"Picketwire?"

Beau looked out the window, stalling. The answer was very clear.

Wherever they put Hogeland, Gabriel Picketwire would find a way to get to him.

"Tell you the truth, Doc, I think the guy will come after you. I think he'll do whatever it takes to get you."

Beau watched the ground coming up. It was an honest answer, and it was probably going to get him killed.

The doctor's face was heavy, his eyes hidden. His hands moved on the stick, and the little jet started to climb.

"Doc, there's nowhere to run to. And if you take me down, that's a real killing. Doc . . . Doc . . . "

Hogeland pulled on the stick. The turbines kicked in, and the jet rose, banked, rolled right, and fell away through the black night. Cold stars rolled across the windshield, and the earth rose up to meet them like a flat denial of metaphysics, vast, limitless, solid as death.

26

2100 Hours – June 19 – Billings, Montana

Vanessa Ballard could hear the sound of a television set as she came down the hallway toward the heavy wooden doors of Doc Hogeland's office. Mrs. Miles, the doctor's secretary, was waiting for her outside the doors, lines of concern and uncertainty marking the satiny perfection of her face, her hands clasped tightly across her stomach, elbows in, her posture rigid with anxiety. Beside her, a large young man in a security guard's uniform stood with his arms folded across his chest, a Maglite in his hand, a large pistol visible at his belt. His face was flushed and shiny.

Other than the sound of the television from inside the office, the suite was silent and dark, the only light coming from concealed spotlamps that cast a dim yellow glow over the oil paintings in gilt frames that lined the oak-paneled hallway.

"Thank you for coming, Ms. Ballard. This is Frank, the night guard. He's the one who called me."

Vanessa nodded and looked past Mrs. Miles and Frank at the heavy wooden doors, the brass cartridge cases hammered into the wood.

"Is he still there?"

She dipped her head once, a birdlike gesture. "Yes. I've tried to reach him on the intercom. He won't answer."

"Can you open the door?"

Frank spoke up. "We can, ma'am. But I'm not sure we should. I've talked to him once, over the phone in Mrs. Miles's office. He says if we try to break in, he'll hurt himself. What I think, ma'am, I think we should wait for the police. I think the guy's a little unstable."

Vanessa considered the man. "If we call in the police, they'll turn this into a sideshow. Right now, he's done nothing illegal—"

"Criminal trespass, ma'am."

"Not really. His father's the director here. Dwight's firm is on retainer to the hospital. He used a key, didn't he, Mrs. Miles?"

She nodded briefly.

"Then it isn't trespass, Frank."

"He's been drinking, Ms. Ballard. I could hear it in his voice. My recommendation would be, let the cops have him."

Vanessa smiled at him. "Let's just see how it goes, Frank. He asked for me, and here I am."

Frank grunted and stepped away from the door. Vanessa reached up and knocked on the wood panel. "Dwight, it's Vanessa. Open up."

The sound of the television cut off abruptly.

"Vanessa?" Dwight's voice was muffled, slurred.

"I'm here. Now open up. It's late, and I've got a lot on my hands right now."

"Are the police with you?"

"No."

"Is the guard still there?"

"Look, Dwight, I want to answer a skill-testing question, I'll stay home and watch *Jeopardy*. Now open up, or I'm going back to the station."

A few seconds passed. Then the doorlatch buzzed and clicked. Vanessa twisted the steerhorn handle and stepped inside. Frank tried to follow her, but she turned and put a hand on his chest. "Thanks, Frank. If I need you, I'll call."

Doc Hogeland's office was in darkness, except for a small green-glass

lamp on the big oak desk, and the flickering blue glimmer of a television
set in the bookcase. The desk lamp illuminated a pair of hands holding a
glass full of amber liquid. Beyond the desk, the city lights of Billings glimmered in a haze under a broken moon. Past the lights, the bluffs on the south
bank of the Yellowstone bulked dark and massive, cutting into the stars.
Vanessa walked over and sat down in the old leather armchair in front of
the desk.

"Drink, Vanessa?" Dwight leaned forward into the light. His tie was
loose and his shirt undone. His bruises were fading, but he looked gray and
sweaty.

"Yes. Scotch, if you've got it."

Dwight reached down beside him and picked up a silver bucket filled
with ice. He pulled out a bottle of Laphroaig and poured a shot into a glass.
He pushed it across the desk.

"Your health, Vanessa."

"Cheers."

Dwight gestured at the television. "You're missing all the excitement."

On the screen, a female reporter was talking to the camera in front of
a low cinder-block building. A sign beside the building read KBOY TV. A
crowd milled around in the background, and a line of Highway Patrol cars
was drawn up in front of the entrance, red and blue lights flashing crazily.
Rifles were out, and uniformed officers were walking the perimeter. Vanessa
could see Frank Duffy in the background, in the middle of a crowd of men
in gray suits and tan overcoats.

"So are you, Dwight. I expected you to be right in there. The ACLU's
all over this, and Maya BlueStones has a whole crowd of SPEAR members
there."

"I see a few people missing."

"Beau's coming back from Los Angeles."

"Oh, yes. That I heard. Dad's flying him back."

Vanessa kept the tension out of her voice with an effort. "So Eustace
says."

"Yeah. I don't see Meagher around, either. I guess he's out at the
airport, waiting for Dad."

"I guess."

On the television, there was a sudden stir as a convoy of cars and pickup
trucks appeared, coming up the highway outside the television station. A
Highway Patrol car was leading it. The cameras bobbed and jumped as the
convoy pulled into the curved driveway. Hard white lights played over the

lead vehicles, a white sedan and a battered old pickup. The pickup was full of Indian men carrying rifles and shotguns. The white sedan was driven by a man Vanessa recognized as Charlie Tallbull.

Maureen Sprague was sitting in the passenger seat, staring straight ahead, her face stiff with fear. Ice clinked in his glass as Dwight drained it and poured himself another shot.

"There she is, *la belle dame* herself. We ought to be listening to this, Vanessa." He picked up the remote and keyed it. The television burst into loud chatter.

"—just arrived. According to authorities, this is the woman who was named by the SPEAR spokesperson. We're told her name is Maureen Sprague. She's a nurse at the Julia Dwight Clinic in Hardin. We're going to try to talk to her—"

The female reporter came back into view, jogging along in front of a crowd of people, talking breathlessly into her mike. They came alongside the white car as it pulled up in front of the station doors. The pickup parked behind it, and several Indian men got out, rifles at port arms. They gathered around the white car, facing the surrounding policemen and federal agents. The reporter was being pushed and jostled. The image jumped and bobbled. She shouted questions into the crowd around the cars, finally cornering a wiry older man with ritual braids and a beaded headband.

"Can you tell us what will happen now, sir?"

The man blinked in the harsh light. "She's going to talk to all of you inside."

"You're talking about Maureen Sprague, the nurse who has been accused of stealing babies from the clinic?"

Dwight laughed once, and took another drink.

"She is part of it. Charlie Tallbull is the man you want to talk to. He's—"

"Did you attack the policeman yourself? Are you a member of this gang?"

"What gang? Lady, will you—"

"We're told there are others involved. Can you tell us who? Can you give us names?"

"You'll get them inside."

"Are you all members of SPEAR? We see a lot of guns around. Do you think there will be violence?"

"No—look, that's it, lady."

"Is SPEAR condoning the kidnapping of this woman? Is SPEAR behind the assault on the police officer at the time of the kidnapping?"

The man brushed past her and into the doors. A cordon of police officers held the crowd back as Maureen Sprague walked into the station building, flanked by Indian men carrying Winchesters and hunting rifles. As she disappeared inside, the reporter stepped back into the picture.

"We're told that there will be a televised press conference in just a few minutes. As you can see, the scene here is pretty wild. I've counted at least six different news crews here, and you can see all the police. So far, the authorities are being pretty silent about the charges, but sources close to the case say that this is the end of an ongoing FBI investigation spearheaded by Special Agent Frank Duffy. We're also told that charges are being drawn up that will implicate individual staff members at clinics in at least two reservations in South Dakota. We can't tell you any more until the conference begins, other than to say that apparently the nurse we have just seen here, Maureen Sprague, is involved, that she was kidnapped in a violent assault earlier today, during which her police guard was seriously injured. She's being turned over to the FBI here by members of the militant Indian group SPEAR. I guess we'll just have to wait for more details, since the police aren't—''

Dwight shut the sound off.

They sat in silence for a while, watching the woman talk. Dwight shifted, and Vanessa heard a scraping sound. Yellow light flared up briefly.

"You quit smoking, Dwight."

"Not anymore. Maybe this is where you tell me what's going on?"

Vanessa exhaled, smelling the cigarette smoke, watching the blue cloud curl into the darkness above the green desk lamp.

"I'm not sure I know, Dwight."

"You know more than I do. I'm getting used to it."

"This isn't about you, Dwight. Don't get maudlin. There are more important things at stake than your opinion of yourself."

On the silent screen, the camera was panning across a newsdesk as several people filed into the scene and took their seats behind it. There was Frank Duffy, crisp and brisk and freshly starched, and next to him Maya BlueStones, in a traditional Ojibway doeskin dress, her expression bright, her black eyes full of calculation, reading the room. Charlie Tallbull stood behind her, flesh sagging over his hard-boned face, his broken arm out in a brace, bruises and scratches over his right eye. Maureen was sitting next to him, looking up into the glare of the studio lamps, clutching a sheet of white paper. Her green eyes glittered, and she looked leathery and old in the brutal white light. Around her neck, a heavy gold chain sent back shards of yellow fire as she moved. At either side of the newsdesk, solemn-faced Indian men stood with their weapons visible, facing the crowd beyond the lights.

"Look at her," said Dwight. "What a piece of work. Five bucks says she comes out of this with a six-figure advance for a book, an hour with Oprah, and the cover of *People*."

"She'll be lucky to come out of this at all. They haven't handed her over yet."

"There's no way she did this all alone."

"Well, we agree about something."

"I got a call from a cop named Moses Harper. He wanted to know about Merced. Asked me about Dad's Cadillac and his plane."

"Did you tell your father about the call?"

"Yeah."

"What did he say?"

Dwight sucked on the cigarette, exhaled in a burst. "He said, 'Thank you, son.' "

"That's it?"

"No. He said, 'You take care of yourself.' And he told me he loved me, said he was proud of me."

Vanessa said nothing. She was thinking about Beau, up in the night sky with Doc Hogeland, about that shiny blue missile against a field of cold stars.

"Doesn't sound like my dad, does it?"

"I don't know, Dwight."

"Does Meagher think I was in this? Do you?"

"I don't know, Dwight. Were you?"

Dwight coughed, inhaled again. "Vanessa, I don't even know what *this* is."

"Somebody's been dealing in fetal tissue—or worse. It's hard to imagine that you could be that close to it all and not know *something*."

Dwight was quiet for a few beats. Vanessa watched the screen. Maureen was reading from the paper in front of her. Vanessa wanted to hear what was being said. But hell, they'd play it over and over again. And anyway, a case like this, the DA would take it over. He'd never leave it on her desk. To be honest, she didn't even really want it. It was dirty, one of the dirtiest things she'd ever come across. It would mark anyone who came near it.

"I guess . . . I guess I knew there was—something. Dad was having me set up these holding companies. I couldn't see what he wanted with Merced.

And a freight company? It wasn't like him. All these years, it had always been the hospital. The Hogeland Wing, more equipment. The clinics. Then suddenly, he's into beef and shipping. I asked him, why the shift? He said it was an investment in the future. In my future, he said."

Meagher had told her what he knew, and what Beau had found at 220 Ditman in Los Angeles. About Danny Burt and Farwest Beef. About Beau's suspicions. By then, Beau was already in the air. It was too late to stop him. She'd had the chance. She could have taken a leap, told Eustace he could have his warrant. But no, she had to play the cold-blooded, square-the-corners, by-the-book assistant DA. Now it was too late to keep Beau out of the plane. She'd have to live with that, whatever happened. Now here she was, sitting across from a man who was just now finding out that his father might be a monster, and all she could think about was how *she* was feeling and what it meant to her. She'd lost a lot over the years. Tonight it was becoming clear to her that perhaps she had lost herself. She felt a rush of sadness, for all the people on the reserves, for what those women had suffered and lost, and even some sadness for Dwight.

She lifted her glass and finished her drink, feeling it burn down her throat. She set it down carefully on the desk.

"Dwight, your father—no matter what he's involved in, that doesn't change all the good he's done in his life."

"No? If he's done what it looks like he's done, I'd say that's *all* there is. He's . . . not human. And I'm his blood. Maybe I'm hiding behind the law all the time because I'm afraid of what I'll do if I haven't got the rules in front of me, in black and white. You don't know what it's like, living with a legend, and now the legend turns out to be a lie."

"Yes, I do. I know all about that."

"Oh, sure. Vanessa Ballard. You know what they call you, around the courthouse? The Tactical Nike. Everybody jumps when you come into a room. There isn't a man in town wouldn't open a vein to get your attention—me included."

"Sure, I'm popular as hell. My social life's a mad whirl. Ever wonder why?"

"We all do."

"Nobody gets to me because my father . . . my father was a monster too."

She couldn't say it. Not even for Dwight. She didn't have the strength or the mercy.

Dwight lit another cigarette.

"I'm sorry, Vanessa. I forgot about your father."

That rocked her. Dwight sat forward in his chair and looked at her through the smoke and the green light, his eyes in shadow, a pool of yellow light lying on his hands on the desktop.

"Mom told me about it a long time ago. She said that's why Bonnie drank, because she knew that at night, your dad would get out of bed and . . . Mom said Bonnie would lie there at night in the bed, and she'd try to get up and go stop him. But she couldn't."

"Oh, yes. Poor Mom."

"Yes. She—she failed you. Maybe, these days, maybe it would be different. But back then, people looked away."

"If you knew this, then how could you bring those charges against Beau? How could you let Maureen go ahead with that charade?"

"Because . . . because I thought it might be true."

"Beau? Beau McAllister? Even I wouldn't buy that. I *know* Beau. I mean, I know the kind of man."

"Like people knew Augustus Ballard? Or the great Doc Hogeland?"

Feelings welled up around her, and she felt her eyes start to burn. Dwight saw that. He got up and came around the desk, stood beside her, uncertain. Finally, he put a hand on her shoulder. After a moment, she reached up and put her hand on top of his. She watched the yellow pool of light where it lay on the dark wooden desktop. The brass base glimmered and blurred.

Dwight was handing her something. She tried to focus on it. Oh hell, it was a linen handkerchief. She raised her hand to brush it aside, stopped, then accepted it.

She wiped her eyes, feeling the warmth of Dwight's hand on her shoulder. It felt sweet and strange, and she realized that nobody touched her, not ever. She sighed and looked up at Dwight, at his bruised face and damaged nose.

"You know, Dwight, you look better a little roughed up. Gives you some character."

"I didn't bring your dad up to hurt you, Vanessa. I'm sorry. I was trying to apologize. Make it right."

She looked around the room, at the plaques and photos, at the artworks and the antique rifles, then at the skyline of Billings beyond the glass. Out in the darkness, past the city lights, Montana rolled away under an endless night sky. She felt the pressure of all that emptiness, and the weight of all the years that bore down on the ancient hills and valleys. She sighed and stood up, looked at the damp linen in her hand. Dwight's face was drawn, pale with shock and worry.

"That's the trouble with memories, isn't it, Dwight? You don't always get to choose what to remember."

Dwight smiled at her. "Well, Vanessa. I'm going to give it a hell of a good try."

"Yes," she said, gathering herself. "So will I."

27

2300 Hours – June 19 – Over Billings, Montana

Hogeland had the jet throttled back so close to stall speed that the warning
light was blipping red in the control panel, and even then the ground
under the wing was a blurred impression of round hills, sudden flashing
lakes, herds of cattle lumbering out of their flight path, and moonlight flickering like silver fire on hydro lines and the tin roofs of barns and coops as
the Lear thundered over the landscape.

Beau, so tight with fear he found it hard to swallow or talk, watched
the earth rush past his windshield. He had the vertiginous illusion that they
were racing past a huge wall of pale gray hills and valleys.

"Doc, what are you going to do?"

Hogeland wasn't talking, and Beau didn't have a single option.

Hogeland didn't look at him. He had his eye on the altimeter. Beau was watching the hills below them. They flew past under the wings, bulky and rounded, tinted a soft gray by the moonlight.

Moonlight glittered on creeks and rivers threading through the valleys. They looked like bright wires. Little farm ponds glistened like pearls on the strings of the rivers. A grid of lights marked a crossroads. A hard square of blue light was a gas station. Soft yellow circles showed isolated homes and ranches. On a side road beneath them, twin white beams crawled along immense expanses of darkness. Far away to the east, Beau could see ragged tatters of cloud shining against the clearing night sky, the last of the front that had torn up eastern Montana, then gone off to dissipate itself over South Dakota. Stars showed through the rips and the moon rode above it, clear and brilliant, almost perfectly round. He could see the dark shadows of the lakes and craters on it. At the edge of the moon he saw the crater walls and mountains edged in hard light. He had never seen it so clearly. It held him for a moment, transfixed, until Hogeland's voice, packed with strain, brought him back again and he looked down at the ground.

"You're not going to die, Beau."

"What are we doing? Running for it? They'll scramble a jet out of Civil Air, or an F-16 from Rapid City. They want us *down*."

Hogeland was looking at the ground as it blurred past the port window. The jet was a missile at this height.

"Doc, they'll follow the transponder. They'll have you on radar. Come on, man—stop this!" Beau had already tried his cellular phone. Useless, the battery dead flat.

Hogeland had the Lear screaming across the eastern Montana hills, so close to the ground that they could see individual trees and houses in the luminous nightscape.

Hogeland switched on the radio. "We might as well listen to them."

"—five five, repeat, you are out of your corridor, you are in violation of Federal Aviation Codes. Come in five five!"

"Logan, this is five five."

"Five five, you are instructed to return to five thousand feet and assume bearing two eight zero. Repeat, five thousand, bearing two eight zero. We will scramble a chase plane, five five."

"What was that?"

Hogeland shook his head. "They're pissed. They've probably got some calls already, from ranchers or people on the reserves. We've scared the hell out of a lot of stock and rattled windows all over the county."

"So now what?"

"Now we give them what they want. We take the flight path and come in on track. Then we kick out and drop off the screen. Then we kill the transponder and level out at five hundred feet.''

Beau thought that over. Then he thought it over again. Then he tried not to think about it at all.

Hogeland's face was set and rock hard. In the light of the instruments, his skin was green and his deep-set eyes glittered with an emerald light.

"Five five, this is Logan Tower."

"Tower, this is five five."

"Five five, you are cleared for landing. Come around to two eight zero. You are cleared for runway niner four. Wind is southeast at ten knots. Your ceiling is unlimited. Five five, please taxi to the government hangar when you land. Roger?"

"Roger, tower. We are having guidance difficulties but have now stabilized and will assume bearing two eight zero, runway niner four. Wind southeast ten knots, ceiling clear, report to airport office upon landing."

The Lear dipped suddenly. Beau's beer bottle jumped off the floorboards and struck the throttle bars. Beau grabbed it as his belly flew up into his throat. Suddenly the windshield was full of Montana, and it was coming up fast. Beau watched it, thinking this is probably how the newspaper looks to a fly in the last two seconds. Hogeland was making a funny grinding noise. Beau realized it was his teeth scraping together. The jets were howling, and the sound of the wind was like a waterfall breaking on the nose of the plane. Beau focused on a thin black line. There was a pair of headlights moving on it, and a small glimmer of silver light off the roof. It swelled and expanded as he watched it, and then it was moving away to the left and Beau's face was stretching down over his cheeks like wax running.

A bell was sounding in the plane. The gauges were spinning.

Hogeland reached out and flicked a switch. The alarm bell cut off. He wrenched at the controls, and the jet, shuddering, leveled out, and now they were hurtling across the landscape and trees were rushing at them, on them, and flickering by, strobing, and the only fixed point in Beau's existence was that cold clear three-quarter moon riding above the shredded clouds above him. He did not look down now. The ground was too close. He watched the hills rush at them and felt Hogeland correcting; the nose came up and dipped again, and then there was a line of orange lights like a string of Christmas bulbs, and Beau could see the lights of cars and trucks crawling down a flat ribbon of black road, and then it was under the wings and gone, and now they were into darkness again.

"That was I-94. We'll see I-90 in about ten seconds."

Beau looked at the altimeter. Red numerals blipped at him.

650 FEET

Their airspeed was shown in green.

380 MPH

And now there was another thin line of orange lights on the horizon. Hogeland grunted and banked right. The right wing seemed to scrape the earth. He rose to clear a mounded slope, then dipped as the land fell away down the bowl between Pompeys Pillar and Hardin. Hardin was a yellow glow on the black horizon.

"We're gonna strafe Hardin, Doc?"

"No, I'll take it to the east. We better hope nobody's up in his Beechcraft for a midnight flight."

The radio was crackling and hissing with frantic calls. Logan Tower was sending a crash alert. By now, they'd be scrambling the choppers out of the National Guard and sending out Highway Patrol cars.

Hardin swelled to a grid of rectangular lights and the patterns of street-lamps. An ARCO sign showed above a hilltop, and a Shell sign beside that, and a Denny's. Then it dropped away behind a range of hills, and the stars were clear again.

"There's I-90 down there. We'll be onto 212 in thirty seconds."

"Oh, good. What are we going to do on Highway 212?"

Hogeland smiled at him.

"Land on it."

And now they could both see the lamplit intersection. Moonlight glinted off the twin tracks of the Burlington and Northern Railroad, where it paralleled the highway. Two tractor-trailers were making their way up the long low rise toward Garryowen. The Custer Battlefield entrance was a pool of white light, and underneath the forest they could make out the ordered ranks of white stones in the military cemetery. The information house was closed and dark. Beau saw the road rise, and he could make out the tall stone tower that marked the burial place for most of Custer's two hundred and twenty-five men. The ones they could find. Custer wasn't there. They'd taken him to West Point and given him a hero's monument. But the rankers stayed where they had fallen.

Moonlight lay on the slopes and hills of the battlefield. It glinted off the curling ribbon of the Little Bighorn River and glimmered under the cottonwoods. Beau could make out little clusters of white stones hidden in the long grasses, bunched in small groups in Medicine Tail Coulee, or singly up the long slope of Deep Ravine, where the survivors had struggled up away from Gall's Hunkpapas, trying to make the high ground.

They had dragged their wounded and shot their horses for breastworks.

It was hand-to-hand up the long hillside. Custer and the last of his company, maybe thirty men left. Custer turned at Boston's shout, looked over his shoulder up the hillside, and saw Crazy Horse at the crest. Custer didn't know who it was, nor did Crazy Horse recognize the white soldier in the buckskins.

Crazy Horse was in front of his warriors, a plain man in his breechcloth and a single hawk's feather in his hair, red dust on his body and on his pony's flanks, his body painted with zigzag lightning strokes, his left cheek scarred and twisted where No Water had shot him for taking Black Buffalo Woman away.

Then Crazy Horse kicked his pony, and his men came down beside him. Twenty minutes later the last of Custer's men were dead in the long yellow grass and the women were busy at their work in long shadows. A smoky yellow sun was going down beyond the ochre hills.

Somehow it was as real to Beau as yesterday's sunrise or the fight at 220 Ditman. It had always been that way for Beau, a crazy parallax illusion that left him half in his own time and half in the past. The jet banked left and Hogeland pointed to the east. "That's 212."

Now the low hills of the Crow Reserve climbed up on both sides of the highway, and Beau saw the white strobe light on the nose reflected in the puddles and creeks beside the roadway. It lit up the surface of the road like a photo-flash, freezing images in Beau's mind like snapshots—a rabbit in the glare and thunder, flattened into itself and trembling, a windblown scrap of brush, a clutter of beer cans by the side of the road, that strobing yellow line flashing under the nose of the plane.

Hogeland dropped the nose and throttled back. The plane yawed, came back, shuddered, and yawed again. The STALL alarm was sounding, a high-pitched electric squeal. The black two-lane road was rushing under the wing. Beau watched the yellow lines twisting and straightening.

They hit the ground at two hundred miles an hour. The wheels bounced and lurched. The plane rocked and bucked, and Hogeland slammed the flaps down full, braked and released and braked again, and the turbines whirled up through the RPM's in a banshee wail.

On Beau's right, the silver lines of the hydro wires rose and fell as they rushed past, a hypnotically beautiful illusion of rhythmic motion and silver light. The nose dipped down, and all Beau could see was the highway, and the yellow line in the headlights of the Lear. Hogeland was saying something very fast under his breath and then the plane shuddered again and the yellow lines turned into yellow dashes and Beau's seat belt cut into his belly and then they were stopped.

Hogeland shut down the jets.

He let out a long breath.

Beau could hear the sound of metal contracting.

Smoke drifted past the cockpit and eddied in the headlights.

Hogeland leaned back into his seat and rubbed his cheeks. Beau unstrapped himself and climbed around the controls. He went back to the door and hit the red button. The door hissed open and the stairway unfolded onto the highway. The smell of oil came in the door, along with the cool wind off the hills and the scent of sweetgrass. He jumped down to the pavement, legs trembling, and suddenly he was sitting on the ground and his chest was heaving and he struggled to find breath.

He was dimly aware of the old man climbing down the steps and sitting down on the highway next to him.

The night sky was full of stars, and the three-quarter moon rode through shreds of storm clouds like a white gull.

Finally, Beau put his head back against the wheel strut and looked sideways at the old man's profile. Hogeland was staring up at the grassy hillside. Moonlight lay on the blades like a silver mist, and a soft wind hissed in the coulee.

"I guess you can fly that thing, Doc."

Hogeland grinned and slapped his hand on his leg. "Yes, I was always good at it. Maybe those were my best days, Beau. Maybe the boys who never come home are the lucky ones."

"Maybe they'll find us here. Someone will have heard us go over. I don't see what this will—"

Hogeland was holding his hand up, head down, shaking his head from side to side. "Damn, you like to talk, son. Let's give it a minute."

Beau was silent for a long time. The night sounds began to rise around him. Far off in the dark, the sound of music drifted across the hills, and the sweep of traffic from the interstate down the line, and the flutter of a bat as it crossed the starry sky, a scrap of blackness in the moonlight, and the *tick-tick-tick* of the turbines cooling, and the *hush-hush* sound of his own blood pumping through his carotid artery, and the raspy wheeze of the old man's breathing at his side.

And from far away the thump and jingle of a horse, his hooves a steady syncopation on the hillside.

"What now, Doc? Into the hills? Let them run you down tomorrow, or the night after that? Or let the Crow find you?"

Hogeland sighed. "No, I suppose not."

"Then let's get up, go find a phone," said Beau, struggling to his feet on shaky legs, "or use the radio. My cellular's dead. Come on, Doc. We'll sort this out somehow. I'll stay with you."

Beau's voice was thickening in his throat. He felt at once the terrible strength of love and friendship and the sinewy cords of years that bind one man to another, and all men to their town and their times. He held out his hand and the old man looked up at him. Finally, he reached out his right hand and let Beau pull him to his feet, and they stood there, face to face in the roadway.

"I never meant for hurt to come on you, or to touch your family. I would never have opened any door that would harm your girls, or even Maureen. And I have, haven't I? I've hurt my own son, maybe past healing."

Beau could think of nothing to say. He watched the old man's face, the pain in it.

"I think of Julia, you know, more and more as I get old. A woman dies, you've known her all the days of your life, every morning and every sundown is marked with her hand and the sound of her voice, the way she folds a sheet, the colors she likes, the flowers or the magazines, her brushes and her creams in the bathroom, the feel of her beside you at night, warm and sleeping, yours to guard and love, the way she moves around the house. And when she goes, most of you goes with her, Beau, you know this, you've gone through it. What's left is a hollow thing. You fill it up as best you can, and I filled myself up with . . . nothing. An obscenity, and made my name filth in my own county. How will you think of me, Beau? How will my son think of me?"

Beau heard the vibration in the man's chest and felt the strength of his fingers, and the age in his old hands, a surgeon's hands, now ropy and knotted with age.

"Doc, I'll always remember what you did for Alice. You made her life easier while she had it, and you made the leaving of it something she could do in a quiet place, surrounded by friends. No matter what you do or what you may have done, there's a blessing in this, that even though you can't go back and right the things you did wrong, the things you did right, they'll never fade. A man's friends, they'll remember the good things he did, and he'll have a place in their memories, a good place—what he was when he was young and his mistakes were all ahead of him."

"Do I have that, Beau?"

"Yes. As much as it's mine to say."

He smiled and let go of Beau's hand.

"You have a good heart, Beau. You should find someone."

Beau thought of Bobby Lee and Laurel and even Trudy Corson. "I have people."

"A woman, Beau. I should have found another."

"I'll try. Now we ought to get going."

Hogeland looked up at the moon. His eyes were bright and moist, and Beau saw the age in the man, and the skull behind the skin.

"Okay. You're right. Enough whining. I guess I just needed a moment to get my bearings. Thank you, Beau."

"Well, it was a hell of a ride, Doc."

"Okay. Let me get my things."

They walked back to the stairs. Hogeland climbed up and Beau heard the hydraulics whine. The stairs started to fold.

Beau reached for the edge of the door, caught it, and pulled, and his fingers slipped off the metal.

Hogeland waved to him.

"Doc—there's nowhere to go! For chrissake!"

"Yes, there is," he said. The door whined upward and closed with a hissing snap. The latch turned and set.

Beau slammed the fuselage with the flat of his hand. Under the glistening skin, he felt the systems come to life. The turbines started to whine.

He raised his hand to slam it down on the blue skin and held it there, then he stepped back away from the accelerating blast from the engine nacelles.

He saw the old man at the controls, his face green in the uplight from the control panel. He smiled at Beau. Beau backed up the slope, shielding his face from the blast.

The blue jet was vibrating with restrained power, the turbines beginning to howl, a piercing shriek rising as Hogeland held the wheel brakes. The halogen light in the nose flicked on, and a mile-long beam cut through the darkness. Far off down the two-lane road, a pair of green eyes glittered in the sudden light, blinked twice, and disappeared to the side of the road.

The blue jet was moving now, rolling, gaining speed.

Hogeland shoved the throttles forward, and the blast drove Beau backward, staggering in the wash, his eyes burning with the smell of avgas and stinging from the dust, and the jet was a hundred yards away now, the searchlight jerking as the wheels thumped and bumped over the uneven roadway.

There was a deafening howl and the nose lifted, and the jet was suddenly free, and rising, and Beau felt a strange exhilaration as it cleared the rise and shot skyward, two bright blue flames marking the jet exhaust and the red winglights blinking.

Hogeland pulled the nose up. The thunder of the engines shook the hills, crested into a terrible hammering roar, faded as the little plane climbed into the sky. A quicksilver shimmer of moonlight arced across the fuselage. The twin blue fires merged into one.

Beau watched it climb, feeling the rumble of the engines in his chest, the little jet lifting up through the cloud-rack, higher and higher, disappearing into the eastern sky, and the thunder rumbled away. Beau watched the tiny pinpoint of blue fire as it climbed away to the east, still rising, shrinking away to a needle of faint light.

He stood there for a long time, straining to follow the blue glimmer, listening to the sound of the jets as they dwindled to a distant rumor and faded away. In a while, there was nothing left but a soft wind in the grasses and the jet was a wisp of blue fire in a field of stars. Then it was gone.

The horse ducked its head, tugging at the reins, trying to reach the sweetgrass. Gabriel released the reins and slid carefully from the saddle, fighting the dizziness and the pain. Under the broken moon, the black hide of the animal had a silvery sheen. The saddle smelled of soap and neat's-foot oil. He found two more Percodans in his shirt pocket and swallowed them with water from the canteen. The setter trotted up to his knee and whined softly. Gabriel leaned down to run his fingers through the dog's fur. The dog settled down in the grass, panting. Gabriel poured some water into his palm and offered it to the setter. The dog drank greedily, then wandered off down the hillside again.

Gabriel looked back at the starry night.

The little jet was gone now. Even the echoes of its ascent had faded into the night wind. Gabriel looked back down the long slope to the highway. In the moonlight the asphalt surface seemed covered in a shiny skin, silvery, like a lizardskin belt. The big man was trudging away down the middle of it, his head down.

It was the sergeant. McAllister. Gabriel knew him somehow. Charlie Tallbull had said the sergeant was in Los Angeles, that he was coming back in the little blue jet with the doctor. With the Walking Wolf. The man was limping badly, favoring his right leg.

Gabriel drank some more water and eased himself back into the saddle. He prodded the horse into a walk, easing him down a coulee. The horse's hooves thumped on the clay. The sweetgrass swept along the horse's barrel as he cantered up another rise, chuffing a little, the snaffle-bit jingling, a faint bell-like ringing. At the top of the rise, he slowed her to a walk. The cop was still in the roadway, a dark shadow against the metallic sheen of the highway. Every line of the man's body spoke of weariness. His limp was getting worse, and he was hearing nothing around him, his thoughts apparently turned inward. He could be taken now. Easily.

The blue jet had gone straight up into the night. Something about the climb had seemed final, fatal.

Gabriel hoped that it was. It was too easy a death, but it was an ending. Charlie Tallbull had the woman, and now the police would have to deal with it. Tallbull would see to that. Tallbull had also promised to get Gabriel some medical help. He'd given him this horse, a Tennessee Walker, one of the best. By now, the county would be full of men looking for him. Maybe even some of his old friends from the Section.

He settled the horse into a slow walk, breathing in the sweetgrass scent and the chill purity of the night air, the sharp clear smell of the horse, a good smell. He thought about the man down there, trudging along the Lizardskin road, about what should be done with him.

Beau had walked a long way down 212 when he looked up to his left and saw the slope of the battlefield on his left. He turned away from the pavement and climbed up the hillside to the wire fence that marked the monument land.

The stone pillar was a half-mile away. The little gathering of white markers seemed to glow in the moonlight. He climbed over the fence. The sagebrush rustled around his boots, and the sweetgrass smell was everywhere in the air. It took him awhile to walk up the coulee. He was breathing hard by the time he cleared the crest and walked up to the low wrought-iron picket fence that enclosed the hillside where the last of the soldiers had died.

To his right down the hillside, a stand of trees sheltered the formal rows of the military cemetery. A white flagpole rose above the treeline, empty. Each evening they took the flag down, and now and then someone would play the Last Post.

He leaned against the rail and read some of the names in the dim light. Here was Boston Custer's stone, and Autie Reed's. Farther up the slope, in the center of a cluster of stones, a marker with a black shield carried Custer's name. Most of the stones read simply:

U.S. SOLDIER

7th CAVALRY

FELL HERE

JUNE 25 1876

From this sad gathering of stones the land descended toward the valley of the Bighorn River. More white stones were scattered here and there in the grassy decline. Beyond the river there were a few rectangles of yellow light from the little houses around Crow Agency. Down in the valley, the river shimmered under the cottonwoods. Beau felt a sweet sadness for all the men who had ridden over and fallen under this country, the long grass parting to take them in and closing over their heads again, seamless and eternal.

He pushed himself up and walked down the stone path toward the park building. He was halfway down the path when he heard something moving in the dry grass behind him.

He turned and watched as a dog came bounding down through the tallgrass. It was an old dog, some kind of setter. It padded up to him and sniffed him in a friendly way. He crouched down to ruffle its red fur and stroke its ears.

"Hello, pup. Out for a midnight wander?"

It whined a bit, then left him, trotting away back up the hillside toward the crest and the coulees that lay beyond it. He watched it as it rambled up the walkway past the monument fence. It reached the top and bounded away down the other side and was gone.

He looked that way for a while, wondering where it had come from and who owned it, but he saw only the soft hills under the broken moon, and the dry grasses moving in the scented wind, and the cloud shadows drifting over moonlit valleys and gliding down the rolling slopes, and rising again into the higher hills until they passed away into the distance where the curving earth and the night sky blended into a shining mist. The empty land was all around him, and a cold wind on his cheek, and the half-heard sound of a horse and rider, and suddenly, tired beyond belief, chilled and alone, he turned and walked away toward the yellow lights of Crow Agency.

Gabriel watched him go. He was thinking about his own name. There was a river, down on the New Mexico border, east of the Sangre de Cristo range. It was a fork of the Arkansas. It ran through very bad country. The first white men who had traveled it, French trappers, had found it so hard, they named it the Purgatoire, which means *purgatory* in English. When the Americans came, they heard *Purgatoire* and pronounced it *Picketwire*. He had been named for the river. The name was either a curse or a kind of prophecy.

Now the sergeant was almost down to the banks of the Bighorn River. The lights of Crow Agency showed through the cottonwoods.

Gabriel turned away, kicked the horse into a slow walk.

It was over.

Let it end.